Advanced praise for *Emma's Call*

I so much enjoyed being with Emma—walking alongside this minister's wife, meeting her community, watching her reach out—being a blessing. Yet also struggling. Struggling to find a place in a largely male-dominated church society. The end of the story left me virtually begging for more! What happens next? How will she walk into the opportunities opening to her? I am glad this engaging, well-written tale, based on facts of the day, has an upcoming sequel! Can't wait!
—Angelina Fast-Vlaar, Award-winning author of four non-fiction books, stories, and poetry. (www.angelinafast.com)

Emma lives at a time of quiet control over women, even by those closest to them. Emma's emotions vividly conflict, as she accepts the duties she is given. Yet, the pull to lead is strong. A story of a time that has passed. A time on which the stories of women of the present day have been built.
—Lynn Wyvill, award-winning poet and author of *Agnes Annis: Mother and Missionary* and *The Third Season: A Memoir of Considered Thoughts While Aging* as well as numerous published essays.

In *Emma's Call*, we meet a delightful woman who struggles to be the epitome of devoted wife, yet one who wants to exert her independence and answer God's call. Not an easy challenge in the '30s in a small rural community. Emma demonstrates that with faith, courage and conviction, one can attain one's hopes and dreams. A great read to remind us that in all the tough times, with faith, one is never alone.
—Louise Elder, A.R.C.T., B. Music, B. Education.

Restrained by the rules and expectations of a woman living in 1935, Emma is an inspiring celebration of resilience.
—G. Gibson, R.N., BScN

Donna writes in an easy-to-read style, capturing her reader's expectations as they follow twists and turns. What will happen next? Emma, a minister's wife, embraces the concept that women and children should be counted. At the same time, she totally supports her husband and manages to introduce ideas. As Emma becomes vocal about her interest in ministry, she finds negativity and hindrance on all corners. Although doubt lingers, she knows what God has placed in her heart. Your writing is always a joy, Donna. I look forward to the sequel!

—Wendy Smith, LLWL (Licensed Lay Worship Leader)

As a born and raised Ontario girl who loved reading, especially historical fiction, I was so looking forward to reading this book. I wasn't disappointed, and very quickly I was drawn into the work, unable to put it down. Donna has done an excellent job of introducing us to her characters. The people that cross Emma's path help her make choices for the direction her life will take. I cried with Emma, felt proud of her, encouraged her, and wanted to give her a hug at times. All in all, this was a brilliant read and I look forward to reading more of Emma and her calling. Thanks, Donna.

—Marian Fox, Caregiver, United Kingdom

Emma's Call

A NOVEL
A WOMAN OF FAITH, BOOK ONE

DONNA MANN

EMMA'S CALL
Copyright © 2022 by Donna Mann

All rights reserved. Neither this publication nor any part of this publication may be reproduced or transmitted in any form or by any means, electronic or mechanical, including photocopying, recording or any information storage and retrieval system, without permission in writing from the author.

This is a work of fiction. Names, characters, places and incidents either are the product of the author's imagination or are used fictitiously, and any resemblance to actual persons, living or dead, businesses, companies, events, or locales is entirely coincidental.

ISBN: 978-1-4866-1964-1
eBook ISBN: 978-1-4866-1965-8

Word Alive Press
119 De Baets Street Winnipeg, MB R2J 3R9
www.wordalivepress.ca

WORD ALIVE
—PRESS—

Cataloguing in Publication information can be obtained from Library and Archives Canada.

DEDICATION

All women who experience God's call in their lives to take their place in church leadership earn the right to this dedication space. Some of you will have found ways to be faithful to that call, while others have been unable to accept due to various reasons. Regardless, it is the call we celebrate and the women who consistently yearn to respond. You are heroes in the faith.

Gratitude

I could not have written this book with its depth of historical context had it not been for the available research of women evangelists in Canada, especially those in Ontario. Thank you to their families and historians who recorded their life and accomplishments.

I am grateful for women who shared their stories and boldly embodied the call of God to serve in church leadership. Although they were not always welcomed, recognized, or nurtured, they were always ready to preach, teach and lead in the midst of obstacles.

And among many who encouraged me to write this story and read it in different stages, I want to mention my writing group, Sara Davison and Heidi VanDerSlikke, who never gave up on this book and continually walked with me. As well, thanks to The Word Alive staff for their direction.

> "I would have given her [the Church] my head, my hand, my heart. She would not have them. She did not know what to do with them. She told me to go back and do crochet in my mother's drawing-room; or if I were tired of that, to marry and look well at the head of my husband's table. 'You may go to the Sunday School if you like it,' she said. But she gave me no training even for that. She gave me neither work to do for her, nor education for it."
> (Florence Nightingale in a letter to Dean Stanley, 1852)[1]

---

[1] Elaine Showalter, *Signs* Vol. 6, No. 3 (Spring, 1981) Florence Nightingale's Feminist Complaint: Women, Religion, and "Suggestions for Thought"), pp. 395-412 The University of Chicago Press.

DONNA MANN

EMMA'S CALL: A NOVEL

TOWN OF NOBLE

MEET THE GOOD FOLKS OF NOBLE

Emma Taylor: wife of Rev. Bill Taylor, mother of Beatrice Taylor and Bernice Taylor
Rev. Murray Maitland: husband of Shirley Maitland
Rev Brian Lawson: husband of Jane Lawson, father of Jason and Christine Lawson
Louise Ryan: wife of Jed Ryan, mother of Rosie Ryan
Hilda Grafton: wife of Leroy Grafton, mother of Alice, Bobby (deceased) Grafton
Bishop Martin: Presbytery
Doris Abbott: gift store owner
Doc Baxter: physician
Henry Bates: grocer
Irene Trask: mother of Nancy Trask and Susanne Trask
Jack Brett: delivery man, piano tuner
Lizzy Maxwell: telephone operator
Maisie Turner: neighbour
Ruth Fair: bank clerk
Tillie Parson: hairdresser
Tom Tolt: funeral director & chairman of the Church Board
Mrs. Bowman: owner of the Dime Store
Mrs. Densmore: midwife
Mrs. Olen: public school teacher/music director
Mrs. Watson: music teacher
Mr. Henderson: insurance agent
Mr. Polin: license agent
Mr. Arnold: postmaster
Mr. Evans: owner of hardware store
Rev Albert Miller: minister of Hampton church

CHURCH WORKERS:
Bertha Porter: church florist
Cora Morgan: church organist
Eleanor Jackson: choir member, kitchen group
Mrs. Brown: song leader
Mrs. Howard: wife of steward, unit group
Mrs Murray: choir member
Miss Prior: retired teacher
Mrs. Norris: a senior
Mrs. Allen: store clerk
Mrs. Lucy Miles: librarian
Miss Muir: town clerk, elder's daughter
Mrs. Reid: church member
Mr. John Hewitson: church treasurer
Mr. Howard: steward
Mr. Muir: elder
Mr. Denver: Summerville committee member
Emma Taylor's Mission Circle members: Barbara (12), Rosie (11), Belle (12), Susanne (13), Victoria (12)

REFERENCE ONLY:
L.N. Reinhardt: lawyer in Toronto
Mrs. Governing: wife of mayor
Mrs. Greenside & Miriam: store owners
Mary Ann Moore: deceased widow of Reverend Walter, previous minister at First Church

Prissy: cat
Darlin': dog

For we are his workmanship, created in Christ Jesus unto good works, which God hath before ordained that we should walk in them (Ephesians 2:10 KJV).

And they did all eat and were filled: and they took up of the fragments that remained twelve baskets full. And they that had eaten were about five thousand men, beside women and children (Matthew 14:20-21 KJV).

ONE
IT NEVER IS AS IT SEEMS

1935, SOUTHERN ONTARIO

Emma Taylor steadied the plate holding a birthday cake while she attempted to fold icing around its edges. Without adequate butter, the pearly-white substance spread stiffly as moist bread dough. Her breath disappeared into the frigid air of the church kitchen, much like her forward-thinking dissolved into nothingness. But it was the raised voices of three girls in the Mission Circle that shocked Emma. She had left them to work on their African project in a side alcove once used as a pantry, never thinking they would argue amongst themselves.

Susanne's voice resonated clearly from their area. "Mrs. Taylor said forty people might live in the community, so I'll have twenty for mine." At thirteen years of age, Susanne had already become decisive in her interests.

"None of your stick figures have skirts. Are they all boys?" Belle didn't say much during this work period, but she could be passionate concerning family issues. Seeing Susanne's artwork must have touched a painful memory.

"I can show mothers and children, but they won't count if my setting is the same as the scripture story." Susanne stood. "So yes, if I want them counted, they have to be boys."

"Everybody has to count," Rosie complained.

Susanne pushed back her chair, making a screeching sound on the bare wood surface. Her voice elevated. "On Sunday, Reverend Taylor read about feeding the 5,000. Everybody was fed, but the women and children weren't counted." She coughed, almost choking. "He said that. I heard him." She tugged the neckline of her threadbare sweater.

Emma winced. Belle ran to her coat, yanked it on and pulled her scarf from the hook. One by one, the girls countered ongoing comments. Finally, Emma hurried past the cupboard and reached Belle. "Come on back." Emma's gentle voice caught Belle's attention. "Let's talk about this."

Emma had no sooner finished her sentence than Rosie slammed her planning book shut. "If I can't include Momma and me…then I'm not going to work anymore on this."

Belle returned to the table. Her gaze shifted from her village to Emma. What could she say to ease the tension? These youngsters deserved answers to the questions the sermon had raised. But how could Emma explain? Would the count be different in today's world? Emma opened her mouth, but words escaped her. The original Bible story came to mind—a meaningful reflection of a community. *I would have loved being there to carry the baskets.*

She wouldn't contradict what Bill said, nor did she want to interpret scripture. That wasn't her task. If she questioned her husband, he'd say, "Oh, Em, people know what it means."

Emma spoke to the girls about the problem without pause. "For this assignment, put all ages, male and female, into your setting. We'll show them as they should be and, yes, count them all."

The children broke out in smiles and glanced at one another. Correctly placing their village, they moved their assortment of stick figures to designated spaces. They worked with ease as they giggled and talked. Pools of tears filled Emma's eyes. Returning to the kitchen counter, she checked the chart she'd created for the lessons.

The Emma Taylor Mission Circle had met for ten years, from April to October. Emma had started the group when her popular husband, the Reverend Bill Taylor, accepted a call to Noble's First Church. The growing rural district in Southern Ontario had developed on the banks of the Grand River and served the population well. On the east side of the tracks, a compact populace called the Hills still had cottages waiting for water and hydro. Most of their men were employed in the local factory and cared for their families according to their income. However, the last major layoff due to lack of orders made life difficult.

Mrs. Ryan, from that area, frequently invited Emma to lead worship for those who gathered in one of their homes. There and at the Mission Circle were the only locations where she regularly taught in the pastoral charge, and she loved doing both. She'd often reached out to children in the Hills even though several from the town congregation questioned why 'those girls' were involved in activities.

She gave the same response. "They attend school together, so why wouldn't they join our events?"

How could Emma help them feel counted when she didn't always feel that way herself? Others appeared to be supportive of her leadership, but she was never sure. Giving a message from the pulpit or teaching Biblical material made women a target for accusations and questions. And she'd heard a few, although second-hand. No one had said anything outright.

The congregation observed Emma as Reverend Taylor's life partner. For that, she was thankful and asked for nothing extra. But what could she do with God's call placed deeply in her heart and mind years ago except disturb the status quo? And that would intrude into Bill's ministry.

Dabbing her eyes with the corner of a tea towel, Emma glanced out the window. Mr. Tolt, chairman of the stewards and the local undertaker, eased his black sedan next to the entrance. Hopefully, he had come to check the furnace with its pipes resembling spider legs threading under the ceiling. He'd be out of sight, hidden from the fellowship hall behind the heavy divider and would have to walk out of his way to go into the well-equipped kitchen area. The distance, however, wouldn't make a difference if he had a complaint.

Taking a deep breath, Emma resolved to defend Belle's request to bring their winter assignments and meet one week earlier than usual.

The sun slowly began to cast warm afternoon rays across the room, easing the coolness in the air. Emma's arthritic hands gradually warmed as she clasped them. Today was her forty-ninth birthday. Although she didn't expect this year to be any different, she paused to thank God for this precious gift.

A bit of lint clung to Emma's moss-green suit, and she brushed it from the material. One of her mother's brooches pinned to the lapel gave a bit of variety and enhanced the jacket. At least it was warm, although it was old. She owned one lovely beige dress for special occasions, besides a few everyday clothing pieces, and two suits for church wear. On a cool day, this outfit was the best choice from her sparse wardrobe.

Emma had bought a pretty ribbon at the Dime Store for her hat, but that hadn't improved it much. She nudged her hair under its brim, hoping it would hold loose strands that sometimes escaped. It didn't always, as the old headband had to accommodate various braids and buns. The depression, rampant throughout the country, made daily living difficult, from grocery shopping to dressing appropriately.

After setting saucers and forks on a small serving stand, Emma returned to the girls' table to see if the group had finished their task.

"We decided we'd like Reverend Taylor to ask us during mission-time tomorrow why we chose our projects," Belle said. "Is that a good idea?"

"That would be excellent," Emma said. *Surely, they won't mention the topic of the count.* While they tidied their space, Emma wrote several invitations to send home with Rosie to pass on to the other mothers but only after 6:00. By then, Emma would have talked to Bill.

Without notice, Mr. Tolt marched into the area. He appeared as if he had paraded off the front page of a fashion magazine: tall, dark hair and with enough charisma to serve the whole town at once. He was an esteemed example of a businessman.

"And what do we have here, Mrs. Taylor?"

Mr. Tolt emerged at unexpected times to take stock of activities and participants. Thank goodness he wasn't authoritative during funerals. Unfailingly, he was a compassionate man with grieving families. He was patient and sympathetic on those occasions.

"This is the Mission Circle. We're studying the Christian community in Africa."

"And do I know these children?" Standing with feet apart and hands behind his back, he surveyed the group.

Why was he so controlling in a place of love? "Rosie, Susanne, and Belle, say hello to Mr. Tolt." Emma waited until they'd greeted him before she said, "We're low in our numbers today, being our first meeting for the season. When everyone is here, there are ten."

Would he talk to the girls? The two from Noble would be familiar. But he might isolate Rosie with questions, considering her separately because she lived on the outskirts of town. She and her friends often walked in from the Hills—it was vital for them to meet at the church.

"It seems warm in here." Mr. Tolt's stern voice cut into Emma's thoughts.

"I hope so. It's chilly outside."

"But it's too early in the day to have heat on for tomorrow. You must be aware we only start the furnace late Saturday night for Sunday service." He inspected the alcove, frowning as if suspicious. "Do I see an electric heater?"

"Yes, I brought the one from our bedroom when I came over. I thought it would remove the dampness from the air."

"And do you do this often?"

"No, never before. The afternoon sun is sufficient to warm this location later in the spring, but the clouds get in the way sometimes, don't they, girls?"

A wave of laughter helped distract Emma from visualizing Mr. Tolt tallying the added expense.

He turned his head to cough. "Then you should have waited to begin your group."

"Yes, you're probably right. The weather is cooler than I thought it would be."

She'd have to answer for bringing the heater, but it was a small price to pay to meet in a warm corner. If Mr. Tolt caused a problem concerning the use of it, she'd put additional coins on the offering plate towards the cost of maintenance.

"I'm sorry. We simply cannot have this. The stewards purchased that particular piece of equipment for your personal use."

"I'm sorry, too. I'll take it home with me after snacks." Emma swallowed before looking at the girls.

Mr. Told unplugged it from the wall. Turning his back to everyone, he lifted the heater. "I'll return it to the parsonage, as I have something to say to Reverend Taylor."

Emma suppressed a shudder at the egotistical tone of his voice. She took a deep breath, saddened that the girls had heard they were not important enough to have funds invested in their activities. If Mr. Tolt treated them in this way, he undoubtedly related to the rest of the children in the congregation similarly when they shared their opinions.

A man knocked on the counter. "Can I bother you, Tom? The inspector is here to look at the furnace."

"Yes, of course." Mr. Tolt smiled. "Excuse me, ladies, I am needed."

What charm he showed in the presence of others. However, he wouldn't leave the building without deepening the conflict he'd started with Emma.

"Perhaps what we spent in hydro today, we saved in coal."

Mr. Tolt lingered for a moment. "I suppose that's your way to look at it. I'm not sure I understand its relevance." The slight edge to his voice made a clear statement that he was finished talking.

The cluster appeared to glean sufficient confidence from Emma's side of the discussion and continued to draw pictures of their African village life. *Such treasures, these children were: trusting and creative.* Their ongoing conversation proved they were comfortable sharing opinions.

Suddenly, Mr. Tolt returned and spoke from where he stood a few feet from the kitchen cupboards. "Mrs. Taylor, could you please step over here?"

A public-school teacher had sent her to the hall for giggling. This felt much the same. Trembling weakened her as she moved across the floor where he waited. "How can I help you?"

He still held the heater in his hand. "Have you completed your meeting?"

"Not quite. They don't have much more to do on their project, and when that's done, we'll have our cake before leaving." Emma examined his frowning face. "Would you join us? They would welcome your interest."

"This area may grow cooler as the afternoon lengthens. Perhaps you should finish your meeting now."

"Are you telling us to go home?"

"I'm merely asking you to take care of this."

"All right, we'll hurry along." *Nothing he says will make us miss our closing, even if we must pull on our toques.*

Later, as they assembled for their snack, cheers interrupted Emma's thoughts as she divided the portion of the cake she'd brought from her cold room. One flickering candle stood in the middle. "Come on, girls," Emma said. "Let's sing to Rosie on her eleventh birthday."

They gathered at the table, eyes sparkling, glancing from one to another as they snickered to the edge of giggling. When they finished their refreshments, Emma collected their plates and wiped up the crumbs.

"Before you leave, divide what's left of the cake, wrap your piece and take it to your mother." Giggles and chatter erupted. Emma had added half a banana to enrich the ingredients to give the girls their favourite flavour.

They snickered and whispered until Susanne slipped away from the others. She tip-toed back a few minutes later, proudly holding a package neatly wrapped in newspaper and tied with a string.

Setting it in the middle of the wooden surface, she said, "We remember singing to Rosie last year, and on our way out, a friend asked if you had candles on your cake, saying she was sorry to have missed the date. Even though we don't know the exact day, we planned to surprise you on our first meeting."

Tears flooded Emma's eyes as she said, "Thank you, girls. It's today, and this is the best present ever." She opened it and lifted a moss-green scarf. *They do like this suit, or maybe they thought it needed a new look.* As much as the gift, she appreciated their ability to grasp an opportunity and be generous.

"Momma made it," Rosie said.

"It's beautiful." Emma ran her finger lengthwise on the intricate cable stitches. "I'll wear it tomorrow. Please thank your mom."

Their young voices floated across the kitchen as they sang *Happy birthday, dear Mrs. Taylor, happy birthday to you.*

Emma smiled through her tears. Bill's decision concerning the girls' visit to worship weighed heavily. Would they keep their joy regardless of the result?

TWO

The clicking of Emma's shoes sounded like a clock as she marched through the kitchen. Time was crucial. Where was Bill? The hall message board was empty. Needing permission quickly to bring the girls into worship took Emma from room to room. Was it wrong to let the children believe the church welcomed them to take part? Would Bill give his consent?

"Bill, are you home? Yoo-hoo!" His closed office suggested he didn't want the desk disturbed. Emma hurried up the steps to the second floor, hoping he was resting in the bedroom. But no. She'd carefully made the bed in the morning. It was as she'd left it.

Was Bill working on his sermon and hadn't heard his name called? She pushed the door open. There he was—his back to her as he stared out the window. His slight form cast a shadow as he turned. Even in the dimness of the setting, his receding grey hairline reflected spent years. A frown creased his face.

"Bill, I'm sorry to disturb you," Emma stammered. Something was wrong.

"We should talk."

"Is it your heart? Are you not feeling well?" Emma's throat tightened as she walked toward him. Chest discomfort during the last few months had caused Bill to complain. Was he all right? She moved into the centre of the room; the heater sat on the floor beside the desk. "I see you've had a visit from Mr. Tolt."

"He came here after he talked with you this afternoon."

"And did he offend you? Is that why you're in here without lights?"

No answer.

Emma's eyes pricked, but she blinked at tears. "He was upset with me, wasn't he?"

"Yes, I'm afraid he was. He asked that you stop the Mission Circle."

Emma pressed a hand to her waist. Stop it? How could she? "Those were his words? His exact words?"

"Yes." Bill combed his thinning hair with his fingers. "What happened in your conversation?"

Emma sighed. "Mr. Tolt came in and as much as said we were not important enough to provide heat for—"

"And you took offence?"

"Well, I did, but not enough that he'd disallow the meeting."

"I'm afraid it was, love." Bill tilted his head. "Anything else?"

"He came back later and said we should finish." Emma sighed.

"And did you do what he asked?"

"After we had our birthday cake, we left."

The lines on Bill's forehead deepened. That wasn't what he'd needed to hear. It sounded as if she'd defied Mr. Tolt. She hadn't meant to, but it was essential for the girls to complete their afternoon.

"That delay wouldn't make him happy."

"We have to live with it." Emma searched Bill's face looking for support. "Did he speak further about this?"

"He said your group wasn't necessary, as the children learn all they need in Sunday school."

This attitude bordered on control; she'd heard it before. "He did? He said that. What did you tell him?"

"I told him you would discontinue meeting in the kitchen until the weather was warmer. I didn't promise him more."

Emma breathed a sigh of relief at Bill's carefully worded sentence. "Good. You're well-practiced at shifting around Mr. Tolt's requests. Let's take each gathering individually. I'll invite them to come here in April. Our table is hardly big enough, but I can add a small surface."

Being out of the church was disappointing, but there was no alternative. Careful not to hurt Bill's ministry or show disrespect to Mr. Tolt, Emma focused on being positive. He was an upstanding man, but he didn't understand the importance of getting together. Unlike Bill, who was predictable, always thoughtful in his responses, Mr. Tolt wanted to be in charge. Bill had been a natural leader since Emma had met him. And today, he addressed the problem with respect.

"I'm proud of you, Bill Taylor. You cope exceptionally well with Mr. Tolt. This decision is wise due to his lack of understanding of the importance of a variety in children's Christian education. He can be challenging to work with, and you hold your own every time he speaks out."

"I'm sorry you had to go through this, Em." Bill's voice softened. "This is important to you. But…there's another issue." A moment of silence held the words in his grip. "He said you had too much to say." Bill grinned at Emma. "When he gets in this mood, he continually finds pet peeves."

Although Mr. Tolt's comment stung, she didn't feel guilty for participating in her areas of guidance. "We'll survive." She walked to Bill and hugged him. "The only reason I have the girls come to the church is to give them something of their own. It helps them to feel connected to God, the congregation, and the building. With worship, Sunday school and the Mission Circle, they'll have an exceptional faith experience."

"Do you think it's working?" Bill started to turn back to his desk.

"I do." She took a deep breath. "You know what is at the bottom of this, don't you? This is not really concerning the heater or the cost of hydro. This is a direct focus on teaching this group…giving leadership."

"We have to let that go. It's bigger than both of us."

"If I let it go, then how can I teach them to stand up for themselves?"

He placed his fingers to her lips. "You'll figure out a way."

She hugged Bill and then pulled back. "I want us to be a visible example of support, in this case, to women and children. I mean, if we don't, who will model for them how to respond and serve?"

"I see you doing that daily."

"I hope so. But I'm like a shadow in ministry, flitting from the choir loft to the kitchen. I visit the sick with you and breeze by the pulpit without so much as a blink, well, except when Mr. Tolt allows." Emma bit her lip. "I understand. Really, I do. You were called, not me…or even us."

"And anything different would not be included in the covenant between the governing council and me. These vague options such as you are implying are awkward, Em." He sighed. "You're correct. Your independent participation is not part of the covenanting of First's call. That's not how it works."

She said softly, "Whatever happened to the promise that God will make all things new, Bill?"

He patted her on the shoulder. "You can count on that."

Emma reached to a side table and pushed a plant until the weak side faced the window. "Sometimes, I sense I live a double life, one where my undying support of your ministry is visible to the congregation. At the same time, my offerings to the church slump dormant in a pile of unresolved ambitions. They expect you to teach, preach, visit, and make all the decisions while I stand quietly behind you."

"It's the way it is, love." Bill took her hand. "You and the ladies have the opportunity to speak whenever you ask. I always honour your request."

Emma sighed. "Speaking, yes. The elders have no problem with us speaking in worship on Mother's Day. Sharing the latest library and Sunday school news or prayer sessions even gain acceptance." She moved the plant again.

"I often wonder at times if these restrictions make you unhappy, yet you continually stand with me on all corners and overcome the limitations." Bill drew her close and whispered in her ear. "Being a minister's wife is not the easiest role to fill."

"My dear, I'm very happy being this minister's wife." She kissed one cheek and then the other. Unspoken words regarding vocational debate would remain silent for this time. "On a different topic, Bill, the girls referred to the Matthew scripture you preached from last week. You know that passage where the women and children weren't counted?"

He settled behind his desk. "Of course. Is there a concern?"

Emma's eyes narrowed. Did he not realize what he'd said? "The group wondered if you'd ask them during mission time tomorrow morning to explain why they chose the African village project." She hesitated. "They questioned if they needed to keep track of their stick figures or if everybody was important. So exact they are."

"That's good. I'd like them to come and bring their work." Bill nodded as if agreeing with himself. "They're that interested, Em. Who would think numbers mattered to children? Hmm." He rubbed his finger back and forth across his chin. "It'll show they listen to my sermons."

"You don't think this would be too much with us travelling to Hampton in the afternoon? You know, something extra added to the service makes a little more for you to think about."

"No, no. I'm happy to invite them to come and share the time. And, Emma, I'm glad we had this discussion. I haven't felt comfortable with Mr. Tolt's attitude lately, so thank you for standing your ground. It probably made it easier for me at this end."

"Then that's resolved." Emma reached for his hand. "Now come, we'll put our supper on the table. I made a tasty casserole earlier, and it'll be ready for us."

Relief surged through Emma even though Bill appeared to miss the significant point she tried to make. Yet, his response pleased her. If he had declined the request, Emma would have hurried out to Rosie's house before 6:00 to reclaim her note.

Emma swallowed a chuckle. She hardly believed that small electric heater had created more heat than warmth. It'd be worth making this move to their kitchen. Maybe someone will ask why and keep the topic open.

"Oh, and Em. Happy birthday." He hugged her and whispered in her ear, "You didn't think I'd forgotten, did you?"

"One never knows in our busyness. And I thank you."

"But, not just that, I also have a special plate set aside for our dessert."

"You do?" She pulled back and winked at him. "Do you mean that half chocolate cake with the fluffy white icing hidden in the cold room?"

"Half? Ah, so you weren't just peeking?"

"You could say that. I was hoping it was for us." Emma agreed.

"I'm glad you left a portion. It's not the first occasion that something disappeared when you thought it was needed."

"Not on my birthday, love. I confess, I shared several pieces with the girls and a few to take home. And after we have some for supper, the rest will make a delicious contribution to fellowship treats tomorrow."

Bill's teasing warmed her heart. He understood. Her life was full of the unexpected, but she was careful where it led. Well, except for tomorrow—she'd soon find out if she had risked too much.

THREE

The sun warmed Emma as she sat toward the front of the sanctuary invoking memories. While the presence of God surrounded her, the majestic sounds of the organ filled the air. Although the Guild ladies attempted to keep the chancel plain, they provided attractive pulpit-falls according to the season and hung banners elsewhere to tell the old story. It must have been difficult to remove the grape juice stain following the last sacrament as they hadn't returned the covering on the communion table.

A movement from the corner of her eye caught Emma's attention. In the next pew, the girls leaned forward as if preparing to race to Bill. His deep voice interrupted Emma's thoughts. "We have special visitors today. Will the Emma Taylor Mission Circle join me at the front?"

Bless his heart. He sincerely acknowledges my work to the entire church. To see the group's excitement is worth the risk of being reprimanded.

Emma held her breath as the children scrambled to stand. Would they trip over their feet trying to get to the pulpit first? Contrary to their usual playful nature, their orderly conduct surprised Emma. One by one, they walked to the front, carrying their cardboard portraits of an African village. Would they ask Bill why women and children weren't counted in the scripture he'd read? *Surely not. The reason they were here was to share their project.*

As a choir member, Emma didn't often have a chance to sit in the congregation. But today, she wanted the girls to be able to see her and be encouraged, so she'd sent her regrets to the organist.

Although not tall, Bill towered above the children when he received them. He quickly sat on the step to prepare for their discussion so that they could see each other on the same level. Bill asked questions that led directly into a mission story. They responded clearly without hesitation. He spoke as a loving father, which reminded Emma of the stories he'd told their twins, Bernice and Beatrice, when they were young.

Emma had shared a growing concern with Bill regarding young ladies having options for their life's work. Their daughters had recently moved to Toronto, and both had secured excellent management positions. Although they lived a long distance away, it was evident they experienced a sense of accomplishment in their chosen areas.

This was the conviction that Emma hoped for all young women. The Mission Circle often explored possibilities to develop confidence. Hopefully, they'll pass the message to their daughters and granddaughters.

Was Emma an example of personal strength? People expected Bill to lead the way, and she was to follow. He was the focus; she was his support. She didn't lack ambition, but ministers' wives had their vital role to fill. Emma wasn't invited to tea parties or book clubs; she often heard about them after the events. The hosts understood she was Bill's helpmate and knew she cherished that position.

Bill missed seeing that her assistance was a benefit. She wouldn't admit an eagerness to work with him as they'd done in the past. It'd hurt him to know that she occasionally felt deprived of sharing her faith in leadership. Her role was totally supportive of Bill, and Emma had blended into her position. Yet, at times she questioned if it could be different.

When standing for a hymn, Emma grimaced. In contrast to Bill's immaculate appearance, his frayed pant cuffs revealed his scruffy shoes. She'd shone them last night, but the worn leather had absorbed the polish.

• • •

During refreshments, Emma continually greeted parishioners. She received gratitude aimed at Bill's sermon, compliments for the choir's anthem and the skilful piano selection of 'Amazing Grace.'

"It was lovely to see those children taking part in the service this morning." A soft voice surfaced from a few ladies standing to Emma's left.

Irene Trask's voice, curdled as sour cream, rose into the air. "I don't agree with you at all. It's Reverend Taylor's place to speak in church. Having those girls up there would be Mrs. Taylor's influence."

Irene, from one of the groups, was unpredictable in discussions. It was always a surprise how she'd defy or defend any topic. Another voice entered the conversation praising the girls. *Best to avoid this debate.*

Emma moved to mingle, stepping aside for Mr. Tolt. He smiled broadly as he strutted through the assembly carrying the offering plates, obviously eager to count the money. Was the congregation aware of the fine line Emma walked with his scrutiny? If he confronted her in public, would anyone stand with her?

"Mrs. Taylor, Mrs. Taylor." Mrs. Trask rushed forward, spilling tea into her saucer. Would she be looking for a compliment regarding the piano selection her daughter, Susanne, had played? Or did she have a grievance to air? Knowing Mrs. Trask was quick to judge without awareness of the whole story, Emma waited to hear her complaint. "Can you explain why you brought some girls from the Hills to participate in our service this morning?"

"Hello, Mrs. Trask." Emma forced a smile. "Why, yes, I'd be glad to do that. A few walk to our group when it isn't raining. I checked for their mother's consent. At our last meeting they finished their pictures of the African communities you saw this morning. And, well, they decided to ask permission to attend worship to show the congregation their projects. It allowed Reverend Taylor to tell a story why everyone is important." Emma rested a hand on Mrs. Trask's arm. "Our mission quota is low due to the economy. However, that doesn't mean our love has to run short for those in need." She pushed a stray curl behind her ear with her free hand.

"Well." Mrs. Trask observed the room as if caught with her fingers in the cookie jar. "When you look at it like that, it's understandable. But that's not the point, Mrs. Taylor." The woman's red hat capped with orange feathers toppled to one side.

Emma raised her eyebrows. "What do you think the point is?"

"We did fine, Mrs. Taylor, didn't we?" Rosie tugged on Emma's arm. "Reverend Taylor explained the village to everybody so well, and we answered all his questions. I could tell he liked us being up there with him." She chuckled. "That was as much fun as we have in our church. And, and we were all in…included."

Emma smiled at Rosie's singsong voice as she struggled with the big word and then realized that she was referring to their previous debate about being counted.

"What do you mean, 'our church'?" Mrs. Trask asked Rosie.

She tilted her head as if she didn't understand the question. "Well, it's…it's just that we love it when Mrs. Taylor comes to the Hills to lead us. Absolutely love it." She looked to Emma and grinned.

Irene checked the latch on her purse before thrusting it under her arm. "I must be going."

Rosie skipped across the floor to join her friends, obviously unaware of innocently opening an additional topic for Emma to resolve. Mrs. Trask would remember this, and Emma would be prepared to respond.

People milled around the room as she took a mental attendance to pass on to Bill if he didn't come for refreshments. She must speak to Rosie's mother, who'd sat under the sanctuary wall clock. Perhaps she positioned herself this way to be last in and first out. Emma was anxious to find her and show appreciation for knitting the scarf, but the image of that wide-brimmed hat pulled low, covering a portion of her face, wouldn't fade. She was a fascinating woman who seemed so cautious.

Mrs. Trask stopped in front of Emma again and handed her a cup of tea. A gesture of regret? "There's none of your cake left." She tucked her serviette in her sleeve. "You've provided treats forever, and this one was extra special. Anyway, I got a corner piece—my favourite size."

"I'm glad they enjoyed it," Emma offered. This conversation had taken a pleasant tone, which was an unusual experience. Irene Trask moved from one person to another, chatting during laughter. Everyone responded to her enthusiastically. Probably they figured life was more relaxed when she was happy. Fellowship was the perfect place to share Emma's leftover birthday cake if it satisfied Mrs. Trask's sweet tooth.

Sometimes attitudes and wrangling smothered Emma. She anticipated visiting neighbouring congregations, which she often did with Bill. Although degrees of conflict could be part of any assembly, visitors didn't usually get caught in it. Hopefully, this afternoon would be such an occasion as it'd give an opportunity to see an old friend from seminary days.

FOUR

Emma and Bill travelled south to Hampton and sat together in the church. "Bless us as we gather here in your midst." Emma's prayer didn't draw anyone's attention. Four gentlemen in the chancel, posed in straight-backed chairs, scanned the people as if counting heads. Faint giggles floated from three girls sitting in the first pew with parents, likely telling stories.

Emma leaned near to Bill and whispered, "I wonder who's happier to be here, the men or those youngsters."

Bill nodded.

Was there someone in this congregation to tell these children they were important? The countenance of those facing the assembly didn't appear willing.

Reflecting on this morning's worship, the little group and their African villages came to Emma's mind. This was leadership—the illustrations and descriptions had heightened other's awareness. It warmed Emma's heart.

For too many years, ladies had missed opportunities. They were perceived to have nothing to contribute except apple pies and choir anthems, although encouraging conversations this morning concerning the girls' involvement were supportive.

This familiar sanctuary relaxed Emma. A red rug curving on the top of the aisle crossed the entire front resembling royalty. Candles, probably considered by the majority to be the height of extravagance, cast a flickering glow from the communion table. Sunlight splashed through the stained-glass windows revealing multiple shades of colour on the organ's brass pipes. At least having the service in the afternoon saved the price of electric power, as the stewards wouldn't have to turn on the long-chained globe lights. The depression caused everybody to protect the almighty dollar, especially in the Lord's house.

The organist played an old hymn, and Emma viewed the loft where the choir had filled the space while she daydreamed. Hampton had called a colleague, the Reverend Albert Miller, to be their minister. Emma and Bill hadn't seen him much since their seminary days and were excited to renew their relationship.

As District Supervisor, Mr. Tolt entered the chancel from the left, leading the way for Albert. His well-groomed hair was neat but lengthy as he appeared tall in a grey suit that fit him loosely; nonetheless, he was the Albert they both loved. "Oh my, how well he looks, don't you think, Bill?"

"I do, indeed. It seems like yesterday we had our all-night discussions."

Mr. Tolt moved forward; his deep voice vibrated across the large area. "Good afternoon. Welcome to this covenanting service. I regret to inform you that one of our elders had to usher our guest preacher, the Reverend Maitland, from the sanctuary as he took a severe coughing spell. They'll return as soon as possible."

A hum of laments washed through the congregation. He was an excellent teacher, and Emma had been expecting his meaningful words to open scripture. When he spoke, she came away newly inspired to serve. Although she was aware this would meet severe opposition if she followed up on it, his interpretation of the Word still strengthened her.

He would have naturally directed his teaching to the men if he hadn't had the coughing spell. Yet, his messages extended past usual expectations and prompted Emma to respond. This challenge didn't surprise her; it was an echo, repetitive and ebbing. She claimed it for herself when she listened to his sermons.

"And now, I'll appeal to the rest of you gentlemen. Is there one among you who'll accept my invitation to open this service?" Mr. Tolt spoke with expectation. "Do any of you feel led to give opening comments?"

Silence filled the sanctuary, except for whispering and a few creaking sounds from those shifting in pews.

"Bill, is this something you might do?" Emma whispered.

"I'd rather not." Bill shook his head. "It takes a bit of deliberation to put one's thoughts together. I'm not sure I'm up to that today."

Emma counted the broad pine floorboards under her old, polished shoes—anything served to take her mind off the urge to respond to the appeal offered to the men. Did she have the confidence to stand and accept, despite the clearly stated word, gentlemen? If it'd been anyone but Mr. Tolt offering the invitation, Emma would have walked to the front to ask if it was acceptable to assist. How awkward he could make it for someone who, in his opinion, did the unexpected.

"Would you do it, Em?" Bill whispered, his gentle voice hopeful. "You know, as you do for me sometimes?"

She studied the gentlemen facing her. "I've been considering it."

No one accepted. Even though Bill had encouraged Emma to stand and offer, she couldn't make herself do it. It seemed out of place. She was the minister's wife—that was a general understanding.

Yet, there was another side. Was it not the least Emma could do, as Reverend Maitland's messages surpassed usual interpretation and prompted God's leading? Hopefully, the men would see her gesture as supportive.

She slid to the edge of the seat with her hands on the pew in front of her, still hesitant. And then she glanced at Mr. Tolt. His glaring eyes bore through her resembling blinding headlights, defying her to continue. Unwilling now to walk forward, she settled back.

"On second thought, Bill, since it's a special occasion, I'd better not." Emma's opportunity had vanished and by her own decision. Those who observed her change of mind would think her stoic appearance represented her station in life. As in many areas of church dutifulness, their perspective misled them.

"I'll leave you to consider this, gentlemen, as we listen to our accomplished organist's prelude." Mr. Tolt nodded.

Following the conclusion of the music, his voice echoed in the sanctuary as he gazed across the assembly. "Very well then, we'll begin." He prayed and read a few texts from scripture before he opened his hymnbook. "Let us join in singing number thirty-seven."

Emma held back the flood of tears pushing against her closed eyelids. She searched for a handkerchief stuck in her sleeve but couldn't find it. Bill would notice if she sniffed or wiped her face. The beloved lyrics appeared blurred. Opening this service wouldn't have been much different from what she'd occasionally done for Bill in Noble. Or would it?

With music in the background, the commissioning celebration before Emma and Bill left for Africa to serve as a team came to mind. The president of the seminary had laid hands on Bill, while she sat alone. For the first time, Pa's words had echoed as truth.

Much later, the Magola Mission elders introduced them as Mizzer Bill and Missa Emma. They'd preached, taught together and cared for the sick in prayer and witness. Precious memories pushed through the years.

Mr. Tolt came to the pulpit and announced that, in the interval, he'd asked the Reverend Albert to share an experience or two that had guided him into ministry and later brought him to this church to serve. "He has agreed to do this. And as he gathers his thoughts, we could sing number forty-two."

Emma leaned to Bill. "This has to be difficult with such short notice."

"Indeed. I wouldn't want to be called to speak without preparation."

At the end of the hymn, Albert went to the pulpit. He spoke with clarity and confidence. Sharing stories about his family, education, and the decision to apply to this pastoral charge brought him to close with prayer before returning to his seat.

Mr. Tolt thanked him with appreciation, admitting he'd placed him in an awkward position. "I can see you are a man who'll never be lost for words." Bishop Martin joined him, and after a short message, he invited Albert to come forward and take his place beside the communion table. The bishop covenanted Albert with the congregation in a litany of phrases before giving the benediction.

As soon as the organist finished the postlude, the assembly went to the fellowship hall for refreshments. Bill surprised Emma by saying, "Let's not stay for lunch, Em. There is such a crowd, and we probably wouldn't have a chance to talk to Albert, anyway."

Although Bill had provided an easy exit, why had he wanted to leave? Discontentment spread through Emma and saddened her as they made their way back to Noble. She had anticipated the afternoon, but despite her excitement in Albert being close geographically, unhappiness lay heavy on her heart. When Reverend Maitland hadn't spoken, and they'd left without lunch and fellowship, her feelings deepened. Mr. Tolt's disapproving glare added to her ongoing discomfort. Still, Bill's quiet mood during their drive home was unsettling. She sighed. Whatever it was, he'd tell her in time.

FIVE

The familiar scenery of patchwork fields and woodland relaxed Emma as they travelled to Noble. She stretched her legs and slipped off her shoes. It wasn't like Bill to be quiet when he drove, but it seemed appropriate with this afternoon's events. Perhaps he was reflecting on their relationship with Albert.

Without warning, sputtering and vibration resonated through the car as it jerked to a stop. Startled, Emma straightened as Bill pulled on the emergency brake. His hair, damp from perspiration, curled above his ears.

"Whatever happened?" Emma frowned, staring at him. She edged forward.

"Not sure." Bill wiped the dust from the heat gauge. "It was running hot during the last few miles, but I assumed we'd make it home."

"It's too far to walk from here." Emma studied the road ahead, straight as the ladies' quilting lines.

"Don't worry, Em." Bill smiled. "This highway is well travelled. Somebody will come soon."

Her watch showed 4:30. The sun had begun its decline in the western sky, enclosed by a bright blaze of yellow and white. The farmland surrounding them waited spring seeding despite the scattering of snow still visible in the shadow of trees. Yet, the peaceful view of the landscape didn't ease Emma's mind. Would someone come to assist them?

Gripping Bill's arm, Emma said. "Do you have your 5:00 supper pills with you?" His regular medication schedule often dictated their activities.

Bill lowered his eyes. "I didn't bring them. The service took longer than I thought it would." He rubbed his long fingers over his arm. "Hampton's only a few miles south of Noble; we've always driven it without incident."

"Never mind, love. We'll be rescued, shortly." Between Bill's anxiety of being without his medication and feeling abandoned on an empty strip of pavement, his blood pressure would elevate.

Stepping out of the car, he moved with care, as if stiff. After walking to the front of the vehicle, he lifted the hood. Emma slipped her feet into her shoes, opened her door and leaned against it to watch. Bill pushed and wiggled various hoses and wires. When he loosened the radiator lid, he jumped back to avoid the fountain of boiling water and steam. Sweat beaded his forehead, and he wiped it with his handkerchief. "I'm afraid we're stuck where we are; we might as well make the best of it."

Emma eased into the vehicle, but not before Bill pressed a hand to his chest. "Come in and rest." Lately, it didn't take much to cause him distress. Emma grabbed a pillow and an afghan from the back. When he settled in beside her, she spread the crocheted blanket on his knees and wrapped her arms around him to give added warmth.

"I hope the car doesn't need a radiator or hoses. Those parts cost a lot." Bill shifted his position. "We haven't spent much money on the engine, so we shouldn't complain."

Emma grimaced. "We haven't had much to spend on anything since this ungodly depression set in." She touched Bill's arm. They'd made hard choices through these impoverished years. Situations of scarcity had convinced her that a certain number in their faith family considered God's love was enough to keep their minister fed and dressed. Dismissing those thoughts, she said, "But we have God, each other, and a wonderful flock."

"We do." Bill closed his eyes. "A determined one, anyway. The finances worry me, though. The offering can't be the same with everything stretched to make ends meet."

"Don't fret, Bill. We'll get along." Emma's fingers slowly traced his hand.

Bill rubbed his forehead as if thinking. "If the funds don't come in, Emma, the church as we know it will close. Granted, the congregation can still stay together and use the basement or another building."

"Have you been pondering this for a while?"

"I have, but I've nothing to base my concerns on except the direction this country is going. Prices and availability have changed so much over a few years."

Silence filled the car again. Emma stroked Bill's arm. "Let's not waste time on what may not happen. What can I do to make you comfortable?"

Bill's shirt rose and fell with heavy breathing. Whether he wanted to admit it or not, he strained to inhale. He needed to be at home in his bed.

"I'm all right." He rested his head against the seat. "Just feeling a bit weak." He sighed and pulled his hat down on his forehead.

Leaning back, Emma closed her eyes. Family, friends and parishioners came to mind.

Bill stirred. "Do you remember the April rally at Hillson Methodist Church and how your life changed when the Reverend Timothy Nelson preached?"

"Yes, indeed. It was a special day even though it's many years ago."

"It was 1910, I think. That must have been the beginning of something exciting for you, Emma."

"Hmm. Almost immediately, I joined the crusades through Southern Ontario, and churches soon invited me to lead revival meetings."

Bill turned and studied Emma's face. "I recall some of them."

Wiping a tear, she continued. "The image of Pa reading a quote from a local newspaper still amazes me: 'Gifted preacher with an unreserved understanding of God's Word.'" She should find that clipping again. It helped reclaim a sense of self to read it, especially when overwhelmed with a narrow perspective of the ladies' work.

"That sounds as if he was proud of you. And didn't your father say your solos reflected sacred texts?"

Emma glanced out the car window. All of this seemed a lifetime ago. Of course, it nearly had been. Singing musical selections in worship was natural, and if Emma offered to do this at First, it might strengthen Bill's ministry. Perhaps this needed more thought, although he preferred she sang alto with the choir.

"Yes, he often said that." Rally days had humbled Emma when individuals said her efforts changed thousands of lives. Then and now, it was God in their hearts that transformed them. "I remember wanting to speak with Pa concerning the possibility of further education. But the conversation was short and abrupt when I said, "Someday, I will lead a church."

"Didn't he want to talk about it?"

"Oh, he talked about it, but not what I wanted to hear. He responded with, 'Don't count on that. You're a woman. You can lead a revival; they come and go. Congregations call men to their pulpits to preach, teach, and live among their people.'"

Bill cleared his throat. "Those words seem harsh."

"I was sure he'd stopped believing in me. Yet, I couldn't understand why he'd say that as he'd always shown support. In fact, he'd been the first one to see God working in my efforts."

A timely quietness wafted through the car, and Emma closed her eyes. Bill's voice broke the silence. "Was that when he placed his hand on your shoulder and said, 'With your good looks, girl, you'll yearn for marriage and a family of your own.'"

"Yes. That was a compliment as I did want marriage and children. Somehow, I guess I wanted all of it."

Both Emma and Bill settled back as if they'd said enough.

He hesitated for several minutes. "It has to be puzzling, doesn't it?"

Emma stretched. "It is when I reflect on our conversation. I remember Pa adding, 'All I'm saying is, the church will never appoint a woman to the Word, Sacrament, and Pastoral care.'" He'd raised his eyebrows and stared at me. "That's a man's call from God."

"That term must have seemed limiting to you."

Emma trembled. The image of her father's face lingered in her mind's eye, stern, yet his eyes had shown loving compassion with a sense of helplessness. "I thought he'd embrace me. But he took a step sideways and walked away. We didn't refer to it again. It was such a contradiction and remains relevant in my memory."

"I hope you have enough good memories in our ministry to counter those lingering feelings."

"Indeed, I have, Bill. So many wonderful ones." She snuggled in beside him.

A long stretch of stillness lay between them. Emma reached to trace white stubble on Bill's chin with her finger as questions of next week's service probed her mind. It'd be short notice to bring in a supply minister and gather enough money to pay him. She'd offer to help, thinking it might relieve Bill's anxiety. He watched his flock with care. Nothing much missed his keen eye.

"What do I hear, Em?" Bill's voice sounded urgent. "Is there something coming? I can't see anything." He altered his position.

Emma sat upright to peer through the window. The sun hung low into the horizon, leaving a shadowy view of the road with dull lights advancing. "Yes, it's a truck." She reached for the door handle. "I'll get out and stand in front of the car. Maybe they'll stop."

Emma shifted off her seat before Bill could protest. She waved as the vehicle drew close. In a few seconds, it stopped beside her.

"Hello there, Mrs. Taylor." Noble's grocery store proprietor, Henry Bates, gazed out his open window. "Having car trouble?"

"Yes, we're…the car overheated and…well, it stalled. Low on water it seems."

"They've been known to do that," he teased.

She pointed to the car. Bill hadn't stepped out.

"And Reverend Taylor?" Henry nodded. "How can I help?"

"We need a ride to town," Emma said. "Bill is feeling discomfort with all the stress of car trouble, as well as missing his overdue medication." Admitting this weakened her balance.

Henry slid out of the truck without hesitation and walked to Bill. Bending a knee, he knelt to get closer. "What's the best way to make this easier for you, Reverend Taylor?" He lowered his voice. "Can you walk? Or I could go and get Doc Baxter."

"We've been waiting a while for somebody to come along. I'm feeling a little taxed." Bill glanced at Emma. "But I'll be fine to ride into town."

His fearful glimpse begged her attention. Then, trying to comfort him, she said, "The doctor will know what's best."

"Let's get you into the truck." Henry shifted to his opposite foot and leaned against the door. "Can you manage, Reverend Taylor?" Steadying Bill with one arm, Henry shuffled to the truck. Bill's wobbly steps caused him to lean heavily.

Emma touched her chest. In a short time, life had changed for them.

• • •

Henry attempted to talk, referring to the weather and gas prices, but they rode to town in silence for the most part. "Do you want to go to the doctor's house?" He slid closer, narrowing the space between Bill as he slumped forward.

"I'll be fine to go home. I'll take my medication, and then I'll rest."

Bill sounded tired, and Emma bent closer to him. His eyelids were heavy, and his breathing laboured.

"Don't you worry," Henry said. "I'll send somebody from McGregor's garage to bring your car into town."

"Thank you." Emma clasped her hands in her lap. "You're an answer to prayer."

"I've been called a lot of names, but not that." He changed gears as he came to the corner. "I'm glad to help. You've both been angels of mercy countless times to the folks in Noble. First church has led many to safety after having a breakdown and finding themselves stranded on a sideroad of life." He glanced at Bill. "And I'm no exception, as you might well remember my struggle to overcome my addiction."

Emma did, but Bill only nodded and stared straight ahead. Slowing as he approached the driveway, Henry said, "Here we are."

Once he parked, he walked to the passenger side. Taking his arm, Emma stepped from the running board to the gravel. Henry offered his hand to Bill and said, "Let's get you inside." When Bill steadied himself, Henry slowly sauntered with him.

Emma opened the front door. "Thanks so much. Without you, we'd still be stranded. It appears we've entered a different season. I welcome your care…and appreciate your love for the church."

Hearing Henry's story of defeating addiction interested Emma. Would this afternoon's incidence heighten Bill's awareness of his health? He had plenty to overcome.

SIX

Emma hung her jacket on a hook behind the kitchen door and hurried to the cupboard.

Bill sat at the table with a heavy sigh. "Thanks for your help, Em. I'm relieved to be home."

"You're very welcome." Emma brought his pill to him with a glass of water. He put the capsule in his mouth and drank slowly. His face appeared strained even as he closed his eyes.

"Will you call the doctor, or should I?" Emma asked as he placed the container in front of him.

"I'll see how I feel in the morning."

Short and precise in his reply, there was no changing his mind.

Emma stooped to pat Prissy on the head. "Good kitty, found yourself a patch of sun, did you?" Her long, slender, multicoloured body didn't budge, so Emma stepped past her. She opened the cupboard and carried plates and cutlery to their places. "As for supper, how does a few fried potatoes and a slice of pork sound? We can add Maisie's dill pickle relish to it." Their neighbour provided them with treats and a few tidbits they didn't need. Bill didn't trust her friendship, as she seemed to have a love-hate relationship with faith issues, so Emma didn't often mention her.

"Just a bit for me, please." Bill touched his stomach. "I've had a feeling of indigestion with heartburn all afternoon. It must be those peanuts I ate. They always do a number on me."

Emma frowned. He wasn't one to complain but adding this to his earlier signs of discomfort was enough to be concerned.

Their meal proved to be stressful as Bill hesitated to eat. He pushed his food across his plate, nibbling lightly. His colour had lessened to a greyish tinge.

Emma touched Bill's hand. "You're not hungry, Bill?"

"Not really, maybe you can use these leftovers for your next soup." A wide yawn filled his face.

Agreeing to his idea, Emma transferred the dishes to the sink and tidied the pantry while wondering why Bill wouldn't have a conversation with Doc Baxter.

"You're sure you don't want to talk with the doctor before you go to bed?"

"Tomorrow, love." Bill sighed. "I'll contact him in the morning to see if he can make a call." He yawned again. His crooked tie hadn't caught his attention. Bill was usually tidy, always prepared to rise to a need. He'd check his wardrobe to be sure that his two white shirts that Emma faithfully washed, starched and ironed were available. But that hadn't worked lately. Instead, he wore the one he liked for too long a stretch.

Was he telling her everything, or was he holding back from acknowledging his condition was worse than he admitted? He was truthful when asked a question, but he might not want to admit anything. There was no use asking why he hadn't wanted to talk to Doc when they came home.

"Why don't you go upstairs and relax, dear?"

"I will soon." Bill rested his head against his hand.

"The Gospel Hour on the radio is a good way to pass the time."

"That'd be nice, but I'm going to sit in my office for a while."

While he sat in his much-loved room, he'd probably light his trusted pipe. His hand-hewn favourite would be hanging in its holder, waiting for him. He placed it in the drawer when anybody from the church came to see him. If they smelled smoke, they didn't mention it.

Later, Emma joined Bill in lifting one foot and then the other as they climbed the broad steps, both avoiding the middle of the squeaky one that sounded like Prissy complaining.

"Maybe our bed would be better downstairs, Bill." Emma sighed. "It's getting harder to manage this grand staircase as we get older." The charming oak banister wound the entire height of the ten-foot front entrance, including a half turn to enter the second floor. Two colourful stained-glass windows graced the upper hall, shedding a mottled reflection across the wall between the bedrooms. Emma enjoyed this old house, although she hadn't taken advantage of her new sewing room since Bill had renovated a bedroom a few years ago.

"I agree." Bill yawned.

"Or we could say you get exercise when you make this climb. That makes them worth their weight in gold," Emma countered.

"That's better thinking." Bill gripped the railing.

His calm nature helped find the positive side of any situation, even though it made it difficult to identify his emotion and dig through the levels of meaning.

• • •

When they reached the bedroom, Emma pulled the curtains. Bill changed into his pyjamas with effort and didn't bother to fluff his pillow. Neither did he turn on his bedside light or open his favourite devotional. After settling into bed, he rolled on his side and drew up his knees like a child.

"I'm afraid to go to sleep." Tears brimmed Emma's eyes. "I'm worried. I wish we'd called the doctor. Didn't you say you'd do that as soon as we came home?"

"I had a quiet time of scripture meditation and felt rested. We'll call him in the morning. He's probably had a busy Sunday afternoon, as we did." He patted the bed beside him. "Come on, Em." The rich tones of a male quartet singing, 'It is well with my soul," flooded the room.

Brushing her eyes, Emma said softly, "Let this be our prayer." She covered them both with the light quilt and reached for his hand. Bringing it to her lips, she kissed it. "My dear stubborn Bill." She shifted to a comfortable position. "Be ready to say no when you're asked to go here or do this or that? Others can help."

"You are one of those. You can preach, you know, Em. If I feel too tired to go to the pulpit on Sunday, maybe you'd cover for me." He squeezed her fingers. "Would you consider it, love? My notes are on my desk. It's a three-part series. I gave the first section this morning. That'll give you a base without having to think it through."

Bill's suggestion jarred Emma. *Was he giving up?*

He said gently. "There are people out there that say a woman should not preach, that it's a man's world. They'll be a problem for you because they don't understand God's love in distributing gifts." He gently cradled her hand. "But that conversation is for another day."

He took a deep breath and brought the blanket to his chin. "Don't feel you have to read my notes word-for-word. You can give a sermon on your own." Bill loved reflecting on their rally days when they both preached to eager followers who filled the massive tents. This remark gave Emma confidence.

"I could do it if Mr. Tolt would ask." If only they were free to speak about those memorable years in their life. "We'll see how you feel when you've rested before we mention anything." The sheet fell away as she slipped out of bed. "I'll check downstairs and turn off the hall light. I won't be long."

Emma pulled the nightlight chain, leaving a glimmer of light to give a restful appearance. She checked both front and side entrances to ensure they were secure and retraced her steps to their bedroom. When she crawled in beside Bill, his body warmth surrounded her.

Thank you for Bill, God. Keep him safe in your loving arms tonight. And thank you for bringing us home safely. We are both grateful for Henry and his pickup truck . . . and for the unwavering example he is for the men in the congregation.

What would the night hold? Worry, uncertainty and a lot of prayers.

Emma lowered the lamp and settled back into bed. Troubled feelings eased in and out of her mind like dark clouds moving across a horizon. Sleep came and went leaving her anxious.

Out of the silence, Bill gasped. Emma sat up. "Oh, Bill, what is it?" She jerked on her bedside light and studied his face. *A heart attack! God, help us.*

She ran down to the kitchen, pushed the telephone button and turned the crank numerous times. Lizzy Maxwell had the switchboard at the front of her house, close to her bedroom in case of nighttime emergencies. Within minutes, a sleepy voice drawled, "Yes, how can I help?" She yawned.

Emma clutched the receiver. "Quick, Lizzy. Call Doc Baxter. It's Bill. He needs the doctor immediately."

"Oh, Mrs. Taylor." Lizzy sounded suddenly alert. "I'll do that right now. Don't worry—"

"Lizzy, hurry! Please." Emma's voice rose in pitch. She hung the earpiece on its hanger, opened the outside access slightly and hurried to their room.

Her prayers deepened on returning to the bedroom to wait. She held Bill's hand and watched his face. "Oh, Bill, don't leave me. How can I go on without you?"

Bill lay unmoving with his head on the soft pillow. His quiet, shallow breathing resonated in Emma's ears.

The door rattled when the doctor entered. Emma slid out of bed and grabbed her housecoat as footsteps pounded the stairs.

Doc Baxter immediately rushed into the room; his white hair tousled as if he'd come straight from his bed. "Hello, Mrs. Taylor."

Hurrying to Bill's side, Doc spoke gently. He placed the padded ends of the stethoscope into his ears and the flat end on Bill's chest. After listening to his heartbeat, Doc tucked the scope into his satchel. He reached for a bottle and tapped out a pill, lodged it under Bill's tongue and watched him before turning to Emma. "I've arranged to take him to the hospital. The ambulance will be here shortly. It's a heart attack. I'm sorry, Emma. Thank you for your quick attention. You may have saved his life."

A commotion resonated in the upstairs hall. Two attendants came into the room, raised Bill onto a stretcher and covered him with a blanket, tying in the sides.

Why did the room feel so cold? Emma froze as the vibration of boots thudding down the steps faded.

The doctor sounded firm. She shivered, but not from the coolness of the room.

"Come now, Emma. Would you like to get dressed?" Doc Baxter pointed toward the door. "You can ride with me."

• • •

The Noble hospital was not large but sufficient for local needs. If a person needed extensive care, Doc referred them to Hampton. A nurse admitted

Bill to a room filled with blinking lights and humming equipment. Emma stayed with him all night, resting in the big chair at his bedside. She talked briefly with both the staff and Bill. He slept in irregular bouts, occasionally opening his eyes.

Nurses came in and out of the room, nodding to her. Then as the sun broke through the morning haze and brightened the area, Doc Baxter bustled in with a chart in his hand.

After greeting Emma, he walked beside the bed to face his patient. "Good morning, Bill. You rested well during the night."

Bill looked up with glazed eyes.

Doc wiped his brow. "Just to add more information for you. It's not the news you want to hear, I'm afraid. We both know your heart gave fair warning in the last few years that it was weakening. This is different. You'll need greater care. I've conferred with Hampton General's specialist to give you the finest medical treatment. We'll talk when you're feeling better. It's a lot to consider. Do you have any questions?"

Bill moved his head slowly from side to side.

Doc Baxter checked the monitors. "I want you to rest, Bill. I'll be back once I review your medications." He hung the chart on the end of the bed and left with Emma.

"How bad is it?" The scent of disinfectant was nauseating, leaving her feeling faint. Life seemed to hang in the air.

"This differs greatly from former scares. This one could have taken Bill, had it not been for you, Emma. Immediate treatment saved him." The doctor crossed his arms on his chest and leaned against the nurse's station. "Bill needs to separate himself from church responsibilities if he's to recover. I'll talk to him and the elders; we cannot risk taking chances."

Emma's bottom lip quivered. "Should I call the girls?"

"Yes, you should. Why don't you do that now before they go to work? You can use the hospital phone." He gently touched her shoulder to guide her. "Then, go along home and get some rest. It's been a long night, and I've arranged a ride for you with Henry. And Emma, to ease your mind, conflict or yesterday's incident of getting stranded on the road didn't cause this." He offered a slight smile. "Neither did the peanuts. Bill asked these same questions. This has been coming for a while—it's part of the change happening in his body."

"Thank you. I've been wondering."

Doc Baxter nodded and glanced at his watch. "I'll finish my rounds now and see you soon."

Emma went to Bill and talked briefly, assuring him she'd be back later today. But, with each step from his room, the awareness of descending into the unknown deepened. This ongoing transformation rendered her helpless.

Sitting at a desk preparing to phone her daughters added additional angst to Emma's rooted anxiety. She viewed her watch: 7:00. Whoever answered would know it was an emergency. She never called this early.

"Beatrice, dear," Emma said when the ring was cut short.

"Yes, Mom. What is it? Daddy? Is it Daddy?"

"Yes, it is. He took a heart attack last night and is in the hospital."

"Is he all right? I mean, he didn't die, did he?"

Goodness, the girls can be so blunt. "No, he didn't die. But I need to tell you that his condition is serious. The doctor wanted you both to know. You don't have to come immediately but avoid leaving it too long. Just be aware this is different than his previous situations. However, the doctor is looking for a full recovery, but your father's working habits will have to change."

"And you, Mom? Are you okay?"

"I am, dear." Emma wiped tears from her eyes and choked back a sob. "I've been with your father all night here at the hospital, but I waited until this morning to call. You'd have worried until dawn if I'd phoned earlier, and you need your rest."

"Thank you for calling, Mom. I'll be sure to tell Bernice. We love you."

Hopefully, the girls would make plans to come home as soon as possible. Their workdays and social connections gave them a busy life, but their relationship with their father was above everything else.

Being alone was frightening. For now, Emma must see if Henry was waiting at the curb.

SEVEN
PART 2

Henry leaned across the cab of his truck to lift the handle, "Morning, Mrs. Taylor. So sorry to hear about the reverend. I am glad I was able to help last night."

Emma slid onto the seat and closed the door. "Thank you, Henry. You were an angel of mercy in our need. I don't doubt that for a minute." She fidgeted with her purse. "Bill rested well once Doc settled him. He's being referred for special medical assistance."

"The reverend is in good care." Henry glanced sideways to Emma. "And don't you worry concerning trips back and forth to the hospital, I'll pick you up and deliver you whenever you're ready." Then, chuckling at his own words, he said, "I'm well-rehearsed at that, you know, with the grocery store giving me lots of practice."

"Nice to hear your sense of humor. It's been a very sad night." She guarded her eyes against the brilliant sun. "I could walk, but this morning I feel a bit weak at the knees."

Henry slowed down to turn a curve. "I understand. You must rest yourself, as you may need to assist the church while Reverend Taylor is recovering. I hear Doc doesn't want him returning for a stretch."

"So, the rumour mill has begun. Why am I surprised? Do they have him leaving ministry?" That sounded sarcastic. She opened her mouth to apologize when Henry snickered.

"Jack asked me that question when I went to the Post Office." Henry grinned.

Emma managed a smile. Jack provided a variety of entertainment with his antics and sense of humour. Everybody loved him. He seemed to take great pleasure in laughing at himself and his dog to bring sunshine to someone's day. Jack would want to know about Bill, as he sees individuals across town and would report kindly.

"Come to think of it, I'd be concerned if people weren't mentioning Reverend Taylor at every delivery I make." Henry shifted gears to slow the vehicle as they approached a stop sign.

"I wonder what they'll say when they hear Bill won't be at the pulpit for a considerable time."

"Some will say, 'long overdue, the man's been working too hard.' You might also hear, 'the Bible doesn't refer to prophets taking sick leave.' They'll sit tight waiting for a miracle, expecting to see Reverend Taylor next week in his clerical shirt."

"Then they'll be disappointed." Emma crossed her arms. "They must get around Doc Baxter to connect with Bill." The cool breeze from Henry's corner window vent brushed her cheeks, causing her to shiver.

"I hope you're invited to do services so Reverend Taylor can have much needed rest."

Emma stared out the window at the houses and lawns. "I'd welcome that, but the elders will require a man."

"Very prophetic of you, Mrs. Taylor." He glanced at her. "I suppose they'll make the necessary contacts as you'll be busy caring for Reverend Taylor.

"Hopefully, we can work together."

"Well, here we are." Henry pulled into the driveway. "Seriously, it'd be fitting if you get to help until the reverend feels better. I've been to a rare service when you assisted at the pulpit, and I like your style. I listened to the scriptures in a whole new way."

"Thanks, Henry. Nice to hear." Emma swallowed. "It'll depend on what our Mr. Tolt has planned." She sighed. Maybe Henry would turn off the truck and talk for a while.

"I'm glad you go where the good Lord nudges. You can't get sidetracked if you do that. My mother is going to ask Reverend Taylor to preach about Sarah. Irene told me one Sunday that God spoke directly to Abraham concerning a promised son."

Emma shifted to face Henry. "I often wonder if it ever occurred to some that God spoke to Sarah when she swept the floor or hung the wash on tent pegs. Anything God said to Abraham would affect Sarah. At least that's the way it is with Bill and me."

She opened her purse and pulled out a handkerchief to wipe her nose. "Come to think of it, the ladies in the congregation might appreciate listening to life from Sarah's perspective. And if Bill wasn't comfortable exploring those topics, he could ask me or someone from the Mission Unit to contribute insights."

"Ah, Mrs. Taylor, I've often thought the same thing. My mom said it'd be interesting to hear sermons from both sides of Bible stories. Goodness me, there are biblical women who are not named. I'm glad times have changed. I want my wife and daughter to be known by their first and last name. They were given for worthy reasons."

Emma nodded. A recurring dream of people standing in a circle gave peace, and it stirred her when a voice echoed her name, an invitation of sorts. However, the request confused her as there were no replies. She wouldn't tell Bill of it, or he'd suggest she pray for peace of mind.

Perhaps she shouldn't share anything this personal with Henry, although he appeared to understand, given his uncomplicated manner of considering the Holy. He must be close to God to have conquered that desire to drink.

Henry started another conversation. "In those years when I struggled with alcohol, Reverend Taylor asked me and several men who battled the same addiction to meet at the church on Saturday nights. We had quite a reputation, being the initial group in the district to admit we had a drinking problem and 'had the nerve to talk aloud about it' as one of our staunch church members said. I haven't indulged since that time; I'd have to answer to God. . .and to the people."

"It takes a lot of strength to do what you did, Henry," Emma said. "You're a good man."

"Thanks, Mrs. Taylor. My wife would agree. I always enjoy talking with you, but I guess you'll be wanting to go in." He wiped his brow with his big hand. "I hope you can have a nap sometime today. It must have been a long night." Henry jumped out of the truck and darted around to her side. "Are you okay to go in yourself?"

"The cat will be waiting for me, wondering why she hasn't been fed." Emma offered her hand to Henry. "I appreciate the ride. I couldn't go straight into the house alone. It's comforting speaking with you. I really needed our chat—kind of cleared the air for me."

"Conversations can do that. I was thinking earlier today of the night you sat on the running-board of Dad's car and prayed with me." Henry took Emma's arm as they slowly made their way up the sidewalk. "I was pretty hungover…couldn't talk, but that didn't seem to bother you. Even with my dull mind, I recall what you said, and you didn't mince words. You told it as it was whether I liked it or not." He paused and grinned. "To this day, your prayer still strengthens me."

"Thanks for the reminder. It means a lot. We're happy to have you and your family at First." She stood at the front door.

"Me too. See you later." Henry stuffed his hands into his pockets and walked to his truck. He started his vehicle and then lowered the window and called out, "And oh, there was a letter for you at the post office, so I picked it up." He hurried back to Emma and handed it to her. "Here you are. I'll come to get you at 4:00."

Watching Henry's vehicle move out of the driveway, Emma's new strength lightened her step. She waved as he drove away, and then she stuck the letter in her purse. But not before she noticed the return address—University of Toronto.

• • •

Bill had taken short bouts of sick leave throughout his ministry, but an endless stretch was unthinkable. Emma would speak to Mr. Tolt and offer to assist again since he'd make the appropriate arrangements. When he realized the time frame, her interest might appeal to him. It'd save effort when trying to replace Bill as well as an extra cost. Mr. Tolt failed to acknowledge the opportunity to boost the financial committee's depleting funds and contribute to Emma's meagre lifestyle. Although this Sunday was impossible, perhaps he'd consider asking her later.

Invitations to participate or lead worship occasionally came Emma's way, like the Presbyterian's appeal to offer an Advent service or the Legion's request to place a wreath and bring the message. But she'd kept busy helping Bill. Mr. Tolt's obvious determination to discount her assistance during the upcoming weeks continued. In the meantime, she'd do what she could.

Within minutes of greeting Prissy and listening to her welcoming meows, Emma heard a knock on the door. Maisie bustled into the kitchen. "Now I'm not going to stay long. Since you've been at the hospital all night with Bill, I want to remind you I'm here if you need me."

"Thank you, Maisie. How in the world did you find out?"

"You live in Noble among those who love you and put it into action." She hugged Emma. "Now, I'll be off."

As one of the anniversary, Christmas and Easter helpers at First, Maisie was also known to frequent St. Michael's Catholic Mass. Even with brief attendance, she was still a regarded source of knowledge about both congregations. Yet, she refrained from attending either assembly regularly. This lack of commitment bothered Bill, although Emma understood.

Maisie's perspective helped to see through jargon. She'd tackle any topic, any country, any subject, sometimes embarrassing Emma. It was that directness that individuals disliked. Bill had cautioned Emma regarding Maisie's willingness to approach issues often normally avoided. Emma would have liked to talk theology and church with Bill, but he didn't often enter complex matters with her. Those areas he saved for the men. So, with whom could she debate?

Just in case Mr. Tolt asked her to fill in for Bill some Sunday, which would be a pleasant surprise, she'd reread Sunday's sermon. It'd give her credibility in Mr. Tolt's eyes. He seemed comfortable with the idea of Emma speaking when she used Bill's phrases. Mr. Tolt hesitated from using the word *preaching* with her. That was for the men.

Looking into scripture would reap blessings whether she shared with the congregation or soaked it up herself. She settled into Bill's chair and laid out his notes. He wrote well with a natural intent to develop a person's relationship with God. He went into the pulpit with a complete manuscript and referred to it occasionally, claiming the Spirit guided his initial writing. He preached with passion, and people often remarked how that reflected his faith.

When she finished concentrating, the envelope that Henry had given to her came to mind. She lifted Bill's paper-opener from the desk and sliced through the end of the covering. "Dear Mrs. Taylor. I am writing to ask for a reference for Nancy Trask." Emma sighed and closed the letter without reading further. She'd deal with this later. It would take careful thought to prepare something that could face Mrs. Trask's scrutiny.

EIGHT

The telephone rang while Emma was reading in the office. She moved quickly to the kitchen. "Hello…yes. You've been trying to get us? Oh, I'm sorry I missed your call." Following a long pause of listening, she said, "Hilda Grafton? I'll be sure to tell Bill. Little girl, you say. Seven pounds is a perfect weight." She frowned. "Yes and thank you for phoning. Goodbye."

Emma hung the receiver back on the telephone box and retraced her steps to sit and think. Why had she taken the message concerning Hilda's baby without updating Mrs. Densmore about Bill? Considering the town grapevine, she didn't know he was in the hospital, or she'd have asked for him. There was something else—a tone of uncertainty in her voice. She wasn't telling everything, even though she seemed relieved the delivery was over for Hilda's sake.

Emma's inclination was to rush to see her. But no! Today, Emma would rest and reflect on her circumstance until she visited Bill in the evening. Regardless of needs in the church, she'd set them aside for now. These days belonged to Bill.

She paced to the window. After looking out at the street, she closed the drapes to shut out the sun. Returning to sit in Bill's chair, she recalled this was the first night in more than twenty years of marriage that he wasn't coming home. Especially in the dimness of the room, she yearned for his touch and the sound of his voice. Shifting in his soft armchair, she leaned into his favourite pillow and drifted off to sleep.

Refreshed with an hour's rest, Emma called Henry to say she'd go to see Bill around 4:00. The late afternoon trek would give a break to think, identify doubts and most of all, to pray. The scriptures where Jesus healed the sick and helped the lame walk deepened Emma's prayers as she asked him to visit Bill.

• • •

Walking into Bill's room, Emma found him resting comfortably in his bed. The doctor was leaving, so she couldn't speak with him. Bill hadn't stirred from this morning's position. Wires, tubes, pillows and trays crowded his area. Emma's pulse raced as she considered the setting.

She sat in the chair beside his bed for twenty minutes before speaking. "I'm here with you, Bill." She whispered.

No reply, so Emma paused. After five minutes, she said, "Are you awake?" She waited.

Bill broke the silence with a fragile voice. "Yes." He stirred, sighed, and drifted off to sleep. After more time, he continued, his voice soft, "I was wondering where you were."

"I went home to have a rest."

Bill took a deep breath and slowly said, "Are you all right?"

"Yes, don't worry, love. Lots of people are connecting with me and asking about you." Quietness filled the room except for the ticking of the equipment that the staff consistently monitored.

Bill slipped into sleep, so Emma lifted her yarn and knitting needles out of her bag. She glanced at Bill; thankful he was resting. Nursing personnel came in and out of the room; one asked Emma if she'd like some tea.

"That'd be lovely, thank you. Just black, please," she whispered and cleared a space on Bill's bedside table to place the cup.

Emma enjoyed the break from knitting to savour her drink. She stretched and then walked to the window and back to loosen a cramp that caught her leg. Quietly she settled in her chair.

In another half hour, Bill's soft voice interrupted Emma's concentration. "I guess…I'm grounded."

Smiling at his sense of humour, she enquired, "Oh? What makes you think that?"

Time lapsed before Bill added, "Doc said, I've graduated to…the spectator's gallery."

"I suppose that's part of your recovery plan."

Bill didn't answer her and carried on with his thought. "From this bed, I can watch what goes on."

Emma viewed Bill through her tears. "For a while. The church will have to manage without your expertise to guide them."

"They'll do fine." Bill didn't open his eyes, although he reached for Emma's hand. "Maybe Mr. Tolt will call you."

Maybe. Emma shifted closer. "Do you have pain, love?"

"No." He continued in a weak voice. "Discomfort."

"Let's not talk. I'll sit here. Shall I read to you?" Emma lifted a book of Psalms from her purse.

"Yes. Your voice comforts me."

She began softly. It wasn't long before Bill's breathing deepened. After sitting with him for another half-hour, she slipped out of the chair and moved to the door. She'd come back in the morning.

•••

The house seemed empty, so big and vacant without Bill. He was her life. Without him by her side, what was there for her? Emma sat in front of the window and observed movement in the church parking lot. Incidents from the last couple of days crossed her mind and left sad feelings.

What could she do for Bill? Nothing in terms of providing help as the hospital was well-staffed, and he'd receive expert care. But she'd do something special for him in the town.

Was there anything in ministry that Mr. Tolt wouldn't find fault? Knowing the congregation was cared for would please Bill. She could certainly do that. She'd visit as she'd previously done and keep notes. He'd read them when he improved. Yes, that was what she'd do—she'd walk or ride her bicycle. Doing this would keep Bill informed regarding the pastoral side of his work, and Emma would be sharing his ministry. She'd soon hear if it wasn't acceptable.

NINE

Following a few days of sitting with Bill, offering water, reading, and praying for him, Hilda came to mind. Emma packed a couple of pieces of pork from last night's supper and slipped the package into her bag.

Shivering in the fresh air, she hurried up the street to Leroy's house. Tall bushes on the east edge of the footpath kept it shady, so she crossed the road. Flashes of sunlight sifting through the branches felt pleasant.

Recalling Hilda's baby caused memories to tumble into Emma's mind. Images of holding one babe in each arm when her twins were born brought tears of love. Passing the hardware window, a pram and several baby articles sat front and centre. Such practical items to support mothers nowadays, perhaps Leroy would purchase one.

Suddenly, something bumped against her leg. "Darlin', what are you doing? Delivering or retrieving?" She bent to pet a burly black and white dog. "We never know where you're going to turn up. Busy, you are."

He was Jack the mailman's pet, although he wasn't a darling, and Jack wasn't a mailman. It was not a secret that he had given himself that title. But the town loved them both, Jack always and Darlin' most days. Glancing at her pocket watch, Emma must not linger. "Bye, Darlin'! Stay out of trouble."

Crested irises and crocuses peeked through the grass in front of houses, and lawns showed signs of greening. The weathered picket fence at the side of Leroy's yard had endured the harsh winter.

Emma knocked on their door twice without an answer. She pushed it open and stepped into the entrance. Muffled cries followed by a soothing male voice drifted down the hall. Thinking she shouldn't intrude upon such intimate moments, Emma waited.

It wasn't long before Leroy walked toward her. "Mrs. Taylor, sorry you had to let yourself in, but I'm glad you did."

"Thanks, Leroy. Mrs. Densmore phoned to say she'd delivered Hilda's baby, so I wanted to congratulate both of you."

"I appreciate that."

"She'll be happy that it's all over, and she has her precious bundle."

"I suppose so." Leroy shifted so his face was not visible.

Was he worried? Emma didn't want to push him on the subject. "Did you know that Reverend Taylor had a heart attack on Sunday night?"

"No, I didn't know. I'm so sorry. Did he…is he—"

"He's recovering in the hospital. I'll be seeing him later this afternoon. I'll pass it on that we talked." Emma handed the bag to him. "Here you go, Leroy, I brought lunch for you and Hilda. And now, shall I go in to see her?"

"Yes, but—"

"Is there something I ought to know?"

Playing with his fingers, he lowered his gaze to the floor and said, "I knew it! I knew it would go all wrong. The baby is deformed. It's her feet."

"I'm so sorry." Emma responded to Leroy without knowing precisely what he meant.

"And…Hilda feels shame and guilt as if it's somehow her fault." He raised his hand before Emma could speak. "She has no reason to, all I'm saying is, she does."

"I'll go in."

Emma knocked on the bedroom door and pushed it open slowly. As soon as Hilda looked up, she broke into sobs.

Leroy rushed into the room. Leaning over the bed, he held Hilda in his arms until her sniffles lessened.

Emma entered the area. "May I sit down?" She waited for Leroy's consent and sat on a cushioned chair.

Hilda sniffled, wiped her nose and said, "Hello, Mrs. Taylor."

"I came to have a little visit and be with you for a bit. Is your baby asleep?" Emma asked.

Hilda shuddered. "She's in the cradle."

Emma drew the cover back. "Aw, Hilda, she's lovely. May I pick her up?"

"Yes, it'll soon be time for her feeding."

"Have you named her?"

"We're going to call her Alice." Leroy helped Hilda shift her position, plumping the pillows behind her.

"I like that name." Emma lifted the infant to cuddle. She moved tiny fists across her face, searching for something. "She's busy, isn't she?" Emma chuckled. "So beautiful, Hilda."

A long silence followed, and Emma didn't fill it with idle chatter.

Cutting through the stillness, Hilda said, "She's not right. She's deformed. God has punished us again. What did I do to deserve this?" Tears slid down her pale cheeks.

Purposefully concentrating, Emma placed her thumb on Alice's palm and tiny fingers closed around it. "Can you tell me her problem, Hilda?"

"Look at her foot." Hilda's voice rose into a high vibrato. "She's crippled."

Emma unwrapped the baby. While cupping her feet, the right heel turned slightly upward. Emma whispered, "What did the doctor say?"

Leroy sighed. "He said Alice wouldn't have discomfort, and I was relieved by that news."

"That is good to hear," Emma said.

"But why? I want to know why." Hilda's forced voice trembled with anger.

Leroy shifted on a wooden chair. "Doc Baxter said it might be the result of Alice's position as she was developing. I don't think he can help. Either that or he's afraid to tell us the truth."

Hilda clutched his arm. "Don't forget, he also said we needed to watch for signs of further difficulty. Right now, he's calling it a club foot."

"Yeah, I know." Leroy patted her shoulder.

"I'm sorry." Emma covered Alice's feet before placing her in Hilda's arms. "Doc Baxter will have a plan, and he'll care for Alice. It often takes research to assess these conditions and to explore different options." Emma leaned closer to Hilda and reached for her hand. "Be proud of her. Psalm 139 speaks of being 'fearfully and wonderfully made.'"

Hilda spun sideways as if considering the image.

Emma remained quiet for a few moments. With a gentle voice, she said, "Maybe Mrs. Densmore can tell you ways to keep your milk so you can continue nursing. Try not to fret, Hilda—it's bound to create stress. Lots of rest and praying for peace of mind helps." She squeezed Hilda's hand lightly.

Hilda shook her head. "Mrs. Taylor, I don't wish to have kind thoughts today. I'm not peaceful. Right now, I'm not even feeling God's love." She reached for her handkerchief. "I think I'd like to be alone if you don't mind."

"I understand." Emma rose to leave. "I'll let myself out." What else could she do? Had she been too quick to offer her support in this intense situation? It certainly wasn't advice that Hilda needed or wanted. Had Emma intruded into Hilda's relationship with God? What would Bill have done?

Leroy mumbled a thank you as Emma left the room. There'd be no consoling Hilda today, and withdrawing was probably the best medicine. Attempting to be positive hadn't helped. *Had I met her in her fear and grief or overlooked it, presenting my idea of a manageable perspective?*

As Emma walked home, she questioned the conversation with Hilda. It was apparent she still grieved her stillborn infant born last year. Giving birth to a baby that she figured was God's punishment was too much. Emma shivered on the warm day. How alone Hilda must feel.

A net full of struggling individuals came to Emma's mind. Even when Bill was able, he'd direct awkward visits to her. Who would go to these people and bring them God's grace in difficult times if they rejected her?

TEN

Having spare time since she hadn't stayed long with Hilda, Emma walked Main Street to the grocery store.

Henry stood tall and confident behind the counter as he met each shopper's needs. He slipped two oranges quickly into Mrs. Ryan's container—it was acts of kindness like this that the community appreciated during these challenging times. Purchasing vegetables from a Hampton farmer insured fresh varieties. When food ripened too much to sell, Henry gave it away. Noble residents would wait a day or two to see if he favoured them with a bag.

"Hello, Mrs. Ryan," Emma said. "It's so nice to see you. It's been a while."

Henry gathered the items on Mrs. Ryan's list and placed them in her box. "There you go."

"Thank you." She paid him and moved closer to Emma. "I—I had to walk in all by myself, as my bread didn't rise. My supply of yeast was low, and I wanted to bake a batch of biscuits for lunches. I usually come early in the morning with the ladies but couldn't manage it today."

"Now, dear." Emma was aware women from the Hills didn't often come to town in the middle of the day. Willing to lose her place in the line-up, she drew close to Mrs. Ryan as they went outside. "You come in whenever it works for you."

"Thank you, Mrs. Taylor." She closed the top button on her sweater, faced Emma, and paused, "By the way, we're hosting House Church this week. Are you able to come?"

"I'll certainly try, although it'll depend on how much I'm with Bill." Emma set Mrs. Ryan's box in the rear basket of her bicycle. "Did you know he took a heart attack?"

"Oh no, I didn't," Mrs. Ryan said. "Is he all right?"

"He's in the hospital and I suspect he'll be there for a spell."

"I hope he recovers well."

"I'm praying for the same thing." Emma tucked her purse under her arm. "I'll get back to my shopping." She pointed to the muddy road. "Be careful of those ruts."

"I will. Today's been demanding enough; I need not add to that with an accident."

Emma made her way to the counter and gave Henry her list.

"And how are you this morning, Mrs. Taylor?" He lifted baking soda from the shelf and placed it in her cotton bag. "It's a nice day to be out for a walk."

"I'm well, and yes, it is a lovely day."

"And Reverend Taylor?"

"Nothing has changed. Thanks for asking."

He set Emma's list on the counter. "I have everything you want in stock."

"That's welcome news when I'm walking. I didn't dare ride my bicycle downtown; I mean, what would people say?"

"Maybe they'd declare, 'There goes that minister's wife. She's probably off to help somebody despite all her troubles. She can get away with anything because everybody loves her as she is.'"

"Now that'd be nice. That would be very nice." She hurried out the door.

"I'll pick you up at 4:00," Henry called.

"Mrs. Taylor, can I speak to you for a minute?" Mr. Tolt swaggered closer as she was about to cross the street. "Out doing your shopping?"

"Yes, I needed a few things."

"I noticed you were speaking with Mrs. Ryan earlier. Have you always been on such close terms with those from the Hills?" Mr. Tolt peered through his thick glasses.

"Why, I haven't thought one way or the other about this. I'm fond of all of them."

"Really?" Mr. Tolt dragged out the word. "Is Reverend Taylor aware?"

"He recognizes my love for those from the Hills."

"Do you go out and preach there?" He frowned. "Irene mentioned something to me after your Mission Circle girls took part in worship."

"I go out and gather with them. Does it matter if I pray or preach, sing or tell Bible stories? The gospel doesn't have limits to my knowledge. I like to think our effort resembles the early church…where the believers fellowship in their homes."

"Does Reverend Taylor know you do this?"

Mindful he'd overlooked her last few words, she continued, "He understands I spend time with the families. It's not done in secret if that's what you're implying." She shouldn't have to defend her trips to the Hills.

"Oh no, of course not." Mr. Tolt lifted his hat and walked a short distance beside her. "Did I hear Bill took a turn?"

"A turn? What do you mean by a turn?" Emma had heard the term used with the words 'for the worse.' Was that what he meant to say? Was this professional care? Any local undertaker would be interested in such a situation.

"I understand Bill had an attack."

"He had a heart attack, Mr. Tolt, and is in the hospital." *He probably knows all of this.* "Doc Baxter is attending him."

"I'm meeting with the elders again. Doc will also be present, as we need to continue planning worship services. I can see you're informed about Bill's situation, as usual, Emma. For sure, he couldn't be under better care." Mr. Tolt pulled his hat lower on his forehead.

"You can count on me anytime to serve at the pulpit to make it easier for Bill while he's recovering. He'll want everything to go well."

"Of course." Mr. Tolt's face suggested he'd like the road to swallow him. Or her. "But everybody likes their Reverend Taylor."

"Yes, but Bill worries. I'm offering to help—to ease the church's workload. That is, I could assist with pulpit responsibilities and extra duties."

"I'll keep that in mind, Mrs. Taylor. Indeed, I'll keep that in mind." He tugged at his fedora. "I'm heading back, so I'll bid you goodbye for now. Give my best to Bill." He hurried away as though he wanted to widen the space between them.

A horse and wagon approached, sloshing puddles from the rain. Emma waved at the driver. *It sure would be pleasant to have a ride through town in that rig sometime.*

Memories of the girls' surprise earlier visit remained cheerful in Emma's mind. It was such an extravagant effort in coming to Noble from Toronto and then returning on the same day. But they both said it was necessary, and Emma was grateful they were able to make the arrangements.

ELEVEN

Emma sat at the kitchen table with a cup of tea. This was a comfortable room, with its long windows providing a perfect view of Bill's garden. With the circumstances of his health, Emma was confident she wouldn't have the benefit of fresh tomatoes and potatoes this summer.

She needed a recipe to make a stew with the fixings from the pantry shelf. She'd inspected Lizzy's dish at a previous church supper. Stirring the ingredients and lifting a heavy spoon from the broth to see if she could spot different trimmings didn't reveal anything out of the ordinary. Vegetables with bay leaves and chunks of well-cooked pork were usual items. But there was a spice or maybe celery. Beets? No, they'd be too strong. She must stop and pray, "Thou shalt not covet thy friend's recipe."

The telephone jangled an uneven ring, startling Emma. She lifted the receiver.

"Hello?"

"Mrs. Taylor, is it?" The man's clear British voice rumbled in the earpiece.

"Yes, this is Emma Taylor."

"Andrew Maitland from Brookes. I hope I'm not calling at a bad time." He choked away from the mouthpiece before continuing. "Excuse me. Ahem. Got myself a cold. Shirley, my wife, wanted to talk with you at the Hampton covenanting service, but we couldn't find you in the crowd during lunch. After I'd had that wretched coughing spell, I felt better, and we mingled among the folks to chat awhile."

"I'm sorry you weren't feeling well. I always enjoy hearing you."

"Thanks. I appreciate that." He coughed again. "So, my reason for calling is to ask if you'd consider preaching at the next event. It's our annual Mission Week and we've decided to have an Open-Door—a rally. We're planning it for the fourth of May. It'll differ from the one you couldn't join last year. As you're aware, rallies have their own process."

"They're remarkable in that way." That had been an additional opportunity she'd missed. Had she become so accustomed to refusing invitations that she'd forgotten they were given? Perhaps she'd put them out of her mind, so she didn't have to regret turning them down.

"The women have taken on the planning, and Shirley reminds me that you give a heartfelt message. She wants you to preach."

"I'd like to do that, although it's not how folks typically see me serve." Memories crowded her thoughts. "But I can't as Bill had a heart attack and is in the hospital."

"I'm so sorry. He looked well when I saw him at Hampton. Hopefully, he'll recover soon." Reverend Maitland coughed away from the receiver. "If you want to talk to someone, you are welcome to call Shirley or me. We'd be more than willing to visit you and Bill."

"Thank you for your kindness."

"These circumstances will not allow you to take on anything at this time. But, when we outline the next rally, you might pray about preaching at the service—that is if your situation permits. And in the meantime, give Bill my regards."

"I will, thanks. I appreciate you thinking of me."

Reverend Maitland continued, "Shirley will be pleased that you'll consider joining us on another occasion." He cleared his throat. "And the event offering will be directed to families from the Hills affected by factory cutbacks. There are countless people in need throughout our districts, but I understand that community is a particular ministry of yours."

"Yes, indeed. This is a worthy cause and will benefit many." *And he recognized my work as ministry. Thanks be to God.*

They said goodbye, and Emma hung the receiver on its hook. If she was waiting for an opportunity to present itself, here it was. *But the timing is wrong.*

She opened Bill's devotional and read scriptures focusing on perseverance. Those words penetrated Emma's mind. They were valid for her as well. She prayed Bill's health would improve so he could return to his church work. And would she respond to Mr. Maitland in a favourable way when he called again? She closed the recipe book; the stew would wait.

• • •

A breeze pushed against the bushes when Emma strolled along the sidewalk after supper. She'd told Henry not to plan on driving her to the hospital. Walking several blocks would help to relax her and give some thinking time. Maybe tonight, she'd be able to chat with Bill.

When she walked into the room, the drawn curtain limited her view. She pulled the cotton gently aside and peeked into the enclosed area where Bill slept on two raised pillows. Did he look pale? It was difficult for Emma to see his countenance. He didn't appear distressed, so she relaxed and decided to sit with him for a while. A half-hour passed, and he still hadn't moved. She left to walk home in her loneliness.

• • •

Emma had so many questions. The doctor kept a close watch on Bill, assuring her that his symptoms were anticipated, and care was standard procedure.

Keeping that in mind, she walked into Bill's hospital room a few days later. He didn't have oxygen or any tubes, which was a surprise. He moved his head to glance at her when she entered.

"Well, hello, Reverend Bill," she teased. "I've come to make a pastoral call. The nurses tell me at the desk that you are pretty chipper today."

"That's what they say, although I feel like I've been crushed by a steam engine."

"Aches and pains, you mean." His comment startled Emma.

"Not exactly. I have a heaviness in my chest. Doc is watching it, so I shouldn't complain. At least I'm here."

"It's nice to see you have your sense of humour." Would Bill tell her the truth?

"Look behind you to see who else came to visit."

Emma twisted to gaze into her daughters' faces. "Oh, girls, I am so happy to see you."

"We're glad too, Mom." Bernice said. "We hear you're taking excellent care of Daddy."

The twins hugged her at the same time, which made them almost lose their balance. "It's so good to wrap our arms around you, Mom," Beatrice said.

"When did you arrive?" Emma asked.

"On the morning train, and then we came right to the hospital," Beatrice added. "They let us in before breakfast because of the distance we came. So, we had tea and toast with Daddy."

Bernice pointed to a bouquet in a bottle of water on the side table. "We thought he'd appreciate these."

"He will, and I can tell he is surely enjoying your visit." Emma asked, "How long are you here for?"

"The nurse gave us permission to stay past visiting hours, so we don't have to leave until the 6:00 train." Bernice gently reached for her father's hand. "We promise to be quiet and let Daddy sleep."

"This is perfect. I was wondering when you could manage a visit. Even a short one is appreciated. It's endearing to have your father all to yourself. So, thanks for coming." Emma placed her hand on her chest.

One girl took a turn sitting at Bill's side as he napped, and Emma walked in the hall with the free one. Too soon, the bell signified the end of visiting hours, and she thanked her daughters.

"Sorry I slept away your visit." Bill yawned. "It was calming to have you with me."

They both leaned to kiss his cheek. "You keep up the good work and you'll be home in no time."

"I hope so. I'm happy to do what I'm told." Bill took Emma's hand. "Are you praying for me, love?"

"I am indeed—night and morning."

"I sensed you were. Thank you." He sighed. "Could we say a prayer of thanksgiving?"

They held hands, prayed together, and Bill added a few words of his own. Emma talked with Bernice and Beatrice before leaving. They seemed content with seeing their father for the day and happy to stay with him through his supper. This was a special pause for everyone, even though there were no apparent promises for any of them.

• • •

The rankling of the telephone repeatedly interrupted Emma's morning tea. "Hello, Emma Taylor here. Yes, I'm fine, thank you, Ruth." Even though she was a favourite cashier at the bank, as she'd chummed with Beatrice and Bernice through high school, this would not be a social call.

Emma listened; her fingers gripped the receiver. "Overdrawn, you say?"

"Last month, Reverend Taylor deposited half of what he usually does." Ruth spoke clearly into Emma's ear.

"Was that the first time?" Emma asked.

"No, it's happened a few times according to my records," Ruth said.

"There's nothing I can do, but I'll speak to the treasurer to see if he can straighten it out. Did you hear that Bill is in the hospital?"

"I did get that news, Mrs. Taylor, and I am sorry. Give him my best. Goodbye for now."

An exchange with Bill regarding church offerings came to mind, as well as a discussion about Emma getting a job to help with finances. Should she have pressed it further?

The topic of Emma finding employment didn't come up again, as it had troubled Bill. *Maybe if I'd been firmer, I wouldn't be in this position.*

Emma buzzed Lizzy to call John. As treasurer, he apologized and said he'd explore the problem immediately.

Wanting to clear her mind of extra stress, Emma opened her cupboard doors to assess ingredients for a soup or stew. Something light to redirect her worries from the previous conversation would be good. She had a few vegetables and prepared broth to add to her recipe. It certainly would be sufficient for her. And then a quiet and lonely stretch awaited her and Prissy for the rest of the morning.

• • •

Emma walked into Bill's hospital room and stared at an empty bed. Where was he? Had he taken a weak spell? Why hadn't someone told her? An orderly pushed Bill into the room in a wheelchair, and he greeted her.

"Well, look at you, all spruced up." Bill's hair was still moist after a bath. As Emma kissed him on the cheek, a fruit soap scent provided a fresh aroma. "You smell good. How are you? And no wires and ropes, as you called them."

"You're right. I'm glad to be free of that harness. It's restricting. And I feel better in my mind, although weak at times in the body." He patted the arms of the chair. "This rig is my safety net. When they want to take me somewhere, I can't believe how anxious I am to sit here." Bill snickered. "And today, I'll remain where I am to have our visit."

Emma touched the cotton sheets before she settled into the visitor's chair. "I'm surprised you haven't asked for flannelette ones."

"I tried that, but they keep them for special purposes." Bill grimaced. "I'm not an emergency anymore." His tone of voice changed. "Does the doctor say when I can go home?"

"No conversation referring to that yet. But I'll be sure and tell you when I hear news."

"What's new in the town?"

University of Toronto's request for a reference for Nancy wouldn't be of interest to Bill. There was no use telling him that Mr. Tolt had questioned her involvement in the Hills or that he hadn't considered her offer to assist at the church. She'd mention calling on Leroy and Hilda but not discuss her attitude. Bill diligently avoided conflict, fitting well in the town of Noble as the population felt the same way. An excellent example of the prevailing general approach: guardian of the good.

"I went to see Hilda and Leroy and their sweet baby, Alice."

"And how did that go?"

"It wasn't an easy visit, possibly too soon. Mrs. Densmore phoned to tell us that Hilda had delivered, so I wanted to say hello."

"It was probably an easier visit for you than if I'd gone."

Emma observed him. The greyish tone of his skin worried her. Was he tiring himself? They visited for twenty minutes before Emma lifted her purse. "I've kept you up long enough today, so I'll go." They prayed together, and then Emma said goodbye.

"Em, do me a big favour and be careful in the Hills. There's a lot of unrest out there with the layoffs. Will you do that?" He reached out and held her hand.

"Now you tell the pest who's talking that way to think on good things. I'll be fine, love. Don't you worry."

With that, she kissed the top of his head and left the room. Imagine those naysayers giving Bill news that upsets him. But she'd be careful, as she didn't want him to hear anything on the gossip line. Even though he seemed like his old self when she visited, he was still in danger. His visible fatigue was evident today, yet this was the first pleasant visit they'd had without orderlies or nurses doing their duties of caring for Bill.

TWELVE

"Now, what's this?" Emma stepped onto their front porch. She pulled out a note folded into the doorframe. "I had a visitor while I was away." She spoke aloud as if Bill were at her side. Emma pushed the door open and walked into the house. Prissy meowed her welcome and then strutted to her cushion. Emma unfolded the paper.

Dear Mrs. Taylor,
Would you help Susanne with her music? Mrs. Watson has been sick, and I don't want Susanne to fall behind. So, if you would come and spend time, I'd appreciate it.
Respectfully yours, Mrs. Trask

I can spare a half-hour although I have two meetings this week. It isn't like it'll be forever. Emma set the note on the hall table.

If Mrs. Watson decided to retire from teaching music, perhaps she would recommend Emma to continue. Maybe this was the job to assist financially. Surely no one would object to her instructing children. Yet, Mrs. Trask used the word *help*, not hire.

Bill often referred to her attitude. She had not been well in the last few years and had hurt several ladies in town with accusations that proved to be untrue. Emma would have to be careful if she was going to become deeply involved with this family. Since Mrs. Trask had invited her, she should be safe from a reprimand, but she'd keep up her guard.

Best get busy and make supper. Emma's reserve supply of leftovers made hash a possibility. Rather than discard produce when it lost its freshness, Henry often dropped off vegetables to Bill and Emma, knowing they'd use or pass them on. As she pumped the water into the sink to wash carrots for the soup, it reminded her of how love healed when splashed on difficulties. Finally, the ingredients began to heat and send a delicious aroma into the air. It'd taste good, but better if she could share it with Bill.

Be thankful *in* everything. Emma rinsed another carrot in the sink. "I'm thankful for Bill's returning health, the hospital staff, the church and very grateful for our home."

• • •

Emma leaned her head in the crevice of Bill's office chair and drifted off to sleep. She startled herself awake and glanced at the clock on the mantel. Goodness, she'd slept for almost an hour. A scuffling on the veranda drew Emma's eyes to the window. A figure appeared fuzzy, and it wasn't easy to make out who it was. Curious, she pushed herself from the chair and walked to the front door.

"Hello, Mrs. Taylor. I didn't think you were here." Mrs. Ryan stood on the porch, clutching a piece of paper. "I was going to leave you a note. I'd like to talk to you, that is, if you have time."

"Of course, I do. Always. Will you come in?" When Mrs. Ryan entered, Emma pointed to the parlour. "Let's sit in here." She led Mrs. Ryan into the room, guided her to the sofa, and settled alongside. "It's nice to see you. How can I help?"

"I wouldn't be so bold to come except I couldn't figure out how else to speak to you in private."

"I'm pleased you came, and my invitation is always open to you."

"I appreciative the time you spend with us out at the Hills. Your prayers have helped in difficult seasons of life. The community says your presence among us is healing," Mrs. Ryan said.

"Thank you. I'm glad to hear that."

"This isn't really a privilege or title; or whether we live in town or the outskirts, it's how God works in our lives. I'm so happy to be part of this effort."

Emma planted herself on the sofa. "It's such a blessing to see faith in action."

"I agree. It's like a revival happening." Mrs. Ryan looked directly at Emma. "And I'm sorry Reverend Taylor is not well. I wanted to tell you personally. You'll have extra responsibilities with him besides keeping up with your visiting." She placed her handbag by her side. "Furthermore, I'm willing to lead prayer and scripture during House Church. You don't have to come out through this demanding time."

"Why, that's so thoughtful of you. You're right. There is additional support needed. It'll be a long time, I'm afraid." Emma studied her friend.

"In case you're wondering if I'm capable, I have a high school education. When I was a child, we lived beside the parsonage, and the minister's wife often helped me with my homework." Mrs. Ryan's eyes shone with excitement. "She used to pray with me as you do with Rosie and the girls. If the whole truth is known, having you come out to the Hills has encouraged me so much that I want to help. That's why I'm offering."

Emma sighed. Her labour had grown fruit. For this, she was thankful.

"I must go now." Mrs. Ryan stood. "You visit with your husband, and we'll be glad to welcome you when you're free to come back."

Emma leaned against the entrance and watched Mrs. Ryan walk to the street. What a gift. Could this willingness to serve happen across town—and in the church?

THIRTEEN

Emma balanced her daily visits with Bill while managing household duties of laundry, cleaning and baking his favourite scones for the bedside table. Leaving a generous supply at the nurse's station made him popular with the staff. They asked him, "Are you the man who gets these special orders delivered?" And he'd grin and chuckle.

The nurse brought him out to the hall telephone, and he talked to Emma for ten minutes early in the day. Although his countenance wasn't visible, she heard his playful attitude on the line. He sounded good as he rhymed off names of those who had come to visit. Some had shared a few circumstances that surprised her. Why would they worry him? It seemed that he had already settled these situations in his mind, and it gave Emma confidence as she listened to his voice. She had taken several envelopes with her yesterday when she visited, knowing mail brightened his day. Members of the congregation also sent him cards. He'd enjoy all of them as he savoured reading. There was no doubt in Emma's opinion that he was feeling well-loved.

•••

The plaque that hung in her kitchen with words of encouragement and building up one another filled Emma's mind. Yet, her soft knock on Trask's front door suggested caution.

Irene immediately opened it as if she'd been waiting with her hand on the knob. Talking about weather forecasts helped avoid anything that Irene might want to discuss. Emma eased off her sweater and hung it on the hall tree. "I suppose Nancy has talked to you regarding her big educational ideas in Toronto." Irene's voice was thick with disgust.

Aware the letter from the university lay deep within her purse, Emma said. "She hasn't spoken to me about anything in particular." *Now, very thankful she hadn't.* "What is it she wants?"

"I never thought any daughter of mine would want such a thing as education. If she hasn't told you by now, she will." Her voice trembled as if close to tears. "She has an opinion that she'll study theology. As if the church wanted young ladies. I realize they have various interests, but they shouldn't have to take theological studies. Besides, scripture makes women's station in life very clear. She needs to find a proper husband like Reverend Taylor, and then she could be his helper. To get educated for herself seems selfish; I mean, whatever would she do with it? And all that money spent for books and everything else." Irene looked away. "Scandalous, it is. A couple in Toronto has offered to pay her tuition—they call it a bursary, never heard of the word. I haven't even met these people. Of all the nerve."

It was no surprise that she'd feel troubled. How would Emma reply without adding to the dilemma? She said calmly, "I'm sorry this has been upsetting for you. But why is this so bad?"

"I knew you'd think that way. Why would a girl waste money when she doesn't need to learn more? If she asks you for support, don't give it to her." Her words hurt like a slap in the face. It was no wonder Nancy hadn't briefed Emma on this topic. *Whom am I loyal to in this situation, Irene or her daughter Nancy? Should I tell Irene about the letter from the university? Nancy must have gone ahead and applied without her mother's knowledge. She's of-age and using it in this family dilemma.*

Emma was suddenly relieved she hadn't shared facts of her own education. She excused herself and walked down the hall to the parlour giving her thinking time. It should be no revelation that Nancy would want to continue studying. She had always been keen to learn, regularly attending Sunday school and worship. She must have registered and submitted Emma's name as a reference. It was essential to respond to the request tonight and mail it from the outside post office bin tomorrow without a return address. This was between Emma and the university. Hopefully, it wouldn't earn Irene's wrath.

Assuming Nancy chose an accepted profession as young ladies usually do, there'd be few questions. But, if she selected a career in theology, law, medicine or similar areas chosen by men, she might have difficulty. Some universities through the years hadn't promised accommodations, library access, or dining options to women. The exclusion of these privileges reflected Emma's experience too much. How would the church celebrate with Nancy if she responded to God in ministry? Worse still, what would her mother say?

In a few moments, Emma eased into a chair in the dimly lit room. "Hello, Susanne, it's nice to see you. And my, what a pretty dress you're wearing." Emma opened the music book and set it on the rack at the front of the polished mahogany piano. "Let's see what you've been doing."

"This is the teacher's binder, and it shows her remarks for each lesson and what I'm to practice for the next week." Susanne handed it to Emma.

"Very good." Emma glanced at the pages until she came to the appropriate date. "Let's begin, then. Please start with the scales. Key of C first."

Susanne placed her hands in the accurate position, so her fingers rested correctly on the keys. She played a few bars. *Oh dear, the notes sound like they're pushing, grating against each other. Such discord will not do.* "That'll be fine for now. I'll test the octaves." Emma touched all the C keys from the top to the bottom of the keyboard. "As I thought. The piano is out of tune. I'll speak to your mother, and we'll sort it out."

"Momma's not going to be pleased." Susanne spoke quietly. "She likes me to practise and not complain."

"Can I have a minute of your time, Mrs. Taylor?" Irene marched into the room. "I heard Susanne begin and then she stopped. Is something wrong?"

"I'm afraid the instrument needs tuning." Emma repeated the exercise, using the key of D. "This will make it difficult for Susanne to hear the accuracy of the piece."

"Susanne has always prepared her lesson for Mrs. Watson without problems. I'd prefer that you teach her the music and not judge the quality of the instrument. Really, I never heard the likes." Mrs. Trask slowly twisted her swollen arthritic hands together as if wringing delicate linen. "I'm surprised to hear you find fault, Mrs. Taylor. Mrs. Watson didn't complain."

"Has she used it?" Emma asked.

"Well, no. There was no reason. Susanne went to her house for lessons." Irene took her handkerchief and dabbed perspiration from her forehead. "What are you insinuating?"

Caring, Emma said, "I've listened to Susanne play during worship. She is gifted. Why not ask Jack to come in when you see him? He has an excellent ear for music and could have a look."

"I won't have a man in my house, thank you. I mean, what would the neighbours think? And I definitely won't tolerate that dog of his." Irene rolled her eyes. "Darlin'! Whoever named their animal with such a name doesn't deserve one. Why he's liable to take anything he can grab in his mangy mouth and deposit it at somebody else's house." She ended her statement with her well-practiced sigh.

Would this suggestion risk additional reprimand? "I hear he's an excellent tuner. He took an exchange of vegetables for his work at the church. And you plant a big garden; maybe you'll offer him food. He's a fair man."

"Well, I don't want anybody to take advantage of me. How am I to know the cost?" Irene's voice heightened in pitch as if hysteria solved the dilemma.

"Jack is reasonable." Emma sighed. "Why not ask him to give you an estimate?" Bill's warning concerning Irene's instability echoed in Emma's memory. Hopefully, if Irene understood that a tuned piano was vital, she might agree.

"I could. But I have to say," Irene exhaled loudly, "if it needs fixing so much, Susanne wouldn't have been able to get her lessons ready for Mrs. Watson."

"Susanne is a conscientious student and would play the phrases as she read them," Emma said.

"Is she right, Susanne?" Irene directed her question to her daughter. "Did you have trouble? Be honest now."

"I don't think trouble is the right word, Momma. I admit the songs sound nicer at Mrs. Watson's house." Susanne smiled at her mother as if seeking approval.

Turning to Emma, Irene said, "If you insist, Mrs. Taylor, I'll ask Jack, but if I find him offensive in any way, you are to blame, and I don't mind telling anybody in town."

Not missing her emphasis on her surname, Emma said, "I understand. In the meantime, perhaps Susanne could go to the church and practice?"

Irene's lips compressed into a thin line. "If you feel it is necessary. My word, I never heard the likes. She's just playing a few notes. And this instrument is sitting here in excellent shape." She leaned against it. "I've sat here since my young days. I'm proud to say it never needed work." She grimaced. "I don't understand why you're making such a fuss. I haven't been able to use it for years because my hands are crippled with arthritis or I'd, I'd play it to prove you wrong."

Emma listened. "That's not required. I'll do what I can for a few weeks until Mrs. Watson recovers."

Irene moved away from Emma. "Very well. Whatever is best for Susanne."

Emma's definition of pastoral care was broad. It went far beyond illness. Situations of grief, disorientation or unresolved feelings often led to the centre of need. Was this a way of caring for both Susanne and her mother?

"And now, let's leave the lesson for today." Turning to Susanne, Emma said, "Come to the fellowship hall tomorrow after school, and we'll catch up with the scales. The room should be warm enough but wear a sweater."

Susanne walked Emma to the door and extended her arms. Emma hugged her and whispered, "I hope it doesn't cost your momma too many vegetables to get your piano tuned."

"Maybe we should plant a bigger garden, because I want to take lessons forever," Susanne said. "Thank you for coming today."

That challenge had gone better than Emma had expected, although she, Jack and probably Darlin', might get into trouble. At least Mrs. Trask hadn't asked Emma to go home or threaten to leave the church as she usually did in her worst moments.

FOURTEEN

The front window of Tillie's Beauty Shop glowed. Her vinegar recipe with newspaper and elbow grease never failed to polish the glass to sparkle in the sunlight. Since the economy had taken a punch at everybody's pocketbook, Emma often frequented her old friend's location to offer the odd jar of chilli or a loaf of homemade bread.

Today, she had nothing but Irene's threat of telling the town her version of the piano tuning episode plus the possible consequence of writing Nancy's reference. This provided heaviness in Emma's heart as well as adding Hilda's newly formed opinion. These situations and a few financial problems mixed with anxiety served as a reasonable defence to drop into Tillie's. Her shop was a happy place, and today Emma needed a lift.

A bell tinkled from above the door. Tillie was using one of those new curling irons. A sizzling and crackling sound, preceding a burning scent, suggested she was close to frying her victim's hair. Sliding the iron into a wire frame on the counter, she guided her fingers to settle a ripple of waves into perfect lines. Stepping aside, she assessed her work.

"There you go, Cora. You're all set now." Turning to Emma, Tillie said, "My word, Mrs. Taylor. I haven't seen you in a long time. Wait until I finish here. Cora is on the run to practice the organ."

"Your hair looks grand, Mrs. Morgan." Emma touched the organist on the shoulder and rotated her in a circle as her cheeks flushed showing immense appreciation for the compliment. "I do admire that style and such an attractive colour as well."

"Thank you, Mrs. Taylor. I wasn't going to get it done before Easter; there'd be those who'd say, Vanity, yea vanity."

"What, in our church?" Emma teased.

"And how is our Reverend Taylor? Sitting on the edge of his bed ready to come home?" Mrs. Morgan asked.

"He is doing well, but the doctor protects him from stress. His room sometimes has a *No Visitors* sign to slow the number of callers."

Cora Morgan sighed. "He'll be getting good care." Setting a bit of change on the table, she glanced back. "There you go, Tillie. It's the usual forty cents? And there's a little extra for working me in today since you're busy." She opened the door and stepped out onto the sidewalk.

The beauty shop was empty. Mrs. Morgan was kind, but she hadn't figured out that Tillie's business was hurting in the failing economy. In hard times, a haircut was a luxury. If Emma trimmed her ends, she could roll her hair in a bun and secure it with pins.

"I'm so glad you stopped by to give us an update on Reverend Taylor." Using a red broom to gather clippings, Tillie dumped them in the wastebasket. "I'm ready for a break. I worked all morning, but I don't have anybody for the rest of the day. Why don't you come to my kitchenette? It's cozy there, and I'll listen for the bell."

Emma followed her and sat on a chair beside the small chrome table.

Tillie set the kettle on the hotplate. "How are you getting along? You must be run off your feet trying to keep up with everything."

"I have to admit life is busy. I do what I can."

Tillie poured tea into two cups. "Did you want a cut today, love?"

"Well, no, I wasn't planning on it. Do I need one?"

"You need to do something." Tillie raised an eyebrow and grinned.

"Aw, I don't have a cent on me, so I shouldn't—"

"Nonsense. For all those goodies you drop off for me to enjoy, let me give you a treat."

They had their tea and ate chocolate cookies before going back into the front of the shop. Tillie ushered Emma to the sink. "Come on, I'll give you a sudsy wash with a sweet fragrance, and when you go to see Bill, he'll think you smell like a flower."

Within minutes, Emma sat in the chair, a soft orange towel wrapped around her head. "Have you always had these mirrors, Tillie? They seem to stretch from wall to wall."

"You haven't been in for a while when you ask that question. An old gentleman came in from Hampton and asked if he delivered, would I have use for them? His daughter had a dance practice room when she was young, and since his wife died, he's selling the house."

"They make your place look elegant."

"Maybe, although, it can be confusing."

"How is that?"

"A woman was sitting under the dryer. I tapped her on the shoulder, flipped the hood and said, 'Your hair is dry, you can come to the chair now, and I'll remove your rollers.' She gazed at herself in the mirror and said, 'Take that old lady over there, I don't mind waiting.'"

Emma almost choked. "Tillie, one of your jokes is enough to lift my spirit for a week."

"Yeah, funny, eh?" After washing and fluffing Emma's hair, Tillie said, "Now what can I suggest? Want waves? They were popular in the 20s, but lots of ladies are still fond of them."

Emma shook her head. "I'd love them, but I'd better stay as usual. Just trim to make it easier to manage."

"Now, Mrs. Taylor, how can you refuse a free cut and style?" Tillie tipped Emma's head to the right and then to the left. "If you like them, then I'll do it. Interested?"

"There's nothing wrong with staying safe, Tillie."

"That's a truth." She grinned. "However, there is nothing wrong with trying something new, either. I promise I'll keep it modest."

Emma settled in the swivel chair. "Well then, go ahead." An hour and numerous stories later, Emma bid her friend goodbye.

"Thanks, Tillie. Until the next time, be kind to yourself."

This couple of hours lifted Emma's mood that had been relatively low due to concern over Bill's health. She was thankful for prayer that continually lowered her anxiety until she began to ponder the changes in their life. Accepting the offer of a free cut gave Emma a new spring hairdo.

At least she wouldn't be as noticeable in the choir as the organist. With her back to the congregation, they'd have a perfect view of her different style.

• • •

Emma joined a few women pausing on the curb for a car to pass. Men's voices from behind rose above the street noise.

"And consider my embarrassment in Hampton when Albert was covenanted."

"That's a while ago. Let those incidents go." A respectful tone of voice interrupted. "It doesn't do any good to hang on and bring them up."

"I was relieved when she relaxed; it appeared she'd come to the front and accept the invitation I gave the men to begin the service. What is one to make of that?"

"As you know, she's opened worship here at First Church when she'd offer a welcome and share the announcements. Sometimes she'd speak for a few minutes when Bill was away or wasn't able. I'm sure she'd have thought it was the same."

So, they were talking about her. Again, the smooth voice of persuasion that she knew belonged to Mr. Tolt responded. "But there was a big difference. I mean, we had guests."

"Ah, Tom, you get anxious concerning little things. Bishop Martin visits various churches, some without clergy. And don't forget he promotes equipping the saints. He'd be grateful to see appropriate lay leadership so Albert's covenanting could carry on without interruption."

Cars went through the intersection, causing Emma to miss parts of the conversation. As the last car rattled by, she continued onto the street.

"My goodness, Tom. Look! Is that Emma Taylor, ahead?"

"No, it couldn't be. That woman has a mass of those ungodly waves. Not Mrs. Taylor's style at all."

Guarded laughter churned in Emma's chest. Why did fooling Mr. Tolt make her so happy?

He echoed the attitudes of the dark ages and reflected the narrow thinking of a woman's place. Maybe he should learn the importance Jesus placed on them and their stories. Had Mr. Tolt forgotten that they stepped in at every turn for the men who went to war? And since the women had the right to vote, they had a voice and had learned to use it.

Who was the accompanying man? Given a bit of time, Emma would identify the friend. When she did, she'd thank him, and they'd have a chuckle.

• • •

Emma was thrilled with her hair and decided to visit Bill. She strode into his room and straight to his bedside without a greeting. Immediately, Bill's face broke into a wide grin. And then he noticed her hair. "Very nice. Didn't you say the old crockery was empty?" He snickered.

"Thank you, Bill. I'm glad you like it. And yes, nothing in the jar and it's been that way for a long time. Tillie said it was payback day—for all the treats I gave her. So, it was free."

"It sure looks nice on you, Em, and this is a pleasant surprise. It pleases me to see you treating yourself."

As much as Emma enjoyed Bill's compliments, his complexion disturbed her. A knock on the hospital door interrupted their conversation, and before either of them responded, Mr. Tolt strolled into the room. Emma pressed her fingers to her mouth. Now he'd see her hair and figure out she'd walked ahead of him at the crosswalk. Still stunned from his cruel words, how would she accept his apology if he offered one?

God, give me patience with this man. Even if he is one of your children, he hasn't been listening well to Bill's sermons.

Emma pushed backward into the curtain. Thinking the Hampton covenanting service might be on his mind, maybe he had come to apologize for the way he'd shunned her.

Mr. Tolt strode to the side of the bed. "Good evening, Bill. I'm glad to see you looking so well. Sorry to barge in, but our treasurer told me there was a mix-up at the bank. I apologize for that, and I'll tidy the files tomorrow morning. Honestly, Bill, it bothers me that this was left so long before someone notified me."

"Thanks for your concern, Tom," Bill said. "Emma filled me in. I'm sure it's been straightened up by now."

"So, you mean it's all been corrected?" Mr. Tolt rubbed his forehead. "I don't understand, as I haven't been to the bank."

"Don't you worry, Tom. That's why we have a treasurer," Bill reassured him. "Can you stay awhile?"

"No, thank you. I thought the problem needed to be straightened out. I have another call to make, so I'll go. Have a restful night." With the ease of an ice cube dissolving in hot water, he strolled out of the room.

Emma was not the reason he'd come. The financial situation was critical to him. He sounded disappointed that he hadn't had the chance to set the figures right at the bank but didn't seem concerned that he hadn't set relationships right with her. Of course, he wouldn't think he'd done anything wrong.

Emma moved back to Bill's bedside, noticing his pale skin against the white bedding. "Congratulations, you are consistently ready with a few words, even with our Mr. Tolt. However, you've had plenty of excitement for one day, so I'll hurry on home."

"Before you go, Emma, are all the arrangements made for Easter at the church?"

"I suspect they are. I haven't heard anything regarding a preacher for the day, but Mrs. Morgan is practicing lovely new pieces with the choir." Emma considered Bill. "There is nothing you'd like better than to walk up the steps to the pulpit and give God's blessings to your beloved people on this hallowed day."

Bill's eyes clouded. Emma reached to place her fingers under his chin, drawing him near to her. "You'll miss this special time, Bill. But it'll make next year exceptional." Perhaps he'd find this an encouraging thought. Would the months and years ahead of them be any different?

He guided her hand to rest in his. "Emma, I think the next Easter day I see will be in heaven." Tears filled the corners of his eyes. "And except for leaving you and the girls, I don't feel so badly in filling my space there."

Emma reached to hug him. What had he just said? Was he thinking that way now? His chest rose and fell more deliberately than usual. Perhaps he was keeping his sobs contained. She kissed his lips and caressed his cheek. "Visiting hours have finished for tonight, but I could ask to stay a little longer. We could talk for a while."

"No, dear. Enough for today. We'll get to this at another visit."

That was a good decision as this discussion needed the proper invitation to lead into it. "In the meantime, I remind you that you're the love of my life."

An orderly opened the door to their room and came to Bill's bedside, probably unaware that he'd interrupted their privacy. "Come on now, Reverend Taylor. I want to settle you for the night. Say goodbye to your wife and I'll come back in five minutes."

Emma offered a bedtime prayer and then hugged Bill. "Goodbye, love. We'll talk again tomorrow." Tears pricked her eyes, knowing that Bill had begun to ponder these things. Because of his comments, their conversation shed light on the days to come.

FIFTEEN

Church life continued as usual during Bill's absence. Emma sang in the choir, contributed to other ministries when possible and made her routine calls to those in need. Some probably defined those efforts as her interest rather than complementing Bill's pastoral care, but she was never sure. She did not, however, get an invitation to come into the pulpit.

Easter came and went. Emma kept Bill informed with the details. The progress of people's health and their activities always interested him. She visited him daily, and they deepened their conversations about everyday topics when they were together.

"Good morning, Bill." She opened the window in his room early in the day. "What nice weather. Are you comfortable?" The morning sun ushered in a bright beginning to the day as it spread warmth. "I brought you breakfast."

"You constantly make Sunday mornings unique with your cooking. Your delivery service gets lots of attention. The nurses tease me daily."

Emma unfastened her basket, happy these treats gave the staff something to make Bill feel special. She set the meal on his bedside table, and Bill reached for his fork.

"This looks tasty. My appetite comes and goes, so I don't know what to expect. But this morning, it's normal." Bill took a bite of his scrambled eggs. "And how is Prissy? You haven't said much regarding her."

"She misses you and lets me know."

"I was happy to see Beatrice and Bernice." Bill chuckled. "Aren't those surprises nice? They arrived late yesterday afternoon and came straight to the hospital to see me. If you'd stayed ten minutes longer, you'd have caught them."

"I think they wanted you all to themselves." Emma nodded her head. "They had this planned aware of my timetable."

"They look great. I had a perfect visit with them, as the nurses invited them to stay with me after visiting hours."

"Those unexpected blessings are exceptional. I'm relieved the excitement didn't tire you. The girls continually add their city news to our ongoing Noble episodes. They were like two teenagers in their room last night, giggling and talking a mile-a-minute. At one time, I was sure they were having a pillow fight." Emma snickered. "And they'll be right in over the lunch hour to see you again."

"That's good." Bill drank from the juice glass that the staff had added to his breakfast menu. "And I had a wonderful twenty minutes with Albert, although it was short, as he left when the girls arrived."

"He seems to make his way up from Hampton regularly to visit. You like his company."

"I certainly do. He's as much the prankster as he was in seminary." Bill pushed his tray away and settled back on his pillow. "Now tell me some news. How is Hilda getting along with the new baby?"

Neither Leroy nor Hilda had been out much. They were probably keeping to themselves to avoid questions. Hilda's words still stung, but Emma would call on them soon. However, there were helpful things to tell Bill.

"Doc Baxter has a record of the foot examinations." Emma placed an afghan on Bill's legs. "He'll order an apparatus for Alice to wear three hours each day when she's older. Those efforts will ease Hilda's earlier questions."

"And relieve Leroy's worries," Bill countered.

"They will." Emma took a couple of bites from Bill's toast before brushing crumbs from her skirt. "Anything helps Leroy. He has difficulty when something happens out of the ordinary."

"And how is Susanne doing with her music?"

"Excellent. She's a delightful student. Jack is going to tune her piano. Susanne practices at the church and likes it. I hope to ask Mrs. Morgan later in the spring to include Susanne regularly in services."

"Is Irene pleased about that?"

"I am certain she is. She sees great talent in her daughter, but Irene doesn't realize the obstacles she puts in Susanne's way."

Bill appeared to let that go and proceeded. "And your Mission Circle?"

"We met on Saturday. Two birthdays. No doubt, the group enjoys our time."

"Henry came to visit me several times. He's a strong-minded young man." Bill paused. "So good to see."

"Isn't it, though? Lately, the town council asked him to deliver hot meals to local seniors. And the church provides ample counter space for an assembly line to prepare the plates. Adequate use of resources, I'd say."

Bill glanced out the window. "When the cold weather comes, they'll have to make different arrangements."

"Agree. We're on guard remembering the fiasco with the Mission Circle and Mr. Tolt. In the meantime, renting out the kitchen provides revenue to make him happy."

"I noticed when John came to visit that he wasn't using his cane anymore. He's so faithful in counting the offering; such a conscientious treasurer he is. And he relates well to Mr. Tolt which must be difficult at times."

"I suspect it is."

Bill's interest in the surrounding area always gave him something to talk about. "You know one benefit of being in the hospital is that you get lots of pastoral care from loving people," Emma said.

Bill grasped her hand. "You work wonders in the community. I hope you're aware. It's an exceptional ministry on all levels."

"Thank you, Bill. I'm beginning to realize that. I guess I've never paused enough to consider it."

"When you go around the town, you walk a sermon a mile long."

"This is nice to hear. When I was reading the Bible, my underlining and margin notes referring to the poor, the prisoner, the blind and the oppressed stood out in ways I hadn't observed so much before. It seemed God was reminding me of something important."

"I'm so glad to hear that, Emma. I often thought you wanted the old rally days back, when all of those mentioned would be present in the multitudes." Bill held her hand and turned her worn wedding band on her finger. "You are a perfect pastor's wife and the Lord's foot soldier answering God's call wherever you are. That's true ministry."

Tears ran down Emma's cheeks, and she didn't move to wipe them. "This is a priceless blessing. And it means so much coming from you."

Bill shifted in his position. Had he been waiting to say those few words that meant so much to Emma?

She checked the clock on the wall and then leaned to him. "It's hard to leave you, Bill, even though you'll get a service on the radio. I'm singing alto in the choir, so I must get along." Parting was awkward; guilt trickled through her mind as she buttoned his sweater. "It must be difficult to hear news and not be included. Rest in the truth that your people will be waiting for you when you're well enough to come back and be with them."

Bill gently touched her arm. "You go ahead. The supply minister needs all the support he can get. He's such a scholar and so caring. I enjoy his visits—he talks church with me."

Emma moved aside, so that Bill couldn't notice her countenance. He didn't see her as someone who liked to have those discussions. She understood. Man-to-man were his unspoken words.

"You know, Em, sometimes I get the feeling that I'm never going to get out of here." He raised his hand when she began to speak. "Now hear me out. I don't believe in signs, but there is common sense, which I trust. The fact is my heart is not getting stronger. I am compensating by hardly asking much of it. All I'm saying is to prepare yourself for whatever happens."

"Would you like me to stay, and you can tell me what you're thinking?"

"No, no. I'm planting seeds for thought. This bed is a good place to reflect on our previous conversations and make a mental note of personal topics to discuss. We should make a list of them, Em."

Bill considered religious and worldly issues to debate with the men, and he saved personal concerns for private discussions with Emma. She pressed a kiss to his cheek. "I hear what you're saying. We can talk about this when you want to."

"I think we should. You have probably written an inventory of possible subjects." He chuckled. "By the way, I heard it's Irene's turn for refreshments. Bring me one of her butter tarts since they're my favourite."

It was not unusual for Emma and Bill to process thoughts in the same way. They used to tease one another concerning topics. Bill often said, "What I didn't think of—Em did." But she didn't want to brood over what Bill was considering. And yet, some conditions shouldn't be dismissed.

SIXTEEN

The sanctuary filled to the back door for Mother's Day Sunday morning service. Emma stayed with the choir until she sang her part in the anthem. She then walked down to join her daughters in the family pew, not wanting to miss this rare privilege. Although Bill didn't often sit with Emma, the pew's emptiness beside her brought tears. It was always special to share a hymnbook and listen to their voices blend.

"And how are our city girls today?" Doc Baxter extended his hand during the fellowship time.

They echoed each other's greetings. "Good morning. We're both well." They turned to a few friends that circled them.

The doctor moved toward Emma to allow space for other people to move around them. "It's nice to see you."

"You, too."

Seldom did she have an opportunity for a discussion with Doc Baxter in such an informal manner. Usually, he was heading one way, and she the opposite.

He avoided a couple walking with coffee in their hands. "The congregation appears to be counting the days until Bill returns to the pulpit."

"I agree. I'm happy the elders accepted the supply minister. Yet, I've received written notes and cards leaving the impression that Bill should hurry and get well."

Doc Baxter laughed. "One woman said she's putting off dying until he returns, as nobody else can do her funeral."

"I'm afraid they can heighten the pressure." Emma raised her hand, palm up. "But I'm careful not to let them make Bill feel guilty for taking the necessary interval to heal."

"He strains against hospitalization like a dog resisting a leash."

"Yes, Doc. He does."

He nodded to her. "Mrs. Taylor, you're probably aware that your Mission Circle gets great reviews from my patients. It's excellent work you're doing there."

"Thanks, I always enjoy hearing that. I've been mentoring Mrs. Ryan to share the leadership, which frees me to be with Bill."

"You won't be too far from that group. I know how special they are to you."

"Yes, indeed." Emma shook his hand. "Enjoyed our chat, Doc. I'd better go as the twins want to see their father again before they walk to the train station."

• • •

Beatrice and Bernice showed great emphasis in their parting words late Sunday afternoon as they stood side-by-side in Bill's room. When they had spent their time, Beatrice bent to her father and kissed his cheek. "Do take care of yourself, Daddy." Turning to Emma, she said, "And Mom, you too. You are both much loved. And even though we're adults now, we need you equally in our lives."

After a few words of parting, they left the room, and Bill swiped at a tear.

Emma rested a hand on his arm. "Are you all right, Bill?"

"I am sad to say goodbye to my girls today." He shifted from Emma. "One never knows." He wiped his eyes with his handkerchief and tucked it into his pyjama pocket. "I'm thinking of the psalm that tells us of the grass that grows and looks fresh in the morning, but in the evening is parched."

Emma slid her arm under his. "We'll plan to be in the morning. Why don't you have a rest. This has been a busy weekend for you. We can talk later."

"That's a good idea. Perhaps I'll enjoy my supper more." Bill rubbed his eyes. "Why don't you ask for a sandwich and a cup of tea, so we can eat together when I wake up."

When Emma returned, Bill was sleeping. She sat by his side and drank her tea, saving the rest of her snack until his meal came.

When he stirred, he looked at her and yawned. "I guess it's time for supper." He ate most of his food but gave his dessert to her. This gesture was odd as apple pie was his favourite. The staff gathered his plates and left him a magazine from the auxiliary cart. After flipping through it, he closed his eyes and fell asleep, ending their conversation abruptly. They stayed quiet for a long while.

Bill broke the silence. "I fear for you, Em, if I'm not here."

Emma moved closer and leaned to rest her head on his shoulder. "Don't worry, love." His comment was not a new thought. She listened carefully to Bill's wishes and supported him in decisions. She often woke up during the night when doubts surfaced, and she wept. His voice softened to a whisper. "I can't think of not having you by my side."

"I'll be here as long as you need me." This response appeared limp in acknowledgment of Bill's bold statement. It had almost rendered Emma speechless. Is that what he's thinking now? Had he said goodbye to his daughters? Tears glazed her eyes.

The loving face of her husband of numerous years challenged her. He was handsome in the pyjamas the girls had bought him, yet nervous as he continually played with the buttons.

Bill adjusted his position in his bed. "I realize life is altered for me."

"It is, my dear."

"Funny that I'm not anxious. I have more peace than I've ever felt when I was active."

Emma slipped a few strands of hair back from her face. They'd snuck out of her bobby pins and irritated her. "I'm relieved you're feeling peaceful, Bill. That's so much of who you are. We live our days as well as we can manage."

"And should we think of three-score and ten years?"

"We have a stretch to reach that goal," Emma teased.

Silence surrounded them. "I wonder if we get in the way of God's promises. I might have to finish living this one out in my eternal life." Bill raised his eyebrows as if asking her.

With a heartfelt tone, she responded, "And I hope you have many perseverance years—with me." She sighed. "I appreciate my favourite pastor, too." *Perhaps this is an entrance into the next level of conversation when he chooses to talk further.*

The sun began to set. Was it time to leave? This visit had been a longer one than planned. A nurse pushed her medicine cart to Bill's room and walked to his bedside. She enquired about his day and gave him his pills with a glass of water. A few minutes later, an orderly entered the room, straightened Bill's covers and fluffed his pillow. "Mrs. Taylor, if you don't mind, please turn off the light when you leave." He left the door ajar, decreasing the noise from the hall.

Emma and Bill talked until he shifted to the far side of the bed and patted the mattress. She hesitated, then slipped under the soft sheets to lie beside him. He hugged her.

"I believe we're probably breaking hospital rules," she said.

"I suppose we are, but there are a few words of encouragement to honour one another. Consider husbands loving their wives as Christ loved the church." His arm tightened around Emma as he whispered, "And I do love you, Em. I love you with all my heart."

"And my love for you is eternal. Here at this moment and forever." Silence filled the room, and then Emma continued, "Let's lie here for a while. Thank goodness, the orderly almost closed the door."

Experiences came to mind, taking her through special times moment by moment. How firm Bill had held her when his father-in-law minister said, "Kiss your bride, Bill." And a year later, Bill's countenance of love as he observed his twin girls and said, "They are so small." Those precious moments appeared like a slow-motion picture-show.

Emma altered her position and laid her hand across Bill's. "We were never much for adventures. Always satisfied to be at each other's side."

"Yes, you're right." he whispered slowly. "That's still enough."

"We have lots of memories."

Time was still. It seemed like they were in their old bed back in the parsonage. All they missed was Prissy curled at the bottom of the quilt.

Emma prayed for Bill and gave thanks for the ministry with which God had entrusted him. She'd drift off and dream they were embracing—

she could feel the warmth of his body. Such peace it gave her. She slipped from Bill's bed much later and padded down the empty dim hall to the nurse's station to call Henry.

SEVENTEEN

The next day was busy with a funeral for which the Presbyterian minister came to preside. A mix-up with the Sunday school teachers' list took Emma a while to straighten. The stove in the church kitchen failed when the women wanted to bake for the men's supper, plus a few other problems.

During the night, Emma decided she'd make soup and take it to Bill in the morning. She'd had a sweet fryer chicken for a meal, and when she removed the meat, it'd be the right size to put in water to boil.

At the correct time, she slid the chicken's bony frame beneath the water's surface. Later she rolled its skeleton in old cardboard to discard in the garbage where Darlin' wouldn't find it.

After bringing several carrots and an onion from the cold room, she peeled and added them to the broth. Turning the burner lower for the vegetables to simmer, she prepared a basket, including a thermos, which she would fill with Bill's favourite meal. Searching cupboards for preferred spices, she discovered she had none. Numerous shelves were bare, so she needed to make an inventory of necessary items.

A wave of appreciation poured through Emma as she caught the movement of Maisie slowly pushing a newspaper under a corner of the back-door mat. Although news of the depression consumed the headlines, Emma took the weekly to the hospital, as Bill still liked to study the few pages.

•••

Going to visit him was a step out of life's busyness into a circle of care. He snored as Emma slipped onto the familiar chair by his side, hoping not to wake him. She'd learned he'd been out for X-rays this morning and was probably catching required rest.

When Bill awakened, Emma loosened the newspaper from under her elbow, and said, "Here you are, love. See if you can find something interesting in this." After a half hour, she set his lunch out in attractive order and suggested, "Why don't you sit up and I'll put your tray in front of you? When you're finished, you can lay in for a while."

Bill yawned. "So nice, Emma. Like you used to do at home." He stretched. "I stood for a few minutes when I came back from my tests, and then with help, climbed into bed." He straightened his pyjama top. "I don't want you to pamper me. The doctor encourages me to move, which I will after you spoil me again." He chuckled.

She fluffed his pillow behind him. "Maybe you'll get moving this afternoon. Have you been more tired than usual?"

"I have. I've been chalking it up to boredom. Not much to do here." Touching his nose with his index finger, he said, "Do I smell your chicken soup?"

"You might," she teased.

"You are a perfect nurse, Em." Bill shifted in his bed to ready himself for the tray. When settled, he spooned small quantities of the delicious meal into his mouth before sipping his coffee. "This reminds me of home. Perks me up. I admit I'm feeling a bit sluggish." He finished half of his lunch, leaned on the pillow and sighed. "That was so good. It's been an effort to get going the last couple of days. I don't know, Em. Sometimes I feel sheer exhaustion."

"Have you mentioned this to Doc Baxter?"

"Not yet. Let's take this as a nudge to rest more."

"Now, Bill, don't name your diagnosis. When the doctor makes his rounds, please ask him." Emma pushed his cup closer to him.

"I waver from total weariness to a desire to solve all the world dilemmas." He drank a few sips before he pushed the container aside.

"The latter sounds like you." Emma set her book of Psalms on his bedside table. "Remember, God comforts us through changing times. Lie back now, close your eyes and concentrate on the Psalms. You find great consolation in those passages."

Emma tidied Bill's tray while acknowledging a niggling fear of his health. Prayers began to fill her mind. G*od, ease his anxiety to make the hours easier. Strengthen him to meet the day, even as he rests.*

A deep quietness filled the room.

"I often wonder if I've been faithful to this great task of ministry. I mean, what's my favourite theological truth, Em?"

"Jesus loves me, this I know, for the Bible tells me so."

"Do our folks know this?"

Emma placed her hand on Bill's. "Yes, they do because they see it in one another's life. You shine a light to everyone you serve, a path when they are lost and a shelter from storms. People respect and care for you because you equip and inspire them to see God's ongoing love and that supports them in daily problems. And so important, Bill, you reach out to those who disagree with you without being preachy. I commend you."

Emma straightened in her chair and leaned toward Bill. "And you walk with them on the Damascus Road to change their hearts. When they're ready, you take them on the Jericho Road and teach them how to assist others. Whenever they reach out to you in their suffering, you travel with them on the Via Dolorosa. Then you go with them on the Emmaus Road to see Jesus resurrected. You're a man of grace—you are, and I love you for it. You're my better half, no doubt of that." Emma patted his hand. They sat silent.

Bill's face flushed. His overly bright eyes watched Emma, and he remained quiet. Finally, he opened his mouth as if to speak but didn't. She brushed back a strand of hair that had fallen over his ear. "I appreciate your love for me. Yes, I do. My dear husband, you share out of the fullness of your faith. As for your effort and spreading God's grace, I give you an A-plus for both. You offer people assurance, redemption and salvation. When you help them get going in the morning, draw close to God and encourage them to meet the problems of the day, you are faithful."

Emma sat quietly, gently rubbing Bill's fingers one at a time, pausing on his wedding ring. She raised her hand to the window and softly said. "Every person on the mission field and here in Noble, knows God loves them if they have listened to you. If anything, maybe they need a little practice in exercising love with each other, so they don't spend all their energy basking in it. But at least they know the truth as you understand it."

Bill closed his eyes and smiled. "I love listening to you. Very convincing. You ought to be a preacher, Em."

She nudged him playfully. "The newspapers gave me that status when I went from town to town for tent meetings. It's a long while since that bit of history."

"Yes, indeed," Bill said. "And you were a master at preaching. I was often in awe of your ministry. I loved working with you in those gatherings. When you led worship, it was the best kind of pastoral care. I think ladies do that much easier than men." He took a deep breath. "Thank you for those memories, Em. I feel better. What would I have done without you?"

"I could say the same thing, love." She moved the top of the blanket to fit against his neck. "But for now, we've talked long enough."

"I feel relieved, somehow. It settles me to speak on these things."

"You rest, then. I'll sit here for a while and read our devotional to you." Emma had spent a significant portion of the day encouraging Bill. After the reading, she offered a prayer, comforted that God had covered them both with a warm blanket of love.

EIGHTEEN

Several days later, the doctor called Emma to meet him at the hospital to discuss Bill's condition. Although he was growing weaker, he kept up with self-care and conversation in a slow, ordered way. Speaking with Doc Baxter would focus on details, which would be helpful. So why did she dread the meeting?

As soon as Emma arrived, the doctor invited her into the consulting room. "Emma, I've checked Bill's progress and compared his results with my comments in previous weeks. He's working so hard to breathe that it weakens him. Yesterday, I gave him medication to lessen stress. When I went to see him after visiting hours last evening to discuss how his heart was failing, he had a certain peace as we talked. His countenance changed, and in his way, he was preparing himself for what was ahead."

Emma wiped her eyes and sniffed. Doc Baxter took her hand. "Bill has it figured out. He was waiting for me to trust him with this recent information. Emma, you have guided him in whatever adjustment he's experiencing. I commend you." A heavy silence fell between them. "Bill told me how much you comforted him and helped him move day by day to what he's now facing." Doc Baxter hung the stethoscope around his neck and opened his palm toward the door. "Let's go and see how he is this morning."

Emma's fingers grasped her purse as they walked along the hall. Was she entering another phase of her life? Her legs felt weak, as if they could close as an accordion. When they came to Bill's room, Doc ushered Emma into freshness without the usual antiseptic scent.

The curtains pulled to the centre of the window allowed a slice of sunlight to filter into the area. They both watched Bill. Was he sleeping? Doc indicated for Emma to sit in the chair. "He'll want to wake up and see you there. He's told me what that feels like." Doc nodded his head and left.

The sun must have slipped behind a cloud as the room appeared shaded. Emma studied Bill. "How are you getting along today, love?"

Minutes passed, Bill's voice strained to speak, "I…I don't think you want…to hear this."

"I want to hear anything you'd like to tell me, love." Emma reached for his hand. And he held hers.

"Thank you…for being with me. I'm going to rest and…rest." Following a long pause, Bill continued slowly with a trembling voice. "I'm warm…no pain. You were…with me…all of this. I love you…Em." Through the next hour, his breathing changed but remained relatively steady, although weaker. Emma whispered to him, prayed and dabbed her eyes clear of tears.

Nurses came into the room, carried out duties and left. Emma sat beside Bill for three hours and read aloud his favourite psalms. His raspy sounds deepened. It was a waiting time. Should she call the girls? No, there was nothing they could do. After arranging to come to Noble, hoping to see their father—he'd be gone. It wouldn't be long now, and Emma laid her head against his shoulder, confident he had begun to cross over.

She should go and get Doc Baxter, but that'd mean leaving Bill's side. The doctor shuffled quietly into the room, acknowledging Emma with a nod. He examined Bill, shook his head and spoke softly to her. Just as the doctor hung the stethoscope around his neck, Bill gasped for breath. Doc took his pulse, and Emma knew. Bill's eyes stared at her, and he slowly began to relax.

Emma's chest tightened. "Oh, Bill. Not yet." She bent over the bed and held him. Sobs rose in her throat, spilling out in moans. Then gazing into his eyes, she quieted herself and soon found the words to whisper,

"Thank you, Bill, for everything you've done for me and for sharing your life." She let go of one hand to tug a handkerchief from her pocket and patted her tears to see Bill without hindrance. "I love you and will forever." Deep sobs wracked her body.

Bill's fingers relaxed in Emma's and finally went limp. His eyes remained locked on hers as the light dimmed within them.

Emma murmured, "The Lord is my Shepherd, I shall not want."

Bottomless pain gripped her chest. She wanted to go with him.

"He's gone, Emma. I'm so sorry." The doctor lifted the edge of the bedsheet.

"Don't cover his face, please," she urged. "Leave him with me…as he is."

"Very well." Doc Baxter folded back the sheet. "We'll hold this dear man close to our heart. The church and the town will miss him." He covered Emma's hand with his own and stood beside Bill. "I'll contact Mr. Tolt and be at the nurse's station to finish my paperwork if you need me."

Fear and uncertainty crept through Emma as she waited for the undertaker to come. How would she go on without Bill? He'd cared for her and led the way. Who was she if she wasn't the minister's wife? Her identity was in Bill.

She slid her fingers across his hand, and tears fell on it. This hospital room had been the one place they had called their own away from public view and the congregation. *Oh death, where is your sting now that Bill is with the Lord.* It was right for Emma to be by Bill's side when he died. She loved and had been loved by him.

First Church had provided more than a house; it was a home, a faith-filled circle, and a total sense of belonging. Bill had given his life to those who needed him; he shared without resistance. Both Bill and Emma were part of a larger family. Would she still fit without him?

Keeping her grief between them, Emma moved closer and laid her head on Bill's pillow. Deep sobs racked her body. Alone with memories and new sorrow—at the mercy of all the loving people, she raised her head. Bill was at peace and this image comforted her.

NINETEEN
PART 3

Mr. Tolt entered the front hall. "Hello, Emma, Beatrice and Bernice. My condolences to you. And how are we today?"

Emma's gaze focused on his use of the word 'we' and glanced at him to see who else he was considering.

"Thank you. We're doing well." Beatrice took his hat and jacket to place over a hook.

Bernice said, "We appreciate your prompt attention."

"We're holding together in light of our circumstances," Emma added. "And you?"

"Better now that the weather has warmed." Mr. Tolt viewed the room as if wanting to begin his task.

"Come to the kitchen." Emma and her daughters walked ahead of him.

He sat and drummed his fingers on the table's wooden surface as if eager to get on with business.

Emma opened a small book that held loose papers. "Thank you for taking the time to come over. Bill and I completed our plans with you when we met last year. However, you'll be wanting to confirm our previous arrangements as well as the information for our tombstone."

"Yes, of course," Mr. Tolt said. "I'm happy to assist with planning." He opened his briefcase, took out a piece of paper and pulled a long silver pen from his jacket pocket.

"Bill knew that." Emma nodded. "He always liked working with you at funeral services."

"That's nice to hear. The feeling was mutual." Then after a long sigh, he said, "Bill went rather quickly, Emma. I'm so sorry. He told me when I visited him one afternoon that his heart condition was serious, and the doctor had told him another attack could be fatal." Mr. Tolt shifted on his chair, rubbing his elbow with slender fingers. "Even as he referred to the danger of further problems, he seemed to fear he wouldn't recover."

Beatrice put her arm around Emma's shoulders as if shielding her from Mr. Tolt's chatter.

"Bill mentioned he wanted to finish the discussion we started." Emma opened a small calendar. "I assured him that I'd be able to accomplish this at the appropriate time."

"Leave it to you for tidying up business," Mr. Tolt said. "It'll set your mind at ease knowing this is all completed. I had entered a tentative appointment in my book after we previously met. Didn't realize back then it'd fall into such a critical period for you." He stacked his papers. "However, we all hoped for the best and we're sad it didn't turn out differently. No doubt in my mind, our much-loved pastor was appreciated." Mr. Tolt nodded and glanced at Bernice and Beatrice. "I'm glad you had a recent visit not too long ago."

"Indeed, we are too. We are." They echoed their words as they spoke.

Why was Mr. Tolt beginning his consultation with random conversation, as he seemed eager to start his business when he came?

"Bill expected healthy days ahead," Emma said. "He used to say, 'there's a lot of work to do, and I need to get at it.' And then he'd smile and add, 'and do it slowly.'" She swiped a few tears and said, "Shall we begin our task? You'll have a busy day."

Mr. Tolt wrote on a blank sheet of paper, folded it and then said, "I do. I have most of the information. Bill's age was—"

"Fifty-one," Bernice responded.

Mr. Tolt read a revised list of options, which Emma had heard before. She took mental notes considering the expense.

He tugged a white handkerchief out of his pocket and wiped his temples. "We have to keep up a good appearance, don't we? I mean, Reverend Taylor had acquaintances across the townships. All the churches have been neighbours with us. It was a known fact that the entire community would gather if anything happened to either one of you. We should be proud."

Should we? Showing off would be the furthest from Bill's mind. Hearing God's word, enjoying a tasty lunch and seeing old friends would be foremost rather than putting on a show.

Mr. Tolt sighed. "Yes, Mrs. Taylor, I'll see to everything."

Listening to him in his many responsibilities was stressful enough without having to sit through his persuasive speech here in the kitchen, especially in their grief.

"Shall I print what we decided to have engraved on the tombstone?" Emma lifted a pencil from the table.

Mr. Tolt handed her a piece of paper. "It's ready except for names and dates. I'll add the full information for Bill, and yours when appropriate."

Emma printed in large letters: William James Taylor, B. 1884, D. 1935, and Emma Fay Russell, B. 1886. D… Together forever.

Mr. Tolt read it. "Are you sure you want to use your maiden name, Emma? You've been Em Taylor a long time and that's how you're known."

"I believe you record your proper, full, given name on your tombstone, Mr. Tolt. It's 'Emma' and not 'Em,' and it's 'Russell' for this part. When I'm lying there beside Bill, people will figure it out."

Both girls snickered softly.

"I understand." Mr. Tolt's tone of voice changed. He glanced at them. "I can see you've thought these things through. It's always good to do this with family. I'll make the necessary arrangements." He dropped the papers into the briefcase and closed it. "Be sure to call if you have further questions."

Emma followed him to the hall. "Thank you for your guidance, Mr. Tolt."

He shook her hand. "You're welcome. Again, my condolences." Stepping aside, he said, "To you both as well, Bernice and Beatrice. I'll see all of you later."

With that, he closed the door behind him. Now, if only Emma's feelings of uncertainty would disappear as quickly.

"Another job off your list, Mom, and that's what's important now." Beatrice took a deep breath. "Well done."

"I'm impressed with you," Bernice said. "You can hold your own with Mr. Tolt. And I speak from hearing Daddy say that's not easy." She pulled her mother close. "I love that strong-minded side of you. Why don't you practice it more?"

Emma smiled. She had been protective of Bill and the plans they'd made, and it was comforting to know that the girls appreciated that effort. "Maybe I will." She sighed and opened her arms to enclose both daughters.

• • •

During the wake, mourners lined the street and the sidewalk to the parsonage's front door.

"My goodness, everybody has come to pay their respects!" Mrs. Howard, a member of the women's unit and a steward's wife, leaned close to Emma as she stood at the entrance to receive condolences. "But it's Reverend Taylor. Such a fine man. Now, be encouraged, dear; God only takes the best. You can't argue with God."

Emma grimaced and shook her hand before passing her to the girls. Thoughtless remarks jarred her. A long afternoon of greeting and accepting both kind and questionable comments was exhausting. Needing to take a break, Emma sat on the chesterfield and looked at the polished wooden coffin. Although Bill's hospital stay seemed like a waiting game from one day to another, these last few days faded into a blur of hours, bringing her to now.

Bill rested at home for this final time. So fitting. Mr. Tolt suggested this change after the conversation at Emma's kitchen table. She'd show gratitude for this extra care and write a kind note to him next week. He had guided her professionally, for which she was grateful.

Maisie came into the parlour and scanned the faces of the crowd.

Emma waved. "Over here, Maisie."

She dropped into the chair beside Emma and leaned over to embrace her. "I am so sorry, Emma. Oh, we'll miss him, won't we?"

"Yes, we will." Emma's throat tightened as she wiped away the tears.

"I just returned from visiting my sister in Windsor." Maisie patted her hand. "I wish I had been here for you."

"I know, but I'm doing well." Emma took a deep breath. "The girls have been helpful, and Mr. Tolt directed me through difficult decisions."

"I knew there'd be people coming and going." Maisie glanced across the packed room. "Has it been this busy through the day?"

"It has. Everybody has come and I'm so glad about that." Emma paused. "Although some of the words our friends are saying confuse me. Where do they get such lines? Not from my Bill's sermons, I can guarantee that. They all seem to speak God's thoughts. I doubt God can get a word in edgeways. And they keep talking about losing Bill. Goodness, I know exactly where he is."

"Now, don't let it bother you," Maisie said. "Let others comfort you in their way and set the rest of it aside for now. It isn't fair but welcome their conversation. Don't allow their comments to drag you lower than you are feeling. Sometimes people are so overwhelmed by their own grief, they say what comes into their mind without realizing how it sounds."

"Thank you," Emma squeezed her hand. "And I'm glad you're back."

"Come now, dear. You have to bear up." Miss Prior, a retired public-school teacher, slid in beside Emma. "Everybody's trying to help. Why, they've put a benefit box in the library for you. Oh, now, I shouldn't have told you. You might be embarrassed knowing we're all concerned how you're going to cope, you know, without Bill's salary and all."

"Yes," Emma said. "It'll be difficult, but I'm sure I'll manage." Carefully folding her handkerchief, she glanced across the room. "Now, you must excuse me. I'll go and stand with the girls again. There are many people waiting to come through, and it's almost supper time."

Later, aware the end of the visitation was growing close, Emma beckoned to Bernice. "Can you accept the final condolences and say we'll see everybody tomorrow at the funeral. I'd like to spend a few quiet minutes with your father."

"Of course, Mom. I'll look after it."

The room quietened. Colourful garden flowers, especially the lovely arrangement of wild blue lupines that must have come from the Hills, issued the scent of honey. They matched the navy velvet flounce around the coffin-stand. Emma wept that she could no longer be with her beloved husband. His countenance was peaceful as if he'd never been sick. Emma was thankful that Mr. Tolt had hidden the frayed cuffs on

Bill's grey suit coat as appearance was something he was always conscious of when in public.

Exhausted by the task of responding to challenging remarks by kind and loving individuals, Emma brushed her tears away. Scripture taught that God had a special love for widows. When would these friends begin to show it?

• • •

After the church service, Emma and her daughters carefully walked on the damp, soggy earth, and followed the pallbearers to the family plot. It had rained earlier in the day, and now the sun broke through the clouds to dry the puddles. Friends formed a semi-circle near the grave to say their final goodbyes. The family stood together.

"Are you cold, Momma?" Bernice asked as Beatrice moved in closer to fasten the button on Emma's jacket.

Cold as stone. The grey-buffed tombstone placed boldly at the head of the coffin drew Emma's attention. As she read the words, tears formed and dropped on her hands. Mr. Tolt had skilfully finalized the arrangements. The site was ready. Could she stay and be alone—sit with Bill? But no, it wouldn't happen. People had been giving her orders all day, telling her to move here, stand there, shift across in front and every-which-way.

Clutching her modest black handbag, she traced its broken threadbare corners of imitation leather. Why had she brought it as she never carried money? Bill had bought anything she wanted. He could guess before she asked.

"Earth to earth, ashes to ashes, dust to dust, trusting in God's great mercy…." Reverend Albert's voice cut into Emma's thoughts as Mr. Tolt tipped a small brass shaker close to the coffin. A generous amount of sand fell on its surface in the shape of a cross. By the time, she'd listened to the benediction, most of the particles had disappeared on the shiny wooden crease, vanishing as life itself.

Bernice offered the palm of her hand under Emma's elbow to usher her forward to stand closer to the coffin.

"Say your last goodbye to Daddy." Bernice touched her tears with a handkerchief.

"I did, dear," Emma said. "I said my goodbyes. I did it in the hospital, at home during the wake, and again at the funeral."

"I know, but can you do it again? Everybody expects it here. Do your best. This will soon be over."

Land's sake, why did she have to do what others needed to see to make all this real for them? She'd like to do what she wanted, what was crucial. It'd be nice to sit here and think for a while, alone. No more words; there'd been enough already. Maybe she could linger behind.

"Come on now, Mom." Beatrice put her hand on Emma's. "It's time to go. Nobody will leave until you do. You know how it is."

"Yes." Emma swallowed. "I do." The mourners would wait. They'd expect the family to lead the crowd from the grave. Everyone would follow.

The family had meant Bill, Emma, and the twins even after they moved to the city. It was how they'd gone through life. In a few days, the girls would catch the train to return to their friends and careers. Prissy and Emma would be all that was left. Tears filled her eyes, and she dabbed at them with a handkerchief.

The snail-like movement reflected Emma's resistance as she hid behind her hat's veil. Holding back sobs as her daughters ushered her along, she'd do what was expected—proper, pleasant and fitting.

A few birds in the overhanging branches chirped, in contrast to the sorrow evident in the air. The slick earth from last night's rain, and the moisture in the grass and weeds bordering the cemetery driveway, left a pungent scent. Mud seeped in under Emma's heels as if she were walking on a muddy sponge. Before she stepped into the car, she attempted to remove the dirt until she noticed newspapers on the matted floorboard.

The sleek black car's engine hummed as Mr. Tolt drove out the cemetery lane. Beatrice and Bernice pressed against Emma as they sat in the back seat, overwhelming her with their attention. Thoughts of stillness and daydreaming surfaced as they slowly made their way toward the church. Tears began again as she saw CLOSED signs hanging in every shop window. Main Street resembled a ghost town.

She leaned on the seat and rested her head on a soft velvet cushion. Her thoughts strayed to home. The image of Bill's favourite chair with his flannelette pillows propped against its back passed across her mind. His pipe would hang in its stand with a few ashes beneath it. And his red plaid shirt would drape on the hall tree.

Prissy would meow, expect him in all their familiar places and settle on the front rug to wait. Emma expected a similar courtesy when she got home later today—but first, the funeral luncheon.

TWENTY

The sound of chairs scraping across the floor mixed with chattering voices rattled through the fellowship hall as Emma entered. She checked to see if the jacket button she'd picked from the cemetery grass still lay in her pocket. It did. Hopefully, her action had gone unnoticed.

The girls would mention Emma's faded navy suit at the end of the day. Maybe it would entice them to take her shopping before they left. Removing their coats, they hung them on the wooden hooks, already layered.

Individuals from both the congregation and the town sympathized with Emma again as she waited inside the entrance, ready to receive them. They extended their hands for a formal handshake and said they looked forward to seeing her following this time. Beatrice and Bernice came to stand beside Emma, receiving additional condolences.

As the minister's wife, she was expected to accompany Bill to funerals and later to comfort grieving families and their friends. She'd never grown accustomed to hearing continuous death litanies. Well-meaning individuals frequently said the same overused statements they'd drawn on for years. It seemed they had to say something and continually repeated themselves.

All those lines were so overworked from funeral to funeral. Time-worn words like, 'He's in a better place' filled exchanges. Emma agreed being with our Lord would be the ultimate. Yet, she grieved that Bill's years of service were finished at the age of fifty-one, and somehow, God might join her in that thinking. And no, God didn't need a messenger. She needed Bill, the girls, the church and the community as well. He loved being a messenger here on earth, and God used him daily.

Bernice interrupted Emma's thoughts. "Mom, you've been greeting people too long. We think you should have a break."

"I'm ready for that, thanks. My feet have begun to ache, and I'm relieved to step aside."

Sighing, attempting to dislodge faintness, she walked to the closest table and pulled out a chair.

Mrs. Howard came up from behind Emma and touched her elbow. "God is in control, my dear, and he knows what's best. Just trust."

Did they say those phrases to gain an understanding of a situation because they were unable to put it in their own words? Mrs. Howard rambled on, and Emma caught the phrase, "Everything happens for a reason, you know."

Emma's jaw tightened. No doubt. Bill died because of a heart attack. Using someone else for a sounding board seemed to make it easier for most to cope with their grief. For whatever motive, she grew tired of listening to all of it. This day ought to be one of comfort, not to enter theological debates. All those short, overused statements had a ring of truth, but did they have to be used as a chain in conversation?

When there was a funeral, it was customary for Emma to make sandwiches and then attend each service and luncheon, often eating her prepared food. Descriptions of the freshness of bread or lack of same and the acceptable amount of egg salad amused her. Although nobody expected her to serve today, how many would do double duty? There were never enough workers to do all the tasks. The kitchen crew wouldn't expect Emma to work, but she'd donate funds to show appreciation for the women's efforts, as everyone else did.

"My dear Emma." Mrs. Murray, one of the choir members, sobbed in Emma's arms. "I feel so sad. Reverend Taylor was such a precious man. We all loved him. Now you take care of yourself." Her blue velvet box hat wobbled on her forehead, making it appear like a balancing act. "God must have needed a right-hand man. That's why he took Bill so young.

You should be happy about that." Goodness, hadn't Emma heard those exact phrases from several friends during the last hour?

Emma took a breath to respond, but words escaped her. Mrs. Murray sighed, leaning her bosom into Emma's shoulder. "And be thankful, my dear, that Bill didn't have to suffer as some do."

Emma pulled a dainty embroidered cloth from her suit pocket to wipe her eyes, relieved she had tucked in a spare one.

Mrs. Murray sobbed into her handkerchief, lifted it to rub her nose and dab her eyelids. "Why doesn't God call our Mr. Hankerman home since his stroke. He's been lying on the same cot for six months now." She bent closer to Emma. "I suspect he's got repenting to do, and it's taking him a long time. Maybe God is trying to teach him or the rest of us a lesson."

Emma didn't even attempt to respond before Mrs. Reid, one of the regular members who sat in the back pew on Sunday mornings, elbowed her way in front of Emma. Her grey hair lay coiled into a semicircle, and her breath smelled as if somebody had put too much garlic in her egg sandwich. Yet, her comments were well-intentioned.

"Lands sake, Emma, whatever will you do?" She sighed. "Imagine Sam dying and leaving me. I wouldn't know where to turn. You'll be lost without Reverend Taylor. Don't forget, dear, you've got friends, lots of them. None of us can do much, but we're here."

Mrs. Miles, the local librarian, came out of the kitchen and poured Emma a hot cup of tea. "Here you are, Mrs. Taylor. Enjoy."

"Thank you," Emma said. "I appreciate this." Could she tell Mrs. Miles the importance of these much-needed interruptions? Accepting a minced ham with pickle sandwich and taking a bite helped satisfy Emma's hunger.

Mrs. Miles set the teapot beside her. "I wanted to say the choir sang like angels and the decorations were extraordinaire in the past weeks. The preachers, well, I admit they've been captivating, but nothing in comparison to your Reverend Taylor."

Emma thanked her and thought how far-reaching Bill's reputation as a preacher stretched.

"Mrs. Taylor. I want to mention, well, you held us together during his hospitalization. So, thank you for loving us as you did." She patted Emma's hand and hurried away.

Before Emma took a bite of a sandwich, Mr. Howard, a steward, sat beside her and started referring to the parsonage yard. "Don't let the lawn cause you any worry. Young Adam will charge you five cents to mow it. It's not parkland or anything. We'll sure miss all the work Bill did, both in the house and with the grass."

Adam had often come to the side door selling his mother's garden produce. Emma always purchased a few items to assist them. Extra pennies would enable him to contribute to the family's needs. She liked the idea.

Geraniums she'd grown from seed and the asparagus ferns she'd nurtured through the winter filled the old metal containers at the front of the residence serving as welcoming sentinels. Bill's lawn gave him a chance to putter. He had mowed it weekly and never asked for assistance from the church. He'd bought and repaired his lawnmower and kept the entire property from his earnings, replacing everything from the front steps to light bulbs.

"Of course," Emma said. "Whatever you say. I'll manage fine." She took a bite of her sandwich. She wouldn't have to prepare any supper; the lunch would be sufficient if she could manage to eat. She nodded and thanked folks as they stopped to offer condolences. They'd been friends for a long time, yet they would soon think of change. And Emma would be introduced as 'our former minister's widow.'

Maisie slipped onto the empty chair at the table. "Are you being looked after?"

Emma turned to face her. "For sure, such a tasty lunch, all of it. You've been run off your feet and haven't stopped to have a bite."

"Ah, I'm fine," Maisie said. "You must be getting tired. What a crowd, eh? Does it comfort you to acknowledge how much your Bill was loved?"

"It does, Maisie." Emma wiped her eyes. "We sure loved him, didn't we?"

"And we still do. Our love will go on as long as we have breath." Maisie stood. "I must keep going, dear. We'll spend time soon."

She had to do her part as one of the kitchen team, although Emma liked her company. Maisie made it easy to linger and chat as she endlessly replenished the plates with food, filling every need in the room.

Mrs. Greenside and her sister, Miriam, joint owners of The Emerald Shop, sat prim and upright on a bench. They must have shopped together, as both appeared perfect, polished like porcelain dolls in their similar pastel linen outfits. Their patent leather shoes reminded Emma of headlights of an oncoming car. She smiled through her sorrow.

Oh, if life could be so flawless. Emma hadn't found it that way—it was a challenge from morning to night. Between her and Bill, they accepted the conflicts in the same breath as the blessings.

TWENTY-ONE

One of the kitchen workers stopped to talk, filled Emma's teacup and then placed sandwiches on her empty plate. She hadn't eaten very much for breakfast and was famished. As she sipped her tea, she stopped to listen to two ladies sitting at a small table to her right. Frowning, she stared at her hands. *Surely, they are wrong, or perhaps I misunderstood.*

New voices joined the mix as Mrs. Howard, and Mrs. Allen, a clerk at the grocery store, joined in the discussion.

"But they must tell her; life moves on. We've had to get numerous supply preachers. We couldn't afford it when Reverend Taylor was sick, and we can't afford to keep Emma now. She'll understand." Mrs. Howard's voice sounded like high keys on the piano.

Maybe someone would come and hang on to Emma with a hug. At least that would take her attention from the discussion that caused more grief.

Emma listened to the conversation focused on diminishing funds and the steward's recommendation that services be held in the basement if things didn't change by fall.

Mr. Tolt standing in church and telling the congregation of the cost to bring in preachers still disgusted Emma. Goodness, did he forget they had three men teaching Senior Sunday school every week? Why hadn't he asked one of them?

He'd probably decided on his own that Emma wouldn't be available, as he hadn't invited her. Not once, and it wasn't because he wasn't aware she wanted to fill in, as she and Bill could have used any funds the stewards might offer.

"I hope she understands. Still, we don't want to hurt her either. She's been here for us, all of us, at any time. We have to be kind."

Whose voice was that? Who was the woman sticking up for Emma? It took a lot of courage to be the one voice among many who differed from the common attitude voiced by several.

"Customers are hoping she'll figure it out," Mrs. Allen said. "This situation has to be managed with care."

What were they saying? At the funeral luncheon of all places. The earth wasn't dry on Bill's grave. What were they considering? *Lord, give me patience and keep me sitting where I am, or I'll draw my chair into their circle and get in on the dirt.*

Over the next half hour, friends stopped at Emma's table; some sat to talk or shake her hand and then excused themselves to leave. As soon as they moved on from their conversation, the ladies' voices discussing Emma's future once again echoed in her ears.

"We'll all join in, and she'll have ideas of what she can do." The same considerate unidentifiable voice spoke.

Could I swivel my chair and join them?

"I expect she's seen this coming." Mrs. Howard's voice rose above the exchange and laughter at the tea table. "Maybe she and Bill decided before he died."

Again, in a quiet tone, someone said, "I hope so. This will hurt her."

"The stewards will leave this for a couple of days, but they must visit as soon as possible." Mrs. Howard's voice remained firm. "I'm sure Reverend Taylor would have been frank with her. Besides his pulpit presence, straightforwardness and honesty were two more of his strengths."

"I agree, but when you're telling your wife she'll have to fend for herself, it might be a different story. We'll see. Pray for her and then leave it with God. Oh, here, let's have another one of these lovely treats." Mrs. Allen's voice softened.

"It's fine to say, 'leave it with God', as long as we're mindful that God may use us to answer our prayers," Mrs. Howard countered.

Emma rubbed her arthritic fingers and sighed deeply. Several women from the kitchen interrupted her eavesdropping with a bag of carefully cut sandwiches.

"Here's a few of those minced ham on homemade bread," Bertha said. "The ones you like—and cookies. You take them with you, too. It'll save you from cooking when the girls are home, and you'll have something prepared when people call on you."

"Thank you. I appreciate your kindness. This will be helpful."

Emma gathered her purse and scarf together. Cora's gentle voice filled the circle. She'd be thinking of Emma's well-being in a caring way.

Escaping to sit and think awhile was one option. This news provided too much to absorb. Could it be that she'd wake up, discover it as a bad dream, and Bill would come in the door happy to see her? But it wouldn't happen, and Emma must continue one day at a time.

Bernice and Beatrice laughed and talked with school friends. A decade in a town developed a large circle of acquaintants; the girls had done this and more. Emma encouraged them to stay if they wanted, and after collecting her food she hugged them before leaving. She said her farewell and began her planned exit, weaving around the tables. Using the side door would save her from more goodbyes and tears.

Miss Muir, a town clerk, breezed in, her bright yellow scarf blowing freely behind her in a trail of lilac perfume. "My goodness, Mrs. Taylor. It is time to go, isn't it? Such a lovely service. Well, as far as funerals go, or, well, you know what I mean. If I can help, please call me. My number is 112 ring 1-3."

"Thank you, Miss Muir. I'm sure I'll manage with the girls at home. But I'll keep you in mind if we need assistance."

"I hope to hear from you. You'll be overwhelmed with all the packing and everything."

"Packing?" Emma blinked. "You mean Mr. Taylor's clothes and personals?"

"Well, yes, and whatever is yours," Miss Muir blurted, her cheeks flushed.

"As for Mr. Taylor's things, I won't be touching them for a while. This task demands some thought before I start." Emma positioned herself in the doorway, watching Miss Muir. "But what do you mean, 'whatever is yours?'"

"Haven't the stewards told you? I wouldn't have known any of this if my daddy wasn't a member of the board. You know, it isn't common knowledge or anything like that, but they've got a minister coming. They'll tell the congregation on Sunday. And well, you're totally aware of how much there is to do to clean a big parsonage. And it's only natural that it should be spotless for the family. Yes, it has to be bright and spotless—"

"I agree." Emma nodded. "Spotless." She stared at her hands. Words could be cruel when offered without thought. Her wedding band, dulled from years of hard work and dishwater, was not bright and spotless. Still, a pleasant reminder that Bill would be in her memory forever. The house wasn't bright and spotless either. Comfortably messy served as a better description.

Reassuring words held a sense of reality. She wasn't alone. *"You'll be fine, my dear; don't worry."* Bill's voice filled her memory.

Miss Muir shrugged. "I shouldn't be bothering you with these things. You have enough worrying to do without our problems. We've got plenty by the sound of church news, with money, the parsonage and getting a different man in place." She placed her hand on the door. "Careful, don't let it slam on your fingers. That'd hurt." She scurried away.

Yes, it'd hurt.

• • •

The past few days seemed like a nightmare. Emma did what she could with the girls' help. Leaving Bill's clothing for a while to sort would be ideal; however, with the pending news, she'd have to begin immediately. Preparing to move would be a colossal task, and she needed her girls' help.

"We'll go through your father's dresser and closet," Emma said. "Include his suit and those two sweaters." She pointed to the clothes folded on the bed. "And there are socks and personal items that can go in the box."

Beatrice added her father's clothes and old favourites to the rest and folded the cardboard flaps.

Emma pulled Bill's flannel plaid shirt close to her face. She sobbed quietly into the soft fabric and said, "I'll save this to wear when I need to feel his arms around me. We can't give the clothes to anybody in this town, but there's a Salvation Army store in Hampton where you can drop them off. That'd be helpful." She wrote the address on a card. "Drive your father's car, and that delivery will complete the job."

When they filled the boxes, Emma gave them the car keys. She hadn't mentioned her fears concerning the future. So much of this had yet to reveal itself. The church would assist with necessary changes, so Emma encouraged her daughters to make their travel arrangements. Their work and connections in Toronto would be waiting.

Bernice missed a long-time friend and often spoke of returning to the city, while Beatrice planned to marry a nice young man in two years and looked forward to seeing him. A sob surged in Emma's throat as she realized that Bernice and Beatrice wouldn't have their daddy to walk them down the aisle. Bill had often referred to being the father of the brides and not the officiant.

Now, he'd be neither.

The girls said their goodbyes to go back to Toronto on the evening train. They promised to take Emma shopping the next time they visited. This was Emma's new life—alone, depending on others, yearning for Bill and thankful for God's presence. A memory came to her mind about not afflicting a widow or orphan. She acknowledged this as God's promise.

The tired old house boasted items generously given to ministers by the congregation through the years. Hand-me-down furniture, second-hand dishes and much-used books filled the rooms. All of this and the few items she called her own would comfort her until she had to leave. By the sounds of what she'd overheard today, her departure was close at hand.

TWENTY-TWO

By Sunday, Emma's eviction from the parsonage would be old news to the congregation. They wouldn't understand if she delayed the process of moving. A dim future with no direction faced her. What would Bill tell her to do if he were here?

Emma cleared her breakfast dishes, took off her apron and powdered her nose. Would she attend worship this morning? Thinking of such an effort frightened her. It was too soon after Bill's funeral to come out of the house. A woman stayed home to provide an appropriate mourning period when her husband died. Emma straightened and took a deep breath. *But we can't always do the acceptable when a crisis needs attention.* By the conversation at the lunch, she had enough immediate personal work ahead of her to warrant going among the membership.

Besides, the girls had returned to their Toronto home. Stillness filled the corners. Loneliness fell into the shadows of each room. Who was Emma's family other than those gathered on Sundays? Would it be out of place for her to enter the sanctuary this morning? She touched her handkerchief to her nose to hold her sniffling.

The church was the only kinfolk accessible to Emma. She wouldn't reach out to strangers. The members were brothers and sisters in the faith. Could she count on them to open their arms, to walk with her in sorrow, or would they persist in relating to her as their past minister's wife? Even though that was her status, she had no idea of the boundaries of that relationship. Maybe they were also confused about Emma's status or how to relate to her. Perhaps being in their midst through worship would make it easier for them to learn about these things.

She climbed the front steps; the elders opened doors and greeted her kindly. They asked to hang her jacket and mentioned a few events of local news. Alone in the pew, tears pricked as isolation overwhelmed her. Watching the choir file into their places brought sniffles as memories of happy times rushed through her mind. Would she be able to hold back her sobs?

How could she pretend to be comfortable among them? If she left during the first hymn, people would know she'd gone home, where she should have stayed. And they'd be right. Today was too early for any widow to venture beyond her front porch. Some would think attending made a spectacle of herself.

However, there was no choice. Emma was here accepting her identity as different from other widows. Responsibility drove her—independent of opinions. Today and in the next few weeks, her actions would be similar.

As she listened to the introduction of the melodic anthem, strength poured deeply into her body and sustained her with confidence. Her voice softly joined the alto part where she sang with conviction and responded to those beloved words of Russell Kelso Carter:

> *Standing on the promises I cannot fail*
> *List'ning ev'ry moment to the Spirit's call*
> *Resting in my Savior as my all in all*
> *Standing on the promises of God.*

When the choir finished with a complex amen, Emma sank into the warmth of the Spirit. Nothing else mattered—she'd stay.

Mr. Tolt came to the front and cleared his throat. "Good morning. With prayer and contemplation concerning who would fill our present vacancy, it is with great pleasure I make this announcement. The Reverend Larson has accepted our invitation and will bring this morning's message. We are fortunate that he is between churches and can accommodate us. You'll be familiar with him as he filled in several times when Reverend Taylor was on sick leave."

Heads nodded, and the members began to whisper. The room dimmed. *They've moved on.* Emma checked the surge of bitterness, knowing it had no place in her heart. This congregation had extended love and concern to her and Bill. She whispered a word of thanks, praying the transition would be easy for the Larsons, the faithful folks, and for her.

Mr. Tolt persisted. "We are grateful to Reverend Taylor and his wife Emma for their ministry through the past decade. As well, we remember their loyal and devoted service. We'll be offering continual prayer for God's grace to comfort Mrs. Taylor with the changes ahead."

Turning to Emma, he said, "Rest assured, we'll do everything possible to help you cope with these unexpected circumstances. With your permission, the stewards would like to visit you tomorrow morning to discuss options and opportunities."

Emma had to give Mr. Tolt credit, although his words held levels of meaning for her. She nodded her consent to the inevitable appointment. She read, prayed and sang the various parts of the service. Reverend Larson's message fed her hunger for challenge and reassurance. He'd fit in, and Emma would pray for him, his family and the congregation. He'd continue to strengthen this community of faith through his ministry.

• • •

On Monday, the expected callers—the stewards and an elder—came to the front door. They sat at the kitchen table and discussed several topics with Emma. She waited for them to get to the real reason for their visit.

"As you know, Mrs. Taylor, we've had to make hasty decisions that affect you." Mr. Tolt clasped his hands together. "For this, we are sorry, but we couldn't avoid it. You met Reverend Larson yesterday morning. We're fortunate to get such a God-fearing man. Our choice invites him and his wife, and their two children to move to Noble as soon as possible. It'll be nice to have a family with children in the parsonage; you know how excellent this is for the membership and community. They bring families—people their own age." He scratched his head as though trying to offer another argument.

Emma leaned toward the table. "I understand, Mr. Tolt. But your words 'as soon as possible' place pressure on me. I'm not used to being without Bill, and now I have to make plans to leave our home." She studied the faces of the men. None of them met her gaze. "That is what you are getting to, isn't it?"

"How did you…well, we don't mean to…."

"What, Mr. Tolt, to rush me? I apologize if I'm not as gracious about this as you'd like me to be. But Bill gave everything he had to all of you at the church. He may have worked himself to the grave on its behalf. It seems his wife might have earned a few weeks of grieving before being forced from her home." Prissy strutted around Emma's ankles, tail high in the air, making soft short mews as if adding to the conversation.

Silence stilled the room. The cat lay across the toes of Emma's shoes as if to quiet her. The stewards looked uncomfortable, and Mr. Muir walked to the window. This response would make Bill chuckle or offer a commendation for using the spunk he liked to see Emma apply.

She drew in a breath. "Gentlemen. I don't wish to complicate matters. You have always been kind to Bill, and to me as well. The church has been incredibly thoughtful during this challenging time—I cherish this friendship. And I realize that decisions must benefit the congregation. One person living here ties up necessary change."

"I'm glad you understand that." Mr. Tolt unclasped his hands and pressed both palms to the top of the table. "It wasn't easy to come here and speak with you."

"I don't know why. Some have been practicing how to give me the news ever since Bill died."

"Whatever do you mean, Emma?" Mr. Muir twisted from looking out the window, his eyes wide.

"I overheard a conversation on this exact topic at the funeral luncheon," Emma replied. "People are talking. Decisions should be kept in confidence. It's not helpful to hear confidential information that causes pain and discomfort to others tossed around in gossip." These words opened the previous exchange with Miss. Muir that had hurt beyond this steward's visit.

"Now it's my turn to be sorry." Mr. Tolt's cheeks flushed red. "This is unfortunate. Why do these things happen when we are so careful? Please forgive us. We don't want anything to come between our love for you and what we must do."

Even in her sadness, Emma appreciated his kind words. "What's done is done." She waved her hand. "So, what is the actual date you're asking for an empty house?"

"I realize it doesn't give you much time, but the Reverend Larson could move at our scheduling. We don't want to hurry you at all; take a week if you need to." Mr. Tolt shuffled his feet as if uncomfortable in his shoes.

Emma blinked. The men appeared fuzzy in her view as she scanned the room. She couldn't believe his words. The church demanded first place again. This time it sucked her dry and robbed her of what life she had. She swallowed. Anger surfaced in her throat as a volcano ready to erupt. Similar situations had happened in different ways. Demands, stress-related duties and ongoing, constant, nit-picking details nauseated her.

Goodness sake, what would Jesus say? She'd like to find a table to tip. And what would Bill add? In his easygoing, patient manner, the words, *"Don't worry, my dear. You'll find a way. You are loved, and you know to whom you belong,"* echoed in her memory.

"Thank you, Mr. Tolt," Emma said, her voice cold. "I'll use the following few days to rest and collect my thoughts. And there are events that I'm committed to with music and cleaning. It'll be healthy for me to do this as planned. So, in three weeks, you can have the house, clean it, air it out, do whatever you have to do to prepare for the new minister and his family." There she'd said it. Probably this was the first time she'd confronted Mr. Tolt, and he listened without discounting her words.

John said, "This won't be easy for you, Emma, with missing Bill and now having to make challenging decisions. It'll be stressful, and we understand that adding this to other unresolved areas of your life is hardly fair to you. Please be assured we'll stand with you any way we can."

"I'll need assistance," Emma said. "But right now, it's necessary to think, to figure out what is helpful." So, there was someone verbally on her side. That mysterious voice at the crosswalk, checking Mr. Tolt about his comment concerning Emma's waves, belonged to John. She should have known. He didn't say much, but when he did, everyone listened. "Thanks, John, for your kindness. Sometimes we need someone to speak up for us."

"Very well." Mr. Tolt made notes on his writing pad. "We'll send the ladies as soon as you are ready for this next step." He pushed his chair away from the table. "They'll do whatever has to be done. You shouldn't have to finish this work by yourself. It's too much after what you've been through."

Why didn't she feel ministered to or cared for during this interchange of words? What a considerate statement, yet it was needled with piercing emotions, sharp as the barbed wire fence surrounding Joe Locum's cows out at the Hills.

Emma rose to her feet. "This requires thinking. There are unlimited questions without answers now that we've come to this turn in the road. Gentlemen, three weeks and not before."

Perhaps Emma had finally said what she'd wanted to say for a long time. No one would push her anymore. She needed to pause and identify the dates that worked for her.

"If you think I don't have much to move because we came with little, you're right. We haven't been given personal possessions, nor have we bought anything to increase the number of items to take with me. But I must consider what was ours and is now mine, as well as allow time for appropriate judgements."

"Of course, Emma." Mr. Tolt stood. "By all means. We'll delay until we hear from you." A moment of silence hung between them. "You do what has to be done and inform us if we can be of assistance."

"Thank you. I'll have to find a place to live. Paying for my housing is a great concern. With some support, I can fill my boxes. Seriously, I appreciate your help. For now, gentlemen, I must get to my work."

Mr. Tolt and his group departed, leaving a bitter taste in Emma's mouth. She paced from room to room, viewing the pictures, touching familiar pieces of furniture and listening to Prissy's consistent meows. The grain in the staircase needed cleaning. Emma, Bill and the girls had continually polished the wood to keep it shining. Over the decade of living in this house, the work had collected ahead of them. Cracks in the upstairs bedroom walls and the patched ceiling had caused plaster to fall. And then there was the water-stained drapery on the parlour window. Mr. Tolt and the stewards handled the complicated financial matters, and the parsonage committee had been no help. They'd have a lot to do before anyone could move in. Would the monetary resources rise to this?

The house had to be made ready for their new minister. If Emma weren't busy getting her own life in order, she'd be the first one offering to assist. Settling these folks would be an exciting time, and she, still an essential part of the congregation, would do her share to make the transition easy. She cared deeply for them as they'd been loving and kind to her and Bill across the years. She'd talk to Mr. Tolt next week or go to the board meeting to give back her keys. *He's a good man. His attitude gets in his way, sometimes.*

Chuckling, she conceded. The keys wouldn't matter much as the locks hadn't worked since they came to this house; still, she shouldn't make his request complicated. The opportunity to set her misgivings aside and strengthen the faith community as much as possible was Emma's goal. She must make her plans and call her friends to see if they could spare a few hours; the sooner she completed the packing, the better she'd feel. Only then would most of the tasks be accomplished before Mr. Tolt sent in his troops. But she would not begin this formidable job yet.

•••

Emma baked a batch of cookies, walked to the hospital and left them at the nursing desk with a note of gratitude. She paused at the door of what had been Bill's room and wiped tears as precious memories flooded her mind. Later at his desk, she wrote letters to those who would appreciate notification of his death, and she called Beatrice and Bernice despite long-distance charges. After a few days of sniffling and muttering to herself, she returned to the assignment before her.

Looking at boxes of pictures, personal documents, and old stationery from a closet shelf gave her thinking time. By the third day, she'd begun to sort and discard finding contentment to do this on her own without having to consult others.

There was a world out there. Bill would not like her to labour too diligently or hide in her memories but value the church's comforting words. Indeed, the congregation was the Body of Christ here in this place, and Emma welcomed their healing touch.

TWENTY-THREE
PART 4

Opportunities to view the church in a different light pleased Emma. Bill had guided his responsibilities before he died. It was not as thorough as he wanted, but at least he had done it. But no one had asked her to give leadership or accomplish any of Bill's duties. She hid her disappointment and continued the pastoral care that Bill held dear to ministry, even though some might not think that way. If it had been important to Bill, then it still was to her. It wasn't vital that others understood.

Emma had planned to ask Bill when he got stronger if he had recommended her to Mr. Tolt. Bless his heart, Bill didn't always look for opportunities, and Mr. Tolt wielded a lot of power. At times this totally undermined Bill. She sighed. All of that was secondary now. It was in the past. It was a new day.

Creative activities occurred with open invitations, and attitudes regularly changed. Maisie, Tillie, Louise Ryan, and a few of their friends had shown astonishing possibilities by reaching out. Men offered their thoughts and made significant suggestions. Children assisted in their own ways. Mr. Tolt had been relatively quiet, which seemed to give much-needed permission to anyone thinking they'd join the teams.

The spring-cleaning effort, although a little later than usual this year, brought all ages to the church property. The board extended an open invitation to come and clear winter debris while the ladies polished the building's interior. People came from across town—those connected in any way joined with regular members. They carried garbage bags, buckets, rakes and shovels.

Determined to enjoy the fellowship and the beautiful day despite her sorrow, Emma took a deep breath and walked the path to the kitchen door. She wasn't going to miss this, and she'd delight in it as much as possible. Surely being with those she loved would lift the grief that weighed heavily on her heart. She grasped a small spade in one hand and a bouquet mixed with pussy willows and mauve lilacs in the other.

"Hello, Emma." Bertha lived on the other side of the road and led the women's work. "I'm so glad you came. We're happy you're getting out." She touched the edges of Emma's spray. "The blossoms are lovely. From your yard, aren't they? And I noticed you brought the geraniums over. They sure thrive in your care all winter."

"They do well, don't they? It's time they came back. They get necessary light here, different from being in the parsonage cellar."

Bertha was also the caretaker of flowers and continually found a place for them. "They're beautiful, and perfect for the front step on anniversary Sunday." She folded the fresh flowers into her arms. "And I'll put these in water for you." She paused. "We sure miss Reverend Taylor. It's not the same without him."

Emma brushed her hands together to shake off the soil. "You're right, it's not."

"I've been wondering why you didn't assist with the odd service when Reverend Taylor couldn't be at the pulpit." Bertha set the flowers on the counter.

She had been the first person to bring this up, and it deserved an honest response. "Mr. Tolt didn't invite me."

"Wouldn't Reverend Taylor have requested you? That'd make it simpler."

"I'm not sure who makes the decisions, or how they do it." Emma twisted the tap to wash her hands. "I don't go to their meetings."

"Maybe I should speak to the stewards." Bertha nodded. "Yes, that's what I'll do. I mean, it would have saved money."

Emma wiped the water off her hands with a kitchen cloth. "I wish you wouldn't address this topic. It makes it uncomfortable for me."

"Well, to be fair to Mr. Tolt, perhaps he thought you'd be too busy… with the reverend sick and all." Bertha's tone softened. "But you never require much lead to do whatever people ask of you. It always appeared you were ready, even with short notice." She frowned. "So be it, but I'd like to give you the stipend Mr. Tolt paid the old gentleman who preached a while back. Bless his heart, he tried. But how many times did we go around the mountain?"

"He did appear to labour." Emma washed the windowsill and wiped it with a clean cloth.

Bertha walked to the sink. "Come here, will you? We need your wisdom. I think some pests visited this spring."

Emma crouched and peered into the bottom of the cupboards, "You're right. The nerve of them, eh?"

"Should we scrub or give it a fresh coat of paint?" Bertha asked.

"Emma will go for scrub…and paint." Eleanor, a heavyset woman from the ladies' unit, marched into the kitchen, wiping her brow. She could be abrupt, yet the others appreciated her sincere and honest judgement.

"Yes, if you're asking me what to do," Emma said, "I'd say do both."

"Nice to see you, Mrs. Taylor. So happy you came out to join us." Turning back to Bertha, Eleanor continued, "What'd I tell you? Now you know why this area looks spick and span. Emma says, 'Paint it. Mr. Evans will donate it.'"

"He says it's one way he can help, since he works daily in his store." Emma bent to pick leaves off the floor.

"And we'll soon have a delicious meal as well as sparkling cupboards." Bertha viewed the abundant assortment of food.

"I'll start these stews heating now." Emma pulled the pans onto the front burners and turned them to low.

Eleanor walked to the stove to view the promised buffet. "Wonderful as usual." She lifted the lids. "And don't they smell delicious? People will enjoy them at the end of their workday. Did Lizzy bring one of them?"

"She did," Emma said.

Eleanor inhaled the aroma coming from each stew. Then she straightened and grabbed a wooden ladle to stir the ingredients in a cast-iron pot. "This one is Lizzy's, I'm sure of it. I'd die to get her recipe. I can't figure out what she puts in it. But it's heavenly."

Emma grinned. The women and a few of the men, shared Eleanor's sentiments. Many in town would like to read the fixings used in the process of that delicious offering.

Mrs. Norris pulled open the door and carrying a bag, she joined the little group. "Hello Emma. So nice to see you." And to Eleanor, she said, "I brought over some cleaning supplies. I don't need them anymore. I'm living in two rooms of my house now, so I thought you could use them."

"Thanks, we will for sure." Eleanor accepted it from her. "How's that working out for you? Smaller quarters, I mean."

"It would have been a good idea to make the change five years ago. It's hard to deny what you talk yourself into thinking you need." Mrs. Norris said. "I have done nothing today, but I hope I can join you for supper."

"You certainly can. All the years you slaved here deserves returns." Emma took a bowl from the cupboard and handed it to her.

"Living alone is not for everybody. So happy I have the church." Mrs. Norris gripped a spoon and stirred the contents in a stew pot.

"And we're your family," Eleanor said. "So, bring a chair. The crew will be in when they're finished outside, and it'll get noisy. Sometimes the fellowship at the potluck is as important as the jobs accomplished during the day."

The homemade soups, stews and freshly baked bread sat on the warming surfaces of the stove. Later, the ladies brought the containers and the pies to the serving table. Everybody entered the room and stood behind chairs lining the long table. When the shuffling ceased, Mr. Tolt, speaking in a clear, distinct voice, complimented the work party on their efforts inside and in the yard. After he asked for God's blessing, the workers lifted their plates and walked toward the food. When the line at the kitchen lessened, Emma sighed with relief. The muffled sounds and the odd laughter suggested they were enjoying their meal.

"I'm glad you came out today, Emma. Can I speak to you for a moment?" Lucy Miles, who had joined the broom brigade, wore a wrap-around apron and frowned under a halo of white hair. She leaned her sweeper against the wall and sat on a chair.

"Is everything all right at home, Lucy?" Emma asked. "The grandchildren?" Lucy had taken them into her care when problems developed in the younger generation.

"Yes, we're all fine. Just the usual coughs and sniffles for this time of year."

"They seem to make their rounds," Emma added.

"I wanted to mention those in need. I understand the mission group received a letter assessing someone as unworthy. Some think we don't have resources to support those thought to be outside our walls, but despite that attitude I'll write a list as we need to be diligent." Lucy began to jot down names.

Emma thanked her. "You're the perfect person to take the lead on this. Thanks for that information. I'll pass it on to others who'd like to help. Setting an example that no one is left out of God's love often causes certain people to criticize."

"I wonder by what standard they judge. We must stand firm and extend our welcome." Lucy coughed. "I'm also wondering about the Ryan's and if there's any way, we can show support."

Emma agreed. "I've been thinking the same thing. Three children there and no garden or root cellar, plus Mr. Ryan was laid off from the factory in the recent cutbacks."

"So unfortunate—another worry for them." Lucy patted her arm. "Do you think we can start a grocery bin in the shed? Extra food can be dropped in."

"You have an excellent idea, Lucy. And it could also be a resource for the community meal that's getting attention." Emma took off her apron.

Lucy persisted. "Did you hear the news regarding the O'Neils?"

"I did. Someone can speak to this on Sunday."

"We heard enough of Reverend Taylor's sermons on helping wherever needed, we'd be doing a great disservice if we didn't share," Lucy said.

"As well, Reverend Maitland from Brooks is asking for a freewill offering during his upcoming rally. The Hills will gain from the donations. Now that Louise Ryan is leading the House Church, I don't get out there as often as I used to, but I still manage to take a pot of vegetables and broth when I go. It all helps," Emma said. "Thankfully, we can discuss these topics and initiate action."

TWENTY-FOUR

The excitement about the tasty supper, shiny windows and sweet-smelling pine floors caught people's attention. As they put away the chairs, they praised the work of those responsible for keeping the building so welcoming. A few women planned to make curtains from the edges of some recently donated worn cotton sheets. Emma frowned when the kitchen ladies referred to the parsonage committee's yearly check-up.

Eleanor moved closer. "They want to get it all done as soon as possible, so the house and property will be ready for the new minister. Tomorrow does seem to be early though, considering—"

"Tomorrow, Eleanor?" Emma pressed both hands to her cheeks. "Did I hear you say tomorrow? Nobody has told me yet."

Every year this happened. The committee gave one day's notice before they came to inspect. It'd be helpful if they reflected on the fairness of their visit because of Bill's hospitalization and death. Soiled cloths lay on the cellar floor beside the wringer washer from a previous cleaning binge. When they viewed this, they'd be sure to comment that it was no wonder Emma didn't have time to assist on Sundays. *Mercy, as if housework was one of my gifts of the Spirit.*

She grimaced in disgust. Did they enjoy catching her off guard? She didn't have the energy to figure it out.

"Mrs. Taylor," Mr. Tolt said as he walked up behind her. "I'm so glad I caught you before you went home."

"Hello, Mr. Tolt." Emma took a deep breath and turned to face him.

"It's good that you are out and getting back into the stride of life. Great meal, as always." He cleared his throat as if preparing to make a speech. "I hope it'll be okay if the parsonage committee drops in tomorrow afternoon. We'll do our usual inspection so we can send the report on to Presbytery. As well, we need to consider what has to be done for Reverend Larson."

"Of course, but this doesn't give me much notice."

"Now, don't you go to any trouble." Mr. Tolt said. "We know you do your best."

"I do. It's an old residence and, well, your committee hasn't been able to contribute to the maintenance during these bad times."

"We understand." Mr. Tolt nodded. "We'll see you at three o'clock, then?"

"Four would be better. I'd appreciate it." Emma didn't wait for a reply. Lifting the damp cloth, she went back to her task of cleaning. *Oh dear, that man does try a person's patience.*

An image of the cookie jar came to mind. Thank goodness she'd filled it with fresh oatmeal sweet cakes. That would take their attention off what the house should be and unfortunately wasn't. She wanted to leave an appropriate impression for Bill's sake even though he wasn't here to see it. He had done more than his part with the upkeep and had said, 'Don't mention the eavestroughs; the church will get to them'. The committee had examined everything, including cracks and corners, when they previously visited. Was it necessary every year? According to Mr. Tolt, it'd be another assessment, only this request was for a different reason.

• • •

The inspection came too quickly, and Emma was not ready. At the exact time, a loud knock sounded. Sighing, she brushed the front of her dress and opened the door to see four serious faces.

Mr. Tolt took the lead. "Good afternoon, Emma. I hope we're not late."

"Come in." She ushered Eleanor, Jack, and Irene Trask into the hall. "Would you like to sit for a few minutes before you begin?" *Who chose Irene to serve this year? Is this still a confidential committee?* Looking for Darlin', it was easy to see that Jack had left his dog at home. Otherwise, half the items on the front porch might be found anywhere in town in the morning.

Mr. Tolt tilted his head as if considering where to begin. "I think we'll go through the house, Emma. You don't have to escort us." He chuckled nervously. "This is the tenth year; we won't get lost."

"I have the list of repairs I put together following last year's walk-through. Would you like a copy, or perhaps you have your own?"

"List? I don't have a list." He shuffled the papers he held in his hand. "Are you sure there was one?"

"Yes, I wrote it in case the committee forgot the items to which we'd agreed." Emma took a deep breath. "Nothing has changed in the house, but if you'd like to go through, I'll lead the way." Emma proceeded slowly past Bill's closed office. "You are all familiar with this space."

Mr. Tolt looked in briefly, scanned the desk and bookshelves from the threshold, not entering probably to show respect.

As they climbed the steps, Irene touched the bottom of the wooden railing with her index finger. She was correct; it hadn't been dusted. At least the guest room was welcoming because of Beatrice and Bernice's recent visit. That much was in Emma's favour. A week's wash lay folded on the chest. Unfortunately, the fresh scent from blowing on the backyard clothesline would have faded, but the soft texture from the consistent wind would still be evident.

Mr. Tolt said. "Anything you can tell us about the bedrooms, Mrs. Taylor?"

"No, everything is the same as you would have seen before." *Surely, they'd purchase a mattress for the Larsons.* When Emma told them the springs were protruding, the committee had promised to look after it, but Mr. Tolt suggested a heavy mat to cover the coils. That had worked.

"There's really no need to go in." Emma walked ahead. "Nothing has changed."

Irene shoved the door wide open. "My, this is different. And such a quaint lampshade."

She obviously hadn't figured out why she was here as she checked the quilt the Ladies Aid had given Emma and Bill when they came. Shouldn't the committee make plans to paint the ceiling stains?

A half-hour later, they made their way into the kitchen and then to the cellar entrance. "The basement is exactly as you remember it." Emma switched on the light. Since Jack and Irene were new, they'd want to go down to the lower level. "Bill regularly checked to be sure nothing was leaking. It's not the nicest area in the house; if you don't care to inspect it this year, I understand."

"I think we should see for ourselves." Mr. Tolt gestured for the team to go ahead. Emma decided not to join them. If they needed to talk by themselves without her, the cellar would be the place to do it. While standing on the earth-worn floor, they couldn't miss the dampness within the old stone foundation.

When they returned to the first floor, Mr. Tolt said, "That's fine, Emma. You've kept a nice home for Reverend Taylor. Don't you worry, I'll write the report."

Did he think her housekeeping was on trial? She and Bill had been respectful of the property, but Presbytery must be informed if the pastoral charge maintained the house and did the upkeep. It's a common thought that the provision of a furnished parsonage kept their minister's mind off material possessions. *If they knew us better, they'd know that was the least of our worries.*

"Perhaps you'll report that you were unable to do the repairs as you'd agreed. Would you like to include the list?"

Mr. Tolt shook his head. "No, there is no need."

Emma handed him the paper. "Maybe you should keep it for your records."

Mr. Tolt didn't take it.

Emma lifted it closer to his hand. "I wrote out two additional copies. With the economy the way it is, Presbytery will understand why the residence wasn't maintained as agreed."

Mr. Tolt accepted the list and glanced at it before slipping it under the bottom of his papers.

"I'm glad you feel Bill and I have done our part." Emma opened the door for the small entourage to leave. It wasn't until she closed it that she realized she hadn't offered them some sweet cakes. That might have helped the tense situation.

TWENTY-FIVE

Prissy jumped onto Emma's lap, purring a contented song. She stroked the cat's thick hair, considering how quickly she'd adjusted to being Emma's sole companion.

The congregation and community spoke with her on different subjects. Certain topics were easy to share. Relationships that caused riffs during Bill's era surfaced daily. It wasn't Emma's role to approach or solve them so they lay unattended.

It was a risk to think Mrs. Trask hadn't publicly chastised Emma for speaking out against the piano; everybody in town would have her version. This account wouldn't be complimentary to Emma. Although she hadn't heard anything, she'd been centred on her grief and might have missed it.

Torn between concern of the impression she may have left with Mrs. Trask and chuckling about overhearing Tom Tolt on the street corner, Emma busied herself with her morning work. Breakfast, watering the plants from the rain barrel and preparing the vegetables for a supper casserole took most of her morning.

Images of Hilda's tear-filled face came to mind. She was a gentle natured woman, and Emma considered her hostility as pent-up anger. Heaven only knows what some had said concerning God's will for the baby. Emma would wait for a while to visit Hilda.

Making a mental note to return to the Dime Store, Emma began to make a list of what she needed. Leaving it too long would convince Mrs. Bowman that Emma was travelling to Hampton for supplies.

Amid these concerns, an underlying dialogue reminded her of declining Reverend Maitland's invitation to preach at the rally. What would she say if he called again? She simply had to pray about this.

Irene's negative comment regarding women's leadership in the church caused Emma to consider excuses to tell Mr. Maitland, and there were a few. She'd told him she couldn't accept his recent request because of Bill's health. Seeing his face brighten when she entered his room was enough reason to give him direct attention. Such sweet memories. Why was it challenging for her to be counted when doing something important? It niggled her that she found it essential to empower others yet had difficulty crediting her efforts.

Although she had defended Susanne to her mother and was prepared to stand with Nancy, Emma didn't confirm her delight when achieving. In moments like this, she could not avoid facing herself.

How many times had she dreamt of sharing a level of ministry and prayed for God's lead? She'd talked to herself concerning possibilities. The idea brought back memories of previous leadership, now years removed. Until Reverend Maitland called, the opportunity to serve in that capacity had seemed impossible. But it had come, and she needed to consider it, as well as identify her true feelings.

She couldn't seem to escape harsh opinions that women ministering was somehow self-serving. Are people giving her a distinct message that God only spoke through men? Did it come to admitting that others' words and lack of understanding created barriers? Had they smothered the flame of God's call in her life? If so, she'd allowed it. Should she thank Irene for sharing her negative opinion about Nancy's application? No, that'd never do.

Between Emma's spurts of organizing items that stay in the parsonage and those that go with her, she visited several families in need, sent business to Mrs. Bowman's Dime Store, and supported the girls in the Mission Circle. She'd offered encouragement to the Hills and inspired the church prayer sessions. Was that all God was calling her to do?

For now, maybe.

Peace filled Emma. Had she missed something? Mr. Tolt hadn't said anything negative to her, so she'd keep Bill's work a priority in the community until Reverend Larson arrived. Even though she realized it wasn't Bill's ministry anymore, she hesitated to confess this focused on her needs.

So be it. Was God still preparing her?

Be faithful in little things.

Emma stopped thinking of other accomplishments. Was she serving exactly how God asked? Was she disappointed? Was she satisfied? Not really. Did she think God had let her down? No, not at all. Peace flooded her.

This isn't forever. It's a step forward.

Emma nodded. *I'm learning lessons here in this place.*

"Anybody home?" Maisie's voice was music floating on sun rays. Prissy raised her head and stretched, acknowledging a familiar sound in the room.

Maisie bustled into the kitchen carrying a cloth bag. "This will brighten your day." She placed a peach-coloured miniature flower in the centre of the table beside a crocus. "And there are tasty recipes in these home magazines."

"I'll enjoy them all." Emma accepted them and flipped through the pages. "Now if my casseroles compared to any of these, I'd have people standing in line to buy them."

Maisie moved back and stared at Emma. "I noticed your new hair style but didn't get a chance to tell you. It looks, hmm, as nice as I've ever seen it."

"Thanks. Tillie did it a while ago. But I take it you weren't fond of my previous hairdo?"

"It was always attractive mind you, but a change is refreshing."

Emma raised her fingers to her waves. "You sound like Tillie. She promised to give me a brand-new look."

"And she did. No wonder, even with the price of gas high as it is, a few still come from Hampton to our hairdresser. Tillie's the best, and it's such a happy place to go." Maisie smoothed her pleated skirt. "Now, I've complimented your haircut and I've delivered my parcels, so I'll go and do my dishes."

Loneliness crowded Emma. Maybe Maisie would stay longer. "Are you in a hurry? I made a fresh pot of tea. Could you sit for a few minutes?"

"I can. Something troubling you?"

"Well, not exactly, but…" She paused; a tone in Maisie's voice caught her attention. "Should there be?" Emma took a deep breath as she lifted the teapot.

"It's a good idea to tell you Irene Trask hasn't been happy." Maisie peered over her wire-framed eyeglasses. "I haven't said anything because you had enough to cope with during the past weeks. Don't be offended by this information. Sometimes, it's important to be aware of what's in the rumour mill, that way you have a choice how to deal with it."

Leave it to Maisie to consider fairness and integrity when contemplating an issue. It was that raw honesty that had bothered Bill. He wasn't sure how to examine a problem that way. As for Emma, she liked to understand both sides of any concern.

"I was afraid of that. So, she went across town with her peeve." Emma grimaced. "Well, I'm sorry she's upset, but I'd do it again…and again, if need be."

Maisie leaned forward in her chair and frowned. "My goodness, you said you wouldn't help Susanne with her music, regardless of how nicely Irene asked?"

"She forgot to add 'on her piano until it was tuned'. The poor girl couldn't recognize her melodies when she practiced at home."

Maisie nodded. "Figured it was something like that. I'm glad you're defending Susanne. Somebody needs to. She has real talent."

"That's how it was. I was honest—just told the truth."

"Feel strong enough to risk being the subject of conversations?"

Emma sighed. "I'll work with the positive and do what I can to build Susanne's confidence. People can decide accuracy for themselves."

"I as much as told Irene that, but I didn't push it, just said enough to suggest that others might see the situation differently."

This was a side of Maisie that Emma trusted and needed. A hard knock resonated and echoed through the room.

"Yoo-hoo, anybody home? Hello?" Irene's voice resembled a whistling kettle.

Emma shot Maisie a look before standing and crossing to pull the door open. "Mrs. Trask. This is a surprise. Will you come in?"

"No, no, I mustn't disturb you. I wanted to…to apologize. I should have come long before this, but with everything you've been through,

I didn't want to remind you of my problem, so I waited." Irene leaned toward Emma and, with a softer voice, said, "I hope you're doing well without Reverend Taylor. We all miss him too." She took a deep breath and continued. "Forgive me for being short with you at the house a while back. I hadn't been feeling fit. I didn't understand what you were saying, and after you left, well, Susanne said I was rude."

And Maisie had cleared the air for Emma as well. *Good work, friend. I'm relieved to have someone defend me, even with the damage done across town. People will have to choose which story to believe.*

"This sometimes happens." Emma slid her arm around Irene and gave her a sideways squeeze. "And thanks for remembering Bill. All of this helps."

"You'll be interested that Jack agreed with you." Irene's favourite frown appeared on her face as she gave a long sigh. "He said he didn't know how anybody could play a song on a piano such as mine."

Emma suppressed a grin. "I'm happy you spoke with him."

"And he'll take a basket of produce for two weeks as payment, my choice when the garden is ready."

"Well, there you go. You worked it all out."

"That's all I came to say. That and adding my condolences. I'll go now." Irene left with a wave of her hand.

Maisie lifted her empty cup as if toasting the situation. "That was a surprise, eh, Emma?"

"Indeed, it was. And nothing makes me happier than to see a peaceful bond."

"So, you can handle extra friction?"

Emma pressed a hand to her cheek. "Now what did I do?"

"I wouldn't say anything, but you're up to it. The rumour mill has it that Hilda Grafton dismissed you when you said her baby's condition was normal."

"Well, that's not exactly as it happened. But perhaps I need to revisit her and apologize for whatever she thinks I did wrong."

"You are a courageous woman, Emma." Maisie paused. "I also hear that Hilda doesn't hold her baby."

"I'd better go sooner than planned. Thanks so much, Maisie, for telling me. I mean, how would I know if somebody didn't pass on the problem?"

"I hoped you'd feel that way and not think I'm gossiping. I didn't mention it to anybody else."

"It's not gossip. It's caring for people. And it also informs me of what I'm getting into." Emma re-filled their teacups.

"Am I'm staying a while longer? You have something else on your mind?"

"I actually have a few things." Not knowing where to begin, she decided to wait. "On second thought, maybe we'll drink our tea and come back to this discussion later."

When they finished, Maisie said goodbye and left by the side door. Should Emma go to the elders and share Hilda's grief and fears? This was pastoral care. Was it fair to expect one of the men to call on her?

TWENTY-SIX

A warm breeze played across the front porch as Emma sat in her wicker chair. An old saying referring to facing the wind and finding the truth crossed her mind. The gusts had been harsh and Bill's heart attack and later his death had led her into a tremendous emotional storm. It was strong, swaying her from one side of her balance to another. She had questioned different thoughts, wondering if they were stable. But now, the wind in her back seemed to support an inner strength to steady her foothold. This was no surprise to her as she settled into a solid faith and assurance of God's presence.

The sorting of objects and filling boxes progressed nicely. Emma savoured these precious moments while reflecting on special times with Bill. Bare necessities would be sufficient for her use until the designated workers arrived to finish her packing.

Two children chased a ball out on the street, causing a driver to stop his vehicle and speak to them. Jack and his dog Darlin' jogged on the other side of the road, probably delivering something from the post office. Henry drove by, tooted the truck's horn and waved as Leroy walked toward Emma, his countenance sad.

"Morning, Mrs. Taylor." He sat on the step and stared out at the street. "How are you getting on? I'm so sorry about Reverend Taylor."

"It's nice to see you, Leroy. I'm doing fine. Receiving lots of help. And thank you for your condolences."

When he didn't look at her, Emma added, "Is everything all right with Hilda and the baby?" Leroy swiped his eyes and stuffed his blue striped handkerchief into his pocket.

"You can tell me," Emma prodded.

"It's just that…well, I don't know exactly what to say after how Hilda treated you."

"Don't worry, it's all forgiven. What is it that you'd like to tell me?"

"Hilda doesn't want to hold the baby, only to feed her. She has it in her head that she's bad luck for Alice." Leroy covered his face with both hands before looking up to continue. "She's got this confound idea that she triggered the baby's death last year, and now she's caused Alice's club foot." He sniffed and wiped his hand over his mouth. "I can't change her mind. And I wonder what'll happen when her milk runs out. Likely, she won't want to touch Alice."

"I'm sorry, Leroy. Have you talked to Doc Baxter?"

He glanced at her. "I have, and he's been talking to Hilda as well." He pushed to his feet. "I'm here to ask you to come to the house. In spite of her words when you were there, she needs you."

"Of course, I'll come," Emma said.

"Maybe this afternoon?"

"Yes, I'll go promptly."

"I'm so relieved. Thank you. It means a lot."

With that, Leroy strutted down the sidewalk as if he'd stretched an inch or two. *This must be difficult for him. Only God can open Hilda's heart and grant her peace.* Emma prayed that the process had already begun.

• • •

In the late afternoon, she knocked on Leroy's door with trepidation. Had he told Hilda that he'd asked Emma to come over? It'd make it easier if he had. But even if he hadn't, Emma was eager to talk with Hilda.

She answered immediately, and her eyes widened. "Hello, Mrs. Taylor. Come in." Hilda's stiff manner opposed her invitation.

Clearly, Leroy hadn't told his wife to expect Emma. *Well, I'll make the best of it. If Hilda asks me to leave, I'll go.*

"I'm…I'm glad you came over," Hilda stammered. "I didn't think you'd ever speak to me again. I mean, I treated you badly. Whenever I looked at Alice, I thought of how I rejected your phrase. What was it? *Fearfully and wonderfully made*; yes, that's it. I'm so sorry. Please forgive me. I've been beside myself knowing what I'm doing to Alice…and what I did to you."

"Hilda, I forgive you. You were upset. Sometimes we say words we'd like to take back."

"Thank you. I was hoping you'd understand."

Leroy joined them and welcomed Emma. He pointed to the hall. "Why don't you go into the bedroom, Hilda, and show off Alice. I'll make tea for both of you."

"We'll enjoy that." Hilda turned to Emma. "Come with me." She led Emma to the back room. Wallpaper of white background with yellow daises made the small area look spacious. Little green leaf-like cords held citrus-coloured curtains in place. When she gazed at Alice in her bassinet, Emma said, "She's grown, hasn't she? What a treasure."

"I watch her, and I'm frightened that she's dying. I hardly lift her and cuddle in case I break her. And then I want to gather her close to my heart. I couldn't go on living if she died. But there are times when I'm afraid of getting too attached."

In Emma's softest voice, she said, "She's not going to break, Hilda. She looks content and healthy, so she'll just keep growing. You're doing fine in strengthening her. Still nursing, are you?"

"I am, but when I get upset, I think my attitude worries her because she frets too. It's almost as bad as when I eat cabbage. She tells me about that too."

Emma chuckled. "Babies are practiced at finding ways to get their point across to us. Why don't we sit here? When she wakes, can I hold her?"

"Yes, that's a perfect idea."

"I brought my knitting." Emma eased herself into the chair, opened her purse and lifted needles holding stitches on a pink bonnet. "I can probably finish this before I go."

Within a few minutes, Leroy placed tea and two cookies on a small table. Emma knit for a half-hour as they visited, cut the yarn away from the ball and darned in the ends.

"It's like separating a babe from her momma." Hilda watched as Emma spread the finished project on her knee.

Alice stretched, yawned, and waved her arms as if welcoming attention.

"It is." Emma bent to tuck the bonnet on Alice's head. "There she is, such a sweetheart." A matching pink sweater lay on the arm of the chair. Emma rubbed her finger across the baby's cheek. "You'll have lots of encouragement in our town. You are loved, Alice."

"Thank you for this, Mrs. Taylor, and for your support." Hilda sniffed. "I'm beginning to realize how much you mean to me. And this knitting is adorable. So pretty. I do feel better. I…I don't want to cave in and say everything is fine."

"I understand. Be kind to yourself. I'm happy to visit and see your baby. Take a day at a time. Be proud of Alice. She's a precious gift."

"Yes, she is, isn't she?" Hilda paused. "But Bobby comes into my mind. That's what we called the first baby. Because he didn't live…I didn't give him a name, well, until you suggested it."

"But he did live. For nine months he drew nourishment from you as he prepared to come into the world."

"I blamed God for his death for so long, I got tired of hearing my voice inside my head. I kept thinking God was trying to teach me something. Or I wasn't a good Christian if I didn't accept Bobby's passing as God's will."

"Do you ever wonder if God cries with you? Tragedies happen. God's love and comfort help us during our grieving time."

"I've never thought that way." Hilda pressed her palm to one cheek. "I feel encouraged knowing."

"It might be a relief if you asked Doc Baxter to explain the complications of Bobby's birth and death."

"I can do that?"

"He'd be happy to tell you if he knew you were concerned in that aspect of the delivery."

"I will, yes, I'll do that when I go to see him. That would help, wouldn't it? For me to know, I mean. To understand."

Hilda seemed to be talking to herself with a convincing voice for this information to plant peace. She was obviously tired of being angry and confused.

"You'll survive all this extra stress and be stronger in spite of it." Emma stroked Hilda's hand. "Women have a God-given inner strength they seem to draw on in times of trouble. Part of the problem is not always being able to identify it." She drew her handkerchief from her pocket and coughed into it.

"Mrs. Taylor, we've already exchanged thoughts on this, but have you given any consideration to midwifery work? I've been so encouraged by your words. You don't give up. And even today, your advice helped so much. Mrs. Densmore is still as busy as ever, and there are a few mothers in town who would really benefit from your skills."

"Thanks for your compliment. I agree, and it's a pleasure to visit them. However, I'll stick to helping in whatever situation arises." Quickly, Emma added. "Have you considered this, Hilda? Is this anything you'd like to do? Work with Mrs. Densmore when Alice gets older?"

"I don't know. I'm interested in the families in town. You know, those who need encouragement in some way."

The suggestion seemed to fit, and Emma would support Hilda on this matter. "Read everything you can find on the topic and ask Mrs. Densmore if she has magazines that'll give you information on the subject."

"I like those thoughts. Doc Baxter might have ideas as well." Hilda reached to touch Emma's arm. "Thank you for stretching me into thinking I have something to offer to others."

"You're welcome. Talk to Leroy. His support is vital when you're considering changes inside your routine."

"I wouldn't want to do anything that'd upset him or make him think caring for our family wasn't important. Besides, if I went out during the night with Mrs. Densmore, Leroy would have to be on the team to care for Alice." Excitement filtered through Hilda's words.

Even though Emma hadn't accepted Hilda's challenge, perhaps there was additional work to do if God led that way. In the meantime, she could listen to Hilda and assist Leroy in seeing the positive side of her yearning. A midwife assistant would be a great asset to the community.

TWENTY-SEVEN

Preparing for anniversary resembled a beehive, although no different than any other year. The June days warmed, and by the weekend, the children would play their Sunday school games on the lawn.

These last-minute checks happened often, and Emma took advantage of them to mix with her friends. Sorrow filled her mind when she sat home alone, so she deliberately tried to step into the activity while she could.

She prepared notes to keep track of her packing accomplishments and accepted all the invitations that came her way. Leaving for somewhere undecided would come soon enough. And next year, she wouldn't have the opportunity to attend and support these yearly events, so she'd get involved wherever she was needed.

Cora Morgan poked her head around the cupboards. "I'm looking for Emma. Do you have her in here?"

Eleanor pointed to where Emma knelt, examining the shelves. "She's giving this a once-over, and us, helpful counsel." Eleanor hummed a lively melody and moved from one space to another. She pointed out areas that needed cleaning and did her share in scrubbing.

"That's our Emma. Do you think I can borrow her?" Cora asked.

"Emma, there's someone here to see you," Eleanor said. "Can you break yourself away from organizing shelves?"

Cora Morgan's daily life mirrored her music in terms of precision. She would not want to wait. Accuracy and detail defined her character.

Emma swiped the dust off her skirt. "I'll leave you to continue your good work, Eleanor. You accomplished a great job in the spring."

Emma followed Cora into the sanctuary. "How can I help? I'd much rather talk harmony than scrub away mouse droppings."

"I hope so." Cora offered a wry grin. She didn't waste any time getting to the reason for her request. "I'd like to look at Sunday's service with you if you have the time. The guest minister, the Reverend Miller, chose a few selections that make me wonder." They walked to the front. "I'm concerned about the melodies." She eyed Emma as if ready to interrupt should she attempt to speak. "It's not that I can't play them, mind you; it's just that they are not familiar here. Maybe the Hampton folks sing these pieces, but we don't."

At the organ, Cora handed Emma the list. "What do you think?"

After finding the numbers in the hymnbook, Emma considered the question. "I see what you mean. I suggest you keep the hymns as the verses support Sunday's scripture. It's a way of hearing the old story from different sources. And change the tunes to familiar ones listed in the back index. It'll be fine."

"We'll still have choir practice tonight. I do hope everybody will be able to come." Cora flipped through a large binder. "I'll need you to sing soprano for the first anthem. We're short of music; perhaps you can share with Eleanor." She pointed to one of the pages. "And for the second one, could you play the piano with me as a duet? It's nice to hear these instruments together."

"I'd be happy to do it," Emma said. She had always responded when Cora needed her and was glad that hadn't changed. "See you later." Appreciating an opportunity to assist in worship, Emma returned to the area where she had been working.

The congregation had begun to use Emma's first name, and she enjoyed dropping the word Mrs. in conversations, especially with friends in the kitchen group. It was confusing when people fell back into their old habit of using the formal manner. Emma would follow what seemed most comfortable with others.

• • •

Soft laughter mixed with the hum of voices as the sanctuary filled on Sunday morning to celebrate the 75th anniversary. Anyone coming in late would have to sit on a chair in the aisle.

Emma went to the stove to put water on to preheat, so it'd be ready to bring to a boil to make tea following the service. The women had brought wrapped sandwiches from home and placed them on plates. Two tables covered with white cotton sheets provided the space for a lengthy buffet. A colourful assortment of desserts filled decorative dishes, although the variety was less than last year. The ladies had contributed to the pile of cotton serviettes propped against one another that resembled a lopsided rainbow. Emma nodded. They were ready.

Melodious sounds in the staircase made the choir easy to find as they practiced complicated harmonies. Emma joined in the singing, as the songs were familiar. Pulling on her robe, anticipation filled her mind. She looked forward to seeing those who didn't attend regularly. Would previous ministers return for the celebration?

Each anniversary, the congregation mentioned their dear Reverend Moore. He and his daughter died in a car crash five years after the family had moved here. Mrs. Moore had left the parsonage following the accident and gone to Toronto to find work.

"I still have tears when I think about how her days ended." As if Eleanor had read Emma's thoughts, she leaned closer wiping her eyes. "Nothing in her life went right after she left here."

"It was kind of several members to visit her," Emma said. For a lengthy period, Mary Ann's profound grief had mixed openly with Bill's call to the church.

"She suffered from that terrible depression. Whenever she'd get unresponsive, she was admitted to the Ontario Hospital in Toronto. Apparently, that didn't benefit her. Poor girl, she took her life, you know."

"She might have been better to stay in Noble where kindness and love would have surrounded her," Emma offered.

An elder broke into conversations and led the choir in prayer before opening the door to the sanctuary. Emma followed the procession into the loft just as the Reverend Albert Miller slid with ease onto the pulpit bench. He had agreed to take the whole service on short notice, for which Emma was grateful.

Albert laughed—not usual behaviour. A growing hum rose, interrupted by an occasional burst of laughter. People were obviously happy to see him, and he responded. The choir whispered, and members giggled. *What was going on?*

With her elbow, Eleanor nudged Emma in the side. "Look! A dog has come up the aisle."

Darlin' dragged a mat by his side sometimes stumbling on it. *Oh, my goodness.* Emma put her hand on her mouth. *From whose front porch had he brought his offering?* Poor Jack, when he realizes what many are laughing at, he'll be mortified. The dog shifted and slithered along the wooden floor which appeared to enchant those who watched. *He'll get slivers in his belly if he's not careful.*

A sharp bark caught Jack's attention, and he jumped from his seat and rushed to Darlin's side, gripped his collar to turn him, but that didn't work. The dog broke free and sprinted to the front, still dragging his mat. Then he flopped on the floor, watching Jack with big eyes while thumping his tail on the wood surface as if he'd won the conflict.

Men and women either eyed the incident over their glasses or held their heads so high they could count the rafters. Some responded out of character by laughing aloud. Darlin' thumped his tail harder, apparently enjoying the whole drama.

Reverend Miller gripped the pulpit with both hands, clearly ready to begin, even with the dog in the building. "Good morning." His strong voice filled the sanctuary. "Greetings to this celebration of 75 years serving your membership and this community. I want to welcome all of our guests, particularly the unexpected ones." He shot a glance at Darlin' as Jack coaxed him out the side door leading to the driveway.

Hopefully, those who came to church once a year on anniversary Sunday understood the minister referred to the dog and not to them. "I am the Reverend Albert Miller from Hampton, close friend of both Emma and her beloved husband, the late Reverend Taylor. I offer to you, Emma," he twisted to face her and then turned back to the congregation, "and to you dear folks, my deepest sympathy."

Midway through the service, the choir member next to Emma slipped a note into her hand. She scanned the words: *Pass the music to me.* Emma gazed at Cora, who raised her eyebrows in expectation. Emma shook her head.

The action appeared to intensify Cora's panic. She lifted a book and whispered, "Do you have it?"

What does she mean?

Lowering her eyes, Cora scribbled on paper. When finished, she passed another note to Emma. 'Do you have the binder for the first anthem?'

No! She'd been told to stand with the sopranos and sing with Eleanor. Perhaps the pages were left where they'd practiced earlier. When Emma shook her head again, Cora pressed her hands to her cheeks and closed her eyes.

At that precise moment, Albert nodded to invite the choir to sing. Emma rose from her chair without hesitation, stepped down to the floor, and walked to the piano. She sat, placed her fingers on the keys and began. The introduction was weak as she fumbled three notes but covered them gracefully by adding trills to emphasize the rhythm. She had heard the melody enough and understood it, but she had to guess at some of the chords.

Would her well-developed ability to play by ear accept this challenge? It had saved her embarrassment many times when someone handed her a piece with sharps—how she disliked them. She managed to provide an impressive accompaniment as the multitude of voices offered perfect harmony and finished with Amen.

With one hand on her heart, Cora smiled at Emma as she made her way back into the choir loft. She nodded, hoping the rendition was pleasing.

Reverend Miller delivered his sermon with great passion. One hymn and then another gave opportunity to harmonize, and Cora's second selection went well with Emma at the piano accompanying Cora on the pipe organ. The reverend thanked the group for their music, stating his appreciation for an up-tempo choice, even if they were in church. This coaxed a few chuckles. He included words of gratitude to the elders for their invitation, to the kitchen ladies in anticipation of the lunch and then offered a blessing on the food before giving the benediction.

Emma and Eleanor slipped out at the last hymn to make the tea. An added year of faithfulness had been celebrated.

• • •

The regulars and visitors filled the spacious fellowship hall. Obviously created by Irene's hand, centrepieces of bright green ferns from the sideroad lent colour to the room.

"Reverend Miller, what a grand message you gave to us." Irene reached for the guest minister's hand before turning to Emma. "Of course, we're used to heartfelt messages, aren't we, Mrs. Taylor?"

Emma stepped back. "Why yes, yes indeed. I'm so glad you were able to come today, Albert. It means a great deal to me and continually solicits memories."

"I miss seeing Bill." Albert touched his chest with his open hand. "We liked to talk about our seminary days. We did share delightful semesters, didn't we?" He gripped Emma's hand. "I'm afraid we gentlemen gave you girls a difficult time. But you didn't weaken by our opinions. If anything, you gained momentum in the debates."

"Why, Mrs. Taylor, is he suggesting you went to seminary?" Irene frowned.

Cora promptly interrupted. "You are pleasant to work with. Why, we were a real team. I could tell you and Reverend Taylor trained in the same school; you are so alike in your style."

"Thank you; I appreciate your kind words." Reverend Miller stepped aside to include someone into the circle.

Irene stared at Emma. Finally, she blurted out the words, "He said our Mrs. Taylor—"

"I'm so glad I caught you before you got away." Mr. Tolt reached for Albert. "Very good, my man. Very good. I enjoyed your message so much." Offering a white envelope, he continued, "Here's a token of appreciation for your hard work. Go out for supper on us."

Emma winced. Did Mr. Tolt have to be so assertive with the honorarium? It was probably his way of being proud the stewards could pay for the services of a visiting minister.

"Irene," Maisie interrupted. "Can you help us put a few short tables in place?"

"I…I can, except I'm in a conversation here about—" Irene wiggled closer to Emma.

"We do need you, Irene," Maisie persisted. "Now, if you don't mind. Some are standing and trying to balance their tea and food. It's not appropriate hospitality."

"But…" Irene crossed her arms over her chest as if she had no intention of budging.

"Here, would you take the end of the table for me?" Maisie winked at Emma as Irene exhaled and gripped it.

Emma suppressed a smile. Maisie was so intuitive.

Nancy Trask walked by as if she was alone in the room. Emma called to her. "Nancy, I'm so glad to see you. How are you getting along with your schooling?"

Nancy threw Emma a quick glance before dropping her gaze and escaping.

What did that mean? Surely, she'd want to inquire if the University of Toronto had contacted Emma.

The reception lasted a couple of hours. People visited with each other, obviously enjoying shared friendships. The workers hurried back and forth, carrying fresh plates of sandwiches and small trays with an arrangement of cookies to pass among the tables. The shortage of sugar and flour always rendered a little less lunch than planned.

Emma excused herself and moved across to talk to Bertha and Eleanor, still working in the kitchen.

"Are you getting worn out?" Emma asked. "Can I come in and help you?"

"Goodness no, Emma," Bertha said. "You made most of these sandwiches everybody's enjoying. You don't have to do this."

"Now, when did we become one-job workers?" Emma cupped Eleanor's elbow. "You look tired. Why don't you both go and have a cup of tea and an egg salad on brown bread that you're so fond of? Come on now. There are a couple of chairs against the wall."

"Ah, Emma, who'll work in the kitchen?" Bertha gazed longingly at the seats.

"I have someone in mind who's done enough visiting. I'll ask her to come and join the brigade for half an hour." Knowing she'd have to explain the topic Albert opened, Emma joined Irene and invited her to come and help. *I might as well get this over with right now.*

"I'd be glad to, as I'd like to check with you further regarding Reverend Miller's comment on you and seminary."

Emma led Irene to the sink. "I've known him for a long time. There wouldn't be enough days in a week to listen to all his stories. We spent lots of hours together when we were younger."

"I'm not interested in his stories. I want you to clarify his comment about seminary."

"That'd take time and more than we have. Better give it up for now, and yes, we'll get back to it." Emma handed Irene a tea towel before she set sudsy cups and saucers on a tray. "Oh dear, our dishes are getting ahead of us."

"Did you talk to Nancy?" Irene raised her eyebrows and scrutinized Emma. "Did she tell you her crazy idea to go to Toronto? That city with streetcars, drinking rooms that admit women and store windows with the kind of clothes that—" She trembled as though she couldn't bear the images. "I never saw the likes. Did she bring up her plans?"

"I haven't talked to her lately." Had Nancy intentionally snubbed her? Maybe she was saving Emma from Irene's abrasive probing. "She walked by, but I think she was in a hurry. Perhaps in the coming weeks, we'll catch up."

People put on their coats and started to leave while saying their goodbyes, adding their gratitude for an outstanding service and tasty lunch. The fellowship hall soon emptied.

Emma sat amid others, taking a much-needed break. As she drank the remainder of her tea, Nancy scurried by, waved and winked at Emma, lifting her index and middle finger in the shape of a V. Emma chuckled. Would this silence heighten Nancy's chance of securing further education?

TWENTY-EIGHT

The dull day reflected Emma's mood. The sun hid behind heavy clouds except for showing unexpected bursts of brilliant diagrams on the floor. Facing the inevitable was a difficult choice. She couldn't continue to contribute to church activities as time was passing.

Those occurrences provided a safe place; they strengthened her confidence and energized her motivation. She recognized what she had to do and when it had to be completed. Focusing attentively on the work waiting in the parsonage brought better results when she mixed them with other interests, but she must focus on packing.

Early in the morning, Emma climbed the attic stairs to sort, discard, hoping to manage her way down to the kitchen side door. She sat on an upholstered three-legged stool and regarded the space carefully. There wasn't much here, but what there was, she needed to clean and tidy.

The sunshine seeped through old lace curtains. An islet effect of diagrams spilled across the pine boards. Prissy sprawled diagonally on the rag mat and claimed a patch of sun rays, sending dust into the air when she thumped her tail on the floor.

The pungent scent filled Emma's senses as she gripped Mary Ann Moore's leather-bound diary. The former minister's wife had suffered shattered dreams and disappointments that must have driven her to this room to retreat.

Shortly after learning of her death, Emma had found the book. While reading the words aloud, she wept. She whispered them and held the texts to her heart, sensing the broken spirit of a woman whom God had called to lead but whom her father had shunned.

Mary Ann's diary gave details, names and events. Emma understood how all of this was possible. She had lived in similar periods of the continuing saga. The power of those phrases introduced a familiar rhythm. She could have written the lines. They had depressed and angered her comparable to how lost opportunities limited Mary Ann. Today, Emma read the words with a new understanding. They energized her.

Suddenly, Maisie stepped into the attic, totally catching Emma off-guard.

"You scared me. What are you doing climbing all these stairs?" Emma planted her hands on her hips. "Your blood pressure will go sky-high."

"I called you on the telephone and nobody answered. I followed all the hallways until I found you. And here I am." Maisie took a deep breath.

She brought a familiar scent of lilac cologne when she came to visit. She also carried hot tea biscuits and homemade jams to the back door. Appearing at the strangest times, during the eleven o'clock news, or in the morning for breakfast, it didn't matter. Maisie seemed to know when Emma switched the lights off at night and raised the blind in the morning. This care and constant vigil did not go unnoticed.

"What would I do without you, my trusted friend?" Emma chuckled.

"You need somebody to answer knocking, so you don't worry your neighbours." Maisie sighed and scanned the room. "My goodness. What are you doing here in the dust? It's enough to take a body's breath away."

"Awh, you're exaggerating." Emma grinned.

"Are you packing?"

"I haven't got to this space, yet. Spending intervals up here reading and thinking."

"Well, my dear. Don't let those stewards rush you into anything. You'd be welcome to stay on in town, you know. Maybe find yourself a little house or share accommodations."

"That big question of the cost of living enters here. What would I live on, Maisie? We have no savings. Bill didn't get a big salary. But I can't complain; overall, everyone has been generous. They shared at times from their shelves with eggs, preserves, and cuts of ham. However, this dissolved into daily living, not into our bank account."

Emma motioned for Maisie to sit. Brushing the dust off a leather seat, she pulled a small bench closer.

"But what about now, Emma? What'll you do now?"

"I don't know. Bill may have had a meagre pension. The church doesn't make much provision for widows. He used to have an insurance policy of which I'll enquire. In the meantime, I don't want to live with my girls. They have friends of their own. I'm in a dilemma, I'm afraid."

"I'm sorry. You don't deserve this," Maisie said. "You're an intelligent woman. You'll think of something. You've worked alongside Bill all these years. You've been his right-hand helper."

"I have. But it doesn't help me now. I've got a box of hymns that I composed, scribblers full of my own Sunday school material, and essays I've written through time. But I haven't any ideas about how to sell them or find interested parties."

Maisie shrugged. "I don't have any opinions on that."

"A while back, when we were having money problems, I suggested that I get a job," Emma said. "Just for a few hours to help out a bit."

"You actually had the energy and time to do that?" Maisie's eyebrows rose.

"If I planned my day, yes. I thought I'd like something of my own, and of course, it would have helped our situation financially. Bill had replied to my suggestion with a firm no. He said, it wouldn't be right for me to get a job, and it'd make a statement against the church."

Maisie asked, "Did you believe that?"

Emma shrugged her shoulders. "I guess so. He added that they'd think we needed to reduce our spending, which we did—in addition to what we were doing."

Maisie's quiet watchful eyes gave nothing away of what she was thinking.

Emma viewed her. "That made me wonder if he agreed to take a lower wage. If people couldn't afford a donation, the effect would ripple outward."

Maisie remained silent. *Did she disagree?*

Emma began speaking again. "It was around the same period that Bill mentioned the phrase, 'we give so others can serve' that we sing at offering time." He said he felt guilty when he sang those words. Sometimes he didn't want to hold out his hands to receive their money or pray over it."

Maisie lowered her head.

Emma cleared her throat. "We knew the stewards didn't have much more than it took to pay his salary."

Maisie didn't respond. Did it sadden her as well? Several seconds passed before she broke the silence. "Some things are difficult to understand."

When she didn't say anything to add to the memory Emma shared, she went on to say, "I'm comfortable with figures and statements; maybe I could do bookkeeping for a local business."

"And you'd work for a man? You'd hear 'minister's wives don't work for men' and 'bookkeeping is men's work'. I can hear it now: 'you shouldn't rob a job from the breadwinner.'"

"Maisie, this is 1935. The town will determine that I'm the breadwinner for Prissy and me. And as painful as it is to say, I'm no longer the minister's wife, am I? Besides, women have laboured in factories during and since the war. Why would anybody say they don't work for men? Where would they get that? It's nonsense."

"You'll hear, 'Things can happen when they're together.' I've heard stories."

"I'd tell them I've heard stories too, and I don't intend to be the subject of any. But, I could get employment out of the house. My goodness, I have to eat."

"You must be prepared for criticism, Emma. If you run a business in your home, you'd have people, including men, traipsing in and out."

"Maybe, but maybe not. It would depend. Would it be acceptable if I were a schoolteacher or a nurse? So why not something of my choice. I'm a good judge of character. The public would have to trust me."

"I'm glad I'm not in your shoes."

"I wish I wasn't, sometimes. But I can't lie down and die either. I'm forty-nine years old, and I still have longings to do and be. I feel there's a lot unfinished. If I had the money, there are places I'd like to see."

"But you couldn't travel alone."

"Oh, for Pete's sake, Maisie."

"Now don't chew my head off, I'm trying to think of safe choices." Maisie squirmed on the bench. "In time, and not for a while, you might consider getting married again."

"Never! Don't even mention such a thing?" Emma's indignant tone of voice caused Maisie to sit back.

"I'm sorry. I'm only thinking it's easier for a woman if she's married. It gives her status," Maisie said. "I speak from experience on this topic."

Emma nodded. "I could teach music. Irene asked me to help Susanne while Mrs. Watson was sick. So, I see an option to give lessons. You know, not taking students from her, but rather beginning a list of those interested in having a tutor for a fee. No one has come forward with musical training, and there are children in town who would benefit. The church's piano would be available to me."

"Would that be wise?" Maisie shifted her position. "You know, being there during the day with the new minister going in and out raises difficult issues."

"I can't disappear into thin air, Maisie." Emma sighed.

"Besides, they only turn on the heat for Sundays in the winter months, and you'd have to let your students go."

Emma walked to the window to draw the curtains. Her arthritic knees and hands ached; she must purchase some liniment to take care of the pain.

Maisie pursed her lips. She didn't say anything, so Emma proceeded. "I've always loved books." She let the curtain drop. "I wonder if I could get work in the local library or a bookstore in Hampton."

"As far as the library, Mrs. Miles protects that collection like a mother hen. Besides, you don't drive, Emma. How would you get there? You'd have to walk rain or shine."

"I can drive. But I'll have to get a license. It should be the first task I do. Bill's car is sitting out there, waiting."

Maisie was silent. Did she disapprove? Her eyes widened. "Are you ready for what will be said?"

"Yes! Would the town suggest I sit on my thumbs, helpless and dependent on others? Maybe they don't want me to stand on my own."

"Are you looking for a piece of the truth, Emma?" Not pausing for her to respond, Maisie continued. "They won't expect much of you."

"Hilda was supportive when I helped her think through the stillborn birth." Emma fumbled with a pencil she picked from the floor. "She suggested that I become a midwife, as women might benefit from my assistance. She also mentioned that Mrs. Densmore is busy, and that I could assist her or build my own clientele."

Maisie took a deep breath and crossed her ankles. "So, you're thinking you'd teach music and midwife around town to stretch the dollar. I'm sure you'd do well in either of those vocations. However, is it your calling?"

Emma didn't answer immediately. Somehow it didn't surprise her that Maisie would use the term *calling*.

"No, it's not," Emma mumbled.

"Can I tell you what I think?" Maisie asked and paused for a moment. "You give old topics fresh energy when you enter into conversations, and also when you stand in that pulpit and show us God's love. You make us sigh and draw in needed air to make our breathing easier. You offer insight and clear the fog when we're trying to look ahead. You put music in our hearts with your encouragement and unconditional love. You're a midwife and a teacher of important topics. There, that's my opinion."

Emma opened her mouth to speak, but Maisie raised a hand. "Let me mention an additional detail. These women trust you with their anger and disappointment, but they wouldn't have gone that far with Reverend Taylor. It's your willingness to identify with their pain that frees them to be open with you."

That was another reason individuals had difficulty befriending Maisie. One never knew what stand she'd take, but it'd be an honest one whether they wanted to hear it or not.

And she was right. Maybe it took someone outside the church to balance the options, some more obvious than others. Yet, Emma had to defend herself at times for thinking in a similar way.

"Yes, Maisie! That's exactly what I prayed to hear. But how do I proceed? I mean, I can't expect the elders to accept the pastoral care I give or invite me into the pulpit. The congregation has expectations. I have to be asked, and they have to be aware of their choices before they even think of requesting my support." Emma coughed into her hand. "But not all is lost because I occasionally offer pastoral care, coach the girls in the Mission Circle and at times join Mrs. Ryan to teach those who gather in the Hills. And what I'm going to tell you now fits exactly with what you're saying. Do you recall Shirley Maitland? She sang at a service a while back?"

"Can't say I do." Maisie leaned back. "My attendance isn't regular."

Emma's question was unkind, but she couldn't retract it. Fortunately, Maisie wouldn't feel guilty, as she remained firm in her decisions.

"The Reverend Maitland phoned to ask me to lead a rally for the ladies' group."

"Nice, Emma. They must know in Brooke how well you open scripture." Maisie pushed her glasses higher on her nose.

"Well, for whatever reason, they want me to come."

"And you said?" Maisie coaxed as an invitation.

"I said I couldn't. Bill's health came first to me, and I planned to be with him as much as possible.

"I can see that would be your priority. What did the Reverend say?"

"He offered help, said he was sorry concerning Bill's heart attack and we left it there."

"So, what's your problem? It sounds like you were honest with him, and he understood."

"I was. I admit that I wanted to accept. But Maisie, that's not all. Would I actually be able to go on my own? This invitation made me think. The truth is, I'm frightened."

Emma hadn't cried much since Bill died, although she shed tears when she stopped to chat downtown or when she peeled potatoes for her stew. Suddenly, she began to sob—and veiled her face with her hands.

Maisie didn't stir. She sat, and Emma wept and then quieted herself. Maisie broke the silence. "Well, I'm glad you let that go. And this is a safe place to do it with someone who knows the love of your life died, your heart is broken, and you're feeling alone without a strategy to move ahead. You deserve to cry, holler, lament, pound a pillow, or whatever else you need to do. Your entire existence has changed and thank God you are aware of it. And secondly, you've admitted your yearning toward ministry, even though you're timid of what the future holds."

Emma sniffed and then blew her nose. "Thanks, Maisie. That's been coming for a long time." She wiped away tears with her fingers. "Now, to answer the question you asked earlier about what the problem is. I'm afraid of starting something new, although I know it's necessary."

A sense of frustration heightened as memories exposed how others had directed her. *Where does God fit? What about God's plan for me? I've been faithful and served as Bill's wife for such a long time. Isn't there anything for me now?*

"That's normal. Thinking this way might lead you to an answer." Maisie raised her eyebrows as if expecting a response.

Emma spoke softly. "I am who I am. This may all be different to me, but I'll learn."

Maisie folded her hands in her lap. "You'll be a power to behold when you get your life figured out."

"I've got to start now. I can't give up. Bill wouldn't want me to." She rubbed the tears off her cheeks. "Work drained much of our time, Maisie. We had little enjoyment, except what we gleaned from our day-to-day activities. We gave and gave to the church." Emma shuddered, opened her handkerchief and sniffed.

Maisie squeezed Emma's hand. "That you did. Come on, I think we could use a break. I brought a few of those tea biscuits you like."

"Before we go down, there is another alternative to my choices that might shed some light on decisions."

Twinges of tension generated uncertainty in her mind. Could she share further, or would it get her in deeper?

TWENTY-NINE

The afternoon shadows stretched longer. Maisie and Emma continued to share options.

"My goodness, girl, you're a woman ahead of your time. You are full of ideas." Maisie said. "But I sense decisions are difficult."

"It's also guilt or fear of being seen as self-centred. I mean, wanting to serve God apart from where others are used to seeing me. This might seem selfish to some. It also means I'd have to explain…defend myself."

"Where does all that come from, for goodness sake? Bill didn't stand in your path."

"I agree, but he didn't sweep the way clear for me either, and I didn't expect him to. We all knew Bill was slowing down. His appearance had even changed, but Mr. Tolt didn't suggest he take a Sunday to rest. During the time he was sitting in a wheelchair with oxygen and managing daily medication, I could have been serving in an accountable manner. But it didn't happen."

It hurt to admit Bill would stay neutral for the sake of the church rather than open doors for her. And in some ways, she loved him more for that. It was a form of protection. He kept them both safe from those who wouldn't understand.

"So, what's prompting all of this?" Maisie paused. "Want to tell me?"

"I'd like to do that." Emma took a deep breath. "There's an important area of our lives that neither of us shared in public. Maybe this'll shed light on my willingness, as well as my hesitancy." Emma sat on the edge of her seat. Would Maisie accept what she had to say? Emma had to trust her.

"In 1910, we had a new king, Father's Day was given a celebration date, and the fifty-cent piece was on the market. Canada celebrated a different period in history. I had been on the revival circuit for a few years, and I met Bill in Elford in 1912. That community and Bill's fellowship had a joint meeting, and we began to lead collectively. Bill and I led tent services then, together and individually."

"You led them?" Maisie's eyes twinkled with delight.

"I did." Emma leaned on the side of the chair. "It took Bill a while to understand that I was competent. He asked me how long I'd been leading, and I told him I'd been serving for two years. Later in our friendship, I showed him numerous statements and letters from well-known religious personnel recognizing my work. I also had formal invitations from across Ontario to come to their towns."

"He was impressed, right?"

"I'm relieved to say he was, although he said little. In those days, rally leadership met to unite the people in Jesus' name. Those tent meetings were exciting, energizing and full of the Spirit of God. We confirmed God's love every night. There were signs, wonders and miracles to behold. We counted money, conversions and attendance. Sometimes we ran those rallies four and five nights in the same town. If we were invited, we held them for a month. I'd preach, sing, play my autoharp and pray. And Bill led a similar form."

Maisie clapped her hands. "I might have known. I loved it when you took the odd service when Bill was away. You are a great speaker. I often wondered how you could share experience and scripture with such ease. When you got a chance, you managed to tell the woman's side, showing it as normal and natural. I know those who listened were touched to their core."

Silence stilled the room until Emma said, "I preached and sang and often sold a dozen or so of my hymnbooks filled with verses and sheet music. Sometimes, there'd be forty plus conversions in one night. Men and women who had never heard the gospel came forward and decided to follow Jesus."

Maisie took Emma's hands. "It must have been exciting years for you."

"It was," Emma said. "I had my personal writing stationery: *Emma Fay Russell, Evangelist*.

"I'm impressed." Maisie leaned back. "Did that involvement make it easier for you in the church?"

"Not really. Revivals are one of a kind. Everybody in town came to them. It was an indisputable spiritual experience for many and entertainment for others. We had tremendous crowds who gathered to hear the music and message. And then the strange warm feeling John Wesley taught would come over them, enough to make them weak at the knees. When the time came to make a decision, they'd come to the front. And a lot of them would begin to attend worship. I used to think we were like John the Baptist, you know…preparing the way."

Maisie shook her head. "Incredible. Was your preference ministering in a sanctuary or a revival?"

"The revivals were different and meant to be distinct. We worked with churches a night or a week or a month if invited, and then we moved on." Emma took a deep breath. "They offer all levels of leadership from administration to services and pastoral care. It has a consistent relationship with the membership and takes them much deeper in their faith."

Maisie chuckled. "I can hear the passion in your voice when you explain this."

"It was exhilarating, no doubt. But people get confused. I mean, how much does it take to get revived before they believe the Lord is serious in sending them out to serve?"

"I see your point. Do you miss the rallies?" Maisie asked.

"No, I don't. It was a season in my life. I'm glad I did it, but I don't crave it."

"Will those days ever return?"

"I don't think so. The events Shirley and Reverend Maitland organize will come close, but they won't be the travelling crusades in which I ministered."

"You loved working with Bill."

Emma paused. "Indeed, I did. And I'd like ladies to have leadership opportunities."

"Is that what motivates you to keep trying—to be available to assist?" Maisie tilted her head to one side. "And to attempt to balance the elders between men and women?"

"Yes, but neither has gone far," Emma said. "There is no such category as a woman elder in our denomination…yet." She waited, and Maisie stared at her. "I want to be free to step in anywhere from janitor to greeter, musician to preacher. It doesn't matter to me."

"I have to give you credit, Emma. You have perseverance."

"Thank you, Maisie. I appreciate that. It's all about God's gifts—the openness to accept and the willingness to use them."

"Your passion and conviction of faith are changing ideas regarding our identity, although some may not have discovered what God is calling them to do."

Emma nodded. "That could be half the problem and our greatest task. Being the Body of Christ here and equipping the saints to do God's work sounds right. Change will come. Women are the first at the cradle, and the old story tells us they were the last at the cross. This gives me courage to find my place as an example for others to seek theirs."

"Now that you've decided to prepare your passage towards a new life, are you going to bring out your autoharp and sing for the congregation?" Maisie raised her eyebrows and regarded Emma.

She held her hands in her lap. "I doubt it. But I admit, we should share our gifts. Mrs. Ryan is one who has accepted her organizational ability and directs it to the opportunities provided. She does that so well despite her surrounding conditions."

"And you're thinking if we all did that, individuals would reach out to others and grow in their faith?"

"Absolutely! Reflect on the words mission and witness in scripture."

"I'll leave you to do that. You'll do much better than me." Maisie paused. "And when you decide, I'll come to listen." She walked to the door. "You know, Emma, you don't give yourself enough credit. You do ministry daily, perhaps not what you'd like, but it's still ministry. I think you are exactly where God can use you. And not only that, but you're also laying important groundwork. Believe me, goodness will follow. Be patient."

The quiet attic provided thinking space for Emma. Did she tell Maisie too much? She had never been that open before, and now that someone else knew her thoughts, Emma felt more accountable to God. What if preaching wasn't only a season?

Even though it was impossible to accept Reverend Maitland's current invitation, she'd consider it for a future occasion. Paul's words to the Ephesians referred to being *created in Christ Jesus unto good works, which God hath before ordained that we should walk in them.* A warm feeling flooded her. What had God ordained for her? And did she have the courage to follow?

"A lot of my resistance to taking the step forward comes from my father's negative attitude. That discussion is for another time. Let's go and have our refreshments—we missed our lunch. My days always make sense after talking to you."

"I'm glad. Anytime." Maisie led their descent to the ground floor.

"There's a whole range of ministry surfacing to catch my attention," Emma said.

"Is this what you were referring to a while ago?"

"It was something I wanted but was out of my reach."

"And now, is God challenging or encouraging you to be ready?"

"It's like God is saying 'first things first'. Learn this before you do that. Prepare yourself to be faithful to do my will."

"And did God use Bill and his gentle manner to teach you?"

"Perhaps some of this is still to become obvious." Emma raised her head to listen. "Am I hearing things?"

Maisie paused. "All this flattery has gone to your head and bells are ringing. Anyway, I've stayed long enough to distract you from what you were doing."

"Never! I'm glad to have your company; besides I'm more on track than I was." Emma stepped beyond Prissy and walked to the front hall. "I better go and see who's there. We'll get our tea and biscuits later," she called back.

There had been surprises during the last few days. Was this another one? Emma would have a better chance of understanding whatever waited for her because of Maisie's questions which opened a window of hope.

Would I rather follow in Bill's footsteps or make my own way? She'd face this question when a deeper truth surfaced through the fog between cold fear of the unknown and the warm touch of God's hand.

• • •

A tall person stood on the veranda in full view through the lace curtains. Reverend Maitland. Panic flooded through Emma. *What date is it? Did I promise to get back to him? No, I declined his invitation.* So much had happened in the last while that it often left her confused.

She twisted the knob on the door and pulled it open. "Reverend Maitland. Won't you come in?"

"Hello, Mrs. Taylor." Removing his hat, he continued, "I'm sorry I didn't call first, but I hadn't planned on coming over. And when I realized I had a visit farther north, I decided to swing around to Noble and save postage plus the effort to send the rally information." He grinned. "I want to keep you informed with our plans."

"I'm glad you came." Emma pointed to the kitchen table. "Can you sit for a few minutes?"

"Thank you." Emma pushed a chair towards the reverend. He placed his hat on the nearest seat. "You cannot know how much we're looking forward to having you come and share God's word with us when you're ready."

Emma settled across from him. "You are kind. Thanks. I'm glad you dropped by to bring me up to date."

The reverend stuck his hand in his pocket and tugged out a piece of paper. "I can't stay long, but I have something for you."

"Reverend Maitland. There...there is some bad news I must tell you."

"Now is a good time to talk. I must ask about Reverend Taylor. When we spoke, he'd had a heart attack, and you were taking well deserved days to spend with him in his recovery period."

"That's right." Emma sighed, wringing her hands in despair. "It's what I want to discuss." She shifted on her chair. "While in the hospital, he appeared to steadily grow weaker. He often seemed like himself, interested in events at the church and in town, but then his energy drained with the smallest exertion. And he…he died in his bed. Gasped for breath and within a few moments he was gone."

Reverend Maitland's face paled. "Oh, Mrs. Taylor, I am so sorry. I had no knowledge of this."

"You'd not have any way of knowing. With his death and all that went with it, I was led from one day to another."

"This would have been such a tragedy for all of you."

"It was, and then the stewards informed me that they'd called a minister, and he and his family were ready to move any time." Emma wiped her eyes. "I've been sorting and packing."

"It's an enormous task. Do you have help?"

"I've had lots of offers, but when you live in a place for ten years, you collect a few items you have to consider before discarding or setting them aside." Emma straightened in her chair.

"I understand." Reverend Maitland held the piece of paper in front of him. "Shall I leave this with you in case we plan a rally next year? You'd still be our first choice to give the leadership." He sounded hopeful.

"I have no idea where I'll be living or what I'll be doing. I can't see that far ahead. The congregation would assume I couldn't wait for Bill to die, so I could go out on my own." Emma swallowed a sob.

"Public opinion can be harsh, and I understand you wanting to be careful. A widow has to pause before making obvious changes."

"Yes, I'm afraid you're right. But I'd like to look at your plans." Emma reached for the paper. "Just to see what I'll be missing."

Reverend Maitland held it out to her. "I hope you stay in an area of ministry as you have done in the past. Perhaps now, it'll be your choice. So many folks I meet praise your work in the pulpit and in the community. Watch the advertisements in church magazines, and when you find your feet, tell them you have something to offer."

"I appreciate that encouragement. I needed to hear it." Emma glanced at the pamphlet with interest. "This resembles holy ground."

"Thank you. Your opinion means a lot to me." Reverend Maitland stood and reached for his hat before shaking Emma's hand. "May the Lord give you peace in the midst of all the turmoil surrounding you."

The heavy load Emma had carried since Bill's death lightened. "You are a gracious man."

They walked toward the door and the reverend opened it. Tipping his hat, he hurried down the front steps.

God's grace often comes in surprising packages, and today it shone brightly through a friend, making it easy for Emma to continue packing and sorting. When considering the future, a slight spark of confidence surfaced. Reverend Maitland's remarks regarding ministry resonated in her mind. *Maybe I can deepen God's call when the time is right.*

THIRTY

Another day—more conclusions. Different challenges appeared. Important memories surfaced, and Emma savoured them to consider later.

Maisie arrived earlier in the morning than Emma expected. They walked to Bill's closed door. "Do you go in here, Emma? Into Bill's workplace?"

"No, I haven't been in since he died." Emma grasped the knob and held on to it for a moment. "But I think it's time. I must clean it out. Will you come in with me?"

They stepped into the dark, stuffy room. The leftover scent of stale tobacco hung in the air. Emma loved the aroma, although it had soured. The parishioners would frown on Bill smoking, but he often sat and read in here while enjoying his pipe.

Emma opened the water-stained drapes, letting the sun flood the windows. The image of Bill slumped on his desk in the early morning of his first heart scare flashed through her mind.

She placed her hand on the back of his chair. Other clergymen had sat here before him, a few probably well-known for their fiery, expository sermons. Bill's teachings were definitive, gentle and personal. Members of the congregation had often said, "He talked directly to me this morning."

Emma's clergy father reflected Bill in many ways; they both had lived in the black and white of life. Yet, when Emma told him she'd stood up to her father and said she would lead a church, Bill rejected his father-in-law's harsh comments. Emma's mother had been the typical minister's wife, asking only to be a dutiful spouse. This example had set a particular plumb line for Emma to stay within the norm.

Where had the time gone? It seemed like yesterday she and Bill had entered this house. They had come directly from the mission field to serve in Noble.

Maisie ambled down the length of the office, frowning at the oversized frames hanging on the wall. "Emma, what are all these certificates? My goodness, this is a Rogue's gallery."

"They're Bill's Bible college and seminary degrees. He was proud of his achievements, and rightly so."

"I'm impressed. It's too bad to store them. They are beautiful. Will you hang them in your new place?"

"I don't think so. They are reminders of Bill's hard work and recognition of scholarship. They tell a story—significant milestones."

"That's a gratifying way to look at it." Maisie removed them from their nails and leaned them against the wall.

Images of earned, yet hidden seminary certificates, filled her mind. She'd never hung hers, hadn't even glanced at them from the time when they were packed.

Emma bit her lip. "Maybe…maybe I should bring out mine and hang them. They've been in boxes for over twenty years, and I haven't seen them since."

"You've got diplomas? Whatever for?" Maisie raised her eyebrows.

"For academic achievements." Emma smiled at her. "Isn't it why you usually get them?"

Maisie signed a long breath. "There's still a lot I don't know concerning you and Bill."

"You're right, I suppose."

Maisie turned her head. "And you never drew on your schooling?"

"Not in a visible way. Whatever one learns remains in memory to a certain extent."

"Never told anybody?" Maisie shook her head.

"No." Emma nodded toward the east wall. "Come with me and I'll show you."

She opened the bottom doors of the pine corner cupboard and pulled out a long box. After lifting the lid, she unfolded several pieces of fabric and raised three frames. Each one sheltered a large certificate with bold antique writing—dated to 1915, the year she and Bill had graduated.

"My goodness, Emma. This is hard to believe." Maisie pressed a hand to her chest. "You are an educated woman."

"I am."

"That's why you made such an excellent partner for Bill. You understood what he wanted and helped him do it."

"Yes, I suppose that's correct."

"And the church got a terrific deal. Two for the price of one." Maisie covered her mouth with her hands.

"They did."

Touching one of the frames with a finger, Maisie murmured slowly, "And you put them away. It looks like a two-sided mirror—what you offered, and what they missed."

"Although preaching and leading music in rallies defined a particular era, it generated rewarding work." Emma stuck her hand into her apron pocket. "These certificates represent my academic endeavours. Being a minister's wife is different. It's a supportive role. It made me happy to be with Bill to further his ministry." Emma paused. "You know, Maisie, scripture tells us that as people of faith, we're ordained into the priesthood of all believers and equipped with spiritual gifts to do what God calls us to accomplish."

"You're right, Emma, but you'll have a hard time getting forward-thinking past our elders."

"We need to continue recommending the nomination of women." Emma folded the pieces of cotton.

"You've previously referred to that, but it hasn't happened. There will be many who are steeped in the passage that women should be silent in church."

Emma was quick in her reply. "And some should be."

Maisie waved a hand towards Bill's certificates. "So, tell me what you're going to do with these."

"Times are different. This kind of ministry fostered happiness. Teaching others, you know. This was a huge part of my seminary training."

Emma blinked and refocused to read the wording before running her fingertips along the grain of the wooden frame. "I felt left out when the college had an ordination service for Bill and other men. I mean, we were called to the mission field as a team. But I knew in my heart that any acknowledgment of what God had planned for us wouldn't be recognized here. It was not the era to identify the concept of God's call on a woman's life for leadership. It wasn't discussed and I didn't initiate it."

"Looking back in history, you've been in ministry for a long time. There's a big difference calling a woman as minister, and women having a ministry." Maisie hugged Emma. "There's always another side to every story, isn't there?"

The framed certificates appeared to stare at Emma, and she moved her hands across in front of them. "What'll I do with all these credentials?"

Ignoring Emma's question, Maisie concentrated on the frame she held in her hand. "Well, I'll be darned. You are sure full of surprises." She rotated a frame and read, "With *Distinction for Preaching*. This is amazing. You told nobody this, either."

Emma began to slide the diplomas back into the box until Maisie touched her hand.

"Leave them out, Emma. Let's hang them up. It's about time."

"What? Are you serious? Do you think so?"

"Yes, do it for the short period you're here. But first, let's boil the kettle and eat the rest of those biscuits.

The morning had given Emma a feeling of anticipation. Did she have the nerve to put the certificates in full view and deal with the consequences? It was a risk she had to take.

THIRTY-ONE

The following morning Emma was making tea when Maisie knocked on the side door and walked in. "Look who I found." Maisie ushered Tillie into the kitchen. "And to think she's looking for a job."

"Hello, Tillie. Day off? You won't get any blisters if we don't accomplish more work than Maisie and I did yesterday." Emma chuckled. "Not that there isn't lots to do. Would you like tea before we begin?"

"I would, thanks."

They settled at the table, and Emma lifted the lid off a plate of treats. "I have a few biscuits a caring neighbour gave to me."

"If they're Maisie's, they're good." Tillie picked up one and began to eat it. "Is there anything we can do for you this morning? Pack or discard?"

"I have difficult choices to make." Emma frowned. "There are boxes of items I haven't opened for years and wonder if I will again."

"Like recipes and letters?" Tillie buttered a biscuit.

"No, I'm thinking of music. There is a box full of words and melodies. During the rallies, I wrote and sang many hymns."

Maisie finished stirring her tea and set her spoon in the saucer. "I'm captivated now. You've shared some, although I wasn't aware you had a large number."

"Bill preferred I play the piano and sing the music with the choir as the organist suggested. I used to teach the children my tunes and sing the words for them. I took part in whatever area I was needed. It didn't matter what I did as long as the church benefitted. This is a wonderful congregation, although they could have waited a few more days before asking me to move. But, overall, they love us."

Emma opened the closet. She stretched to her tiptoes to pull a battered wooden case from the top shelf. She placed it on the table, observed it and sighed. "This hasn't been unlocked for years; it might be rusted by now."

Maisie clasped her hands. "Open it."

Emma unfastened the metal guards on the side and raised an eyebrow. Strings set across a redwood instrument reflected the sun shining through the window. "My goodness, it's as beautiful as the day I put it away."

Tillie's eyes widened. "Play it, Emma. Please?"

Emma slipped picks onto her fingers and pulled the harp to her chest, wrapping her arms around it as if hugging a beloved friend. She picked and strummed. Her voice carried a melodious *Amazing Grace* throughout the room. When she finished the final note, she gripped the harp before placing it back in the box. It fit tightly, resting on a collection of papers.

"That was so beautiful. And to think you were not asked to sing a solo in church." Maisie grimaced.

"Cora wouldn't have known. Joining the alto section suited me fine."

Silence hung like a heavy morning mist. Maisie wrapped her fingers about her cup of tea. "You told me you were an evangelist when you met Bill. I've been wondering why you had to go to seminary if you were already ministering."

"Bill and I married in 1913. He preached in the district at the same time I did. We decided to take further training together. I applied to several Canadian seminaries for a theological degree, but was always rejected, so we went to my cousin's denominational school in the United States for four semesters."

"Were you allowed to attend classes with Bill?" Maisie asked.

"Yes, although he liked to sit with the other men. We studied the same courses. I majored in Biblical Theology, and my graduation certificate added a second degree in Pastoral Ministry." Emma straightened her apron. "Bill received his diploma on commencement day."

"And you didn't?" Tillie frowned.

Emma shrugged. "That was predictable. It's not like I'd need it. Many years later, Bill encouraged me to request it. The college sent it without question. And when it arrived in the mail, I wept."

Quietness filled the space between them.

Maisie's lips thinned. "I'm sorry. Not everything makes sense. Good for Bill for urging you to take that step."

Tillie moved to the edge of her chair. "Did you get good marks?"

"I couldn't have received any better. My professor gave me a hundred percent on each examination I wrote."

"I don't wonder from the way you interpret scriptures." Maisie said. "You opened them at our ladies' meetings and in church that caused some of the women to talk about your teachings for several days." She clapped her hands. "Here, we had two scholars in our midst and didn't know it."

"I didn't use the academic title, but it gave me confidence knowing what I had achieved. At least the school gave me as much as they could."

"Indeed, Emma," Tillie said.

"Funny how everything worked out." Emma lifted the teapot, and the dark liquid filled their cups. "My father expected me to follow my mother's example and marry a man of the cloth. I wanted to be a missionary; this was not acceptable to him. He gave his approval when I became an evangelist because I was part of a team."

"You did that. And you arrived on the mission field through a different approach than your original plan." Maisie took a sip of tea.

Emma smiled. "I did."

"Come on, we've talked long enough." Maisie rubbed her hands together. "Let's go to Bill's office and fill boxes. And bring your tea."

How easy it was for everybody to keep thinking Bill was still in their midst.

• • •

Tillie walked through the parlour. "This is stunning." She touched the woodwork. "I appreciate Carpenter's Lace. Someone was trained on the tools."

"I've often thought the same. I like this room, too." Emma spoke softly.

Beautiful carving edged the area and created arches of filigree artistry, providing a highlight in the old house. "Bill didn't ignite the fireplace, as smoke instantly filled the area every time he put a match to the paper-bed under the wood."

Maisie cleared her throat. "I understand the mantle is treasured by the people, and I admit it gives an elegant appearance."

"It's a cozy room. It was in here that Bill presided at events such as weddings with only the bride and groom and their witnesses." Emma drew in a deep breath. "A great deal of ministry happened here."

She opened heavy curtains revealing two large arched windows. "These lined drapes aren't very attractive, but they keep the heat in during the winter and the sun out in the summer. Besides, we both loved to view the opaque stained-glass design along the top window panels."

They walked into Bill's office. "But all of that pastoring was Bill's, wasn't it?" Maisie pulled a book off the shelf. "Be honest, didn't you accomplish more on your own when you were single?"

"Those were the days when we worked with men—the concept of who had power or the lead wasn't critical. We used the gifts God gave us and shared them equally with others." Emma touched the edge of a bookshelf.

Maisie raised her eyebrows in surprise. "And you brought none of your experience into worship or to our elders? You could have created a history of your own."

"Perhaps I did in supporting Bill. He was the minister, I understood that."

"And you were happy to be his wife and share in ministry when acceptable," Tillie said.

"Yes, I was." Emma slowly moved her arm across the room. "This is a man's space—consider the leftover pipe scent to stacks of magazines and books. I can tell Bill loved it. His domain. And the church, eh? A man's world."

A slight frown creased Maisie's forehead. "Very different in Grandma's time from my understanding. And unlike in ways when I was a young woman. There was freedom for us in some circles; now the parameters are established, and we work within those boundaries created for us. It's not right, but it's the way it is." Maisie set two books on the desk.

"All of this makes me feel sad," Tillie said. "It'd be natural for a minister and his wife to have similar interests and skills. That's probably why they're attracted to one another in the first place."

"Why didn't Bill tell us about your education and experience? Wasn't he proud of you?" Maisie asked.

"He was in his own way. Bill didn't speak of either, as people aren't always ready to hear facts and findings if they're contrary to what they believe. They like to hear confirmation of what they already know and have their minister build on the familiar. Bill was aware of this and mentioned these conversations at times through the years. He referred to them several days before he died, and we talked about this in our last discussion. In fact, he made it like a deathbed prayer, hoping he'd done all he could to give the people a broad scope of knowledge and faith."

"My goodness." Maisie blew on the cover of a book, raising particles of dust. "He felt that strongly about his ministry, did he? We weren't aware of what we were missing, so we couldn't appreciate what you had to offer."

"That's the point." Emma opened a file and fanned the sheets. "There are interesting facts to learn. Had Bill lived, he might have discussed these topics with the elders." A couple of pages caught her interest. "When I unpack these boxes, I must take time to read this material. It'll hold more interest for me now than in my previous position."

"Ah, I believe you will." Maisie brushed her hand across the blank space on the wall. "Promise me you'll consider hanging your certificates to honour those special years."

Emma slowly nodded her head. "I'll consider it."

"You're far too modest, Emma. If you were Mrs. Governing, you'd have hung them around your parlour so the whole town would be sure to see them."

"Well, she is the mayor's wife." Emma snickered. "Does that count for something?"

Maisie raised her hands with the palms facing Emma. "Just teasing; you know how she holds her large gatherings to 'bless the congregation'. I think she shows off her silver and linen and—"

Emma covered her mouth to stifle a chuckle. "No, no, not nice."

"But I'll admit she has favourite lines like, 'Since the Lord gave me such a beautiful house, why shouldn't I share it with others?'" Maisie dropped into Bill's armchair. "That's as good a one-liner as any. She'll invite you when her flowers are at their best and when her cleaning ladies have come and gone." She smirked. "And then she won't issue an invitation until she wants to impress the town."

"May the Lord bless her anyway." Emma set a box on Bill's desk and lifted a lamp along with a picture into it.

"Emma, you never cease to amaze me with the grace you extend to people." Maisie straightened her skirt. "One added question before we go to work. Doesn't it say somewhere in scripture that some women amazed the men? You should preach or even write on that subject, Emma."

"Mm, in my spare time." She grinned.

"Why don't we discuss these topics?" Tillie asked. "I regret we didn't consider this years ago. Everybody would benefit from reading the gospels with an open mind."

"Bill would have agreed. And to gain the courage to reach out without being self-centred is essential. I used to ask myself, 'Did I touch the hem of his garment this morning?' That continually helped me to believe I had something to pass on."

Emma and Bill had had this same conversation several times, but Emma didn't tire of examining it. The discussion of ministry and the distinct roles they represented connected her to Bill in a positive way.

Voices faded into the background as Emma focused her mind on the certificates. Would she abandon them in the box or hang them? Should others see them? Maybe not if she continued to live in this town. The news would be on everybody's lips by noon on the first day. Yet, to return them to the drawer denied a significant season of her life. The diplomas reminded her of Bill at that age, teachers, assignments and fellow students such as the Reverend Albert.

How she loved writing those essays—excitement filled her senses. She'd get them out, too. She hadn't seen them for years. Perhaps she'd discarded them. No, she wouldn't have. But where were they? She'd find them by the time she was ready to move.

Painful grief overtook her. *Oh Bill, if only you were here to talk to me.* Wiping her tears with a cotton handkerchief, she turned to her friends. They worked for another hour, clearing Bill's desk and dividing his books, except for those Emma wanted to keep for herself.

"Let's leave the bottom row for Reverend Larson." Emma stretched to review the titles. "And the ones on the third shelf I'll take with me."

Tillie closed the lid on a box and placed a hand on the small of her back as if it ached. "What do you say we quit for today? I don't think we can do any more."

Maisie stretched. "Contrary to what it might look like, we got a lot done…besides thinking, that is." After laughing through her words, she said, "Call us if you want to fill boxes."

"Thanks. I will." Emma waved to them. "Put your feet up tonight. You two deserve a rest."

Alone with uncertainties and choices, nobody could resolve any of this but Emma. The old favourite line, *I don't have to decide today*, didn't work anymore. She had to make decisions, and soon.

Guilt feelings gripped Emma as she considered moving on without Bill. But new plans were necessary, and he fit in her memory. There was room for him there. Niggling questions wouldn't allow her to rest. She could not continue to pack, discard, or give away anything before she decided what had been central to them both. It was time for careful choices. That had to come first, regardless of how long it postponed the process.

THIRTY-TWO
PART 5

Rivulets of water streamed down the outside of Bill's office window as if racing each other. Beyond, fogged by mist, a tall cedar hedge appeared smudged against the bleak horizon. Emma squinted to see the images clearer, but better vision didn't help.

Could she see through obstacles to set goals? They were as unclear as the trees across the street. Yet they were there—only weather conditions came between her and them. Her grief, uncertainties, empty plans, and sometimes lack of awareness held her captive. Would she have to ask her girls for financial support or worse yet move in with them? Emma had tested herself with these questions dozens of times, but she was still at a loss.

And now there were new queries regarding her future. How does she get a license? Would she have enough confidence to charge a fee for music lessons? And was starting a bookkeeping business a possibility?

Questions without answers swam in Emma's head as fish in a pond. Bill's pension was a bit of a mystery that needed to be solved. The insurance money was an issue. How would she apply for it, and how long would it take to come? Maybe she should write a note to the company. Funny, Mr. Henderson, their agent, had attended Bill's service and had not mentioned the policy.

People would introduce her as Bill's widow, and she'd have to meet their expectations if she continued to live in this town. But what if she struck out on her own? *It seems like it's you and me, God. You know the way, and I'm stumbling, trying to find it. Show me, please.*

Bill had found a source of strength and comfort in this room; perhaps she would, too. She walked around his desk, sat in his chair, and then placed her hands on the well-worn wood of his working space. It was here that he'd prepared for the following Sunday, funerals and teaching opportunities.

The recently cleaned surface didn't reflect Bill. He worked well in chaos and mess, but his presence had mirrored a refined appearance until lately. Various pictures, posters and lists stacked to one side begged acknowledgement. Notes of unfinished work on the side table added to the familiarity of Bill's effort. Inside the middle drawer, pens, notepaper, and pins lay in a heap. A few papers revealed nothing of importance.

Shifting her position, she opened the top right compartment and then the second. The third one exposed several boxes with mission cash and an offering from the Friday morning men's group. Mr. Tolt would be glad of all of this. He commented on how each penny helped.

She sifted through various envelopes until one with her name stuck out from the rest. Could it be a letter from Bill? It lay on a pile of what looked like receipts encircled with an elastic band. Perhaps he had left instructions to give the funds to a particular need. The writing on the note revealed an example of Bill's penmanship: immaculate and steady.

My dearest Emma,
You'll read this in the event of my death. We have said our goodbyes, and I am confident you'll put considerable thought into planning your future.
Please accept this money and use it as you see fit. It is not for the church. We gave it twenty years, and God blessed our offering. This humble present, my dear, is for you. I have gathered a little at a time and saved it here.

Emma held the stationery to her heart and, with the other hand, wiped tears from her eyes. This action was true to Bill's nature: preparation and protection. He'd found a way to continue his support of her. Lowering the page to see it fully, she continued to read:

As you will know, we don't have savings, and changes often happen without much notice. You may need to make plans quicker than you'd like. I hope I live a long while and you do not require these reserve funds. If this is the case, we can spend them in our old age.

However, since you are reading this letter, it means you are going on alone. I've added to this little pile every month so that you can be independent. This thinking will be different, but God has equipped you. Thank you for loving me all these years. I'll see you when your work is done here on earth.

Now, go and find your way. And do it with these gifts God has given you: faith, knowledge and preaching being three of countless others. In more than two decades of sharing life with you, I've seen God bless you with the Word, music, and pastoral care. They will sustain you in making a new beginning.

Love to you always, Bill.

Emma sobbed as she clutched the letter. She wiped her eyes and reflected on Bill putting away money to provide for her in this hour of need. *Thank you for protecting me.*

As daylight faded, she placed the letter in the drawer with the cash, notepaper and a calendar. Collecting old memos and scraps of paper used for bookmarks, she stuffed them into the wastepaper basket, already full to overflowing. "I must empty this and straighten my mess," Emma said aloud with untiring vigour. "The sooner I clean this area, the better."

Thunderbolts crashed one and then another. The afternoon was dull, and clouds covered the sky, dimming the room. This place would serve as Emma's goodbye. Pushing back her shoulders, she determined to finish organizing her thoughts as soon as she could manage. These finances encouraged her to consider new opportunities and possibilities. She had Bill's blessing. The words that inspired her during this challenging time were, *"You'll be fine, Emma. You are loved."*

She'd deposit Bill's gift in the bank. Lifting the mission contribution and the men's offering, she slid an elastic band around their edges and placed them beside Bill's envelope of money for her. She'd see to all this tomorrow.

THIRTY-THREE

A fresh breeze blew through the leaves as Emma strode along Noble's main street. She'd complete her business at the bank and then go to the furniture store to give Mr. Tolt the envelopes with money for the groups.

When she opened the heavy door, it occurred to her she hadn't been here. Bill had done the banking, and she hadn't given it much consideration. A few people nodded before she hesitated at the end of the line-up. Would the teller have Bill's account number and the information she needed?

When Emma's turn came, she moved forward. "Good morning, Ruth. Nice day it is after the rain." Relieved to see her at the wicket, Emma relaxed.

"Indeed, it is, Mrs. Taylor." Ruth pushed papers aside. "How are you doing? Getting along all right?"

"I'm learning something different daily, and banking is on the list today." Emma said.

"What can we do for you?"

"I have money in this envelope. I'd like to put it in our bank account—the one Bill used."

Ruth leaned in close to the wicket. "Do you have your bankbook with you?"

"No, I didn't bring it," Emma said. "Come to think of it, I'm not sure where it is."

"We'll need it to deposit the money."

"Of course." Emma wiped the perspiration from her forehead.

Ruth checked her filing system. "I'm sorry, Emma, but that account has been closed. This is normal procedure when someone dies. You wouldn't have been able to deposit or withdraw as it was in Bill's name."

"Oh!" Glancing back, it was easy to see that the line-up curved to the wall.

"What I can do for you this morning is open an account in your name," Ruth said with a sincere smile. "Would that be satisfactory?"

"Yes, thank you." Relief swelled through Emma. "What do I do?"

"I'll tend to it for you." Ruth pushed forms past the wicket and drew large x's on a few lines. "There we go. Sign where I've indicated. The number on your account is right here." She pointed to the spot with her pen. "And this is your bankbook. I'll enter today's transactions when we've finished."

"Thank you, Ruth." Emma pressed a hand to her chest. "This is all new to me. I'm afraid I'm not thinking straight."

"You're doing fine, Mrs. Taylor. Now, you said you had money to deposit?"

"Yes, I do." Emma fumbled, pulling out bills one at a time.

A familiar voice cut into her thoughts with abrupt certainty. "Are you all right, Emma? The line is getting long. Is there anything I can do for you?"

Emma observed the number of people in the line-up, her heart hammering. "Hello, Mr. Tolt." She yanked the rest of the bills out of the envelope. "I'm sorry to hold everybody up. I had my first lesson in banking, due to Ruth's kindness." Emma laid the bills on the counter in front of Ruth.

The frayed wrapper fluttered from her fingers onto the floor, and she bent to pick it up.

Mr. Tolt snatched it and scanned the words as he handed it back to her. "Doing church deposits, are you? You don't have to worry yourself. The stewards keep track."

"No." Emma shook her head. "This has nothing to do with them. Bill must have used an old envelope. He often did."

"I see." Mr. Tolt frowned and stretched to check her figures before moving into the line-up. Excusing himself to the first person, he said, "I'd better help Emma with her banking."

Ruth pushed a document under the window for a signature. Emma shielded the paper with one hand to keep Mr. Tolt from reading the amount and she signed with the other. Collecting her bankbook, she thanked Ruth for her assistance and shuffled from the line-up to tidy her handbag and secure her thoughts.

Mr. Tolt followed her. "Are you certain you don't need help, Emma?"

"No, thank you. I'm fine. Oh, there is another matter." Emma pulled two remaining envelopes from her purse. "I found these in Bill's desk. They contain money for a couple of groups. I planned to bring them to you later, but you can have them now."

Mr. Tolt glanced around the area and lowered his voice. "As I said, Emma, the stewards will look after the financial end of tidying Bill's affairs. You don't have to worry yourself concerning any of this."

Emma took a step back. "As Bill's wife, I read my husband's papers. If I find something directed to someone, then it is my duty to be sure he gets it. Now, do you want these envelopes, or shall I go to your furniture store later and leave them there?"

"I'm sorry, Emma." Mr. Tolt held out his hand. "You can give them to me now. You said there were two?"

"Yes." She lifted them into the air. "There are two."

"But you deposited funds from another envelope." He looked to the wicket where Ruth was now helping someone else. "Was there...well, is there anything I should attend to from that deposit?"

"No, I have everything under control." Heat flooded her face. "What my husband left for me is mine to do with what I choose."

Emma began to walk, but Mr. Tolt said, "I do apologize. I had no right to question your judgment of what you were doing with those funds."

"I was following Bill's instructions."

Mr. Tolt nodded. "If you say so. Good day, Emma."

With her head lowered, she walked past several people to the street. *The nerve of Mr. Tolt to underestimate me and be so public about it.* His doubt of her ability was not new to Emma. Bill had given the instructions, and she followed them. Two envelopes for the church and one for her. Was Mr. Tolt questioning Bill's integrity? Where would this lead?

The incident churned in Emma's mind with a mixture of embarrassment and regret. Those watching would surely understand she hadn't delayed them on purpose. Suddenly, she had no interest in window-shopping. How easily those words of condescension drained her confidence.

The sign, *'Thomas T. Tolt: Funerals & Furniture'* sat squarely in a semi-circle of grass. The letters needed painting. At the extreme right of the property, a lovely cottage with dark green shutters nestled beside a hedge of Forsythia. Although not in flower, its beauty in past years burst into spring with bright yellow colours. *Thank you for redeeming images.*

• • •

Completing more errands while on Main Street as planned didn't appeal to Emma as much as going home. What could have been a positive and celebrative step in her newly found independence had been suppressed by mistrust. Although unnerving at the time, she'd acted according to Bill's request, and she shouldn't have to apologize. After entering the house and shutting the door behind her, she opened her purse and pulled out her new bankbook. *Thank you, Bill. I'm grateful for your thoughtfulness.*

She switched on the stove and placed the kettle to boil. Fixing herself a cup of tea and eating one of Maisie's biscuits would clear her head. When her drink was ready, she carried it to the table, sank onto a chair and drank deeply. She turned to her notepad and wrote a long to-do list, then a shorter one for the group who had offered to pack.

She would explore Bill's insurance. The proper etiquette would be to go to Mr. Henderson's business, but not wanting to walk downtown again, a telephone call would suffice. She gave Lizzy the number. Within a few moments, a calm voice said, "Hello? Mr. Henderson, here."

"Yes, hello. It's Emma…Emma Taylor."

"How are you, Mrs. Taylor?" Mr. Henderson replied. "Are you keeping well?"

"I'm fine. Thank you for asking." Emma took a deep breath. "I'm putting Bill's financial records in order and decided to make an appointment to talk to you concerning his policy."

Intense silence filled the line.

"I'm…I'm sorry, Mrs. Taylor," he stammered. "There is no policy."

"Are you certain?" Emma sighed. "Bill made regular payments every three months."

"Perhaps he arranged for a policy with the other insurance office in town."

"No, I'm sure he would've done his business with you." Emma's knees weakened, and she sank onto a kitchen chair. "I...I came in myself several years ago and gave you a payment."

"You did that, but Bill cancelled his policy when the new company bought out the initial one, and he said...well, he said he couldn't afford the premiums. I'm sorry Emma, the file has been closed."

The words *the file has been closed* echoed in Emma's mind. She clutched the receiver to her ear. "Thank you, Mr. Henderson." Her voice broke. "Ahem. I apologize for bothering you."

"Not at all. Bill had a concern that the money from the policy might have to go toward any final expenses, and he didn't want you left without means."

The envelope! *Yes, Bill had even planned that.*

"I understand." She rubbed her forehead.

"So, are you saying everything is okay?" he asked. "Mr. Tolt was in here a while ago and mentioned that you were making deposits with church envelopes and, well...."

Emma twisted in the chair. She shouldn't need to defend her business at the bank. Mr. Tolt had formed a wrong impression. She quenched her anger and would revisit the unfairness of his actions at another time.

"I hope you straightened him out, Mr. Henderson," Emma said. "Mr. Tolt has a way of defining facts to give his own suspicions leverage. Be assured he received the envelopes Bill had instructed him to get. The remaining one that Mr. Tolt questioned had my name on it."

"I don't doubt you, Emma. I understand, totally. I thought I'd mention it."

"I'm glad you did. Thank you for your assistance. It appears I have unfinished business with Mr. Tolt. So, I'll go now. Good day."

Emma hung the receiver on the telephone's hook as tears fell on her cheeks. Mr. Henderson's words left her in a panic. Bill's funds must have been limited, and he couldn't afford the insurance payments, so he regularly put money in the envelope as he could manage. It must be so, but why hadn't he told her? And was this why the bank questioned Bill's partial deposit from his monthly salary? This dilemma was one problem solved.

An additional gnawing question kept probing Emma. Did Bill have a pension? He had referred to it once, but she'd never seen any paperwork from the treasurer.

Lifting the telephone receiver again to buzz the operator, she asked Lizzy to connect her with John. He had his financial facts foremost in his mind and would help her. On the third ring, he answered.

"Hello, John." Having to check on Bill's business troubled Emma. She didn't even like the sound of her voice. "It's Emma here, Emma Taylor. How are you?"

"I'm well, and you?"

"I keep working at getting all of Bill's paperwork tidied up. And that's why I'm calling. Did Bill have a pension?"

"No, I'm sorry. I wish I had better news for you. There has been a discussion, but nothing has been finalized."

"I guessed as much, but I decided to inquire."

"Is there anything else I can do for you?" John asked.

"Not today. And thanks for your information. I won't keep you any longer. Goodbye."

Emma put the telephone receiver back and sighed. "At least I know."

She walked into Bill's office, seeking to feel his closeness, but an empty room waited. *What'll I ever do without you? Sometimes I feel I'll wither and die.*

Emma sat at Bill's desk again and opened the side drawer. Her forehead wrinkled. Where was his letter? Pencils, erasers and stationery filled the area. Various pieces of paper still lay scattered. Bill's note wasn't anywhere to be seen. Desperate lunges under layers of documents disclosed nothing of interest.

Besides the message being proof the money belonged to her as a gift, she wept for losing the precious words of love and care. She peered into the garbage pail; grey metal faced her. She had taken the contents to the kitchen trash yesterday and burned it in the backyard bin.

THIRTY-FOUR

Emma studied Bill's picture. She'd brought it from the parlour to the kitchen table and placed it beside her tea. Taking her handkerchief from her apron pocket, she dabbed her eyes free of tears. Although Bill didn't delight in heart-language, he did his best. His private manner was protective in many ways. He constantly said, "Em, keep our business between us and God."

Is it just you and me now, God? Emma drank deeply from the cup and then placed it on its saucer. This dilemma of basic survival wasn't church business. It was hers, and it continued to require discussions and decisions.

Trusting Maisie with her personal problems seemed appropriate. Emma certainly couldn't go to anyone from the congregation. How easy it was to love Maisie as her friend and neighbour. Bill's voice resonated in her mind, *'You don't really know her well enough to share our information. If only she'd commit one way or another in terms of church attendance, it'd solve a lot for me.'* This was one counsel that Emma disagreed with Bill. She'd already begun sharing deeply with Maisie during the last few days. Her suggestions seemed extreme to what Emma had ever allowed herself to consider. Not feeling guilty anymore, the words, I'd do it again, filled her mind.

Emma lowered her head to her hands to think. Maisie was a tactful listener without judgement, and her honest response to different topics that Emma had introduced and dismissed was fair. These discussions were life-giving; without them, she wouldn't have a deep level of understanding of her dilemma. An abrupt noise caused her to stand and walk to the window.

Maisie dragged pieces of wood towards the street. Opening the back door, Emma said, "Hello. When you're free, come in for a cup of tea."

Maisie accepted the invitation, and within five minutes, she sat at Emma's table. "I removed the end of the veranda; it was so rotten. I hope someone can use it for firewood."

They discussed local events for a while, filling in time. Finally, Emma said, "Why do you think I'm hesitating from responding to a natural incentive to do something for me?"

Maisie was quiet for a moment. "Well, let's apply this thought: people still see you as Bill's wife and helpmate. And you don't want to change that, right?"

"I was careful not to influence Bill's ministry with my longings."

"Or by something you've always wanted to do, or have been called by God to do, but might seem contrary to other's opinions." Maisie paused as if thinking. "And also, you should stay in Bill's shadow and resist achieving anything through your own efforts?"

Maisie twisted her position in the chair. "And you were careful not to give Irene Trask any grist for the rumour mill?"

"It must seem to you like I'm well-practiced at doing the right thing, but I neglect to consider that was then and now is today." Emma sighed.

Maisie continued, "There is truth in this. You crave the openness to go to Brooke and lead that rally if the invitation comes again or do what needs to be done to bring home the bacon for you and Prissy."

"Oh, Maisie, you have such a grand way to explain situations." Emma's voice lightened.

"Whenever, and whatever you take on, you'll handle it with expertise and common sense, and everybody will benefit. Am I right?" Maisie leaned over the table, her hands flat on its surface. Not waiting for an answer, she persisted. "So, there you have it. You want to be counted as someone who can contribute to your well-being as well as others. You know what you don't want and what you do. I ask you again, why the hesitation?"

Silence. *Yes, I want to be counted and not feel guilty.*

Maisie tilted her head. "Well?"

Emma grinned. "When you put it that way—"

"Emma, there's no optional way. You are getting messages from God, colleagues, and now a friend. You have no choice."

Tears rushed to Emma's eyes; thankful she'd brought Maisie into complete confidence. "Then I'll pick myself up after tripping on my own feet." Emma hugged Maisie and then walked to the sink clutching both cups in her hands. "When we have time, maybe we can talk again."

"I'll look forward to that. In the meantime, I'll finish my job."

This exchange had been revealing. "Definitely all this awareness makes extra to process. Adding it to an already complex situation doesn't help."

"It will. You think about it, and we'll come back to the topic."

Maisie left, leaving Emma with a sense of hope. Deep conversation always did this for her, although today, she'd omitted Bill's opinion. Maybe it had to be like that. Was this a turning point in her life?

THIRTY-FIVE

Two women arrived the following day to help Emma fill boxes with items to take with her. As they worked, they moved from the kitchen to the cupboards along the hall and into Bill's office.

"Shall we bundle Bill's books for you, Emma?" Mrs. Allen, a faithful member, pointed to a shelf.

"Yes, if you have time." Emma picked up a large box. "You can put these items and papers in here, and then they'll be all together." She lifted a cardboard container and placed it on the desk before pointing to a row of hardbacks. "These will fit in here to go with me. I don't think it'll be too heavy."

Mrs. Howard turned a volume and examined the spine. "Why would you be interested in theology?"

"You never know what I might do in the next few years," Emma said, aware the statement was a risk.

"You'd have to have a minister's mind to read these." Mrs. Allen flipped through a bulky book.

"Yes, that'd help," Emma said.

Mrs. Howard walked alongside the certificates hanging on the wall. "My goodness, Reverend Taylor had a lot of these."

Emma deliberately stood beside her and took a deep breath. What would be the backlash if Emma told the truth? Would she be able to defend herself? Was it important to share this information and risk consequences? In a short time, she'd leave town, and diplomas wouldn't matter to these friends. But despite that, it'd be crucial for others to understand the story. After taking a deep breath and offering a short prayer, she said, "Those are mine. I brought them out and decided to hang them for the remaining period I'm in this house."

Mrs. Howard's eyes widened as she stared at Emma. "Yours? Why would you have certificates?"

"All students who graduate earn them."

"But women? How can a woman earn one?"

"By meeting course requirements, the same as the men." Emma squared off with her.

"But..." Mrs. Howard shook her head. "I'm confused. What would all of that have to do with you?"

Did Emma have the courage to continue this conversation? "Years ago, I attended a seminary." Her voice seemed too soft to participate in this discussion.

Mrs. Howard drew in a quick breath. "You did, Emma? A real one?" When she spoke again, her voice held a hint of sarcasm. "Minister's wives don't go to seminaries."

"This one did." Emma eyed Mrs. Howard, as if defending the young woman who had loved every class, welcomed a debate, and maybe most of all, researching and writing assignments with Bill.

"As a married woman, you went—" She pressed her hand to her chest. "Oh my, I don't believe it. And we didn't know any of this. What would the elders think?"

Emma raised her chin. Her discussion with Maisie must have been practice for this. "Would it have made any difference to you or the congregation?" Emma asked. "I worked beside all of you and my Bill."

"I'm not saying anything against your work with Reverend Taylor and the church. It's just that theology schooling, it's...it's something women, Christian women, don't do."

"I'm sorry to disappoint you, but this Christian woman did. And there was another godly Christian woman in my class as well. Particular groups of Christianity understood that John Wesley encouraged both men and women to study, preach and give leadership."

"Are you certain?" Mrs. Allen, who had been quietly listening to the dialogue, leaned in to consider a diploma behind the framed glass.

"Yes, I'm certain. At times, I wish I'd dared to share this when I served at Bill's side. But I chose to set my experience aside and support him as everyone expected."

"Well, I, for one, am glad we weren't aware of this, Emma. The elders might have spoken to Reverend Taylor regarding you taking as much part as you did." Mrs. Howard straightened.

"I doubt it. Sometimes the men-folk find it easier to make these adjustments."

"Well!" Mrs. Howard pressed her apron flat with both palms. "How many ladies were in this…this class?"

"Back in 1914, in Bill's denomination, St. Matthew's Theological Seminary admitted a woman preceding my years. That effort paved the way for the rest of us. Yes, to respond to your question, women answered God's call by studying, achieving and serving." She squared her shoulders. "There was a time when they were empowered to preach, teach and care for people."

"I never knew," Mrs. Allen whispered.

Emma relaxed as if honesty had lifted a ton of weight from her. "I wouldn't have hung these certificates at all, knowing they would bring difficult questions, except Maisie suggested I do—for a short time—for my personal pleasure. There's no harm in showing them now since I'm not your minister's wife anymore."

Mrs. Howard's eyes narrowed. "Maisie is, she is of that nature. She'd encourage you in something like this."

These two could chew away on Emma's achievements or failings all they wanted, but to imply that Maisie's character lacked integrity proved too much. Emma took a deep breath and said, "They look suitable hanging there. I believe I'll leave them until I go."

Emma had gone too far to hold back. Hearing her voice defend ministry and the woman who had encouraged her to be authentic by admission and visible proof warmed her heart. It did more than that. It created opportunity to lead the way for others to acknowledge God's invitation to minister, nurse or teach among other stations in their life.

"Maybe I ought to offer myself to a church."

Both stared at Emma in silence for a minute. She gulped. That forward-thinking plan embedded itself firmly in her mind by her own words.

Mrs. Howard elevated her hands in the air as if reaching for an answer. "Why, whatever would you do there?"

With this newly formed appreciation of inner courage, Emma surged forward. She met the other woman's gaze. "I'd minister in every way I was asked or given permission."

"But who would have you?" Mrs. Allen slowly pressed her fingers to her throat. "I mean, you're a woman."

Perhaps she asked this question to initiate a valid response hoping to understand the dilemma they'd opened. Emma took a deep breath and smiled. "Are you asking if a congregation would give me a chance? I can't be certain. All I can do is find a way to be available."

"I don't know of one church that would have a woman as their minister." Mrs. Howard's strong dismissive tone stung. She nodded once as if that closed the matter.

"My point is, I can try." With her finger, Emma slowly followed the bottom of one of her framed certificates. "These kinds of procedures take time. Sometimes we have to wait until new understandings are experienced."

"It's different for you. I mean, you have those papers from a seminary." Mrs. Allen's gentle nature encouraged Emma. "Whatever all of that means."

"You're correct." Emma conceded. "There was a period in our Christian history when women had freedom to preach. Levels of opportunity and leadership changed their participation, but that's in the past. This is 1935 and if I try, I might surprise myself and a few others as well."

"You have gumption, Emma Taylor," Mrs. Allen said. "It'd take more than I have."

"It's not gumption," Emma said, gently. "It's the Lord's call. There's a lot of difference. I'm not seeking ordination, but women ought to be free to accept the direction God is calling. They should be counted. Their voices should be heard." Her tone softened and slowly, she asked, "Don't you want the same for your daughters?"

Emma glanced to the door watching for Maisie to walk in. They'd discussed ministry, and she'd supported Emma in this new consideration and would stand beside her against all opposition.

Silence filled the room. The conversation had taken a severe turn, and coolness permeated the air as though someone had eased on a slow fan. The negative comments didn't discourage Emma, even though she'd shared this information with the worst audience in town. But her words were strong, confident and honest. It was enough.

"We've accomplished a great deal this afternoon. I'm very thankful for your help." Emma lifted the last box down from the desk. "Let's leave this for today. You'll have supper to get on the table."

As if Mr. Tolt hadn't stirred enough gossip, this interaction would keep people busy passing on the news over the next few weeks.

Had it been wise to have such a discussion? It could be of no benefit in minds without knowledge. Their resistance demonstrated an unwillingness to learn. All the reasons men were accepted emerged in Emma's memory. She had repeatedly heard them since her academic days. Her father had said as much thirty years ago, and professors had echoed similar truths. Parishioners also had the same advice. But scriptures surfaced and warmed her heart where women excelled in ministry.

Numerous congregations interpreted passages to mean they shouldn't teach men, preach, lead or speak in certain circles. Emma understood the culture, tradition and positions of power from which those statements were informed. The scripture was clear in these areas.

There were multiple examples in board minutes where committees had chosen men, and Emma encouraged that, knowing it was essential and expected. She respected male leaders, and she yearned to hear a woman teach the Word as well.

A favourite passage in the gospel of Luke reminded Emma that this face of God displayed courage and honesty. If a woman had several coins and lost one, would she not search for it? Of course! *We'd be that way in leadership. There'd be no troublesome attitudes and misgivings hiding in the corners.*

Emma had prayed, even cried out for understanding. God's encouragement resonated daily in her prayers. "Ah yes, we've lost many opportunities to minister, teach and preach through the years." Her phrase echoed in the room, so empty now that she was alone, although the awareness of Bill's absence seemed to transfer into energy to move onward.

The future could be different for her as she had savings in her bank account and many years of experience. Certificates proved her education, and obedience directed her to Jesus' great commandment to love God with her heart and mind and strength and love her neighbour as herself. This truth settled in her heart, motivating mission.

James' message about faith and works serving together coupled with fresh determination energized Emma. She loved the invitation to give sight to the blind, visit the prison, help the lame walk and free the oppressed. Would people accept her, a woman, to minister? She had her education, but would a pastoral relations committee call her? In the end, the decision wouldn't be hers. It'd be up to the church and probably men. Although, hopefully, it'd be in God's will.

THIRTY-SIX

Even though Emma had completed packing her assortment of boxes, there were still a few items in the attic. Several books and magazines that had brought her pleasure sat stacked on the floor. Perhaps she should remove them, so the space would be clean for the new family.

She made her way up the staircase, running her hand sideways on the broad oak banister. Opening the door to the left led to a landing with narrow steps to the attic. Winded, she dropped onto the stool to rest for a moment. She scanned the large area until she saw Mary Ann Moore's diary beside an empty cup. *I have more to ponder than I thought. What'll I do with her private writing? Will I take it with me? Would it be stealing? It isn't mine.* It had been there when she and Bill moved in. Maybe she needed to think about leaving it for others to read. Emma frowned. Somehow that didn't seem right.

She opened the dust jacket: a slight protrusion under the side flap, previously missed by her earlier curiosity, suddenly caught her attention. Hesitating, feeling as though she was intruding on privacy, she slipped her fingers deep under the cover and slid out a folded paper addressed to Mary Ann along with five one-hundred-dollar bills. A business card fluttered to the floor. Emma bent and picked it up: L.N. Reinhardt, Attorney at Law, Box 303, Bloor Street, Toronto, Ontario. *What's to be done now that I've found this?*

According to her notes, Mary Ann was an only child, and her clergy father had opposed further education. This money must be old family currency, because he wouldn't have had funds to give away in those years.

A piece of stationery lay folded in between the bills. She could not bear to abandon it unread, even as a heavy burden of guilt rested on her conscience. She unfolded the paper.

My dear Mary Ann,
I am sorry we have not been able to see one another during my challenging health problems. Your responsibility is first to your husband and daughter, and the miles between us are many. However, I have things I need to say. I'll write them in this letter as I do not know how much additional time my health will allow.

I have been remorseful about denying your request to gain further education when you graduated from high school, although as a woman, you might have found this difficult. I should have encouraged you to seek options. I was unable to think beyond my fears of the possibility of you marrying outside the church or moving from your mother and me. How foolish. I ask you to forgive me. We were happy when you married Walter. I had hoped your marriage and family would satisfy any vacuum left from missing the opportunity to attend college. Yet, I hear your pain within the words of your correspondence.

Secondly, if you have an opportunity to study, I'd like to give you this gift to fill the void you might feel due to being deprived of further learning in your early years. This does not in any way replace a future inheritance.

I love you.
Your father

Emma shook her head in disbelief. She had to decide concerning the diary and consider the letter and money. Thoughts of passing the envelopes to Mary Ann's cousins, aunts or uncles pressed her mind, but where were they? Would she have to donate the funds to the stewards? She'd found it on this property. Did it belong to the house like the second-hand furniture? Perhaps she'd call Mr. Tolt and ask his opinion, but he'd wonder if she'd given all of it to him. He'd use it to pay for the supply ministers he'd called during Bill's illness. The money was an offering. But what do you do with an offering if you have no place or person to receive it?

The business card indicated that someone else was aware of this situation. She'd write to Mr. Reinhardt today.

Emma flipped each page of the diary and slowly read:

"If you find this diary–you are to keep it.
It is not to be given away.
It now belongs to you–whoever you are.
Because you are the one reading this,
knowing will give you peace.
If you gain strength from my words,
they are gifts to you because you understand them.
As for the money, it's meant to enrich the mind.
Use it wisely, be grateful for those who believe one needs
to be inspired through verse, prose and informative topics."

Well, there it was. From across the years, Mary Ann had given the book to Emma as well as the money. Could she achieve what Mary Ann had left undone—to be an inspiration to herself and others with verse, prose and informative subjects?

Regardless of Emma's decision for her future, did she need to include Bill in the big picture? Should the steps in her plan reflect him in some way? In considering Mary Ann's gifts as Emma was the next person to read the diary, her choices would naturally mirror wisdom that surfaced during that time. Yet, did the options that surfaced in her mind make the statement of being happy to leave her present life to focus on a new future? Yes, but!

What a dilemma she found herself in.

Mary Ann had given Emma a challenge, and she had the opportunity to accept it? The money, letter and verse were incentives for Emma to go forward. She reread the prose to see if she'd missed anything.

After long consideration, Emma emotionally and physically received Mary Ann's gifts. Now to assess possibilities to use them to contribute to the world on her behalf. Emma needed to further Mary Ann's call so that this venture would reveal her love for scripture. These gifts were given with trust. Emma's accumulation of treasures remained visible as she added to them. So many results, some opening portals to new beginnings, the rest firmly closing the entrance into the past.

Prissy raced through the attic doorway and jumped onto Emma's lap. The cat purred herself to sleep; the consistent rhythm expressed contentment. Many thoughts stressed Emma's mind until they quieted too.

THIRTY-SEVEN
PART 6

On Emma's final day in the parsonage, she sauntered around the rooms. It wasn't her home any longer; the removal of her items left a different appearance.

Once the Larsons moved in, happiness and generosity would continue. Emma wrote a welcome note, placed it in her favourite china teacup and set it in the middle of the oak dining table.

She had meticulously cleaned, scrubbed and dusted each level of the old house. Everything shone; even the staircase had been freshly oiled and polished. Relieved and exhausted, she vacated, feeling she was handing over a much-loved gift. Carrying Prissy, Emma walked across the driveway to her neighbour's house.

There wasn't a rental space available in town, so Emma had accepted Maisie's invitation to move in with her and since she didn't have a car, there was room for Bill's in her lane. Maisie's house would be a perfect location, a protected environment to consider the next step. Prissy would adjust easily as Maisie's voice was familiar from her frequent visits. As well, the cat could often be found sleeping in the sun on Maisie's porch or drinking water or milk there. This house also reflected a safe place to grieve Bill's death and a secure haven for settling into the status of widowhood. Widows had an elevated position in scripture reflecting care, but Emma was happy Bill didn't have brothers. Didn't the Word have something to say about remarrying?

From the window of her bedroom, she observed the committee arrive with their crew at the parsonage. Stewards and church ladies appeared with mops and brooms, scurrying like ants covering an anthill. Their mission of preparing for the new minister seemed to drive and excite them. Emma prayed for energy to finish their task. It didn't surprise her that they were there for an hour and had obviously completed the deed.

• • •

The following day, Emma sat on the back veranda enjoying a second cup of tea when someone backed a large truck in the driveway. A car followed, and all four doors opened at the same time.

A tall man with a broad smile got out the passenger side and raised a hand in Emma's direction. "Good morning." A deep voice sang into the air. "I'm Reverend Larson. Brian, to my neighbours, and this is my wife, Jane. These are our children, Jason and Christine." Jane shut the driver's door and waved at Emma. She returned the greeting, thinking how friendly the introduction sounded. She warmed to Jane, standing taller than her husband.

"Hello," Emma called back. "I'm Emma Taylor, and this is Maisie Turner's house. She'll be out in a few minutes to greet you."

"It's nice to see you again so soon, Mrs. Taylor," the reverend said. "I recall you from the church service. I see your move proved successful. We appreciate all you've done to make our transition comfortable and speedy."

Maisie's musical tone of voice preceded her as she pushed open the screen. "Did someone call me?" Looking toward the new family, she continued, "Welcome neighbours. It's wonderful to see all of you."

"Pleased to meet you again." Reverend Larson waved in acknowledgement. "Hope we don't clutter the driveway too much with bicycles, hockey nets and baseball bats. You never know what you'll have to step on or maybe trip over in our driveway."

Maisie laughed. "That reminds me of my family years ago. It'll be fine. Don't worry."

Emma sighed. Maisie would fortify the Larsons with tea biscuits and hot casseroles during their busy days. And she'd defend them when people chewed a fresh chunk of gossip. Yes, she'd be like a guard dog. She'd offer the same depth of friendship to the Larsons as she had to Emma and Bill. The sun came out from behind a cloud as if God gave a blessing on the beginning of Maisie's bond with the Larson family.

• • •

Emma walked beside the garden to the back veranda. The birds played in the cedars as they flew in and out between the branches. Flowers attractively lined a border at the edge of the lawn, and ferns poked between the boards of the wooden rails, some probably reaching for sunshine. Rustic hinges and pastel-coloured plants decorated the attractive window boxes that had already become familiar to Emma. Red buds floating in a sparkling bowl of water on the small lunch table had attracted a butterfly that continually flited in and around the blossoms. The intricate crocheted edge on the bright red tablecloth showed Maisie's handiwork. The entire scene provided a delightful place for conversation amidst nature's best.

"And happy-today to you. We missed the July 1st celebrations, so we'll have our own." Maisie's cheerful voice filled the space as she carried a tray of muffins with white crumbled candies tucked into red icing. "Imagine the country throwing a party for you in light of your decisions."

Emma winced. "That's nice of them especially since I haven't figured out my tomorrows at this point. But I'm sure the sun will come up in the morning."

Maisie arranged the tray on the table. "Give yourself credit. You've sorted and packed boxes, claimed ideas of what might work for you, dismissed a few and made plans. That's progress."

"Okay." Emma smiled. "I agree with you. My heart is still heavy with grief, but in the middle of that, I try to be pleasant. There are days I succeed better than others."

"There you go. You're recovering, so that's something to celebrate." Maisie unfolded a serviette. "Deep sorrow changes a person forever. It's the price for loving. You'll find comfort in figuring out what's normal for you when the time is right." She wiped icing off her fingers with a moist dishcloth. "It's important to decide what is vital, what you need to settle yourself without Bill. But that will come."

She lifted the teapot and poured tea into Emma's cup. "Are you regularly writing your notes? You know—your activities and feelings? Journaling deepens your thoughts. Gets rid of lots of confusion from here," Maisie pointed to her forehead, "and puts it on paper, so your mind can interpret it."

"I do my best." Emma took a sip and set the cup on its saucer. "And speaking of writing, what should I do with Mary Ann Moore's diary? Does it belong to the parsonage? Do I put it back where I found it?"

"You could." Maisie pulled out the chair across from Emma. "Maybe Mrs. Larson will get comfort from it. It's not like Mary Ann is here to give you direction."

Emma squirmed in her seat. "Well, in one way, she did that."

"Indeed! How?"

"She wrote a poem," Emma said. "She stated that the diary belonged to the first person who read it. Since we were the next family to occupy the house, I suppose that means me. The cleaning crew between Mary Ann's departure and our arrival hadn't bothered to move the pile of books in which her journal was sitting."

Maisie removed her eyeglasses. "There's no question then, is there?"

"But that's not all," Emma said, twisting her hands together. "A letter from her father and money he'd sent in 1923 were both in the diary."

"1923? And she didn't spend it or take it with her?" Maisie froze with her teacup halfway to her mouth. Frowning, she placed the cup on the table. "Did grief win over, and she forgot, maybe left it by mistake?"

"That crossed my mind. The poem clarified that the money and the diary were to go to the next person who read it. Mary Ann must have hoped it would be important to the reader and that he or she would gain strength from it. It seemed her situation should help someone else, as she'd also left her father's letter as a further explanation to the state of her affairs."

Emma took a deep breath and continued, "She tucked the business card of a Toronto lawyer into the book probably hoping this would serve as guidance. I wrote to him, but he hasn't replied. I hope he will before I leave. I prayed and then brought it all with me. If Mary Ann wanted this reader to have the diary and the money, it seemed easier this way than going to the Larsons and requesting it."

"Seems fair, Emma." Maisie ran a finger around the rim of the teacup. "I can see you've spent a long time thinking. But it's cut and dried as far as I'm concerned, so why are you fretting?"

"I feel guilty," Emma said. "What if the lawyer writes and says the diary needs to stay with the house?"

"Then you go to the parsonage with it and say, 'This belongs in your attic.' But that won't happen because it would contradict what you've told me."

"Maisie, you can make a problem seem like an opportunity." Emma clasped her friend's hand. "And that's what this is."

"If it feels right to you after prayer, don't fight it. It's actually honouring Mary Ann."

"It is. Yet, I'd still feel better if the lawyer wrote to me." Emma sat back in her chair. "Do you ever feel there's more to your beliefs than your understanding?" She poured honey on a muffin.

"At my age, shouldn't I have it all figured out? Faith and God and all the rest?" Maisie winked at Emma. "Doesn't wisdom come with maturity?"

Emma set the jar beside the sugar bowl. "How old do you think a person has to be before they get this wisdom?"

"I suppose there are many ways to gain it. When you reflect on your decisions and actions and learn how to identify them in your life, you are getting close. Or, when you realize you're thinking differently from the way you used to, that might be a hint. Thoughts will fit with what you're planning, or they'll create a challenge," Maisie said. "Then, you're getting near."

"So, a person wins both ways?"

Emma connected with Maisie's ability to think past the unexpected and remain open-minded as they were the same age and shared similar understandings. Maisie wasn't afraid to search out new dimensions of faith and experience. Her appreciation of freedom was evident, and Emma pursued that kind of sincerity.

THIRTY-EIGHT

Going to the Post Office to get the mail was first on Emma's list this morning. There would be 'Thinking of you' postcards and a few letters. Sure enough, Mr. Arnold, the postmaster, handed her a bundle. Warm tears blurred her vision. People in town occupied her thoughts as she put their greetings in her purse and continued her errands.

Emma rounded the drugstore corner and almost bumped into Rosie Ryan. She walked with her head lowered, sliding pennies one by one across the palm of her hand.

"Hello, Rosie, are you walking to school?"

"Not today." Rosie counted slowly with her index finger.

"Do you have a note for Mrs. Olen?"

"Nope, I don't need one." Rosie frowned.

"It's always a good idea to give a reason for your absence. That way, your teacher doesn't think you're skipping."

"I'll get one next time. I promise."

Emma tilted her head. "Mrs. Olen won't be happy."

"Momma's sick. I'm staying home with her."

"And are you going to get her something with your pennies?" Emma asked.

"Yes, I want to buy pain pills."

Emma asked, "Can I help?"

"Yes, Mrs. Taylor." Rosie showed her money. "Do I have enough for a small bottle?"

"Not quite. But I do." Emma directed Rosie. "Let's go in." The few coins in her pocket felt heavy.

After buying the medication, they came out into a warmer day. Emma lifted her hand to her eyes to give shade from the sun. She studied Rosie, happy the Ryans had such a capable daughter who could help. Living in the Hills wasn't easy for anybody, and Rosie assisted in her own way.

"Would you like me to go with you to see your momma, Rosie?" Emma asked.

"No, Ma'am. I'll be fine. And so will she." Rosie raised the bottle. "And if her mig…migraine headache goes away, then I'll go to school." She ran along the road toward the Hills with her precious bag and hollered back, "Thank you, Mrs. Taylor, and Momma thanks you too."

Emma waved. Such a determined girl deserved encouragement.

Although Mrs. Ryan wasn't on the church visiting list, Emma made a mental note to drop by. She wouldn't disturb her, but if she was still suffering, Emma would call Doc Baxter. He could go to the house and settle her. If there was an extra cost, Emma would cover it.

• • •

Cleaning the kitchen and sweeping the floor took Emma an hour. She decided to visit Mrs. Ryan to see if the pills had helped. But first, she crossed the street and entered the Dime Store, the bell chimed above her. A rubber boot scent drifted in the air, but it wasn't as strong as the irresistible homemade caramel bars fresh from Mrs. Bowman's candy-maker. She priced those treats too high, and even as they pleased Emma's taste buds, she moved directly to the counter.

"Good morning, Mrs. Taylor." Mrs. Bowman's distinct voice filtered from behind a stack of containers.

"It's a nice day to be out," Emma replied, looking for the owner.

"I'm glad you think so." Mrs. Bowman's agitated words echoed one by one into the air. "What can I do for you?"

A tall, slim woman scowled under dark, wide eyebrows. Her cheeks mirrored polished apples as she came from behind the counter and towered above Emma. As the proprietor, Mrs. Bowman ran this business with ease, thinking she knew what her customers wanted.

"With this weather, you'll still be needing seeds for your garden."

Mrs. Bowman was an ambitious salesman, but she had a reputation for sending merchandise home with people they hadn't planned to purchase. Her intentions demanded the customer's attention.

Emma chuckled. "I might need them, but I'd like yarn today."

"What are you knitting? I have lovely bright colours. They came in yesterday." Mrs. Bowman walked behind the counter and lifted a few skeins. "Is this for you?"

"I'm taking one to Louise Ryan. She'll be running low on her supplies." Emma slid her fingers through the fibre and nodded. "I like this mauve. It'll make into bibs, leggings or whatever else she chooses."

Emma set the yarn aside and then touched the coins in her pocket. Would she have enough?

"Only one ball?" Mrs. Bowman sounded disappointed. "Maybe she could use smaller skeins for lap rugs."

"This is kind of you. But, if she requires more, I'll tell her where I bought it. I only came in for this." Emma remained firm. Mrs. Bowman often seemed to have difficulty understanding that customers knew what they wanted.

"I know you persuaded her to enter knitting and crocheting in the fall fair." Mrs. Bowman wrapped the purchase.

"And she sold her items for a profit. All of this helps in this economic slump."

Handing the paper parcel to Emma, Mrs. Bowman said, "How in this world do you keep in step with everybody? It's not like Mrs. Ryan will ever support you or anybody else, and here you are spending money on her."

This topic was not a favourite one from Mrs. Bowman's perspective. Emma sighed as she accepted the package. "It doesn't hurt to be kind to someone."

"Sorry to say, I haven't found much kindness in the church. My daddy made me go on Sundays, so I think I've had enough for a lifetime."

This subject was one Mrs. Bowman always chose to challenge Emma. "Even in public school, we learned, 'do unto others as you would have them do unto you.'" Emma pushed the parcel under her arm. That was the deepest she'd go into a faith discussion.

"Do you find that in scripture?" Mrs. Bowman responded quickly.

"I do. It's helpful to keep the verse handy in my mind."

"So, you do all this kind stuff around the town, so you'll get caring deeds done to you." Mrs. Bowman sniffed and put her handkerchief to her nose.

"That's not a bad idea." Emma grinned. "But no, I don't go looking for ways to help. It happens. Besides, the congregation accepts my support, and I assist as much as I can." She slipped the soft package into her purse on top of the cards.

Mrs. Bowman piled the remaining colours into an attractive circle. "Thank you for your business, Mrs. Taylor."

Emma walked toward the door. "You aid people too. Keep up the good work."

"I try." She moved away from Emma and proceeded to speak. "I guess you'll be thinking my daddy's church impacted me."

"Something's working." Surprised that Mrs. Bowman began another conversation, Emma paused.

"I don't appreciate you giving them credit for anything I do. If that were so, this town would support me rather than going to Hampton to buy goods. Besides, I give because I want to…and when I want to."

The scripture of being created to do good works that God prepared in advance passed through Emma's mind.

"Thank you for coming to Bill's funeral. It was kind of you. And to close your store for the day—well, I was touched."

"I wanted to mention him but didn't know if I should. He was an honourable man and will be missed."

Before the day was over, Mrs. Bowman would have helped a half dozen people, as well as those who didn't need it. It was a blessing to see God's grace surpassing difficult situations. Emma was uneasy with the direction her discussion had taken but relieved it ended up on a positive note. At times, Mrs. Bowman seemed bent on being hard on herself and Emma.

THIRTY-NINE

Ryans' cottage was on a back street at the edge of town, tucked behind a cedar tree. A quaint sign, *Welcome to our Home,* hung a little crooked, as did the open gate in front of a lilac bush. Like other buildings in the Hills, the residence needed painting, but Mrs. Ryan's flowers offset that condition. Emma glanced at her watch as she strode along the dusty path to deliver the yarn. Over the last few months, she'd kept a strict schedule and still often became caught up in it.

Relaxed, she stepped up to the Ryans' front entrance and knocked. No one answered. She tried again—still nothing. The blue curtains gathered tightly on the window were not inviting. She opened the door a crack and set her package inside on the floor. Rosie would find it later and give it to her mother, and she'd have something to take her mind off her worries. Besides, she'd have extra supplies to knit for the fall fair.

Jed Ryan sat on an old chair, content and disinterested. He'd tipped it backwards touching a wide board leaning against the house while he tinkered with a small engine. After he drew on the cigar, he kept the smoke in his mouth for a few seconds before blowing it in circles into the air.

Emma braved a conversation. "Nice day, Mr. Ryan." She hadn't had much opportunity to speak to the men in the Hills, except for one or two who occasionally came to the House Church. Finding ways to greet those who didn't attend was also a ministry.

"It is that Mrs. Taylor." He examined his cigar stub and tapped the end.

Where did he get money to buy his smokes? Before she could say anything more, she caught a glimpse of a dark-coloured bottle under the front of the chair. These situations caused Bill to ask her not to go 'wandering around the Hills'. Too much drinking, fighting and arguing involving countless men was his complaint.

Without looking at Emma, Mr. Ryan dropped his cigar on the ground and twisted his shoe over the hot embers. "Sorry to hear about Reverend Taylor. He was a good man. Offered me a quarter when he gave me a ride into town a while back."

Emma turned to look at him. "Yes, he was much loved." Not acknowledging the rest of his statement, she cleared her throat. "It was bad news to hear that the factory closed its metal-plating floor." She waited for Mr. Ryan to respond, but he rocked his chair on the two legs. She continued, "I understand you didn't get much notice. That must have been difficult. You've worked there for years?"

"Ten, Ma'am."

He didn't lift his head, just kept rocking. Louise Ryan must be handy on the scissors as well as the knitting needles considering Mr. Ryan's neatly trimmed hair laying loose in waves over his neckline. A crease in his dark blue work pants and plaid shirt gave him a tidy appearance. Somehow, poverty seemed contradictory for him. What was his family like, and how had he been raised?

"It doesn't seem fair." Was that an acceptable reply? Nothing must seem reasonable to him on any level.

He didn't respond, only kept turning an unlit cigar. Emma didn't want to loiter when she was on an empty street while the afternoon was getting late. Yet, she couldn't walk away and end their conversation, so she said, "Do you think there'll be further layoffs at the factory?"

"Yes, Ma'am." His curt response didn't offer information.

"I'm sorry. It must make it hard for you and the men."

"It does." He leaned forward on his chair, and it slammed on all four legs.

Emma drew in a deep breath and quickly added, "I left Mrs. Ryan a ball of yarn inside the front door."

"Thank you, Ma'am. She'll appreciate that." He studied her as if he expected her to say something. "I wondered if you came to complain about the disorderly behaviour the boys caused last night."

"No, Mr. Ryan. I didn't hear of such. Was anybody hurt?"

"Not that I know of. They have too much on their minds, and in their worrying, they take comfort in their cider."

"I'm sorry for their burdens." It sounded like Jed Ryan hadn't been involved in the conflict. What words could she offer to support him? "If we can assist in any way, please do not hesitate to tell me."

He stood and stuck his thumb into his front pocket. The short man who possibly felt discounted by his status didn't say anything. At least he didn't appear to be dismissing her, but perhaps, in his understanding, it was appropriate to stand because she was leaving.

"We care for everybody in the community." Emma stepped back. "We are here to help."

"Funny, I never thought of the church that way. I figured all they wanted was money."

"I can't deny that available funds keep it equipped to serve. But it's the serving that reminds us we are doing the Lord's will."

"Is that so?" He scuffed the dirt with the toe of his shoe. "I don't think I knew that."

Was Mr. Ryan finished speaking? It seemed he had something else to say; possibly Emma could coax it out of him. "If anybody in your community could benefit from our support, let us know. The church is not the building as much as it is the people." She hesitated. "If we know about others' needs then we can plan ways to meet them."

Mr. Ryan didn't seem to want to say anymore, so Emma left the topic. "It's time for me to go into town. I'm pleased we had this opportunity to chat." A movement caught her attention. Had the curtain shifted? If Mrs. Ryan had observed their conversation, surely, she wouldn't be offended. "I hope I see you again. Perhaps you will attend the House Church discussions."

"Perhaps."

"You'd be welcome."

"Good day, Ma'am." Mr. Ryan sat again and prepared to light his cigar.

As Emma paused at the street, he said, "Heard about the O'Neils?"

"This is the Roman Catholic family? Percy O'Neil?"

"Yeh, that's them."

"I did hear of their tragedy." Three generations lived in a relatively compact house, and they were not well known. "The ladies are wondering how to assist them."

"Their back kitchen, where they had the wood stove, caught fire and took the whole half of the house."

"I'm sorry. They didn't need that."

"They moved in with their neighbour, but it's crowded." Mr. Ryan's voice cracked. "They're building on a room."

"We've made ongoing plans to see what is needed. Pass this message on. It might comfort them through these days to understand we care."

"I'll tell them." He glanced at Emma and then said. "Thanks for your concern. I appreciate this. I mean, it's important to know someone cares."

Emma walked into town with peace flowing from every breath. Mr. Ryan appeared not to mind her words regarding the church, the House Church, or the Lord.

It was not Emma's routine to visit with men. That had been Bill's interest, and he did this kind of outreach well. And true to his nature, he had visited Mr. Ryan, and he remembered it, which showed how much he valued Bill's care. As her conversation took place outside and not in a familiar way, anyone who regarded or heard of the incident could not find fault.

FORTY

First Church in Noble constantly stretched the congregation to contribute, serve and be involved. This year was no different with so much activity in the community.

"I'm done in." Emma reached into a deep windowsill in the fellowship hall to grab her purse.

Maisie stuck her arm into the sleeve of her coat. "You and me both. I'm relieved when busy times come and go."

"Me too. So glad to have you here."

Irene Trask pushed the door open. "Here's where the two of you are. Couldn't find you anywhere."

"Just tidying up. We've been cleaning all the cracks and corners from recent use," Emma said.

"I'm relieved to locate you, Mrs. Taylor. Mrs. Olen has been looking for you. The school's spring concert is on her mind, and she wants to talk to you." Irene wrung her hands together as if she was washing them.

"It's that time. There's been so much going on, I completely forgot."

"You can't do that, Mrs. Taylor." Irene settled her hands on her hips. "Mrs. Olen has counted on you for ten years to make that concert happen."

Maisie faced Irene. "Maybe she won't expect Emma to do it this year with everything she's been through."

"She will. Nobody's told her any different."

"I'll call her tomorrow." Emma pulled on her coat. "She'll understand."

"Mrs. Taylor, I'd hate to prepare a nice variety of food for the box social and not have an attractive container. As I said, you've done that concert for a decade. The attendance will be high because of your organizational skills as much as the shared talent. She wouldn't ask somebody else for fear of hurting you and disappointing the crowd."

"Don't you worry, Irene. She'll understand my situation differs from previous years." Emma reached for the switch and cut the kitchen lights.

"But…but nobody knows Susanne's talents as you do. I want her to have the lead in the community drama, and she's also prepared to play a lovely piano solo for Mrs. Olen's school concert."

Emma took a few steps. "Susanne is a competent musician, and I'll look forward to this as well. However, I'm not sure she's emotionally ready. Lately, she appears nervous especially with the open page in front of her." Did that come from practicing at home with her mother's help?

"There'd be no reason she couldn't have her book. I turn the pages for her, so she doesn't have to worry. Nothing says a student has to memorize her music." Irene nodded as if coaxing a positive response from Emma.

"She seems such a happy child when she's away from the piano, but she's changed. She becomes quiet and withdrawn at the keyboard." Emma didn't like mentioning Susanne. If her mother pondered this, she could be helpful to her daughter.

Irene frowned. "Why, I haven't seen her act this way at all. I stand over her when she practices, tap my toe, and tell her when she makes mistakes. She does what she's told, and I'm happy."

Emma closed the kitchen door and walked to the outside entrance. Maisie and Irene followed until Irene stopped. "If you encourage her, Mrs. Taylor, she'll play. All I'm asking is that she has a chance."

There is nothing wrong with wanting the child to have an opportunity. However, would Susanne prefer a different way of preparation and performance?

• • •

Early the following day, before Emma poured her first cup of coffee, Maisie's telephone jangled. Emma said, "Good morning. Emma Taylor speaking."

"I'm so glad I caught you before you began your daily routine."

"You did. I haven't had my breakfast yet."

"It's Mrs. Olen speaking. I'm sure you figured that out."

Emma sighed. How was she going to tell Mrs. Olen that this year was too difficult to take on something else? But perhaps she was phoning to say she'd already arranged for another leader.

"Yes, Mrs. Olen, what can I do for you this morning?"

"Nobody told me you'd moved, and I bothered the new minster to get this number. I'm calling about the concert and hoping you'll continue in the tradition of taking the lead in organizing it."

"Thank you for thinking of me. I've done it for a considerable time; perhaps someone else might like to take over."

"I'm sorry to hear you say that, Mrs. Taylor. I really count on you. The students love you, and they're looking forward to rehearsing with you. I'd have called you earlier, but with Reverend Taylor's death and everything, you must have been exhausted." She gave another long sigh. "By the way, how are you doing? I think of you often."

"Thank you for your words."

Mrs. Olen coughed. "I didn't realize Reverend Taylor's heart condition was that serious."

"Any kind of heart condition can be critical, and especially when it happens to someone as young as Bill."

"I see, well, er, everything has changed a lot for you." Mrs. Olen cleared her throat as if she was holding back tears.

"I'm afraid it has. Since I've moved, I'm trying to find my way in the thicket of life."

"I'll reconsider your commitment, Mrs. Taylor." Her voice was thick sounding disappointed.

"I'd appreciate that. And, if you'd accept a reduced obligation, I'd be glad to assist in a less pressured area."

Silence and then Mrs. Olen almost exploded. "I knew you'd rise to my invitation. You know what they say, 'the show must go on.'" Mrs. Olen tittered. "I'm so relieved. I'll let you go for now. If you could come into the school later today, we can record those who signed the participation sheet. And by the way, I'm waiting to hear Susanne play at her upcoming recital at the church. I'm sure much credit is due to you."

"Not really. She did the organizing, selection of melodies, and the posters. She is an exceptional student. All the rest of us have to do is show up."

What had she consented to achieve for the school's spring concert? The list was the first step to putting it together, so nothing had changed. Reflecting on what Mrs. Olen said, Emma decided the woman hadn't heard the words *a lesser obligation*.

• • •

Emma knocked on Mrs. Olen's door, and she opened it wide. "Thank you for coming over. This shows the importance you place on this event. It is a brilliant celebration of talent, and the whole town loves it."

Piles of papers stacked across the desk next to brightly painted signs exposed open appointment books. Mrs. Olen's organization for the special occasion had begun.

"You're welcome. I'm happy to get the concert started, but as I said earlier, a lesser—"

"We can arrange that, but for the moment, we should check the list." Mrs. Olen pulled a chair out from a desk before going to the opposite side. "And then there are auditions and, of course, the program sheets. From there, we go into the rehearsal and then the concert." She clapped her hands. "It'll be a wonderful event once again this year."

Although Mrs. Olen hadn't invited Emma to sit, the teacher had placed the empty chair there for that reason. A rap behind Emma caused her to turn. Two pupils stood in the doorway.

"Goodness." Mrs. Olen raised her hands. "So eager these students are for a part in the concert. Come in, come in, girls."

They marched into the room, looking as though they'd received a first prize red ribbon.

"We're not ready for the auditions if that's why you've come. But since you're here, we can listen."

They spun around like they were standing on a top. The dark-haired one, Barbara, came forward. "I can recite poetry, and Victoria will sing."

"Is that true, Victoria?" Mrs. Olen asked the tallest girl.

"Oh, yes, it truly is." She folded her hands in front of her waist as if ready to begin.

"I hope this is all right with you, Emma. These two are so eager to be on the program." Mrs. Olen made a sweeping gesture with her hand.

On cue, Barbara recited a poem with precise enunciation and phrasing. When she finished, she curtsied and stepped back.

"Well done." This girl was talented, and Emma would give her a vote with a level of unveiled appreciation.

"And now, Victoria, are you ready to sing?" Mrs. Olen asked.

"Yes, Ma'am, I am."

The young girl took a deep breath and sang a melody in a minor key. Emma hadn't heard anything so beautiful from a twelve-year-old! This performance would unquestionably top its category.

"Thank you, Victoria. We'll call you when we have finished our auditions and written the list." Mrs. Olen ushered the contestants into the hall. "Don't either of you worry, you did exceptionally well."

They chattered to each other as they left, and Mrs. Olen closed the door.

"That is eagerness if I've ever seen it. We'll have no problem getting a roster. I want to set tomorrow afternoon for auditions if that is acceptable to you.

Emma should immediately correct the extent of her involvement but listening to this talent begged a serious commitment. She'd restrain her activity somehow and keep ample time open to continue her plans. Her heart swelled as boys and girls excelled in their talents and school activities. Victoria and Barbara from the Mission Circle proved they'd carried on their interests. This school event was such a grand occasion to encourage the youth to use their God-given gifts.

"I'll do the first hour of the audition, and I'll ask someone to monitor the second half. I have several young ladies in mind, and I'll introduce them to the process of putting this concert together. Would that be all right?" With permission, she decided to ask Mrs. Ryan if she'd assist. Her management skills would fit Mrs. Olen's needs, and the school would have another volunteer.

That would show both the competitors and those Emma directed into leadership that this was an excellent opportunity for youth to develop expertise.

"Emma. I do hope this participation doesn't tire you. You've been through a lot over the last while." Mrs. Olen extended her arm to touch Emma's shoulder.

"I'll take it easy, and with help, I'll be fine."

The annual concert was a key occasion. It was probably the most popular free entertainment in the town, and people supported it both by their attendance and a few coins in the hat placed on the table at the front entrance. Perhaps an essential and long-standing gift Emma could give to this enterprise would be to staff it with willing and accountable volunteers, so they'd be well-trained to carry on next year.

FORTY-ONE

Boys and girls waited to audition. Susanne Trask was third in the line-up. When it came to her turn, she walked to the front of the stage and announced her selection and composer. After sitting on the piano bench, she placed her fingers on the keys and gave an exceptional performance, bringing tears to Emma's eyes.

"Thank you, Susanne," Emma said. "You played that as nicely as I've ever heard. We'll be in touch as soon as we decide." It was suitable for those competing to go through a waiting period toward acceptance.

Belle, who had attended Emma's Mission Circle, was next with her artwork. She hung three sections of cardboard across the stage and told a consistent story from one piece to another. Her articulation was perfect as she enunciated each syllable with accuracy. Emma was proud to have had a part in her coming-of-age process in such an effective way. Those Saturday mornings around the table had built Belle's confidence as she debated her position.

The first hour of songs, readings and two skits led Emma to introduce Mrs. Ryan as the judge for the second group of auditions. She stepped forward, wearing a tweed skirt and a mauve knitted sweater. Mrs. Olen welcomed the idea of a young woman interested in the process.

"I'll go now, ladies, as I have to do a few errands." Emma waved her hand.

"Thank you, Mrs. Taylor." Mrs. Olen's eyes were bright with moisture. "This has been a positive afternoon so far, and I'm sure the second half will be suitable."

Emma recognized the yarn in Mrs. Ryan's pullover as the identical colour Emma had left inside the house a while back. She must have gone to the Dime store to purchase additional skeins, and Mrs. Bowman had probably given her a couple. It couldn't get any better than this.

• • •

Preparing the program went well. There were no questionable choices as an appropriate number auditioned to perform. Emma had kept her distance from much of the work and managed daily to continue her planning process.

The night of the concert arrived despite a disastrous rehearsal that sent stories up and down school aisles. Anticipation and trepidation stilled the air as Emma and Mrs. Ryan met with the participants in the lunchroom.

Belle scowled. "Did you hear what happened last night—absolutely dreadful."

"I thought it was kind of funny." Rosie giggled. "Especially when the curtain fell on the piano, covering it and Susanne."

"That's a surprise. I knew that a light bulb exploded, and a fuse blew, plus short tempers, tears, and I figured patience got lost in the crowd." Emma snickered.

"Ah, Mrs. Taylor. I didn't mind. There was me and the keyboard in the dark." Susanne giggled.

"Let's be thankful all of that was at rehearsal, leaving the recital to proceed without problems."

Emma had heard the account from Mrs. Olen but didn't feel guilty about not committing her evening. Besides, Mrs. Ryan had identified the events of the rehearsal but didn't seem upset.

Susanne stepped close to Emma. "I'm so happy. I'm looking forward to playing my solo. If you could talk to Momma, I'd be pleased. She, well, she makes me nervous when she stares at me, and worse still when she turns the pages. Sometimes I don't know whether to look at my hands, my music or her frowning face."

"I'm sorry, Susanne, I wasn't mindful she was so critical of you. I'll speak to her, don't worry."

Emma considered the big wooden clock on the wall. "It's ten minutes to seven, and I'd like to pray with all of you before the concert."

The assembly quieted as Emma's strong voice filled the area. Ending with her well-used conclusion, she said, "And all God's children said...." A prayerful amen echoed across the group.

There was no doubt in Emma's mind that Irene enjoyed a notable place in the evening's event. Emma watched for her and explained how Susanne's training prepared her for this three-minute solo performance without a page-turner. Although it seemed to hurt Irene's pride that she wouldn't be assisting, it was the only way to make the point that the recital was about Susanne.

When the speaker introduced her, Susanne went to the piano as planned and began her selection without her book. She played the piece with confidence and started the repeat in perfect timing. Suddenly, Mrs. Trask marched in, ready to take part. She must have climbed the rear entrance and slipped behind the curtain. Emma's heart fluttered as Susanne's face turned from pleasure to disappointment.

Mrs. Trask frowned as she considered the front of the piano and then glanced to Susanne, perhaps looking for the book. She faltered, stopped, and began again, only to blunder several bars. Finally, she crossed her arms on the keyboard and bent over them. Her shoulders shook. Irene reached toward Susanne, she drew away from her mother's touch, pushed the piano seat aside and ran out the back of the stage.

The master of ceremonies rose to his feet and immediately announced the following number: a skit of four young boys who, within minutes, had the audience roaring in laughter.

• • •

Emma quickly hurried down the steps and found Susanne at her locker, crying. She cuddled close as Emma wrapped her in a hug. "I'm so sorry, Susanne. So sorry. She surprised me, too. I spoke to her, but obviously she didn't heed my advice."

"I hate her." Sobs came fast and hard.

"Aw, Susanne. Don't say that. Your mother loves you, and she was only trying to help."

Susanne stopped crying and stared at Emma. Then she began to cry again. "I know. I love her, but I want her to let me be me." She pulled away and wiped her cheeks with her hands. "I knew that song so well, but when she marched out from behind the piano, I lost control and wanted to let her have all the attention. That's what she wants, you know."

"And yes, I realize that." Emma gave Susanne an extra hug. "Come on now. Let's go to our lunch. Your mom didn't appear until the final repeat, so the audience heard you play the whole song through once. And they'll be waiting to tell you what a genius you are at the keyboard."

"But I stormed out of there like I was being chased. I'm so embarrassed."

Emma put her arm around Susanne. How true. When Irene got a bee in her bonnet, she chased everybody. Running was a familiar image to keep ahead of her. Emma had done a bit of it.

As they swayed back and forth, Susanne sighed and then shuddered.

"Think back to the day when Mr. Tolt came into the Mission Circle. It was Rosie's birthday," Emma whispered.

"Yeah—and it was your birthday, too."

"And do you recall Mr. Tolt taking the heater?"

"Hmm, I do," Susanne said.

"We could have dwelt on that incident, but there was a greater matter. And what was it?"

"We wanted to describe our African village to Reverend Taylor during mission-time in the church service."

"Why was that?"

This softly spoken conversation had become like a bedtime story as Emma held Susanne.

"We wanted the women and children to be counted."

"And were they?"

"Oh yes, all of them." Susanne drew back.

"Do you think you were counted tonight?"

"I do, Mrs. Taylor. It was in print. I was number three on the program."

"Indeed, you were. It's important to find ways God remembers you, names you and lights the path on which you walk. Even if something goes awry in a situation, you'll see God's hand of guidance leading you through to the other side."

Susanne hugged Emma. "Let's go to lunch, Mrs. Taylor."

"Let's do that," Emma responded.

They walked into the fellowship hall, where school students served refreshments to those sitting around small tables, enjoying themselves. Suddenly Susanne was circled by individuals congratulating her. Several friends had cards for her. A child lifted a balloon with the words, *Fly High*! scrolled in red paint across its surface. Susanne giggled and bent for a hug. She was counted, and she had overcome.

FORTY-TWO

Emma lifted the telephone receiver to hear Mrs. Howard's voice. "Emma, is it? How are you? Feeling settled in with Maisie? Maybe you'll stay with her for a while?"

Not knowing which question to answer, Emma chose the last one. "For a while. Lovely day we're having."

"Isn't it, though?" The sound of paper crinkled noisily in the receiver. "Going through my lists. I'm calling to invite you and Maisie to a potluck supper on Friday in the fellowship hall for 5:00 sharp. It's a welcome party for the Larsons."

"Thank you. I'll tell her. It sounds like it'll be a grand event." Emma closed the conversation with a few words and then said goodbye.

When Maisie brought the laundry into the kitchen on her way to the washing machine, Emma raised a hand to stop her. "There's a potluck for the Larsons at the church on Friday night. Such a nice opportunity for the congregation to meet them. What do you think we should take?"

"Your macaroni salad would be a perfect contribution, and I'll make a tomato and lettuce arrangement fresh from the garden. Or should we practice Lizzy's stew?"

"That'd be dangerous ground." Emma laughed. "I remember this same supper when Bill and I arrived—it was a grand experience for us." She placed a hand on her heart. "But this is the first social event that I'll go alone."

"And what am I? Invisible?"

Emma grinned. "You are funny," she said. "Okay, we'll go together."

•••

The fellowship hall adorned with coloured tissue trimmings appeared welcoming. Flowered tablecloths boasted sweet pea and snapdragon centrepieces.

"Very nice," Emma said.

"Irene must have decorated using her favourite trim." Maisie untangled two twisted streamers. "The ladies have been busy."

"Girls, I'm glad you're here," Mrs. Brown, the song leader, said. "Let me take your bowls. Terrible disappointment—we find we have no pianist. We were counting on a volunteer to play. Could you…would you accompany us, Mrs. Taylor?"

"Why yes, I can try," Emma handed her the macaroni salad she'd made that afternoon. "Anything in particular?"

"Wait until I take these dishes to the kitchen, and I'll get the sheet music. You can familiarize yourself with it while everyone settles."

This chance to rehearse would work, as Emma wasn't aware of entertainment the committee had planned.

When Mrs. Brown came back, a frown furrowed her brow. "Sorry, Emma. I've examined the cupboards, but I can't find the song. And the choir wrote special words for the Larsons. My, My! You'll be able to follow along, right? You're exceptional at playing the piano."

Her expectations were high and this choir that strove for perfection now looked to Emma to lead them through their contribution to First's welcome. "I hope I can play to your satisfaction." Emma took a deep breath.

People entered the room and gravitated to the minister and his family. The congregation had rallied well following their shock of Bill's death. The folks still loved him, but the church had a new beginning, and today's event would launch it.

"Emma, we're ready." Mrs. Brown waved her to the piano. Emma nodded and walked to the instrument as she had done in the past.

Sitting on the bench, she waited for the leader's instruction. Was she going to say what key to play their song?

"Emma, would you give us an introduction, please?" Mrs. Brown asked.

"Can you hum a few notes of the tune, so I can catch the rhythm," Emma whispered so others couldn't hear. "I need to hear a few bars."

Mrs. Brown moved closer. "I'm sorry, Emma. This has put you in a difficult position. The song goes like this: La la-la-la-la-la. It's repetitive. You'll grasp the timing quickly once we begin."

Emma held curved fingers above the keyboard. "And what key do you think it's in?"

"Let me see." Mrs. Brown hummed a little melody. "Try G. and if I shake my head, then drop it down to F key."

Emma struck the G major chord, did a few arpeggios taking in several octaves. She slipped grace notes between the chords with corresponding minor sevenths and glanced at the choir. They waited with wide eyes and mouths slightly open as if an angel wing had brushed them.

Mrs. Brown began to sing the lyrics. The rest of the voices joined her. Emma caught the song's rhythm and within a few bars, accompanied the choristers with great delight. When they concluded, enthusiastic applause filled the room.

"Thank you," Mrs. Brown said to the gathered group. "And a special thanks to Mrs. Taylor as she stepped in at the last minute when we didn't have a pianist. We've enjoyed her music for a long time, and tonight, without notice, she shared her talents and blessed us."

Again, clapping filled the area. Emma trembled. In all the years she and Bill had served this church, few had pointed her out as making a significant contribution. Pleased she'd had this experience to tuck into her Noble memories, Emma raised her hands to join the clapping. Mrs. Brown had given a gift in her gratitude.

Mr. Tolt came to the front and gave a lengthy speech highlighting Reverend Larson's virtues, and applauding followed. Mrs. Brown handed Mrs. Larson a bouquet and introduced Jason and Christine. The children waved.

"Would you give us a few words, Reverend Larson? I'm sure the folks would appreciate hearing from you," Mr. Tolt asked.

Reverend Larson walked in front of the packed fellowship hall, an excellent form of a man with broad shoulders and a pleasant smile. His dark blue suit and white shirt fit well, and his tie took on a pleasing sheen.

"I brought a quote of Robert Frost's with me that I'd like to read to you. You can tell me if any of it applies to this congregation. 'Half the world is composed of those who have something to say and can't, and the remaining half has nothing to say and keeps on saying it.'" A long pause suggested that the reverend was finished speaking, but then he broke the silence and added, "You'll find out soon enough which you favour."

The crowd burst out in laughter. Emma hadn't heard them sound so amused. The reverend took a deep breath and began to share further.

"Ministers can get on the wrong side of congregations. Sometimes we say what they don't want to hear. Or perhaps they're waiting for us to speak to their heart in a certain way, and we miss the invitation. I hope I say a few words in the next several years in a particular way to you. Maybe you're in the portion of the world who has words to say and can't or won't. I promise you before my time is complete in Noble, you'll be speaking a mile a minute."

Again, a great ovation spread across the room like a tidal wave of fresh water. Those in attendance chuckled and nodded to one another; they appeared to enjoy Reverend Larson's manner. Could Emma's remaining interval with the church produce a long-overdue wonder? *I may be in the half of the world with something to say but haven't realized how to do it yet.*

"We share ministry, folks. Our tradition has been to honour the gifts God has given our laypeople, male and female alike." Reverend Larson viewed everyone.

Emma sat straighter and listened. The congregation would not sway him. Bill, and those before him, provided an excellent foundation for Reverend Larson to continue ministry.

The words, 'It is finished,' passed gently through Emma's thoughts.

Knowing this gives me the certainty that our ministry is complete in this place. Strange, it's the new minister who facilitates this grace. I'll begin to plan and tell Maisie tomorrow.

The men had placed long boards, covered with sheets, along both walls, so all the participants had to do was carry their chairs to place them and pick up a plate. The ladies brought the food to the front table that they'd attractively decorated with the produce from their gardens. There were three stews tonight, with sandwiches and buns. Emma and Maisie set their salad bowls amid the dishes, all of them different.

Emma contemplated the hot options as she walked along beside the table. Did Lizzy bring a stew? Yes, that one appeared to be her container with chunks of meat and vegetables. Using a ladle, Emma lifted the ingredients onto her plate and added salad before including a bun from the basket. Taking a seat between Susanne and Irene, the discussion on the school year was well on its way. Irene had obviously come to terms with Nancy's choice of education, as she mentioned nothing to Emma.

After swallowing a spoonful of stew, Emma paused. *There it is again. Perhaps a nut or…a spice? What is it? Pumpkin? Cinnamon and nutmeg?* Using her spoon to make diagrams through the stew, she noticed tiny black cloves among the ingredients. Emma glanced at the buffet where leaves, paper pumpkins and vegetables created a fitting centrepiece. That had to be it: pork, veggies, spices and pumpkin with broth. Yes! Who would put those items together but Lizzy?

Emma craved leaving the party to go home and try the new recipe. But she'd have to wait. For the time being, she'd enjoy Lizzy's, as it might be her last chance.

FORTY-THREE

In the next week, excitement heightened as individuals anticipated Susanne's first recital. She had practiced an extensive selection of music to perfection and decided to offer it. Jack had meticulously tuned the piano in preparation for this day.

Irene Trask brought colourful flowers for the windowsills and placed several planters of ferns at the front. She'd sewn bouquets of strawflowers for each pew and hung them with delicate lace. Maisie carried four candles and would light them at the end of the recital, as Susanne's final song was a lullaby.

The news spread. No one had offered a performance in the decade Emma had lived in Noble. People attended in high numbers, both from curiosity and for encouragement.

"Look, Maisie. It's exactly 6:30." Emma said as they waited. "The program should last forty minutes, so the stewards will be happy we don't have to use the lights."

Emma leaned to one side to get a clear view of Susanne as she moved to the instrument with confidence. Her ankle-length pink dress fit perfectly, emphasizing puffed sleeves in a lighter colour that matched the bodice. A necklace twinkled, much like her eyes. Silver clips held her curls in place. She appeared relaxed, maybe knowing her mother was sitting with the rest of the guests promised an evening without embarrassing surprises.

Susanne bowed and then sat on the piano stool; the folds of her skirt cascaded to the floor. She stared at the wooden grain of the upper panel, probably to focus her thinking. After placing her hands on the keyboard, the sounds of a lyrical sonata with precise phrasing and intonation filled the church. Each piece won applause, and too soon, Susanne announced her final choice.

Maisie went forward and lit the candles at the front as sunlight dimmed. She whispered to Emma upon returning to the pew. "Perfect timing."

The enchanting melody stilled the sanctuary, and Susanne's light, and distinct arpeggios resembled a gentle waterfall.

When she finished, she stood beside the piano, faced the audience and curtsied. The crowd rose to their feet and applauded. A few calls of "Bravo" resounded from the back. Susanne thanked her guests for coming and then said, "I want to acknowledge my mother for being the best page-turner any pianist would want. She did it so well it enabled me to memorize, for which I am grateful." Again, an applause swept through the space, and Irene took a bow. "She is also to be recognized for the petite arrangements on each pew. And the table centrepieces in the fellowship hall are Mother's designs as well." Again, the applause echoed across the sanctuary.

"Would Mrs. Taylor and Mrs. Watson come forward?" The two of them flanked Susanne as a new wave of clapping swept around them.

"I could not have played for you tonight without the dedication of these music teachers." She hugged Mrs. Watson and then placed her fingers on Emma's elbow. "They not only arranged for this recital, but I understand they have baked five cakes and put the kettle on for all of you to have tea." She nodded to Emma. "Mrs. Taylor, would you give thanks for this night and ask God's blessing on our lunch and time together." Susanne turned to the audience, "Following this, you can go directly from here to the tables in the hall."

Emma drew closer to stand with Susanne after Mrs. Watson returned to her seat. It took confidence to speak to a crowd…and Susanne had done it.

"We are thrilled to have attended your first recital, Susanne, and I hope you'll plan one next year. We have not had such a grand night out since…since I can't recall." Emma prayed heart-warming words and then invited everybody to refreshments. People shuffled out of their pews, sharing conversation.

Emma hurried towards the back stairs to enter the hall and be present when everyone entered. To her surprise, she almost bumped into Mr. Tolt, rushing up from one step to another.

"Such a crowd. Didn't want to miss the chance. I went to get the collection plates." He gasped as he said the words. "The ushers left them in the Sunday school room where they counted the morning's contributions." His face darkened in the dim staircase.

"The concert is over. I have already asked for God's blessing on the food," Emma said.

"But—we need to take an offering."

"Why would we do that? The recital was free."

"Nothing is free in this world, Mrs. Taylor." He began to retreat down the stairs.

"Mr. Tolt," Emma spoke into the unlit staircase, knowing he hadn't yet reached the last step. "The offering this afternoon was Susanne's talent…a God-given gift. And I believe the audience received it with gratitude."

Mr. Tolt grumbled to himself as he opened the bottom door to the hum of voices presenting welcoming sounds.

The ushers had given Susanne a favour by leaving the plates. Emma proceeded to the fellowship hall thinking; *there's something to be thankful for in every situation.*

She lifted the tops off the round containers and poured boiling water into teapots. The cups and saucers were already on the tables, and as people filed in, the chatter and laughter carried a high level of excitement.

Mr. Tolt stood at the end of the table, still waiting for the offering. How long was he going to stand there? He's showing his intentions, not the hospitality of the congregation.

Sitting on a tall holder, a white candle burned above the surrounding rectangular cakes. "Susanne, please come and blow this out." Emma waved her over. "Next year, you'll have two tapers, and maybe when you finish school, you'll need bigger baking pans."

She blew out the flame as the onlookers cheered and applauded. Tears filled her eyes as she hugged Emma. "This makes me so happy. And to think all we needed was to get our piano tuned, so I'd listen to my notes better. This is the best night ever."

Later, Emma walked through the building to check the rooms, acknowledging how the light from the candles reflected Christ's hope and love. To provide the place and opportunity for someone to share talents had to be one of the finest gifts a church could offer.

FORTY-FOUR

Emma sauntered downtown on a bright morning, thinking she'd select a present for Maisie. She didn't want for anything, but to receive a keepsake she wouldn't purchase for herself would give added pleasure. She had refused to take a penny for room or board, and this gift would show Emma's appreciation.

As she neared the corner, she stopped and looked at Mr. Tolt's Packard parked in front of the drug store. She was thankful she didn't have to go in, not wanting to make conversation. As she walked past the entrance, he rushed out with a small bag. Medication? Did he ever need help? Especially medicinal?

"Good morning, Mr. Tolt," Emma said. "It's a nice day."

"That it is, Mrs. Taylor. Are you keeping well?" Mr. Tolt touched his fingers to the brim of his hat. "Happy with Maisie, I hear. She's been a worthy friend to you."

Emma nodded. "It's been pleasant for both of us."

Mr. Tolt opened the car door and placed his package on the front seat before turning to Emma. "I've been meaning to speak to you. Do you have a minute?"

Was he going to invite her to sit in his automobile? He closed the big door. She nodded. "Of course."

It appeared as if he would lean against the car then reconsidered. After snatching his hat off his head, he gripped the brim.

"It's my remark. My distasteful comment I said to you in the bank a while back." He flicked an imaginary speck from his jacket, his eyes not meeting hers. "It wasn't meant to insinuate you were keeping money aside for yourself. I mean, if Bill left you an envelope with funds in it, then it's yours to do with whatever you like. I had no right to question your actions."

"Thank you for sharing those words, Mr. Tolt. I recall your comment and apology, but it did leave me wondering if you believed I'd confiscated funds."

"It has bothered me that you might have taken it that way."

"I can prove it," Emma said. "Bill left currency in an envelope telling me it was mine and that I didn't owe it to the church." Although there had been correspondence, Mr. Tolt didn't have to know she'd lost it.

"Indeed!" Mr. Tolt's head jerked. "I hope he didn't think that anyone would question you."

"Perhaps," Emma replied, making a mental note to set the letter aside when she found it. "Stranger things have happened to widows."

"There is no call to prove anything, Emma. Bill was a wise man. He always paid his debts, and he would have provided for you." Mr. Tolt bowed his head and sighed. "We could all see that."

"Thank you. I'm glad we had these few minutes to talk to each other. It'll make the rest of my preparation much easier."

"Speaking of that, I imagine it's been quite a task." He peered at her. "Have you found a place to settle?"

"No, not yet." That was enough to tell him. She wasn't going to say anymore. The town didn't need to learn her intentions. If the ladies' side of their previous conversation concerning Emma's diplomas produced public attention, it would undoubtedly create a heated discussion.

Mr. Tolt rotated his hat by the brim before placing it back on his head. "I'm sure you'll do well in whatever you decide. God's blessings on you."

There they were—words of reconciliation. Surprised at how easily Mr. Tolt talked to her, she said, "I appreciate your kindness. I trust you and Mrs. Tolt will keep well." She would store his comments in her memory as she moved into her new life.

• • •

The gift shop door had seen better days. Strips of old paint hung loosely on the panels, and the latch sounded as though it needed oil.

"Hello, Doris." Emma walked to the counter.

"Why Emma Taylor, I'll be. I haven't seen you for a while."

Emma loved to hear someone speak her first name. "I rarely buy presents. I used to bake, knit or sew and put a ribbon on it, but I don't have my home now. Besides, I want something special for Maisie. She welcomed me to her house on short notice and has made me comfortable."

"We have several nice options. Are you looking for a particular item?"

"Yes, I had an angel on my mind," Emma said.

"Then I have just the one for you." Doris reached to a high shelf and lifted a figure. Its luminous silk gown fell layered under pale pink wings raised upward in devotion.

"It's beautiful." Emma clasped her hands. "And Maisie doesn't have one." She rotated the gift. "I'm afraid to ask how much it is."

"I've been waiting to take you something," Doris said. "So, I'll sell you this at my cost, which will save you a dollar or so, and it'll also allow me an opportunity to give you a parting present."

"Thank you. Times are hard for all of us, Doris, and I think you're a good businesswoman to make an agreement." Emma set her purse on the counter and opened the clasp. "They should have you on the steward board at the church. You might save them a few dollars."

"If the men ever invite women to share that responsibility, I'll be first in line."

Doris wrapped the angel in light paper. Emma checked her coins and placed them on the counter. With a cheerful goodbye, she left the store to make her way to Maisie's house.

• • •

Emma walked to the back door and heard groans coming from the area of the flowerbed. "Hi, Maisie. Are you ready for a break?"

"Always." She replied as she straightened to face Emma. "You put the kettle on, and I'll be with you as soon as I can make my way out of these flowers."

Emma nudged her purchase toward the edge of the table. From behind, Maisie kicked off her garden shoes at the door.

After pouring the tea, Emma sat and looked directly across the table. "Maisie, I can't show you enough gratitude for all you've done for me." Emma laid her hand over her friend's fingers. "And I'm grateful you coaxed, pushed and pulled the truth out of my head and heart."

Maisie studied her for a moment as if considering how to respond. Emma continued. "We had an amazing time together. I've enjoyed our conversations. We talked into the night, slept to the last acceptable hour in the morning, and we drank a lot of tea at this table. We listened to the birds in the day and the crickets in the evening."

"I hope you're writing this down, so you'll remember me with favour." Maisie giggled.

"I have fond memories," Emma said. "You don't have rules, and it's been such a nice place to relax, reflect and look ahead. I don't think I'd have considered a future had I not spent these weeks with you. But the time has come for me to make decisions how to go on in my life." She chuckled. "People talk about me going, leaving, or moving, showing me that they believe in me. I've decided to step forward although not sure to where, but at least I can begin to set goals and lay out my plans. As I gain self-assurance in this process, I'll add to it until I'm content with the choices I've made."

"That is good to hear. I sense you have a few options playing on your mind and heart. I can see you've begun that in your concentration." Maisie paused and slowly said, "And Emma, it's been my pleasure to have your company."

"You gave me food, tea and the odd apple pie, and you've strengthened my confidence, for which I am grateful." With that, Emma placed the gift in front of Maisie. "This is for you."

"Ah, Emma." Tears slid down Maisie's cheeks as she pulled the paper to reveal the beautiful statue. "I'll cherish it forever."

Emma grinned. "I was waiting for you to say, 'Oh, you shouldn't have.'"

"I've learned a lot from you, Emma. You don't like those one-liners." Maisie turned the angel. "She is exquisite." She touched the porcelain cheek with one finger. "I absolutely love her. I'll think of you with gratitude, and she'll sit in a distinct place." Maisie leaned to hug Emma.

"Now, I have a gift for you, since this seems to be the proper time." Maisie slid a copy of *The Church to You* from under a pile of papers. "I give you this knowing that you'll read this magazine with interest and perhaps choose an advertisement to apply for a ministry position."

She raised the palm of her hand to face Emma. "Now let me finish. There's a list on the last few pages giving names of churches seeking leadership. It'll come to you monthly so mail me your address when you're settled. I hope you'll find it meaningful during the next few years. There are excellent articles. They'll take you past the ordinary—get you thinking of new ways."

"Thank you, Maisie." Emma took the periodical and positioned it over her heart. Reverend Maitland's remarks instantly brushed her memory, 'Watch the advertisements and when you find your feet, tell them you have something to offer.'

"You're right. I'll read objectively, and hopefully I will see something that interests me. But, with this direction, it'll be special." She hugged her faithful friend expressing gratitude for the generous and appropriate gift as well as the encouragement she'd been in her life.

Later that evening, as Emma stood at her bedroom window and stared across the driveway at the old house, waves of sorrow flashed through her mind. She swallowed and took a deep breath. That was then, and this is now. Maisie had said, "Perhaps choose a church and apply to be their minister." Could she do that? Emma wiped her eyes.

FORTY-FIVE

Thunder rolled through the darkness as if chasing the lightning that slashed the sky and illuminated corners of Emma's bedroom.

Stretching, she yawned, contemplating her situation. As the rain fell to give creation moisture and new growth, Emma admitted missing personal renewal opportunities. It wasn't that God had avoided her. There were times she had turned a deaf ear to the Spirit's leading. Emma had stagnated, stood stuck in her tracks, without knowing how to change. As long as she and Bill had done their best for the people they served, they'd been happy. But it wasn't the case now. She must go on alone. It was comforting to accept that God hadn't forgotten her. She would listen carefully to the still, small voice.

No pension. No insurance policy. The ladies' conversation echoed in Emma's mind. "But what church would have you?" And from the other side of the room, "What would our elders have thought?" Irene's disgust of Nancy wanting to study theology, "as if the church wanted women," continually resonated in Emma's awareness.

The reluctant sun hid behind dark threatening clouds similar to her confidence. Could it benefit Emma if she considered the future longer before spending the time planning? *God, walk with me on this blurred journey. Protect me from well-meaning guidance that does not reflect your plan for me.* Urgency showed even in her relationship with God.

Tears fell on Emma's hands. Balanced with prayer, the imaginary wall of resistance still heightened, and the path crowded with weeds and thorns. Emma's life wasn't much different than Mary Ann's. They were both widows. Both had to leave their homes without financial backing, except for what a beloved individual gave them. Neither one was emotionally confident nor prepared for what circumstances forced.

Emma didn't hear Bill's chipper voice in her memory, 'Keep your chin up, Em.' Did she have more to figure out? She'd completed the necessary tasks of moving from the parsonage to Maisie's house. But this refuge was only for a short period. And then, where? Defeat filled her being. Negative remarks echoed in her memory.

Why was she feeling uneasy? She hadn't done anything wrong—not like denying God. But at times, she'd directed her energy totally to Bill's ministry, ahead of her interests. She wasn't sorry for doing that. It had been her place to support him, and she did that well. Now, it was her opportunity to step into a new role. Who would stand with her? This situation provided an opening to make changes rather than turn in on herself and lament her predicament. Did she have the faith to move forward?

Consider a day, Emma. One day.

Living with Maisie had opened Emma's eyes to possibilities. Promises she'd made to herself and the plans she needed to persevere played in her memory. She'd prayed long into the night and again at the break of day for guidance. Peace saturated the morning's laments. She sighed. "I'll serve willingly."

• • •

Emma padded down the hall in her favourite slippers. Maisie had the coffee ready, and Emma poured a cup before sitting at the kitchen table to make a list of options. When she finished, she pulled Maisie's magazine gift towards her and flipped through it.

Today, she'd prepare an application to see who, if anyone, would interview a woman with her credentials. Feelings of relief and tempered excitement swept across Emma's mind.

The category *Pulpit Vacancies* intrigued Emma. One boasted a large adjoining house. No, she wouldn't apply there. Another post stated information describing a pastoral charge with three congregations, which would be too much of a challenge.

Several advertisements invited applicants to contact the secretary of the church board. Perhaps she'd write to them to determine their interest. Mailing one at a time beginning today would work. Doing it that way wouldn't arouse Mr. Arnold's curiosity. Although the post office clerk was knowledgeable, did he enjoy gossip?

Should she use her initials, E. F. Taylor, in her application? That might appear impressive, but they would need to decide if they wanted a woman, and they wouldn't be able to tell from the signature. Over the hour, she crafted four applications with letters of introduction. After placing them in addressed envelopes, she sealed and tucked them in her sweater pocket. She'd mail one as soon as she went downtown.

• • •

Later in the day, she rode her bicycle to the Vehicle License office. Townspeople and rural residents gathered in Mr. Polin's renovated sunroom to begin the process and arrange their driving test. Lots of her friends in town drove without a permit, but Emma wanted to do this the right way. Mr. Polin came out from behind the curtain and invited Emma to come forward. A heavy scent of cigar smoke filled the air, took her breath away and caused her to cough.

"Well, good day to you, Mrs. Taylor," he said. "How can I help you?"

Emma leaned against the counter. "Do you have information about getting a permit to drive?"

"The one wanting to drive is expected to make the application himself."

"I understand," Emma said. "It's for me. I'm the one applying."

Mr. Polin's eyes widened. "Are you not getting lots of offers when you wish to go somewhere? My goodness, remembering everything Reverend Taylor did for us, I'd think folks would line up to be available to you."

"No, it's not that." Emma said. "Friends have been gracious. But I won't be able to lean on them forever. I must fend for myself. Besides, I'm not sure what the future holds, and I wouldn't want to ask strangers."

"Now, Mrs. Taylor." Mr. Polin frowned. "We hope you'll stay in our midst. We like having you here."

"Thank you," Emma said, shifting from one foot to the other, "but can you tell me what I have to do to get a license to drive?"

"If you have your mind made up, we can go ahead. You know, few ladies in town have taken this step. They'll wonder why you need to."

"I can only imagine." Emma sighed.

Mr. Polin led her through the process. He gave her a booklet to study the rules of the road. She'd take a driver's test with Bill's car; if she didn't pass the first time, she could apply again. Now, that was grace. Emma liked second chances.

She thanked Mr. Polin, began to leave and stopped in front of Mr. Tolt.

"Excuse me." She started to walk around him.

He attempted to stop her. "I can't help but wonder what you're doing in this place, Mrs. Taylor. Collecting something for someone? Times are hard; it's helpful to run errands for friends."

Why does he sound so annoyed when he uses my name? "I couldn't agree with you more." Emma slipped by him and went out the door to the street.

Here was another topic for him to discuss with others. Mr. Tolt would ask Mr. Polin what she had been doing here, suggesting that he had her best interests at heart. And, like a spark in a dry forest, it took only one to start a raging fire.

• • •

Emma climbed the steps to the post office to mail her first letter. Feeling optimistic about filling out the license application, plus outdoing Mr. Tolt, charged her courage. If she didn't need help, she'd have used the outside box. But she was here, so she'd make the best of it.

"Good afternoon, Mrs. Taylor. Great day we're having." Mr. Arnold's selection of neckties was popular. Today it was cats; Prissy would enjoy that. People playfully waited in the café to discuss the colour or image he'd charm his customers with on any given day. The prize was a free cup of coffee.

"And hello, Arnie." She set her envelope on the counter. "Is this going to cost me three cents?"

"That's right, Mrs. Taylor." Mr. Arnold reached for it, surprising her as she'd have finished the task. It didn't matter much as he'd have to use his official imprint.

"Now who would you know in Owen Sound? Catching up with a 42nd cousin, are you?" He placed the stamp in the corner of the envelope.

"Could say that I guess." If the church is family, then that was an accurate response. "Will you put it in the bin for me?"

"I certainly will. Now don't you worry. It might take at least a couple of weeks. I hope you find everyone well."

"Thank you, Arnie. You have a nice day."

If that was an example of how he watched who mailed what and to whom, there was no way she could keep her plan confidential. Emma planned to collect Bill's medical records for Doc Baxter from the Hampton hospital. Perhaps she would mail her next application there.

•••

"You've only been practicing for a couple of weeks, Mrs. Taylor." Jack had taken Emma daily for a lesson. Darlin' jumped in the back seat, never showing any signs of anxiety from Emma being at the wheel. "I wouldn't want you to fail your test. Why not drive for a month and practice?"

"To tell the truth, I guess I practiced driving these streets for ten years, giving people rides to the doctor or picking up a few groceries for those in need." She'd also delivered or gathered Bill's items, but those excursions hadn't given her the sense of independence she experienced today. Turning the steering wheel to go around a bend, up a street and across to the next corner with Jack in the passenger seat strengthened Emma's confidence. She patted the steering wheel with her fingers. "But you're the judge, am I getting along all right?"

"Oh, yes, you're doing fine. But I'd be upset if you were disappointed."

"I wouldn't like that either, Jack, but I can do it."

Emma drove on the slippery and muddy streets from the recent rain. "This kind of road gives me a bit of practice of how my tires might be on ice."

"Let's hope we don't see those conditions for a while."

Silence filled the space between Jack and Emma. What was he thinking? "We've missed you at church, Jack." She glanced at him. "Any reason? Are you not feeling well?"

"No, I feel okay." He lifted his cap and placed it in the same place on his head. "You know, I've been a faithful member, but it seems somebody's changed the seating. So, I stay home and do my praying."

"There's nothing wrong with that, Jack, but don't you miss being with us?"

"I can find God, or maybe God finds me right in front of the radio. I always listen to *Today's Christian Hour,* and the singing is really good."

Jack wouldn't desert the congregation. He had a compassionate nature, and Emma sensed his character at each instruction.

"The new minister has drawn different folks into worship. Might be the reason you think the seating has changed." She shifted gears as they climbed a steep grade. "There's lots of room for everybody."

"I know, but we'll see."

"I'm relieved you have your reasons and Darlin' coming to the anniversary service didn't upset you."

"Well, I didn't like it, but no, the last two times I went, somebody was sitting in my seat."

"When you're ready to come back, you tell me, and I'll bake those scrumptious oatmeal squares for fellowship following service. But don't leave it too long. When I get my license, there's a good chance that I will consider leaving Noble."

Jack was quiet, perhaps thinking of her words. Ignoring the last sentence, he continued, "Can I slip in when my radio program is over?"

"Now, what do you think?"

"I know. You make us reason for ourselves." Jack shook his head. "Maybe you tell me when you're making them squares, and I'll come."

"All right, we'll settle for that. And if I make them next Sunday?"

"I might be there."

"And you can sit with me. I'll look forward to it," Emma said.

Jack stared at his hands. "We'll…I'll miss you if you decide to move."

"Thanks, Jack. We have wonderful memories, haven't we?" Emma noticed that he wiped a tear away.

FORTY-SIX

Emma passed the driving test without problems. Mr. Polin handed her the license with congratulations. "I never would have thought a lady could do this with as much ease as you did; it goes to show the world is changing."

"Students need an informed teacher." Emma tucked the licence into her purse. "Jack's patience showed as golden, which made me believe I could do it. My confidence took a step upward through this whole process."

She opened the door of Bill's car and slipped into the driver's seat. Unfastening her wallet to look at the license, it appeared as if it had always been there. Much the same as the day she touched her bankbook for the first time, satisfaction filled her.

• • •

Maisie's indoor plants thrived from consistent watering and a pinch of plant food. Emma watered each one carefully. The ringing of the telephone jarred her thinking. "Hello, yes, Emma Taylor here…oh, I'm sorry to hear this, Jack. Yes, he was a wonderful dog, and everybody in the town loved him." Emma listened as Jack gave her the details. "Of course, I'll come right over."

Maisie came into the room before Emma finished the conversation. Concern crossed her face. "Bad news, Emma?"

"I'm afraid so. Jack called, and his dog, Darlin', died during the night."

"How sad. Jack will be heartbroken."

"He wants me to go over, but the car is getting an oil change."

"Shall I ask Reverend Larson to take you? I'll go if you like."

"Yes, please do." The driveway appeared empty. "He was washing his car earlier. See if he's outside."

"I'll go and ask him."

Within ten minutes, Emma, Maisie and the reverend arrived at Jack's mobile home tucked in behind a large stand of blossoming hydrangeas. A doghouse with the word DARLIN' etched on a piece of wood above the door, leaned against the back entrance.

As they moved out of the vehicle, two more cars stopped. Eleanor poked her head out the car window and said, "A few of us were cleaning the church, and Leroy informed us that Darlin' had died. We thought we'd come over and see how Jack is."

Henry parked his pickup truck and called, "Did Darlin' die? There's all kinds of chatter at the grocery store. I had to come and see for myself."

"Yes." Pleased that everybody was sharing the news, Emma said, "Jack phoned about ten minutes ago. I'll talk to him and ask how we can help." She knocked on the trailer door, but not before more activity on the street drew her attention.

Leroy parked the car and stepped out. Hilda cradled Alice in her arms and joined him. As Emma waited on the trailer step, a dozen people gathered on the patchy grass. The Ryans, Jed included, walked across the front yard carrying a box and set it on a wooden table.

Emma opened the door and entered a space where Jack sat in a booth with a cup of coffee. "I'm so sorry, Jack. Darlin' was a special dog. You know the whole town loved him."

"Yeah...but, I wasn't sure." Jack twisted his peaked cap on his head.

"Come look at your front yard. A large group of your Noble friends want to say goodbye to him."

When Jack peered out the window, his eyes welled with tears. "It's hard to believe. I never knew."

Emma smiled at him. "If they didn't love him, they wouldn't have tolerated the way he left presents on their front porch."

"I guess you're right." Jack swiped a tear on his cheek.

"What would you like us to do? How can we help you say goodbye to your beloved dog?"

"I put him in a box with his mat and carried him to a protected area of the hedge." He focused on Emma with sad eyes. "If you want to go there while I cover him with earth, the rest can follow."

"I think everybody will. We'll all do this with you."

Emma stepped out of the trailer with Jack. Amazed at the crowd, she spoke clearly, "Good morning." Her strong voice reached out to them. "Jack is going to bury Darlin' in the backyard. Please come with us."

They walked back, everyone as solemn as if they were burying their best friend. Jack leaned over the closed box a moment, lifted it above the hole with two ropes and then lowered it.

"We'll always remember your dog, Darlin'," Emma said. "He was the town's greatest entertainer."

As they remained at the narrow grave, different friends shared a time when Darlin' had drawn their attention. Then someone would laugh and begin another story of an antic he had carried out. Soon, Jack was laughing with everybody.

"That dog barked when I came toward him, announcing to the whole town that he was my friend," a man said. "And he used to share my garden tools with the town. He thought I had them on the veranda to lend to my neighbours."

Somebody else called out, "That was Darlin'—everybody's dog." Quietness saturated the space.

Emma raised her voice. "You know, Jack, animals, particularly dogs like Darlin', have a special relationship with their owners. You were a wonderful friend to him. No doubt, he embarrassed you, but I'm safe in saying nobody saw you hurt or scold your dog. He slipped into the drug store with young Rosie Ryan as if protecting her. And I'm sure he enjoyed Reverend Albert's few words dedicated to him on the Sunday he came to church. I suspect he couldn't find anybody in town that morning and wanted to be near friends—those who loved him. Jack, you were his buddy. And I thank God for people who understand animals, care for them and give them a home. Darlin' was part of this town's life." Emma nodded. Quiet applause filled the area.

"Much obliged, Mrs. Taylor." Jack reached out and shook her hand.

The crowd wandered back to the street, murmuring gently to each other. The sound of a mouth organ sent a beautiful, mournful melody drifting in the air. At the end of the song, Emma caught a flash of shiny metal as Reverend Larson slid something into his vest pocket.

Jack faced his friends. "I don't hardly know what to say. So, thanks so much for coming and for being part of this day. I wish my place was big enough to invite all of you in for a cup of coffee, but it's pretty cramped quarters."

Emma shook her head. "That's okay, Jack. They've taken care of everything."

"My goodness." Jack looked puzzled.

Emma raised her voice. "I'm told the ladies brought cookies and cups. And Henry has donated a few chocolate bars, and if you break them in pieces, there will be enough for everybody. As well, the Ryans added a box of sweets." Emma waved to them, and they returned the gesture. "To all of you, thanks very much for contributing treats and coming to share this special time." Pointing to a worktable, she said, "There's a metal pail by the flowers for your wrappings. Help yourselves to Jack's pump water. It's fresh and free."

People applauded, and soon the hum of voices and laughter circled Jack, comforting him as only friends can do.

• • •

Days passed before Emma had a chance to share something that had been weighing on her heart. "Do we have a few minutes?" she asked Maisie.

She put on the kettle. "Would you like a hot drink?"

"I would, indeed." There was no easy way to begin a conversation that Emma had been assessing, and today it had finally come to a head. She had to talk it through with someone, and Maisie would be the perfect listener.

"There we go." Maisie set two cups of steaming cocoa on the kitchen table.

"There are a couple of hitches unsettling my mind. After I hung my diplomas, Mrs. Allen and Mrs. Howard who helped me pack, examined them and expressed words between disgust and bewilderment. I spoke openly about my education, maybe too willing to defend myself. I was sure they'd tell their friends, and then, who knows how far the news would travel. Did you…have you heard any talk?"

"No, can't say that I have."

"I haven't either. I keep thinking somebody is going to confront me. But…I wonder why that hasn't happened."

"Hmm." Maisie glanced down at her hands and took a deep breath. "The first thing that comes to my mind is if that incident was known around town, you'd have heard from Irene. And you haven't." She sat back in her chair. "Secondly, I suspect those two women haven't said a word. Partly because they don't understand, or they are prouder of you than you realize, and they haven't settled on how to tell you."

"That'd be wonderful, Maisie. Wouldn't that be a miracle?"

"And your second concern?"

"I spread the various mailings to search committees across the week—a couple in Noble, and one in Hampton when I was across that way. It was in that line-up at the post office counter when I met Lizzy Maxwell. How in the world did that little piece of news get back to our Mr. Arnold except through her? He told me when I went in to mail my fourth and final letter. Again, he scrutinized it, asking if the name on the envelope was Scottish."

"Aw, I'm sorry that plan seems to be backfiring on you." She took a sip of her drink. "There's nothing you can do, Emma. At least your applications are on their way, and we'll wait until the replies come back."

"I suppose you're right. Hopefully, I'll soon know if anybody is interested in inviting me to an interview."

Emma and Maisie talked until they both began to yawn and decided to turn in for the night. Emma lay awake for a long time. If Mr. Arnold noticed responses by their return address, he'd figure what she was doing. He'd probably tell somebody, maybe even in error, or what he might consider as care. But that'd be all it'd take. Then how would the town deal with it? She flinched and tugged the quilt tightly to her chin.

FORTY-SEVEN

Emma received responses from three of the churches to which she'd applied regarding an interview. All of them said they were sorry, but her qualifications didn't meet their requirements. They offered God's blessings in her search. If the fact that she wasn't a man was a problem, they omitted to say. She'd wait and see if her fourth application attracted a search committee. If a letter from a woman with a seminary certificate intimidated people, she was determined not to apologize. She smiled as she read the reply from Cunningham Square Pastoral Charge, signed by J.D. Cunningham. *Would a few gatekeepers attend there?* Emma chuckled at the thought although there might not be any connection.

It was evident in the responses that not one of her applications had initiated interest. Somehow seeing this was good news. It would be disturbing if a church was confused about acceptance and wasn't informed enough to identify it. So, reading their honest responses was refreshing and saved the misfortune of getting involved with a group that might prove disastrous. Somehow this feeling of relief deserved recognition.

During supper, Emma told Maisie about the three letters. "Even with the replies, I'm no further ahead. However, there is one more response to come. So, we'll celebrate this as well as getting my license and a bank book. Since neither of us are big spenders, let's go for a drive."

"Do you have anywhere in mind?" Maisie said a half-hour later as she settled into the passenger seat of the car.

"Any place you want," Emma claimed.

"How much gas do you have?"

"I've got enough to give us ample pleasure." Emma turned the window down into a rather dismal evening. "There might not be good scenery as it's been a dull day."

"But I can see that's changing. Look there." Maisie pointed to the west. "Want to go to Poplar Hill to see all shapes and sizes of multi-coloured trees? We can view the sunset from there."

Emma drove out of town. Between a line of heavy clouds and the forest stretching upward, the sun settled.

"It's as beautiful and round and bright as if happy to appear for us." Emma leaned forward on the steering wheel.

"And it hasn't shone all day?"

"No, not a blink." She stopped at a farmer's laneway. "Do you ever think God shows us something special for the sake of giving us pleasure?"

"Not really. Do you mean intentional as from God to us?"

"Yes, because then we feel a sense of peace, and open ourselves to goodness. And maybe God makes the statement, 'I am God.'"

"I love the way you talk. But I don't know whether you fabricate these little speeches, memorize from a book or bring them up from the deepest part of your soul."

"Don't worry where I get them. If they ignite your faith, that's the main purpose."

"You've been working at that ever since I met you. By now, it's a wonder you haven't given up on me." Maisie chuckled and glanced across the car.

"You underestimate yourself," Emma said. "God fills your cup on a daily measure. I like to remind you sometimes."

"And it pleases me when you do." Maisie shifted in her seat. "We can walk a mile and watch our feet take step after step, which is a safe way, especially if it's a bumpy road. Or we can saunter, difficult as it can be, and look at flowers, green grass and birds. I can see when a woman stifled by grief and loss of identity through changes beyond her control can sink into depression, experience isolation, and feel lost in a sea of regret."

"You and God stimulate my thinking, drag me from myself to reflect on past obstacles."

Maisie nodded her head. "And you came to the point where you discovered you were looking in reverse and realized you wanted to move ahead."

"Excellent imagery while sitting on the top of a hill." Emma eyed Maisie, waiting for her to retaliate with one of her amusing remarks.

"And God is giving you a picture of what you're attempting to do?"

Laughter spilled into Emma's words. "Glad you said that and not me."

Maisie peered out the side window. "Here comes a car. Now who else is out here looking at the sunset?"

"I don't know, but they're going the wrong way to see it."

The car slowed and drew alongside them. "Are you out of gas, Mrs. Taylor?"

"No, not at all, Mr. Tolt. Thanks for asking."

"Are you having trouble? You haven't been practicing your new driving skills for long."

"No problems. The car is serving me well." Emma patted the steering wheel.

"But it's not running."

"No, that would be a waste of gas—not wise in this depression."

"Exactly my thinking." Mr. Tolt opened his door and leaned out. "Is it Maisie you have in there? Now, Emma, it comes to mind Maisie doesn't have a license, and you shouldn't be driving without a licensed passenger."

"We're fine, Mr. Tolt. You don't have to worry."

Maisie nudged Emma's arm. "Oh, for corn's sake, tell the man you passed your test before he has a heart attack."

"Maisie tells me to inform you that I passed my test and have my license so you can relax."

"Have your license? Now why would you want a license?"

"To do what we're doing." Emma pointed at the view before them. "Any pleasure we have on this earth can be enhanced by finding God's handiwork on an ordinary day. Did you miss the sunset today, Mr. Tolt?"

"He doesn't have a lot of God-language in his vocabulary. You've stumped him," Maisie whispered.

"Don't let us keep you, Mr. Tolt. Good evening to you." Emma rolled up her window and, once again, the sunset boasted its red and golden splendour.

Mr. Tolt sat in his car for a few moments before driving away. Perhaps he was trying to understand the simplicity of the moment in the overwhelming power of God's creation.

Emma drove her car back to Noble, entertaining Maisie with stories of Bill and Prissy. With a new existence bordering on what was now beginning to feel like routine, Emma felt God's lead.

FORTY-EIGHT

Maisie and Emma were sitting on the back veranda watching the hummingbirds when Irene Trask bustled up the driveway in the early evening. "Ladies, I'm so glad you are home. I heard distressing news. And, well, you know me. I had to come directly to you, Mrs. Taylor, and ask if it was true. I couldn't believe it, as it's so unlike you to go behind our backs. Yet—"

"What are you saying, Irene?" Maisie held out a hand, palm up. "What are you accusing Emma of doing?"

"You must understand what I'm referring to, Mrs. Taylor." Irene gently brought her arthritic hands together. "I simply can't imagine what would make you do such a thing."

Emma slid a chair across the space, offering it to the angry woman. "Irene, please join us and tell me what you mean." Had the news of Emma's seminary education finally caught up to Irene?

She sat, swallowed and began to speak slowly, as if not trusting her words. "I have it from a trusted source and not Mr. Arnold that you have been writing to different churches begging them to give you a job." Irene took a deep breath. "And not only that, but you went to Hampton to do your mailing so it wouldn't be as conspicuous as sending a letter from here where you're known." Irene glanced behind her as if an audience might have gathered.

After thumping her purse on her lap, she leaned toward Emma. "Then, as you got letters returned to you from those you'd pestered, you took them outside to open the envelopes as if you were hiding something. Heavens, I find this so…unlike you. What would make you do such a thing?"

Emma frowned at Maisie and shook her head. If this weren't so ridiculous, it'd be tragic. Irene only needed a fragment of information to give her the nerve to retell the incident in an exaggerated form.

"Irene, I'll only tell you this once, so listen closely." Emma paused to take a deep breath. "First of all, I did not write to churches begging them to hire me. I responded to their invitations to apply. And secondly, I didn't drive to Hampton to mail something in secret. Doc Baxter asked me to pick up Bill's medical history from the hospital, so I posted a letter there." Emma smiled at the parishioner. "Does that make sense?"

Maisie leaned back in her chair. Would she join the conversation? Probably not, as she seemed interested in how Emma would get herself out of this.

"I understand everything you said, Mrs. Taylor, except for one thing. If you weren't pleading with them to give you work, what could you want from them? I mean, who are they to you? No more than strangers! You certainly don't have 42nd cousins in every pastoral charge. Isn't that the term you used when you lied to Mr. Arnold?"

Should Emma scream, holler or cry like a baby? She stood. "I'll just say this before I leave this party and retire. We are the Body of Christ. Furthermore, the church is a family, Irene. We are the family of God. In other words, you are my sister in Christ. We are part of an amazing worldwide kinship. And if I said 42nd cousin, which I didn't, or even agreed with Mr. Arnold, as it was he who used the phrase…it'd be familiar in faith language." She shoved her chair into place at the table. "Now, I'll say goodnight, as the hour is getting late."

Emma strode into the house. Within a few minutes, Maisie came in. She considered Emma from the doorway.

"I am so proud of you."

Emma began to wipe her eyes.

"Tears wash the soul, my friend," Maisie whispered.

"Can you believe it? How in the world am I going to talk my way out of this, Maisie? How widespread are these lies? And who is carrying them, tattling to this one and then to another? It shames me. Am I using the church for self-centred reasons?" Emma faced the wall and pressed her palms against it. "What on earth did I do to deserve this humiliation? Would Bill think I sacrificed our name for selfishness?" Emma shifted toward Maisie. "I'm shocked. This accusation will spread through the community as quickly as wildfire. I'll be the biggest joke this side of…" she raised her arms, "wherever."

"Emma, come sit down. Let's talk a bit." Maisie set a dish of peppermints between them. "Here, take the sour taste away. Having to keep your cool with Irene, as you did brilliantly, must have left an unfavourable flavour in your mouth."

Emma sighed. "Maisie, what would I ever do without you?"

"I don't know, but I'm here anytime you need me."

They discussed why some would believe what they wanted, regardless of what Irene reported to them. Maisie said, "We'd better cut our conversation short and head to bed, unless you're interested in a wee hot toddy for medicinal purposes?"

Emma pressed one hand to her cheek. "I must remind you of my Methodist roots, and I am a minister's wi…widow. But you go ahead."

"I'll pass. It's a relief, you know. I mean, I've been wondering when something like this would happen. Now that it's over, we can carry on."

"So, you're suggesting we should let this go and get a good night's sleep so we're ready for act two?"

"Something like that. Are you up to it?"

Emma winced. "I don't know, Maisie. I really don't know."

• • •

Emma pulled her nightie over her head and settled onto her soft mattress. Her eyes remained wide open, staring at the ceiling, as one hour after another gradually passed in the dim bedroom. The bedside clock's hands inched along, spending most of the night. Slowly Emma began to form a change of direction in her mind. She would stay in Noble and do what people expected of her. She'd find a way to live within her means with Bill's financial gift. If she could find a job, she'd be fine with careful planning. Did it take Irene's jolting reprimand to make Emma see clearly? If Irene thought this way, no doubt there'd be others. Emma had received three rejections in the mail, and there was no reason why the fourth wouldn't be similar. Tears ran down her cheeks, and she tugged the cotton sheet up to wipe them. Emma wouldn't tell Maisie for a few days that previous plans had changed. She'd be disappointed to learn that Emma was staying in Noble.

The following week was relatively quiet. Had the town accepted Irene's story? She would have told her assumptions to everyone she met. Emma stayed at home to avoid questions. Nobody approached her. Had Irene's account of the mailed letters failed to draw any attention? What was going on? Are people skirting the issue, hoping not to hurt her? Was she being shunned—disregarded? She'd expected inquiries. But nothing.

The folks would show disappointment when they learned she was staying in town. What would it matter? She hadn't said she was leaving immediately. They would think she was still working out her plans, which would be the truth. There was no need to tell anybody exact details.

When Emma walked up the main street, individuals told her community-centred news. They complimented her on practical choices and presented ongoing support. Since life appeared peaceful, perhaps Irene's hostile visit had been a dream. Granted, Maisie had been there, so it had happened.

Rather than being rejected, it seemed friends overly praised Emma for the slightest effort. She received three greeting cards with handwritten letters enclosed wishing her well wherever God led her. One, on nicely printed paper, quoted, "Hoping your plans work out for you."

Cora gave her a lovely purple African violet, a favourite flower. Reverend Larson promised rhubarb roots for her flowerbed when she settled in her new place. Emma wanted to ask him if he knew something she didn't? Or maybe a question like, "What new place and where?" hoping to open the topic.

Everybody was guessing, and it bothered Emma. All the praise people handed out about her future made it challenging to stay in town. They would be saddened when they realized she had given up. Would she, in time, be seen as rejecting their encouragement? That kind of thinking brought her to tears.

Irene hadn't come back to visit, and Emma wasn't disappointed. She let the incident drop, as she couldn't stand the stress of waiting for the next episode to erupt. Should she attend worship? If folks were aware and didn't think Irene's story was an issue, Emma wouldn't make it one.

Sunday's sermon was powerful. The choir sang two selections in four-part harmony. Mr. Tolt gave the announcements to the congregation in a friendly manner, including the invitation for lunch. Such a strange contrast to the way he sometimes spoke.

Emma studied the pulpit. Why didn't she miss seeing Bill behind it? It must surely be that Reverend Larson belonged there. Emma rested a hand on the pew-pillow beside her and smiled, despite tears. Words of scripture soaked her spirit. Illustrations of encouragement, risk, and assurance pelted her emotional space. Had she given her decision to stay in Noble enough thought?

• • •

A wreath of colourful leaves hanging on the parsonage's new side door caught Emma's attention as she prepared vegetables for a salad at Maisie's sink.

"Hello, Mrs. Taylor." Jack's face showed against the screen.

Emma opened the door. "It's so nice to see you."

"I have a parcel for you from the post office." He handed a box to her. "You might be too busy to pick this up, and Mr. Arnold wanted you to receive it as soon as possible, so I brought it over." Jack examined the package before returning his gaze to Emma. "He asked me to tell you directly that everybody's on your side. There will always be those who have difficulty showing it."

"Thank you, Jack. That's so thoughtful of you. And pass on my gratitude to Mr. Arnold." She reached out for the box. "It'll be different for you these days without Darlin'."

"It is that, Mrs. Taylor. Yes, indeed." He started to walk away and stopped. "So nice of you to speak of Darlin'." He left before Emma could reply.

She squinted as she read the return address, L. N. Reinhardt, Attorney at Law, 303 Bloor Street, Toronto, Ontario. Mary Ann's lawyer. Emma opened a drawer and lifted the scissors to cut the string wrapping the package. *Here it is. Now I'll have instructions about the diary, letters and money.* Disappointment crept into her thoughts. This discovery would dictate if Mary Anne's possessions became part of Emma's life. She ripped the paper from the box. Gripping the lid, she set it on the table. Seeing a leather-bound book led her to proceed. Two envelopes lay beside it. She unsealed the first one, scanned it for necessary words of instruction, and then read each word carefully.

> *Dear Mrs. Taylor*
> *Thank you for writing and asking for instructions concerning Mary Ann Moore's diary and content. I had lost hope of ever hearing from anybody, which led me to think no one had found them.*
> *I knew Mary Ann and her parents well. After she died, they hoped that someone would honour her wishes. She included the exact instructions to me as you read in her handwriting: see additional enclosure.*
> *I hope wherever you are, Mrs. Taylor, that you trusted your instinct and accepted her gifts, as they belong to you. Treasure them, use them, take courage from them and pass them on as you see fit. As for the money, I'm sure you'll find creative ways to use it.*
> *Sincerely,*
> *L.N. Reinhardt, Attorney at Law*

Tears clouded Emma's eyes, both for the words in the letter and Mary Ann's gift. Relief and assurance of her own decision occupied her thoughts. *I'm thankful for receiving this. I'm afraid I'd have to return Mary Ann's work in good conscience, despite her instructions and Maisie's encouragement.*

After placing the letter on the table, Emma reached into the box and lifted a beautiful small hardback. Without delay, she opened it. Words of healing filled each page. *These are new entries. I haven't read any of this before. She's written this following her time at Noble, perhaps in the Ontario Hospital.*

Setting the book aside, Emma reached into the bottom of the box and pulled out a padded wrapping: the will. As she skimmed from one piece to another, she finally found the section. The exact words Emma had read while sitting in the attic appeared in Mary Ann's handwriting. Also, money tied with a red ribbon lay among the typewritten sheets with this instruction: '*If you ever decide to publish my work, or yours, for that matter, Mr. Reinhardt will assist in the process.*'

Emma glanced up at the shuffling at the door. Maisie hustled into the room, carrying a brown bag. "Good morning, Emma!"

"Good morning. You'll never guess what Jack brought me." Emma pointed to the box.

"The lawyer wrote to you?"

"He did. And it's all relevant news. Just as we assumed."

"You knew Mary Ann better than anyone."

Emma put everything in the parcel and closed the top. She'd savour the contents later.

FORTY-NINE

The fourth response to Emma's application came in the mail from the Bruce Peninsula. It was a brief acceptance with a promise from the search committee chairman to telephone Emma. She closed the envelope. Her recent decision to remain in town would make her discussion with him difficult.

When he phoned, Mr. Denver's excitement resonated in every word as he invited Emma to an interview, saying that they would go from there. "We're isolated up here in Summerville," he said. "Everybody needs books, lots of writing paper for their personal use and an adequate radio with batteries. We often lose electricity with the storms." He went on to add, "We have a grocery store, three churches with adjoining cemeteries, a garage, post office and a school. And, oh yes, we're working on building a town hall as the old one burned down. We also have a newspaper and an excellent fall fair. Not much else we need."

Irene's harsh words and others' negative opinions had caused Emma to rethink the opportunity to accept God's call to serve in a pastoral charge. She had made this new discission through tears to stay in Noble and rent a modest accommodation. Emma took a deep breath before telling Mr. Denver of her change of mind.

He interrupted her thoughts. "Now, about the position, if it were left to me, I'd make the motion without hesitation to invite you to come into our community of faith as our minister. So, I'm hoping the feeling is mutual when you meet us. We don't do a lot of the typical red tape, so I hope you're comfortable with that."

This wasn't the usual procedure she'd seen Bill follow when he accepted the call to Noble. What was to make of avoiding the formal tradition of an interview and vote? This conversation was different than any arrangements Emma had heard concerning interviews, appointments and covenanting, but perhaps the process had changed.

Mr. Denver continued in a rapid succession of words, "My mother taught children and adults in our church as a volunteer before she got arthritis and couldn't fulfill her duties. Nobody could tell the stories of Jesus as she could. Yes, siree, I'd welcome you into our midst—that's for sure."

Had he finished his remarks? Perhaps not, as he cleared his throat. "Maybe I'll add that this congregation has only seen a woman in paid leadership at her desk in the school classroom. So, if I were you, I'd be prepared to answer questions regarding why you want to stand behind a pulpit." He paused again. "Oh, dear. That does sound rather unfair, but, well, I thought you should know."

"I appreciate that, Mr. Denver." Emma doodled on the notepad next to the telephone. She must not let Mr. Denver continue. "I need to tell—"

Mr. Denver added, "Come ready to begin immediately. Like I say, if you agree with our conditions, then we can put you right to work."

"But —"

His voice relaxed and began to speak slower. "I—I realize this is out of the ordinary but, we'd like to call you, although I'm not sure what this position will be titled. We'll figure that out later. The two gentlemen who previously served as ministers stayed a long time, so we're doing the best we can."

The Noble community thought she was going somewhere. Mr. Denver believed she was coming to them. And Emma was trapped between his offer of ministry and her decision to withdraw her intentions and stay in Noble. She held a hand to her chest. This moment had caught her off guard. Emma reflected on the brief gap when she'd stepped away from her yearning to pursue ministry.

Numbness covered her like a heavy blanket when she attempted to think about it. She hadn't given this new plan sufficient time to defend it in her mind—so she kept silent. Mr. Denver continued to speak enthusiastically of her arrival. Of course, he wouldn't know she'd changed her mind. She shuddered.

Irene's accusing voice echoed in Emma's memory. She'd heard it on different topics over the years and had learned to understand Irene's nature. What a position of uncertainty to be in. She had wrestled with the opportunity to make a change toward ministry longer than her recent decision to stay in Noble, and she had felt safe in it.

Emma took a deep breath. *I won't let Irene direct my future. I won't.*

"Mrs. Taylor, are you there? Did we get cut off?"

Emma took a deep breath. "I'd be happy to come to Summerville to discuss this further, Mr. Denver. Thank you."

Anybody who gave such an inspiring reference to his mother teaching in the church was enough for Emma. "Thank you for your comments, Mr. Denver. I won't be surprised if anyone on the committee asks about these topics. I'll be there in one week."

"That's good. One week from today: 4:00 in the Sunday school room. I'll get the committee together, and we'll have a bit of an interview to make it official."

For some time after Emma said goodbye, she mulled over a few things Mr. Denver had said that didn't make sense. What did he mean regarding the committee assembling for "a bit of an interview to make it official?" Had he not offered her the position if she agreed? He did say to come prepared to go right to work. Maybe she'd read too much into their conversation, although he'd said that if it were up to him, he'd welcome her and make the required motion to call her to the pastoral charge for the ministerial position. His other statement about the schoolteacher gave her pause and caused confusion. It was typical that individuals wouldn't have seen women in leadership in the community, yet Mr. Denver deemed it necessary to mention that fact. Was that a warning?

Emma had completed her original list. She'd committed herself to taking another step in her plan. It seemed as if the group hoped the invitation and conditions would be agreeable to her. Was she relieved or terrified?

• • •

Later, as she and Maisie sat at the kitchen table enjoying a cup of tea, Emma shared the content of her phone discussion with Mr. Denver, including the fact that she would be going to Summerville for an interview with the committee in a week and if everything went well, she would start work immediately.

Her friend reached out and covered Emma's hand with hers. "This is wonderful," she said. "I'm proud of you."

The departure date proved to be perfect for those offering to help. Reverend Larson presented a trailer which worked perfectly. Friends helped to load her oversized items. Emma had lots of boxes, and they fit tightly into the space. Reverend Larson pulled a canvas tarp across the top, tied the sides and told her to keep the trailer until somebody visited.

Individuals from the congregation and community had showered Emma with practical and financial gifts during the last week, and she had stored them in Bill's car. She'd been firm that she didn't want a farewell in the church, thinking that wouldn't be proper without Bill. She grieved having to leave her friends. This pain was a different sorrow than she felt in mourning Bill's death. She'd add them to her pile of unresolved aches in her heart and face them later.

She had taken people's advice, such as get lots of sleep, pack with care, and give away Bill's clothes. Except for the plaid flannel shirt that she would keep for herself. She'd hang her certificates in her new office and put Bill's books in her bookcase. She planned on needing them. And somewhere in the middle of storing and unpacking, she might find her Sunday school materials, essays, hymns…and maybe Bill's love note.

Emma didn't enjoy goodbyes for a lot of reasons. She didn't want to risk opening entrenched grief in public, so she'd deliberately connected with folks individually and in groups. It wasn't the ideal way to say farewell, but it was the best she could do with the time she had. What would it be like to drive out of Noble with Prissy, knowing home was no longer here? Worse yet, she was between addresses. Shivers gripped her, even in the safety of Maisie's kitchen.

Driving to Summerville would be daunting. Worrying was an emotion that didn't feel comfortable. However, situations of uncertainty surfaced in her mind, causing fear. What if she got halfway there and the car stalled as it did when Bill drove it home from Hampton? Would the gas tank spring a leak? Was there an extra can of fuel in the trunk? What would happen if the trailer severed itself from the car and rolled into a ditch?

It would have been a good idea for Emma to have driven to Leroy's house to prove she had the necessary expertise to drive north successfully. It was too late for that, though. She must not fret all night, or she'd be in no shape for those miles tomorrow. Perhaps she'd go for a practice run before Maisie returned from her errands.

FIFTY

Confident from driving the car around the concession while pulling the trailer, Emma readied herself for today's trip. The sun shone from high in the sky as if blessing the day. Emma admired the new wooden end on the veranda after closing Maisie's door. Colours from various flowers in planters hanging on the railing appeared brilliant.

Emma had said goodbye to the Larsons and Maisie earlier and was eager to get on her way. However, when she placed a foot onto the gravel, she faced a large gathering assembled on the driveway, neighbouring lawns, and the street. Tears began to flow down her cheeks.

Maisie raised her hand. "Emma, you made it very clear we wouldn't be able to entice you into the church for a goodbye event because you didn't want a get-together without Reverend Taylor. If anything, we were afraid you'd pull away in the middle of the night or skip out when you went for your practice drive. We were so happy you came back to leave according to your plan."

Ah, they did know I'd been practicing—probably watched me. Emma grinned as she regarded everyone's faces.

"The community didn't want to miss this opportunity to say goodbye, so a few asked if they could have a moment to speak." Maisie waved through the air. "But first, do you have a few words you'd like to say, Emma?"

Her legs felt like jelly. This surprise left her speechless. Plans to proceed without fanfare or public notice had failed. Emma took a deep breath. "What comes to mind is holding your hands and saying how significant you were to me and Reverend Taylor during our time in Noble. Please know how special you are. Today, I say my goodbyes and hope I'll see you again sometime."

Belle, Rosie and Susanne moved forward, holding a piece of cardboard with "The Emma Taylor Mission Circle" printed across the front in crooked letters. Strings of binder twine knotted at each end held a perfect banner with a large number stitched across the top. The girls hung it on Emma's shoulder and, in unison, as though they were singing, said, "Thank you from our group, including all seventeen of us that attended. You gave us courage and cheered us on." They stepped back, and the crowd applauded. Emma wiped her tears.

Only Susanne remained. "You have shown us how to set our course, make decisions, and carry them out. You have been an example for all of us to stretch beyond the moment and see possibilities." She hugged Emma before giving her a large white envelope with a black music staff scrawled across it.

Susanne had no sooner stepped aside than her older sister Nancy strode to Emma and placed a garland of vines and blossoms around her neck. "At my graduation, you can do this for me."

Rosie Ryan moved away from the rest and came to stand in front of the crowd. She turned and offered a handful of wild daisies to Emma, lingering as she focused on her. Did she want to say something? No, the flowers were enough.

Jack didn't come forward, but he gave Emma a thumbs-up and said, "Thanks for making them squares and sitting with me in church."

Irene walked to Emma. "My voice ought to be the loudest, so everyone can hear me say I should be wearing sackcloth and standing in ashes. I am comforted that the good residents of Noble think you can do no wrong." She reached out and gathered Emma into her arms, and the group applauded softly. "I'm so…so sorry." Her hug tightened as if she was checking sobs.

"Thank you." Emma pulled back and stared deeply into Irene's eyes.

"You're welcome. I hope I can come up to Bruce County to visit."

"That'd be very enjoyable for both of us," Emma said. "Put it on your kitchen calendar."

Hilda made her way through the crowd, pushing a buggy. Lifting out a wheel, she said, "Every one of these spokes represents girls you encouraged to risk a new path to walk. The rim is this town that keeps moving us forward, allowing us to learn and consider possibilities. The hub is faith that holds us together. It's important to say that you gave us confidence. You helped us find our feet. Alice will use hers because of your willingness to stand in the gap."

Mrs. Bowman slowly approached Emma with a large skein of yarn in a beautiful shade of blue. "You have a faith-filled heart, Mrs. Taylor. This skein is for you to knit when you're feeling melancholy, and with each stitch, give yourself credit for all the kind deeds you did in this town." She reached into her bag. "And when the blues leave you, try your favourite pattern and laugh." She smiled a wide grin as she handed Emma a colossal ball of brilliantly variegated shades of yellow. "I know what you're thinking, 'your daddy's church is rubbing off on you.'"

Everybody cheered. Mrs. Bowman was her own hero.

A voice resounded in the crowd. "We are very grateful to be included in your circle of care. We learned the importance of being involved, listening and giving thanks." Emma slowly examined the assembly, wanting to acknowledge the man who had spoken. The only rapid movement in the few moments of silence was Jake Ryan wiping his brow before lowering his hat to shield his eyes from the brightness of the day. Soft applause filled the area.

Mrs. Howard and Mrs. Allen walked toward the front, both with the kind of grin that says, *finally, we get to tell someone this delightful news.*

Mrs. Howard said, "Thank you for the opportunity to talk to you during the packing day. It must not have been easy to share your appreciation of learning with us, and I confess—" She paused as if holding back tears. After clearing her throat, she continued, "Neither of us listened with courtesy...or love. For that, we apologize. We've been doing our homework from Reverend Larson's Bible study. We asked specifically to learn about informed Biblical women, and he gave us a long list of assignments. I can only say we were amazed at our findings."

Mrs. Allen strode forward. "We decided to make these presentations when we learned you didn't receive your diploma upon graduation. And you welcomed it many years later when Reverend Taylor suggested you request it." She handed Emma a framed certificate. "We want this one to be on time. It says, '*Emma Taylor, First Church recognizes ten years of service and ministry...dated September 1935.*'"

Mrs. Howard opened an oblong jewelry box and lifted out a finely carved wooden cross on a silver chain. She hung the necklace around Emma's neck. "When you wear this, remember our shared faith."

Through her tears, Emma hugged both ladies before they returned to their seats. Emma turned toward her friends.

Mr. Tolt stepped away from the rest, followed by the stewards and elders. "I know what you're thinking. He's going to ask someone to take the offering."

Emma laughed. "That crossed my mind; I have to admit."

"You gave an offering in everything you did, Emma. And you've developed determination since you settled on your vocation." Everyone clapped again. "I confess you wear it well."

Emma blushed.

Mr. Tolt continued, "And the rest of us benefitted from every word and act of love you gave. Today we are giving you this envelope. It contains the stewards' words and a cheque for helping us out in the church. It's been a long time coming and, and it includes our friendship and appreciation." Again, loud applause created a wave of noise and laughter. A few "Bravos" and "Here-Here" echoed across the yard.

Blinking away her tears, she replied, "To all of you. I'll keep your kindness in my heart, always."

Mr. Tolt handed her the envelope. "If the north doesn't work for you, I invite you to stay in the cottage on the far corner of our lot. I've had it for rent, but the Noble population likes where they live, and nobody is standing in line for a town property associated with funerals and furniture. I'll hang this picturesque sign that reads, *The Emma Taylor House*. It's yours to use as you wish. While we wait for you to come home to visit, it's available to anybody needing a short-term residence. Although you can't have it for the next three months as the O'Neils will be moving in until the community rebuilds their home."

From the Hills? Was Noble rebuilding the O'Neils' home? *Did I ever think I'd see these two communities come together?* Emma took a deep breath to let Mr. Tolt's statement saturate her thoughts. The Hills and the town were joining in a project to benefit each other. Was it the gift that had touched her or that Mr. Tolt had given it? Most of all, maybe, that her beloved Hills was being recognized. She dabbed her tears of appreciation with a handkerchief.

"Thank you. I am thankful for you and your presents." Emma gazed at the faces she loved. "And, Mr. Tolt, I truly appreciate your kindness. I'll visit, for sure. In the meantime, please don't add the subtitle 'A Place of Rest' since it's on the lot beside the funeral home."

He laughed as if enjoying her comment. This gesture was a sincere contribution to the day.

Mrs. Olen led the children up the driveway, singing a joyous Sunday school chorus. When they stopped, Cora Morgan said a hearty, "One, two, three," and the choir broke into "For She's a Jolly Good Fellow." A great flood of voices embraced Emma with four-part harmony, and she joined the melody. The audience spent the next hour passing on their congratulations and best wishes.

• • •

Emma walked to her car and placed her various gifts carefully in the back seat. After opening the door, she slid in beside Prissy, who waited on her cushion. Emma started the car, waved to everyone blocking the way, and attempted to gradually move down the driveway. People stepped aside and opened the way to the road. Children continued to swarm too close to her car, dragging their hands unhurriedly along the panes of glass and closing the space surrounding the vehicle, causing muted sun rays.

Emma drew in a slow, deep breath as she turned onto the street. A few elderly folks leaned on canes from their porches; some waved while standing in front of their windows while others wiped tears from their eyes. Slowly Emma drove the car away from everyone and everything that had been dear to her. "Well, God, it's you, me, and Prissy…besides Bill in my memories."

With a honk of the horn, Emma made her way up the street, feeling like a new bride waiting for the tin cans to rattle together. At first, the apprehension of dragging extra weight tightened her back muscles. Even with her practice time, the utility trailer filled with her earthly possessions tugged and jerked on the vehicle.

As she drove along, she grew accustomed to the sway and relaxed her tight grip on the steering wheel. A glance in the rear-view mirror confirmed that she had lost sight of familiar scenery and the town she loved. It'd be three hours to her destination, and she'd get used to driving and pulling her load.

She stared at the highway ahead that wove nonstop through the thicket of the landscape and finally out of view. Fields and trees rushed by on either side, providing a blur of colour and shape. The river flowing adjacent to the road was similar to the countryside where this car had overheated last March. The water had been out of reach enough to know assistance had to come from another source beyond their resources.

Despite Emma's raw grief, God's strength filled her at every turn and urged her forward. Bill had taught her essential areas of ministry by example, in his quiet way, and she'd continue if Summerville invited her to minister among them. She had visited his grave once a week, faithfully pruning the flowers and gathering leaves. Eventually, the plot beside Bill in the Noble cemetery would be hers. Until then, she would carry on in ministry, but in a different way and another place.

She rolled the window down enough to let the aroma of the country seep into the vehicle, sweet and comforting. Stretching one arm across the seat, she dug into a bag and shook out her new cardigan—such an original colour, very appealing. It'd be her favourite because Louise Ryan had knit it for her. She laid it on her lap. *It'll keep me warm during cool nights up north.*

As for her unanswered questions, she'd leave those in God's hands. She'd done all she could do to prepare herself for this opportunity. *I pray I'm in your will, God; if not, you'll have to speak louder.*

THE END

BOOK #2
EMMA'S CHALLENGE

CHAPTER 1

September 1935: Emma Taylor's excitement at beginning a new life mixed deeply with the grief of her husband Bill's death. Although this tragedy was unexpected, with the assistance of her daughters and a good friend, Emma painfully managed over time to adjust to single life. Her grief was deep and complex, swaying her from helplessness to certainty. Today she was confident due to the love of Noble's First Church congregation. Thankful to them for being a visible part of the Body of Christ, Emma remembered with gratitude that they had continually invited her to be among them, circling her with love and providing safe opportunities for tears.

The horizon stretched the vast skyline under wispy white clouds wandering from here to there across the blue sky. Long, twisting roads led up hills, down into valleys, and around detours, resembling life.

Emma had driven from Noble dragging the trailer with all her earthly possessions, anticipating a fruitful meeting with Summerville Memorial's search committee. Hopefully, they'd offer her a call to minister among them. This effort was a pioneering step, as it was unusual to consider a woman for this position. For her, it was either accept the ministry to which God had called her or live an impoverished life. The harsh depression years seldom left people with a choice.

Lake Huron reflected the brilliant sun, highlighting elevated whitecaps surrounded by swirling foam—an image of hope amid the turmoil. As she reached the village and turned right onto Main Street, bordered groomed lawns edged a white church with a bell tower standing high above the front entrance. A large wooden cross claimed its peak, making a definite statement of importance in the community. Tall willow trees draped over a white clapboard house with an extended veranda. She drove to the farthest corner of the parking lot and shut off the engine. Several cars and a bicycle parked in a sandy area indicated that Mr. Denver and the committee members had already gathered.

On the front yard, an attractive sign displayed hand-painted letters:

Summerville Memorial Church—Everybody Welcome
Services May through to Thanksgiving 11:00 a.m.

Five and a half months? *Land sakes! Where does the congregation go the rest of the year?* The dates on the sign determined she'd only have a short period to serve from the time the committee appointed her before they closed the doors until spring. What would she do from Thanksgiving to May? And did they miss Christmas worship altogether? *Maybe Christmas doesn't happen up here.*

In their conversation, Mr. Denver hadn't mentioned these dates of their closure interval, nor had he spoken about accommodations. He'd indicated that he'd get everybody together for an interview. Had she misunderstood, or worse still, had she used her longing to interpret his statements as a firm offer? No doubt, she'd have as many questions of them as they would have of her.

Emma opened the car door and scanned the area. The scripture, "Behold, I make all things new," came to mind. Each event had been a challenge during the last few months, yet they had taken Emma forward to this time. Today would be no different. Now was a perfect opportunity to practice the ministry concept that God had placed in her heart.